THE O

SCIENCE F

YEARBOOK

TWO

Also available from Orbit

THE ORBIT SCIENCE FICTION YEARBOOK ONE

THE ORBIT
SCIENCE FICTION YEARBOOK
TWO

Edited by
David S. Garnett

Futura

An Orbit Book

First published in Great Britain in 1989
by Futura Publications, a Division of
Macdonald & Co (Publishers) Ltd
London & Sydney

All characters in this publication are fictitious and any resemblance to real persons, living or dead, is purely coincidental.

ISBN 0 7088 8316 8

Typeset by Leaper & Gard Ltd, Bristol

Reproduced, printed and bound in Great Britain by
BPCC Hazell Books Ltd
Member of BPCC Ltd
Aylesbury, Bucks, England

Futura Publications
A Division of
Macdonald & Co (Publishers) Ltd
66/73 Shoe Lane
London EC4P 4AB
A member of Maxwell Pergamon Publishing Corporation plc

ACKNOWLEDGEMENTS

As before, the editor's thanks go to John Jarrold of Futura, and also to all those who made material available for this collection. They are, as the saying goes, too numerous to mention. Particular thanks, however, to Ellen Datlow, David Pringle and Ian Watson for their assistance.

'Introduction' by Lucius Shepard. Copyright © 1989 by Lucius Shepard. Published by arrangement with the author.

'The Secret History of World War 3' by J.G. Ballard. Copyright © 1988 by J.G. Ballard. First published in *Ambit* 114, Autumn 1988. Reprinted by permission of the author.

'On the Edge' by Sharon N. Farber. Copyright © 1988 by Omni Publications, Ltd. First published in *Omni*, December 1988. Reprinted by permission of the author.

'PrayerWare' by Jack Massa. Copyright © 1988 by Jack Massa. First published in *Full Spectrum*. Reprinted by permission of the author.

'A Short Course in Art Appreciation' by Paul Di Filippo. Copyright © 1988 by Mercury Press, Inc. First published in *The Magazine of Fantasy and Science Fiction*, May 1988. Reprinted by permission of the author.

'Vivaldi' by Ian McDonald. Copyright © 1988 by Ian McDonald. First published in *Empire Dreams*. Reprinted by permission of the author.

'Probability Pipeline' by Rudy Rucker and Marc Laidlaw. Copyright © 1988 by Rudy Rucker and Marc Laidlaw. First published in *Synergy 2*. Reprinted by permission of the authors.

'Peaches for Mad Molly' by Steven Gould. Copyright © 1987 by Davis Publications, Inc. First published in *Analog Science Fiction/Science Fact*, February 1988. Reprinted by permission of the author.

'French Scenes' by Howard Waldrop. Copyright © 1988 by Howard Waldrop. First published in *Synergy 2.* Reprinted by permission of the author.

'Distances' by Kathe Koja. Copyright © 1988 by Davis Publications, Inc. First published in *Isaac Asimov's Science Fiction Magazine*, Mid-December 1988. Reprinted by permission of the author.

'Home Front' by James Patrick Kelly. Copyright © 1988 by Davis Publications, Inc. First published in *Isaac Asimov's Science Fiction Magazine*, June 1988. Reprinted by permission of the author.

'Deadboy Donner and the Filstone Cup' by Roger Zelazny. Copyright © 1988 by The Amber Corporation. First published in *Terry's Universe.* Reprinted by permission of the author.

'The Flies of Memory' by Ian Watson. Copyright © 1988 by Davis Publications, Inc. First published in *Isaac Asimov's Science Fiction Magazine*, September 1988. Reprinted by permission of the author.

'Thanks for Drowning the Ocelot' by Brian Aldiss. Copyright © 1989 by Brian Aldiss. Published by arrangement with the author.

'Science Fiction Novels of the Year' by John Clute. Copyright © 1989 by John Clute. Published by arrangement with the author.

Introductions to their stories are copyright © 1989 by J.G. Ballard, Ian McDonald and Roger Zelazny.

All other material in this collection is copyright © 1989 by David S. Garnett — who denies any responsibility for the cover of this book.

CONTENTS

INTRODUCTION
by
LUCIUS SHEPARD

It always begins for me with a single line, just a line, without any idea or thematic notion attaching. In this case the line went as follows:

> The kid pulled his black Trans Am into the Sunoco station, and it seemed like a cold wind had pulled in along with him, snapping the blue and yellow flags strung between the pumps.

The image of the kid, the black car, and a cold windy day called to mind some evil necessity, and after a few minutes I wrote the entire first paragraph:

> The kid pulled his black Trans Am into the Sunoco station, and it seemed like a cold wind had pulled in along with him, snapping the blue and yellow flags strung between the pumps. He was a scrawny, hollow-chested kid with a hard mountain face. Squinty eyes, sharp cheekbones, and a thin fastidious mouth. His dark hair had been hacked into a patchwork of tufts and stubble, and his arms were mapped with yardbird tattoos: swastikas, a skull cracked by an axe, dice that showed snake eyes. He had on jeans and felony shoes and a black T-shirt with white lettering that read IF YOU LOVE SOMETHING LET IT GO: IF IT DOESN'T COME BACK, HUNT IT DOWN AND KILL IT. The kid had come to swear by those words. He thought they said a lot about his personality.

The energy generated by that paragraph acted like the initial bars of a rock and roll guitar solo, stating tonality and theme, providing the ground upon which the ideas inspired by the passage were to be played out, and I spent the next couple of hours evolving those ideas, sketching out scenes, noodling with plot, realizing that I was embarking upon an exploration of brutality and the dissolute. Then, with this in mind, I began again to write.

There is to my mind an atmosphere of performance about the writing of a short story, an air of enthusiastic purpose and the suggestion of an unseen audience that is urging the author on. If the beginning of the story is handled successfully, if this auctorial enthusiasm is communicated, then the reader may experience an excitement similar to that he might feel upon turning on the radio and hearing a brilliant new song — it will locate him within the world created by the piece, and also, by imbuing him with a sense of dislocation at its finish, will illuminate his own world. That is an overcomplicated way of stating a rather simple verity: that short stories can, like rock and roll, evoke a poignant or spectacular effect within a brief space of time, and can utilize their immediacy to cause a variety of subtle and powerful reactions in their audience. This immediacy has captivated me and keeps me returning again and again to explore the form.

By contrast, the writing of a novel is a highly civilized act, one that requires scholarly patience, seasons of contemplation and activity; its ultimate product, however high-flown or barbarous the materials, becomes the companion of an idle hour, of a leisure whose classic requisites are a quiet study, a pool of lamplight, and something moody on the stereo. The short story derives from a tradition that today finds expression in pubs, over back fences, around campfires, in any venue where two people, one of them with a story to tell, may gather. Though artists of tremendous intellectual refinement have practiced the form, it always has managed to maintain the commonality and accessibility of the tale; indeed, most stories usually involve a single ordinary moment — or a succession of such moments, be they of love or illumination or frivolity — and strive to expose the bright flash of being that is their essential matter. As do we all when we speak with friends and lovers and strangers on trains, trying to tell them what we are and where we have been and what it is we want from them. That is also part of the short story's allure for me, the idea that I am a participant in the art along with, say, a couple of bikers swapping lies about women and a group of men relating different versions of the same football match and three old ladies maligning the pretty divorcee who has just moved into the upstairs flat. And this particular facet of the allure has proved central in my attitudes toward the story that I am currently writing, the one with which I am illustrating this introduction.

Science fiction and fantasy afford me a means of examining the ordinary — pretty divorcees and the like — under the light of the imagined, and through this process it often happens that the ordinary is revealed to be extraordinary, that odd things creep from beneath stones and revelations issue from unlikely quarters. In the first paragraph of my story I have introduced the character of the Kid, a malefic sort who has the capacity to wreak havoc by mysterious means. He is, in effect, the imagined light, and the ordinary upon which I intend him to shine is a seventeen-year-old hooker and drug addict named Faye, whom he picks up in a gas station in Daytona Beach, Florida, which happens to be my old home town. Having established the Kid's bleak persona, my next obvious task was to establish Faye, and this I began to do while they are stopped at an intersection while driving to the Kid's apartment.

> On the opposite corner was a lounge of concrete block painted to resemble a circus wagon, with a sign on the roof that read 24 HOURS TOPLESS GIRLS GIRLS GIRLS; a man in a windbreaker and plaid pants was trying to see in through the frosted windows. Two dispirited-looking girls wearing shorts and tube tops were shivering in the doorway of a T-shirt shop; one started toward the Trans Am, flashing a smile that was pathetic in its falsity, but the kid warned her off with a stare. The wind had drifted sand up from the beach and scattered it across the blacktop in the shape of four enormous white clawmarks, and from one of the arcades, just audible above the crush of the surf, came tinny shards of calliope music, adding an accent of brittle derangement to the scene.
>
> 'God,' Faye said despondently, 'God, I hate this fucking town during the off-season. It's like when the tide goes out and you can see all the weird shit stuck in the sand.'

Before writing this passage, I had not fully understood the materials of the story. I had been improvising, working the notes of the words and ideas into various shapes, playing in fits and starts. Now I realized that the story had to do not only with its central figures, but with my home town, with all faded resorts that have no character of their own and are like stage sets into which a new cast is moved every few weeks . . . except during the off-season, the one time of year when what they really are, what everyone who lives there is, becomes visible. I also realized the story was not merely an exploration of evil, but that it was foremost a love story, that Faye — hopeless and dissipated, with her crude eloquence and flashes of insight — would be an object of fascination for the Kid. As she had become for me. The Kid had originally been my chief focus, and I had intended Faye to be more-or-less his foil. But with the utterance of two sentences, she had asserted herself to be his equal. And thereby hung my tale. And quite a venerable tale it was. Beauty and the Beast. Quasimodo and Esmerelda. Kong and — oh, my God! — Fay Wray. And 'The Off-Season', I decided, wasn't half-bad for a title.

Moments of illumination and discovery, moments in which one's characters take on a life of their own and so forth, occur during the writing of novels; but because of a novel's length, because it is necessary to measure out one's enthusiasm, to pace oneself, it's more difficult to take advantage of the energy that such moments release. In this instance, however, like a guitarist who has just stumbled upon a terrific hook, I got behind the feeling and began to flesh out both Faye and her desolate backdrop.

> Pelican with spread wings perched on a creosote-tarred piling.
>
> Silver Beach Motel, LuRay Apartments, Coquina Inn.
>
> Tanned old man in sweatshirt and shorts passing a metal detector over a patch of mucky sand.
>
> Dead Ferris wheel with seats removed, canvas-shrouded Tilt-A-Whirl silhouetted against the stars. Black sea beyond. Only the arcades still open, and atop them, the miniature golf courses with dilapidated Taj Mahals and King Kongs, old windmills, giant cobras with gaping Hole-in-One mouths. A couple playing the course on top of the Joyland, knocking colored balls across the patched greens. Straining her ears, Faye imagined that she could hear them laughing.

And watching a teenage couple pass the Kid's apartment:

> The girl's blond hair swung out in the wind with the abandon of a pale flame, and her laughter was rich and easy. She had so much that Faye felt less envy than alarm, the way you might feel after seeing something that abolished a fundamental conception. They stopped beneath the streetlight and kissed for a long time.
>
> Love, Faye thought, where is it?

It was all coming together now, plot, character, tone, and I was high on the writing, certain that within a relatively short time I would have a completed — albeit unpolished — piece of work. And that is perhaps the most compelling reason that attracts me to the creation of short fiction — the sense it gives me of riding the whirlwind, of being just a bit out of control, the possibly illusory yet nonetheless exhilarating feeling that I am on the verge of creating something better and wiser than myself, like — once again — a guitarist whose fingers have begun to move faster than his thoughts and is surprising himself with his invention.

The authors of the stories that follow will surely have methods that differ from my own; for their sakes, I hope they are more aware of what they're doing than I. But two things I can guarantee — that they had a very good time in writing them, and that their good time has produced startling moments of insight and poetry. And this in turn guarantees that you are about to have a very good time reading them. However, I won't dwell on this point. An audience can always tell whether or not the band is having fun up there on the stage.

Which is what I am about to do right this moment.

> When the kid walked into the Joyland Arcade, he knew right away that this was going to be his night. The video machines like strange judges with black metal hoods and squealing voices, Guns and Roses raving from the speakers, girls with Dilaudid languor and frosted hair and fat breasts groped by lean pimply speedfreak boyfriends, the blazing fluorescents making everyone look bloodless and sooty-eyed . . . all comprising a single vile image. It was as if the Joyland

was the sky, and the drugged, lost children grouped around the machines were the newly aligned constellations of a hellish American midnight zodiac, and the kid was the rising sign . . .

Nantucket, Massachusetts
January 1989

J.G. BALLARD

J.G. Ballard's first stories were published in 1956 in *New Worlds* and *Science Fantasy*, and his first novel was *The Wind from Nowhere* (1962). Other novels include *The Crystal World*, *Crash* and *Empire of the Sun*; and his short stories have been collected in such books as *The Voices of Time*, *Vermilion Sands* and *Myths of the Near Future*. His most recent books are the novel *The Day of Creation* (1987), the novella *Running Wild* (1988), and the collection *Memories of the Space Age* (1988).

Through stories such as 'The Terminal Beach' and his pioneering of 'inner space', Ballard was the key author in the New Wave revolution of the sixties. This was when he wrote several 'condensed novels' — the most controversial of which featured a protagonist who was to become much more famous later. Now Ballard has returned to this character, as he explains in an introduction which he has written for the *Yearbook*.

THE SECRET HISTORY OF WORLD WAR 3

by

J.G. BALLARD

Introduction

Ronald Reagan has been a long-standing interest of mine. My 1967 piece about him, 'Why I Want to Fuck Ronald Reagan', later published in The Atrocity Exhibition, *led to the first American edition being pulped at the orders of Nelson Doubleday. Yet a cooler reading of the piece, which virtually predicted a Reagan presidency, would have quickly confirmed all his admirers' real reasons for championing the then Governor of California. Reagan has always been a puzzle to the Europeans — how could a man so intellectually third-rate, so clearly incompetent, become chief executive of the world's most powerful and important nation? But the United States exists on a superior and altogether more advanced level to that of mundane Europe. There image is all, and Reagan's image, as it has evolved over the years from opportunist right-winger to national Grandaddy, reveals so much to us in our attempts to grasp the essence of American mass psychology.*

J.G. Ballard

Now that World War 3 has safely ended, I feel free to comment on two remarkable aspects of the whole terrifying affair. The first is that this long-dreaded nuclear confrontation, which was widely expected to erase all life from our planet, in fact lasted barely four minutes. This will surprise many of those reading the present document, but World War 3 took place on January 27, 1995, between 6.47 and 6.51 p.m. Eastern Standard Time. The entire duration of hostilities, from President Reagan's formal declaration of war, to the launch of five sea-based nuclear missiles (three American and two Russian), to the first peace-feelers and the armistice agreed by the President and First Secretary Gorbachev, lasted no more than 245 seconds. World War 3 was over almost before anyone realised that it had begun.

The other extraordinary feature of World War 3 is that I am virtually the only person to know that it ever occurred. It may seem strange that a suburban paediatrician living in Arlington, a few miles west of Washington D.C., should alone be aware of this unique historical event. After all, the news of every downward step in the deepening political crisis, the ailing president's declaration of war and the following nuclear exchange, was openly broadcast on nation-wide television. World War 3 was not a secret, but people's minds were addressed to more important matters. In their obsessive concern for the health of their political leadership, they were miraculously able to ignore a far greater threat to their own well-being.

Of course, strictly speaking, I was not the only person to have witnessed World War 3. A small number of senior military personnel in the Nato and Warsaw Pact high commands, as well as President Reagan, Secretary Gorbachev and their aides, and the submarine officers who decrypted the nuclear launch codes and sent the missiles on their way (into unpopulated areas of Alaska and eastern Siberia), were well aware that war had been declared, and a cease-fire agreed four minutes later. But I have yet to meet a member of the ordinary public who has heard of World War 3. Whenever I refer to the war people stare at me with incredulity. Several parents have withdrawn their children from the paediatric clinic, obviously concerned for my mental stability. Only yesterday one mother to whom I casually mentioned the war later telephoned my wife to express her anxieties. But Susan, like everyone else, has forgotten the war, even though I have played video-recordings to her of the ABC, NBC and CNN newscasts on January 27 which actually announce that World War 3 had begun.

That I alone happened to learn of the war I put down to the curious character of the Reagan third term. It is no exaggeration to say that the United States, and much of the western world, had deeply missed this amiable old actor who retired to California in 1989 after the inauguration of his luckless successor. The multiplication of the world's problems — the renewed energy crises, the second Iran/Iraq conflict, the destabilisation of the Soviet Union's Asiatic republics, the unnerving alliance in the USA between Islam and militant feminism — all prompted an intense nostalgia for the Reagan years. There was an immense affectionate memory of his gaffes and little incompetencies, his fondness (shared by those who elected him) for watching TV in his pyjamas rather than attending to more important matters, his confusion of reality with the half-remembered movies of his youth.

Tourists congregated in their hundreds outside the gates of the Reagans' retirement home in Santa Barbara, and occasionally the former President would totter out to pose on the porch. There, prompted by a still soigné Nancy, he would utter some amiable generality that brought tears to his listeners' eyes, and lifted both their hearts and stock markets around the world. As his successor's term in office drew to its unhappy close, the necessary constitutional amendment was swiftly passed through both Houses of Congress, with the express purpose of seeing that Reagan could enjoy his third term in the White House.

In February 1993, after the first uncontested Presidential election in the history of the United States, more than a million people turned out to cheer his inaugural drive through the streets of Washington, while the rest of the world watched on television. If the cathode eye could weep, it did so then.

Nonetheless, a few doubts remained, as the great political crises of the world stubbornly refused to be banished even by the aged President's ingratiating grin. The Iran/Iraq war threatened to embroil Turkey and Afghanistan. In defiance of the Kremlin, the Baltic republics of the USSR were forming armed militias. Yves Saint Laurent had designed the first chador for the power dressing Islamicised feminists in the fashionable offices of Manhattan, London and Paris. Could even the Reagan presidency cope with a world so askew?

Along with my fellow-physicians who had watched the President on television, I seriously doubted it. At this time, in the summer of 1994, Ronald Reagan was a man of 83, showing all the signs of advancing senility. Like many old men, he enjoyed a few minutes each day of modest lucidity, during which he might utter some gnomic remark, and then lapse into a glassy twilight. His eyes were now too blurred to read the teleprompter, but his White House staff took advantage of the hearing aid he had always worn to insert a small microphone, so that he was able to recite his speeches by repeating like a child whatever he heard in his ear-piece. The pauses were edited out by the TV networks, but the hazards of remote control were revealed when the President, addressing the Catholic Mothers of America, startled the massed ranks of blue-rinsed ladies by suddenly repeating a studio engineer's aside: 'Shift your ass, I gotta take a leak.'

Watching this robotic figure with his eerie smiles and goofy grins, a few people began to ask if the President was brain-dead, or even alive at all. To reassure the nervous American public, unsettled by a falling stock market and by the news of armed insurrection in the Ukraine, the White House physicians began to release a series of regular reports on the President's health. A team of specialists at the Walter Reed Hospital assured the nation that he enjoyed the robust physique and mental alertness of a man fifteen years his junior. Precise details of Reagan's blood-pressure, his white and red cell counts, pulse and respiration were broadcast on TV and had an immediately calming effect. On the following day the world's stock markets showed a memorable lift, interest rates fell and Secretary Gorbachev was able to announce that the Ukrainian separatists had moderated their demands.

Taking advantage of the unsuspected political asset represented by the President's bodily functions, the White House staff decided to issue their medical bulletins on a weekly basis. Not only did Wall Street respond positively, but opinion polls showed a strong recovery by the Republican Party as a whole. By the time of the mid-term Congressional elections, the medical reports were issued daily, and successful Republican candidates swept to control of both House and Senate thanks to an eve-of-poll bulletin on the regularity of the Presidential bowels.

From then on the American public was treated to a continuous stream of information on the President's health. Successive newscasts throughout the day would carry updates on the side-effects of a slight chill or the circulatory benefits of

a dip in the White House pool. I well remember watching the news on Christmas Eve as my wife prepared our evening meal, and noticing that details of the President's health occupied five of the six leading news items.

'So his blood sugar is a little down,' Susan remarked as she laid the festival table. 'Good news for Quaker Oats and Pepsi.'

'Really? Is there a connection, for heaven's sake?'

'Much more than you realise.' She sat beside me on the sofa, pepper mill in hand. 'We'll have to wait for his latest urinalysis. It could be crucial.'

'Dear, what's happening on the Pakistan border could be crucial. Gorbachev has threatened a pre-emptive strike against the rebel enclaves. The US has treaty obligations, theoretically war could —'

'Sh . . .' Susan tapped my knee with the pepper-mill. 'They've just run an Eysenck Personality Inventory — the old boy's scored full marks on emotional resonance and ability to relate. Results corrected for age, whatever that means.'

'It means he's practically a basket case.' I was about to change channels, hoping for some news of the world's real troublespots, but a curious pattern had appeared along the bottom of the screen, some kind of Christmas decoration I assumed, a line of stylised holly leaves. The rhythmic wave stabbed softly from left to right, accompanied by the soothing and nostalgic strains of 'White Christmas'.

'Good God . . . ' Susan whispered in awe. 'It's Ronnie's pulse. Did you hear the announcer? "Transmitted live from the Heart of the Presidency".'

This was only the beginning. During the next few weeks, thanks to the miracle of modern radio-telemetry, the nation's TV screens became a scoreboard registering every detail of the President's physical and mental functions. His brave, if tremulous heartbeat drew its trace along the lower edge of the screen, while above it newscasters expanded on his daily physical routines, on the 28 feet he had walked in the rose garden, the calorie count of his modest lunches, the results of his latest brain-scan, read-outs of his kidney, liver and lung function. In addition, there was a daunting sequence of personality and IQ tests, all designed to reassure the American public that the man at the helm of the free world was more than equal to the daunting tasks that faced him across the oval office desk.

For all practical purposes, as I tried to explain to Susan, the President was scarcely more than a corpse wired for sound. I and my colleagues at the paediatric clinic were well aware of the old man's ordeal in submitting to this battery of tests. However, the White House staff knew that the American public was almost mesmerised by the spectacle of the President's heart-beat. The trace now ran below all other programmes, accompanying sit-coms, basketball matches and old World War 2 movies. Uncannily, its quickening beat would sometimes match the audience's own emotional responses, indicating that the President himself was watching the same war films, including those in which he himself had appeared.

To complete the identification of the President, audience and TV screen — a consummation of which his political advisers had dreamed for so long — the White House staff arranged for further layers of information to be transmitted. Soon a third of the nation's TV screens was occupied by print-outs of heart-beat, blood-pressure and EEG readings. Controversy briefly erupted when it became clear that delta waves predominated, confirming the long-held belief that the President was asleep for most of the day. However, the audiences were thrilled to know when Mr Reagan moved into REM sleep, the dream-time of the nation coinciding with that of its chief executive.

Untouched by this endless barrage of medical information, events in the real world continued down their perilous road. I bought every newspaper I could find, but their pages were dominated by graphic displays of the Reagan health bulletins and by expository articles outlining the significance of his liver enzyme functions and the slightest rise or fall in the concentration of the Presidential urine. Tucked away on the back pages I found a few brief references to civil war in the Asiatic republics of the Soviet Union, an attempted pro-Russian putsch in Pakistan, the Chinese invasion of Nepal, the mobilisation of Nato and Warsaw Pact reserves, the reinforcement of the US 5th and 7th Fleets.

But these ominous events, and the threat of a third world war, had the ill luck to coincide with a slight turn-down in the President's health. First reported on January 20, this trivial cold caught by Reagan from a visiting grandchild drove all other news from the television screens. An army of reporters and film crews camped outside the White House, while a task force of specialists from the greatest research institutions in the land appeared in relays on every channel, interpreting the stream of medical data.

Like a hundred million Americans, Susan spent the next week sitting by the TV set, eyes following the print-out of the Reagan heartbeat.

'It's still only a cold,' I reassured her when I returned from the clinic on January 27. 'What's the latest from Pakistan? There's a rumour that the Soviets have dropped paratroops into Karachi. The Delta force is moving from Subik Bay . . .'

'Not now!' She waved me aside, turning up the volume as an anchorman began yet another bulletin.

'. . . here's an update on our report of two minutes ago. Good news on the President's CAT scan. There are no abnormal variations in the size or shape of the President's ventricles. Light rain is forecast for the D.C. area tonight, and the 8th Air Cavalry have exchanged fire with Soviet border patrols north of Kabul. We'll be back after the break with a report on the significance of that left temporal lobe spike . . .'

'For God's sake, there's no significance.' I took the remote control unit from Susan's clenched hand and began to hunt the channels. 'What about the Russian Baltic Fleet? The Kremlin is putting counter-pressure on Nato's northern flank. The US has to respond . . .'

By luck, I caught a leading network newscaster concluding a bulletin. He beamed confidently at the audience, his glamorous co-presenter smiling in anticipation.

'. . . as of 5.05 Eastern Standard Time we can report that Mr Reagan's inter-cranial pressure is satisfactory. All motor and cognitive functions are normal for a man of the President's age. Repeat, motor and cognitive functions are normal. Now, here's a newsflash that's just reached us. At 2.35 local time President Reagan completed a satisfactory bowel motion.' The newscaster turned to his co-presenter. 'Barbara, I believe you have similar good news on Nancy?'

'Thank you, Dan,' she cut in smoothly. 'Yes, just one hour later, at 3.35 local time, Nancy completed her very own bowel motion, her second for the day, so it's all happening in the First Family.' She glanced at a slip of paper pushed across her desk. 'The traffic in Pennsylvania Avenue is seizing up again, while F.16s of the Sixth Fleet have shot down seven MIG 29s over the Bering Strait. The President's blood pressure is 100 over 60. The ECG records a slight left-hand tremor . . .'

'A tremor of the left hand . . .' Susan repeated, clenching her fists. 'Surely that's serious?'

I tapped the channel changer. 'It could be. Perhaps he's thinking about having to press the nuclear button. Or else —'

An even more frightening possibility had occurred to me. I plunged through the medley of competing news bulletins, hoping to distract Susan as I glanced at the evening sky over Washington. The Soviet deep-water fleet patrolled 400 miles from the eastern coast of the United States. Soon mushroom clouds could be rising above the Pentagon.

'. . . mild pituitary dysfunction is reported, and the President's physicians have expressed a modest level of concern. Repeat, a modest level of concern. The President convened the National Security Council some thirty minutes ago. SAC headquarters in Omaha, Nebraska, report all B52 attack squadrons airborne. Now, I've just been handed a late bulletin from the White House Oncology Unit. A benign skin tumour was biopsied at 4.15 Washington Time . . .'

'. . . the President's physicians have again expressed their concern over Mr Reagan's calcified arteries and hardened cardiac valves. Hurricane Clara is now expected to bypass Puerto Rico, and the President has invoked the Emergency War Powers Act. After the break we'll have more expert analysis of Mr Reagan's retrograde amnesia. Remember, this condition can point to suspected Korsakoff syndrome . . .'

'. . . psychomotor seizures, a distorted sense of time, colour changes and dizziness. Mr Reagan also reports an increased awareness of noxious odours. Other late news — blizzards cover the mid-west, and a state of war now exists between the

United States and the Soviet Union. Stay tuned to this channel for a complete update on the President's brain metabolism . . .'

'We're at war,' I said to Susan, and put my arms around her shoulders. But she was pointing to the erratic heart trace on the screen. Had the President suffered a brain-storm and launched an all-out nuclear attack on the Russians? Were the incessant medical bulletins a clever camouflage to shield a volatile TV audience from the consequences of a desperate response to a national emergency? It would take only minutes for the Russian missiles to reach Washington, and I stared at the placid winter sky. Holding Susan in my arms, I listened to the cacophony of medical bulletins until, some four minutes later, I heard:

'. . . the President's physicians report dilated pupils and convulsive tremor, but neurochemical support systems are functioning adequately. The President's brain metabolism reveals increased glucose production. Scattered snow-showers are forecast overnight, and a cessation of hostilities has been agreed between the US and the USSR. After the break — the latest expert comment on that attack of Presidential flatulence. And why Nancy's left eye needed a tuck . . .'

I switched off the set and sat back in the strange silence. A small helicopter was crossing the grey sky over Washington. Almost as an afterthought, I said to Susan: 'By the way, World War 3 has just ended.'

Of course, Susan had no idea that the war had ever begun, a common failure among the public at large, as I realised over the next few weeks. Most people had only a vague recollection of the unrest in the Middle East. The news that nuclear bombs had landed in the desert mountains of Alaska and eastern Siberia was lost in the torrent of medical reports that covered President Reagan's recovery from his cold.

In the second week of February 1995 I watched him on television as he presided over an American Legion ceremony on the White House lawn. His aged, ivory face was set in its familiar amiable grin, his eyes unfocused as he stood supported by two aides, the ever-watchful First Lady standing in her steely way beside him. Somewhere beneath the bulky black overcoat the radio-telemetry sensors transmitted the live print-outs of pulse, respiration and blood pressure that we could see on our screens. I guessed that the President, too, had forgotten that he had recently launched the third World War. After all, no one had been killed, and in the public's mind the only possible casualty of those perilous hours had been Mr Reagan himself as he struggled to survive his cold.

Meanwhile, the world was a safer place. The brief nuclear exchange had served its warning to the quarrelling factions around the planet. The secessionist movements in the Soviet Union had disbanded themselves, while elsewhere invading armies withdrew their frontiers. I could almost believe that World War 3 had been contrived by the Kremlin and the White House staff as a peace-making device, and that the Reagan cold had been a diversionary trap into which the TV networks and newspapers had unwittingly plunged.

In tribute to the President's recuperative powers, the liner traces of his vital functions still notched their way across our TV screens. As he saluted the assembled veterans of the American Legion I sensed the audience's collective pulse beating faster when the old actor's heart responded to the stirring sight of these marching men.

Then, among the Medal of Honour holders, I noticed a dishevelled young man in an ill-fitting uniform, out of step with his older companions. He pushed through the marching files as he drew a pistol from his tunic. There was a flurry of confusion while aides grappled with each other around the podium. The cameras swerved to catch the young man darting towards the President. Shots sounded above the wavering strains of the band. In the panic of uniformed men the President seemed to fall into the First Lady's arms and was swiftly borne away.

Searching the print-outs below the TV screen, I saw at once that the President's blood pressure had collapsed. The erratic pulse had levelled out into an unbroken horizontal line, and all respiratory function had ceased. It was only ten minutes later, as news was released of an unsuccessful assassination attempt, that the traces resumed their confident signatures.

Had the President died, perhaps for a second time? Had he, in a strict sense, ever lived during his third term of office? Will some animated spectre of himself, reconstituted from the medical print-outs that still parade across our TV screens, go on to yet further terms, unleashing a fourth and fifth World Wars, whose secret histories will expire within the interstices of our television schedules, forever lost within the ultimate urinalysis, the last great biopsy in the sky?

SHARON N. FARBER

Sharon Farber's first story was 'Born Again', published in *Asimov's* in 1978. Fifteen more stories have appeared there since, and her fiction has also been published in *Amazing, Whispers V, Universe 14, Omni* and 'various obscure and forgettable markets'.

She lives in Chattanooga, Tennessee, and says that the following story 'actually began as a very silly story called "A Science to his Madness", about a chemistry student in a universe where Sixties comic books are realistic depictions of everyday life. After neglecting the story for several years, I sat down to rewrite it one weekend, after I'd been working 90 hour weeks as a resident physician in a big charity hospital. Not a single sentence of the original remains.'

ON THE EDGE

by

SHARON N. FARBER

Blue. When she stands, balanced as on a tightrope, and looks below her, everything is blue. Strange and awful winds whipping her hair before her eyes, she turns cautiously to stare down the other way. Again, everything is blue — cold blue ocean reaching up into the endless sky. The air is crisp and dry. Far above, the blue sky fades into a pure black, dotted with alien constellations.

'Excuse me, Dr. Whirtham, I beg your pardon,' said Dr. Raj, with his lilting Indian accent, as half a dozen books fell onto the counter beside her head. 'Oh, I am so sorry.'

'No problem,' Rachel yawned, brushing away a *Manual of Medical Therapeutics.* 'I just dozed off. What's up?'

Raj, leaning precipitously above her, kept reaching for the *Physicians' Desk Reference.* 'There is a patient who was given phenothiazines by his friends.'

'Some friends.'

'Yes, and he took them to relax himself, and now his head is bent like this, and his eyes cannot move.' He twisted his own head ceilingward, in demonstration.

Rachel ran her hands through her hair, trying to return it to some semblance of order. 'Acute dystonic reaction. Fifty of Benadryl.'

Her colleague stopped reaching for the shelf. '*Fifty* milligrams?'

'Works like a charm. Or one milligram of Cogentin.'

'Thank you. It is amazing how you remember all these dosages.'

'Not really. Sherlock Holmes said your mind is like an attic, with only so much storage space. Well, when I was younger I knew the geologic areas, the fifty muscles in the human arm, and who penciled and inked the first eighty issues of "The Fantastic Four". Now all I know is how much penicillin in the butt you get for syphillis and how much for the clap.'

'Ah,' said Bill the charge nurse. 'The romance of emergency medicine.'

Yawning, Rachel stood, draping her stethoscope around her neck. Things seemed too quiet. Midnight, and only one patient in the emergency room? She walked out to the waiting room. A large cockroach scurried past; raising her sneakered foot, she paused. 'No way. Never kill anything that will leave a stain on your shoe.'

Aside from the usual drunk or two sleeping it off, and a chronic schizophrenic they allowed to hide behind the soda machine, the room was silent. Ants and roaches had gathered about a spilled can of cola.

'Enjoy the quiet while it lasts, Doc,' called the receptionist from her iron-barred cubbyhole.

Rachel swung open the door to the outside, immediately hearing the sound of the rain. Water was pouring from the sky, casting halos about the streetlamps. Light-streaked torrents ran down the incline. The doctor had a momentary vision of the rain forming a moat about the old hospital on the hill, turning it into one of those mysterious castles from the comic books: a place of hidden treasures, vaulted halls, treacherous dungeons; ghosts would stalk the halls and madwomen's tears merge with the rain.

She smiled. 'Turkeys don't fly in the rain.' All over town, potential patients were staying inside, out of trouble; it was too wet for brawls or muggings. People would treat their own minor ailments, and even those with true medical emergencies would try to wait out the storm.

She took a step outside, letting the wind whip her graying midnight hair, smelling the acrid odours of the wet street. Suddenly Rachel had a flashback to her dream, understanding now what had seemed so strange. Despite the endless vistas of ocean, fading into the horizon that had been all wrong, there had been no smell of salt and sea.

Far off she heard the first soft wail of an ambulance, taking the winding roads, its siren fading in and out like a jazz vocalist, while the rain gushed into the street and beat staccato on car hoods.

'Hey, Doc!' someone yelled, behind her. 'Multiple crunch coming in!'

After a few seconds, when she did not reply, the voice came again. 'Three cars! At least one dead! Shit, what a night.'

She sighed, letting the door swing shut, enclosing her inside. 'Yeah, yeah. I'll be there.'

She's flying; flying uphill, paralleling the blue flat as a sheet below her. Suddenly she reaches the crest and is flying straight into space, and the blue beneath her recedes down the other way; over the edge, she heads into the stars . . .

'And then I realized it,' she said, reaching to the center of the table and pulling a lump of sugar from the china cruet set. Everything at the Empress' Tea Garden was elegant; the wild-blackberry crepe cooling on her plate was garnished with carved orange and lemon slices. 'I was dreaming about a square planet — a cube in outer space.' She held up the sugar lump as if it were exhibit A. 'Like the Bizarro world.'

She looked expectantly at her breakfast companion. He was her age, in that brief and timeless moment when vitamins, exercise and lotion hold one poised before the quantum leap from youth to middle age. He had a square jaw, wireframe glasses, and a cheap yellow running suit unzipped to show a Greenpeace T-shirt. He sat there, a spoon heaping with yogurt and honey granola poised before his mouth.

'The *Bizarros,*' she repeated. 'You know. The Bizarros were these imperfect copies of Superman who did everything backward and talked funny. "Bad am good to us!" I dreamed that I was living on a box-shaped planet, just like theirs. Isn't that too much?'

'Rachel . . .'

She tossed the cube onto her uneaten crepe. 'Christ, Kent, didn't you read comic books when you were a kid?'

'Rachel, three people died last night.'

'Yeah?'

His jaw dropped slightly, and he lowered the spoon.

'Well, for God's sake,' she said angrily. 'What'd you expect? They were drunk — all the drivers — and driving like assholes in a storm. The Coast Highway's bad enough in good weather.'

'They *died*, Rachel. They might not have if Las Pulgas had a trauma center.'

'You mean, if it hadn't been just me and some camel jockey in that shit excuse for an ER?'

'Exactly! That's exactly what I mean.' Exchanging his spoon for a Cross pen, he flipped open a steno notebook. 'With proper facilities and a decent county hospital, they'd be alive right now. Right?'

'I won't say that. You can't quote me on jack, Kent." She laughed once. 'You know, I did save the dirtball driving the pickup. Homemade tattoos are pathognomonic for sociopath, and he was tattoo city. He was turning blue; I didn't wait for the X ray, just stuck a needle in his chest. Blam!'

She waved her hands. 'Guy had a tension pneumothorax from busted ribs. With these little hands I pulled him back from the edge of death. Couple of months, he'll be able to get drunk and do it all again.' Leaning back, she popped the sugar cube into her mouth and grinned.

'Maybe next time, he can run into a school bus, right?' She began to chuckle uncontrollably.

It is dark, with flickers of light reflecting off the bars on the tellers' windows and the corners of the desks. The quiet bank smells dry and summery, like new money.

Pausing before the vault door, a caped figure raises a gun and fires. The huge circle of metal dissolves, turning into colored mist, while below it a row of intricate wire-sculpture orchids springs into existence. The mist gradually clears, and the view into the vault is unobstructed. Coins glowing silver, piled deep, like water in a swimming pool. You could leap in, dive, and kick back to the surface, coins sparkling in your hair as the dark night flowed onward . . .

With the return of the hot weather came the return of standard chaos to the emergency room at Las Pulgas County Hospital. Dr. Wirtham sat at the counter, small and unimportant in her green scrub suit. Given the proper makeup and a rinse to take the gray out of her hair, she might have looked foreign and mysterious. As it was, she looked chronically weary. 'Ma'am,' said a woman leaning over the counter and pointing to one of the children clustered about her. 'Ma'am, my son here . . .'

'Ask a nurse,' Rachel snapped at the woman, not looking up as she scribbled a history and physical. She paused to stare at her work. 'Shit, *I* can't even read this,' she muttered. The patient's complaint was equally indecipherable. He seemed all right, but what if she had overlooked something? She remembered reading an old comic book, with Superman vowing to expose himself to gold kryptonite, forever losing his powers, if he ever caused anyone harm.

'Rachel?'

She gazed up. 'Kent. What are you doing here? Paper cut?'

'Sir . . .' said the charge nurse, approaching with tubes of blood and urine for the out box. 'Registration is outside. . . .'

'It's okay, Bill.' Rachel tossed the chart down. 'This is my pal, Kent Randolph. He's the ace star cub reporter for the *Las Pulgas Daily Journal*.'

'Have you given any thought to my question?'

'Oh, God!' Bill cried. 'Has he proposed?' He did a quick bump and grind.

'Buzz off,' growled Rachel, grabbing Kent by the elbow and ushering him toward the waiting room.

'Well?' he asked.

'You know how hard it is to get work in California, especially right on the coast,' she whispered. 'Every doctor in the damn country wants to come here. And now you, Mr Front-page Farrell, you want me to sing for your little exposé and lose my job — for what? For these people?'

She propelled him into the doorway.

'Take a good look, Scoop. The only sober person in the whole waiting room is that old lady there, who comes in twice a week with heart failure because she doesn't take the lousy medicine we give her for free! Whoops, I beg your pardon! *That* guy hasn't been drinking or fighting, either. No, he's got endocarditis, infected a heart valve by shooting dope. He needs at least six weeks of intravenous antibiotics, but every time he starts feeling okay, he signs a.m.a., then comes back when he's sicker 'n shit again.' She slammed the door shut.

'What happened to your human decency?' Kent asked her, his jaw muscles rippling over clenched teeth.

She made a show of searching her pockets. 'Beats me. Hey, look! Want a Life Saver?'

It was, as always, broad daylight when she returned home, exchanging her dirty scrub suit for a clean pair. The top was blue, with a deep neckline, the little print below reading PROPERTY OF UCSF.

Too hyper to sleep, she went out onto the porch. The ocean crashed angrily below, and everything smelled of salt and seaweed and mold. Off to the left some children were climbing the rocks, gathering tiny crabs trapped in puddles. Far to the right she could see surfers paddling toward the breakers. She slumped into the lounge, opening up an old comic book entitled *The Geek*, about a hip mannequin brought to life in 1960's San Francisco. When Rachel had sold her comics collection to fund her medical education, the buyer had refused to take the two issues of *The Geek*.

'Certain really bad comics are valuable,' he'd said. 'The same way some of the great stuff, like *Magnus Robot Fighter*, is practically worthless. Anything with bondage or girls in prison sells like hot-cakes. And you know those old *Lois Lane* comics everyone threw away 'cause they were so dumb? Well, now they're rare and worth a mint. But you can keep *The Geek*. I'd have more luck reselling *Richie Rich*.'

Quickly bored by the rackety plot and idealistic sentiments, she tossed the comic down, picking up the *Las Pulgas Daily Journal* instead. Kent's column ran on the editorial page, with a story about an illegal immigrant with pneumonia who'd delayed going to the hospital for fear of being caught and deported. Rachel had heard about the case — ER day shift had intubated the woman and shipped her directly to intensive care, where the police grabbed her family as they kept watch. Bill had described it to Rachel quite graphically, complete with screaming babies and pleading parents, but his rendition had come across as situation comedy rather than pathos.

The column ended with another impassioned plea for the mayor and the board of supervisors to improve health care for the indigent. She threw the newspaper on top of *The Geek.*

'Now, if this were a comic,' she muttered, 'Kent could dress up in a cape and tights and do some real sleuthing. The mayor would be involved in some conspiracy to give all migrant workers pneumonia, and in the last panel, about to shoot our hero, he'd fall into a vat of diplococci and drown.' She tipped the lounge chair back to almost horizontal, closed her eyes, and let the distant crashing of the waves lull her to sleep.

'Great galaxies! It's the Board of Superheroes!'

'Indeed it is, citizen,' replies the mighty muscled man in yellow, emerging from the shadows to confront the derelict. 'Did you see anything suspicious?'

'Yeah, someone ran thataway!'

'Thank you; you may have helped us capture a bank robber and well-known fiend!' Clapping the derelict heartily on the shoulder, the man in yellow looks over his shoulder and calls, 'This way, fellas!'

He runs into the night-blackened alley. The derelict watches, muttering the heroes' names as they pass. 'The mighty Boar! Bald Eagle! Superbman! The Abbreviator, Tiny Terror to Crime! All my former heroes, together again! And they thanked me!' Looking down with disgust at his brown paper bag, he snarls. Then, standing up straight, he tosses the bottle against the wall and strides off proudly as Mulligan Brothers dry sherry shatters on the bricks.

Inside the alley, the Boar holds up his hand to stop the others. 'Look! This back wall has been vaporized!'

'What's that beside it?' asks Flyboy, the Eagle's young companion.

His mentor scratches his scalp. 'It looks like the five-foot shelf of classics!'

The Boar bends down to confirm it. 'You're right, it's the Harvard Collection of Great Books*! This proves Dr. Entropy has been here — we've found the spoor of the chaos gun!'*

'Huh?'

'It's simple, lad,' answers the Abbreviator, himself a scientist who has used his knowledge of non-Newtonian physics to shrink himself, fight crime, and tour the little planets that orbit nuclei. 'You've heard of conservation of order? Well, every time Dr.

Entropy fires the chaos gun and disrupts things, the displaced order forms something wonderful!' He shakes his tiny head. 'What a fiendish device! Once she actually made a silk purse from a sow's ear!'

The Boar shakes his fist deeper into the alley. 'We've got you surrounded, you doctor of disorder!'

In reply a bolt of azure light streams outward, turning the building behind them into an ancient ruin, a stone temple of gods forgotten millennia before the first human history was recorded. To compensate, the ground before them becomes a perfectly ordered rose garden.

'Aiee!' screams the Abbreviator as the thorn of an American beauty materializes beside him, skewering his thorax.

The Bald Eagle snatches him off the thorn. 'No, little pal! Don't let it be true!'

'It is,' Superbman says, gently taking the body from the Eagle and placing it in a shoe box the Man of Style has found in the rubble. 'My superb hearing reveals no heartbeat! But we shall bury him in the backyard at our headquarters, and we shall avenge him!'

The heroes unconsciously strike determined poses, from their shelter in the shadow of the ancient temple. 'This is odd,' whispers the Boar. 'I've fought Dr. Entropy how many times? Fifteen . . .'

'Sixteen,' corrects his friend, who also has a superb memory.

'And no one's ever been killed before!' He clenches his jaw angrily. 'I've been too decent about it! Okay, Dr. Entropy, no more Mr. Nice Guy!' he screams, heading for the back of the alley.

'Wait!'

His friends spring after him. The blue light bursts forth again, turning the Boar's clothes into old rags with wonderfully embroidered edges, but he continues running. A mound of garbage beside him becomes tiny leaping gazelles. The chaos bolt hits Superbman, covering his perfect physique with swamp debris. Paving stones below the Bald Eagle and his ward come alive and begin squealing and running, propelling the pair into a pit of lukewarm bittersweet chocolate, while beside them all appears a table with a ten-course Szechuan banquet.

'Help! Fire!' calls Flyboy. Superbman, washing himself off quickly with jasmine tea and patting dry with napkins, pulls them

out, then licks the chocolate from his fingers. He hopes that the Boar will be all right. Superbman knows of the evil Dr. Entropy, whose father had been a respected scientist, inventor of the chaos star drive. Dr. Entropy had for no good reason blamed his accidental death on the mighty Boar and had perverted the chaos drive into a horrible weapon, using what might have been a boon for humanity only for evil and self-gain.

The Boar rushes onward, unstoppable, like the powerful forest beast for which he is named. He comes upon a crouched, black-caped figure, surrounded by heavy bags of money, who is leveling a pistol at him. He catches up a garbage can lid, and it takes the bolt of light, becoming a circle of yesterday's newspapers. Tossing it aside, where it knocks over a Ming vase painted with plum blossoms, the Boar grasps the chaos gun, crushing it to a fine powder.

Then he lifts the cloaked figure, dangling it over the pavement. 'Now! I've never hit you before, Dr. Entropy, but . . .'

The hood falls back, revealing the criminal's face. 'No, please don't hit!' he pleads. 'I've just had extensive dental work!' The Boar drops him, standing over him incredulously. 'Who are you? Where'd you get that gun? And where is she? Where is Dr. Entropy?'

'I had the weirdest dream last night,' Rachel said. 'There were, like, superheroes in it.'

'Was it erotic?' asked Jack, the doctor sharing her shift. They were gathered by the Mr. Coffee during the predawn slump, when even the roads are quiet; when cortisol levels are lowest and the human body least able to handle stress. They were dressed identically, in soft green scrubs, the loose tops and pajama pants resembling medical judo *gis.* 'You and some hunk from Krypton, right? Or, hey, how about Plastic Man?'

'Or Batman and Robin,' leered Bill. 'They're *my* favorites.'

'Come on. Didn't you ever think how easy things would be if we lived in the universe where comic books take place?'

'No,' said Jack. 'Can't say I ever did. Okay, who's gonna do the pelvic?'

'Not another. Are we having a half-price sale for PID?' Rachel grimaced. 'As seen on channel seventeen: "Women, do you have pain occasionally *down there*? Do you have a purulent discharge that would gag a maggot? Are you bored and listless with nothing else to do this slow Tuesday night? Why not come to the scenic Las Pulgas County Hospital and Cockroach Motel for a fun-packed pelvic examination . . .?"'

'With a cold plastic speculum,' Jack added in a deep announcer's voice.

'. . . and best, it's *free*!'

'Act now,' Bill the charge nurse finished, 'and we'll throw in two million units of intramuscular benzathine penicillin! Doctors are standing by. . . . Honestly, gang, you're nowhere near the record. That was when the cops decided to clean up the Stroll one night. Every hooker in town had nowhere to go, so they came to the ER for a checkup.'

'Sounds like a job for Johnny Quick,' said Rachel. They flipped for it and she lost. After the exam she took a swab to the emergency room lab. This was a tiny room with a laundry hamper, a stack of bedpans, outdated bottles of Gram's stain reagent, and a microscope. It was a far cry from any laboratory in a comic book. She tried to mentally dress it up with bubbling retorts, grinning skeletons, and a madly arcing Jacob's ladder. 'And now, with my microscopic vision, I will see the very fabric of the universe. . . .'

The wet prep of the discharge showed a few clue cells and a triangular trichomonad, waving its single flagellum gamely. 'She's got wigglers.'

Did they have trich in the world of superheroes? she wondered. Surely not. Surely people who could fly to the stars without spaceships, people who could become invincible or incredibly strong, who could see the future or eat metal . . . surely such people would not suffer from *Trichomonas.*

She flourished the slide, glaring evilly at the laundry hamper. Then she heard a crash and a scream.

Turning off the microscope, she strode across the hall, where Jack had been preparing to sew up a laceration.

The sterile tray had been knocked over, and the floor was slippery with Betadine. Jack and a nurse, a small gray woman, were backed up against the wall, Jack with his gloved hands up. Rachel couldn't tell if he was trying to maintain sterility or to surrender. A thin young man with stringy hair and a number of homemade tattoos was holding a gun on them.

'You tryin' to kill me, man?' he was saying. He swung about to include the newcomer under the rubric of the pistol.

'Do you mind?' Rachel asked. 'I'm *trying* to see a patient.'

'A sick little baby,' she added for the sociopath's benefit as he glared at her. 'And if she starts crying, we'll *never* get any peace.'

'He's trying to kill me. Look.' He pointed the gun muzzle at his forearm, where a deep wound was outlined by iodine prep.

'Ooh, that's nasty. Needs stitches.'

'I was trying to get the glass fragments out,' Jack said.

'Shut up, man!'

Rachel shook her head sympathetically. 'He must need something for the pain.'

The sociopath's face lit up. 'I'm allergic to codeine, man. I need Demerol.'

Rachel nodded to the nurse. 'Go get seventy-five of Demerol. Let me see this.'

She gloved up. 'I need a new suture set. Well, give me your arm,' she added, annoyed. 'And get that out of my face so I can work. How'd you do this?'

'Got mad and slugged a window,' he said proudly, letting her recleanse the skin. Jack began to edge for the door.

'Oh, look, there's the glass. I can get it —' She grabbed the tweezers, saying, 'Here, pull the skin back a little. I see it. I've almost got it.'

As the sociopath retracted for her, the gun on the gurney behind him, the police burst in. 'Cancel the Demerol,' said Rachel. 'Turkey. I should sew you up without lidocaine.'

'That was crazy,' Kent said. He'd waited until her shift was over and then dragged her out for breakfast, this time to a diner on the wharf. They watched fishing boats setting out into the fog as they ate hotcakes and home fries. 'Things like this wouldn't happen if the emergency room was adequately staffed.'

'Then I'd have to be crazy all alone. Where's the fun in that?'

O. S. Y. 2—3

He put down his coffee. 'Why the hell did you do it?'

She shrugged. 'Off the record? I dunno. The asshole was annoying me.'

'I think — shit! I think you enjoyed the whole damn thing. That's why you won't help me. You like chaos in the ER.'

'Maybe.'

He sighed. 'Okay, let's do something on the record. Why'd you become a doctor?' He clicked out his pen point.

'You mean the inspirational stuff I told med school admissions about how I wanted to alleviate suffering, work in a free clinic for migrant workers, and maybe even join the Peace Corps? Well, it's all bullshit. Sure I said all that once, I think I even believed it. But you want to know why I *really* became a doctor?'

He nodded. 'Your public awaits.'

'When I was a freshman in college they ran the old *Flash Gordon* serial, one episode every Wednesday, after the Bergman films. Every week, Flash and Dale and Zarkov would get captured by some bizarro mutant types and then be dragged in front of, say, the king of the Frogmen.

'"Ooh, what do we have here?" asks the king. "What a wonderful heroic man Flash is. Throw him in the pit and make him shovel radioactive lizards." Then he leers at Dale. "Ooh, what a gorgeous pure lady. Toss her into my harem; I'll be there soon." Finally he gets to Zarkov. "Ooh, Dr. Zarkov, you're such a fine scientist. Put him in a nice air-conditioned lab, boys, and give him everything he wants." That's why I decided to go to med school.'

He slammed his notebook shut. 'You know, you're crazy.'

She's on the porch, looking out at the ocean; behind her is another ocean, slanting off in the opposite direction. Her condominium is built on the very edge of the planet. Two seas wash its foundations. Her robotic butler enters. 'Madam, there is a gentleman at the door! He is unarmed, and my sensors reveal no superabilities!'

'Show him in,' she says, fingering a small blaster she keeps in the pocket of her dressing gown. Should she fire, the robe will be ruined. These things are unavoidable.

'Dr. Hugo Mayhem,' announces the robot, retiring to a corner. The newcomer is a tall man with a hawk nose, slightly crazed eyes, and hair and beard sadly in need of a trim. He wears blue jeans, an Irish knit sweater, and hiking boots. When he speaks, it is with an Oxonian accent.

'Dr. Entropy?'

'You have the advantage, sir!'

'We met, I believe, at a Corrupt Geniuses League function! The funeral for poor Hans!'

'You do seem familiar. . . .'

Striding to the edge of the porch, Mayhem glances down. 'Such an amazing planet! I have often wondered how they kept it from eroding back to a spherical shape and how its gravity could keep the oceans flat! I should have guessed they were painted on!'

She nods. 'The dry air does annoy one's sinuses, and I tire of having to create water by nuclear fusion each time I wish a bath, but I would not trade this condominium for any other fortress on any other planet!'

'Just so,' he agrees. 'Now I daresay this is why I appear familiar!' He points up at the sky. Looking past his finger, she notices the constellation.

'Why, it's you!'

He sighs ruefully. 'What do you get for the man who has everything? My friends rearranged the stars for my birthday! Unfortunately, they moved Fomalhaut into a low-rent region, with the Gamma Egregians for their closest neighbors! There's a large price on my head as a result!'

He begins to look about nervously. She changes the subject. 'What brings you here, Dr. Mayhem?'

'Oh, the usual! I was fleeing for my life and decided to stop for lunch at Rick's Café Terrestriale! he says, naming a famous restaurant in the capital city of the square planet.

She nods. 'Rick's one-third human; he has the best Earth cuisine this side of Alpha Centauri!'

'Ahh, the broccoli and squid with Sirian sauce . . . but I digress! Whilst there, I overheard some heroic sorts at the next table! They were discussing Dr. Entropy, whom they described as a renegade priestess of the Cult of Chaos and a sworn foe of humanity! It seems that when she disappeared, she gave her chaos gun to a lackey!'

'Severance pay, when I retired!'

'He unfortunately appears to have used it to kill the Abbreviator!'

She gasps in amazement. They stand for a minute in silence, then she sighs. 'For an obnoxious, uptight little twit, he wasn't too bad!'

He puts a sympathetic hand upon her shoulder. 'The Abbreviator's friends have sworn to avenge his death upon Dr. Entropy, following her if need be to the ends of the universe!'

She shrugs. 'Well, so much for retirement! The Boar will find me; he has uncanny forest senses! Plus I had to go and leave a clue, didn't I?'

'Oh, not a clew!'

'Yes, I really did!' She shakes her head ruefully, thinking how closely she has conformed to the unwritten rules of supervillainry. 'I wrote, "I'm going where it's less hip!"'

Her visitor frowns. 'Naturally, sooner or later he's bound to realize this can only refer to the squarest planet in the universe! I'm afraid you blew it, Dr. Entropy! It's only a matter of time before you receive a visit from the mighty Boar! (Such an aptly named character!)'

She pauses in her misery. 'Hey, watch what you say about my archfoe!'

They paged her in the cafeteria, and she ran all the way back to the emergency room. Bill was bent over an unconscious patient, trying to find a viable vein in an arm decorated with old needle tracks. 'Two bullets to the squash,' he called. 'Vitals are stable. Should we call in neurosurgery?'

Blood was dripping onto the floor from the turban of bandages, and the room already stank of unwashed feet and Mulligan Brothers rosé. 'Not yet,' Rachel muttered. 'What happened?'

'Family says he comes home tonight,' a paramedic began, 'and he tells them his friends shot him two times in the head.'

'Some friends.'

'Then he goes, "I'm done for!" and falls down, so they call us.'

'Let's get portable skull X rays, and preop bloods.' Taking a deep breath, she added, 'Check the EtOH level, too,' stealing a glance at the clock. Everyday at about eight P.M., the ER changed its smell from blood and urine and old disinfectant to cheap beer and cheaper wine. The odor seemed to linger until she smelled it constantly, even when she wasn't at work, and the thought of taking a drink made her stomach churn.

Rachel did a quick neuro check; the patient was lethargic, but his brain stem and motor functions seemed intact. She held her breath while staring into his eyes with her opthalmoscope, then leaned back, finally unveiling his head. There was a small scalp laceration, still oozing blood, but that was all. 'Two bullets?' Where the hell were they?

Later, after seeing three more drunks, two bellyaches, and a sore throat, things had quieted down enough for her to go to midnight supper. She was not surprised to find Kent in the cafeteria, waiting like some predatory animal.

'Lemme tell you about this case,' she said. 'Guy stumbles home, says he's been shot, then keels over. I'm in a panic; do you know how brain looks after a thirty-eight? Only, this guy's fine. I keep looking for bullets on the X rays, and there aren't any. I spend five hundred of the taxpayers' dollars on this guy, and he's just dead drunk from too much table wine.'

Kent said, 'Look. We're almost to the point where we can force a hearing. We just need one person from the inside to testify that the place is a pit. You could do it, Rachel. Tell the board of supervisors how it's understaffed, underequipped; how you wouldn't take your maiden aunt's poodle there. And I know you despise poodles.'

'Christ, why me? I'm no idealistic lover of humanity.'

Kent took off his glasses and rubbed his eyes. 'You're my best bet, *Doctor*. Because you're not from some med school in a country I can't even pronounce, and you don't work ER just for a down payment on a Mercedes, and you don't look like an ad for Cocaine User's Profile. *Last accomplishment: saving a life. Favorite snow: Andean flake.*' He looked at her suspiciously. 'Do you have anything you can wear besides scrub suits?'

'I have formal scrubs. . . . Let me sleep on it.' She smiled winningly, thinking it was time to retreat. 'Have I told you about these strange dreams I've been having?'

'Dreams? What's next, astrology and biorhythms?' He

flinched, seeing his star witness dissolving into just another trendy Las Pulgas yuppie.

'Of course not. You know me, I don't believe in anything. It's just, they're so weird. . . .' She tried to describe the dreams: first the glimpses of the cube-shaped planet, then the super-battle, and finally the mad scientists who just stood and chatted.

'I mean, you always knew the heroes must hang out and party together, sort of like old-time movie stars going to Pickfair. 'Honey, let's cruise over to Doom Patrol headquarters and see what's cooking!'

'I guess it makes sense villains would be chummy, too.' She picked at her unnameable casserole. 'My all-time favorite story was *Flash* number 123. That's where the 1961 Flash meets another Flash, who'd starred in the 1940's *Flash* comic book. They concluded that when Gardner Fox, the Golden Age *Flash* writer, had thought he was dreaming, his mind was actually tapping into events in a parallel dimension. God, it was great!'

'Wait a minute. Are you trying to tell me that you're getting news from another world, where superheroes exist?' He leaned away from her.

'You ought to move there,' she told him, annoyance masking her face. 'Crusading reporters are probably all the rage. You could go into your secret lab and invent a superserum.'

'Not me, I flunked chemistry.'

'Yeah, you're more the magic word type. Like Billy Batson saying "SHAZAM." Let's see —' She began to giggle, then said in a resonant voice, 'When Kent Randolph, heroic boy reporter for the *Daily Journal*, says the magic word "WARP," he is mystically imbued with the exposé abilities of Woodward and Bernstein, the popularity of Ann Landers, the wit of Royko, and the power of the Pulitzer prize!'

Kent laughed also. 'And how about you? Let's see, a doctor would need the idealism of Schweitzer, the diagnostic acumen of Ben Casey . . .'

'The sheer humanity of W.C. Fields . . .'

Kent leaned across the table. 'Okay, Wonder Doc. How about starting your quest for truth, justice, and the American way by helping me?'

She shook her head. 'Sorry, physicians aren't superhero material. Research scientists, wealthy playboys, reporters: Those are the folks who become masked sentinels of justice. Doctors just turn into maniacal world conquerors. Dr. Doom, Dr. Psycho, the Brainwave.'

He looked astonished. 'But medicine is so . . . so respectable. It seems made for heroics!'

'Well, yeah, there were a few.' She began to tick them off on the fingers of one hand. 'Dr. Strange. He was a money-grabbing alcoholic surgeon before changing his profession to sorcery. Dr. Mid-Nite. He quit medicine to become a sensationalist writer. Thor. He was so obnoxious that the gods of Asgard took away his memory and sent him to medical school as a punishment. He's the only one who stayed in practice — until all his patients left because he was always off fighting mystic menaces during office hours.'

Pushing back her chair, she stood. 'Excuse me, I've been here too long. I can hear the suffering calling to me from the ER. And you know what they're saying?' She paused at the tray rack. 'They're saying, "Hey, Doc, got a beer?" '

Kent smiled perfunctorily at her joke until she was gone, then began shredding a napkin. 'Dr. Worthless.'

'I hear you're looking for me!'

The Boar spins about. He never expected to find Dr. Entropy sitting in his living room. Merely thinking of the consequences of his secret identity having been discovered makes his heart race.

'How did you know?' he asks, pulling his mask back snug. 'Uh . . . how'd you know I'd be visiting my friend Willard Wasp, the crusading reporter?'

'Just luck! Lucky I noticed that you two are the same height, have the same eyes and chin . . .'

'Lots of people look alike!'

He approaches cautiously. She holds up empty, ungloved hands.

'Sit down, hero! I come in peace!' Waiting until he has complied, she continues. 'I understand you're looking for me! I'm really sorry about the Abbreviator, but you can't blame me; I was two galaxies away at the time! I've retired, turned over a new leaf!'

'I've heard that one before!' the Boar says bitterly. 'Mad

scientist pretends to reform, becomes your best friend. . . . You give him your unlisted phone number or a signal calculator. Next thing you know, it's pow! Your secret weakness, or a piece of your long-lost planet, right in the gut!'

'You know me better than that! Have I ever lied to you?'

He scratches his head. 'No, Dr. Entropy, you haven't — and you're better in that regard than my airhead girlfriend.'

'Admit it, Boar, we've had some good times! Remember when I brought all the statues at the Metropolis Museum of Modern Art to life?'

He starts laughing. 'And the knight was chasing the police cars. . . .'

'Or the time you caught me at the auto show — honest, I was only checking out the new models — and I transformed the Buicks into dinosaurs?'

'Do you know the mess they made?'

'Be thankful they were herbivores! Come on — I just want to sit in my nice quiet condo and work on my memoirs or maybe a unified field theorem!'

'Why should I believe you?'

'Look, let me tell you my origin story! I'm a doctor! I'd invented a ray to cure cancer and psoriasis; the prototype of the chaos gun! But I needed a power source — pure radium! My colleagues thought me crazy! I couldn't get a grant, and I'd already used up my life's savings building the ray!

'So I thought I'd borrow the radium! You know, once they saw it work, they'd forgive me the theft and let me mass-produce the thing! What a boon to a suffering humanity!

'Only, when I went to borrow the radium, I needed help, so I hired these bumbling idiots from the Planet of People With No Vowels in Their Names! The next thing I know, you're there trashing my lackeys, I've turned your Boarmobile into rotten haddock, and I'm a wanted criminal! So what else could I do? I didn't have a job anymore — I had to keep robbing stuff!'

The Boar sighs. 'Have you learned your lesson?'

'Yes! Never again will I hire anyone from the Planet of People With No Vowels in Their Names. No, seriously: I didn't want to be a villain; I just wanted to help! Now I just want to be left alone!'

The Boar rises, holding out a hand. 'You've been a good

archfoe. Remember the time we teamed up to defeat Nowhere Man and his Invisible Army? We did swell — until they were defeated and you changed my boots to peanut butter!'

'Consider it a prophylactic double cross,' she laughs. 'I knew you'd seen me stealing the ether batteries, an offence committed after our truce, and you were probably going to sock me away in jail for that!'

'You're right!' he smiles. 'Well, I promise I'll help! I'll put in a good word, and the judge'll probably give you a reduced sentence!'

'No way,' she snarls. 'Okay, I asked . . .' and she throws a small chaos grenade at him as he lunges for her. She's over the couch and heading for the door, but he's blocking it. Meanwhile his stylish young-professional living room turns into a student hovel, albeit with pure gold brick and board shelving, and the Barry Manilow song on the stereo becomes a catchy tune by the Dead Kennedys. The curtains are now spun crystal.

'You're trapped,' he says.

'Never!' She bolts into the kitchen, locking the door and shoving a chair against it, then looks about quickly for weaponry. If only she'd built a new chaos gun. But then, she hadn't intended to fight.

She pauses, furious at the turn of events. She is caught in a typical bachelor's kitchen, with cookery and spices good for any contingency but a pile of dishes in the sink and Lean Cuisine packets in the freezer. Cockroaches are lunching in the dirty dishes. She tosses a small chaos grenade into the sink; the cockroaches turn to slime, but the dishes become Wedgwood china, embellished with azure silhouette roaches.

'Hope he likes blue,' she says, reaching into the refrigerator. She cracks open a Diet Pepsi and thinks.

All she has to work from is a collection of upscale cooking equipment. That will be enough. Quickly she rewires the Cuisinart, attaches a corkscrew and a set of Ginsu knives, then grounds it with a wooden salad bowl. She can hear the Boar banging against the door; he is hesitant to demolish his own apartment and, besides, thinks her trapped and helpless. Turning the handle of the cheese grater, she watches space and time warp before her and prepares to step through. . . .

Rachel was exhausted. She'd spent at least an hour wrestling with a man who'd been beaten up by some friends ('What's with friends in this town?'). He was encephalopathic from head trauma, unable to understand that he was in a hospital. Not even truly conscious, he'd screamed and thrashed and destroyed a set of leather restraints before forty-five milligrams of Valium had calmed him down.

'Enough to kill a small horse,' the charge nurse had remarked as they'd finally quieted the man enough to get the CT head scan.

'Unless the horse also had alcoholic cross-tolerance,' she replied.

After that and the usual other pleasures of an emergency room on a warm Saturday night when the moon is full and paychecks recently cashed, she returned home. Her clothing smelled of blood and vomit and wine. She showered, changed into a fresh scrub suit (with Centralcity General Hospital's initials prominent on the pockets), and contemplated throwing her dirty sneakers into the ocean. 'Probably kill all the fish and cause a red tide,' she realized, and tossed them on the back porch. Lying on the couch, she closed her eyes and . . .

. . . sees Dr. Entropy emerge from the kitchen. 'It's okay, I come in peace!'

Rachel sits up and stretches. 'I've seen you before. . . .'

'On TV, right? I think Dan Rather covers the superbattles very well — Cronkite always seemed faintly disapproving! I hated thinking Cronkite didn't like me!'

'This is crazy,' Rachel clutches her hair. 'I'll wake up in a minute.'

Her cloaked visitor is examining her outfit. 'CGH. Let me guess! Captain Green something or other! Green's the most popular color motif for superheroes. I hope you realize that!'

'Huh?'

Dr. Entropy points to the initials.

'These are scrubs. Stolen from Centralcity General Hospital.'

'They certainly look more comfortable than what I'm wearing!' Dr. Entropy is clad in skintight black leotards, with red belt, gloves, and boots, a black cape, and goggles. 'You're a doctor and a thief? We have a lot in common! In fact, we even look a bit alike.'

She takes off her goggles and shakes out her hair. They could be twins, except that Dr. Entropy is in better shape from her life on the run and has a more stylish haircut. 'Who are you?'

'Rachel Wirtham, M.D.'

Dr. Entropy sinks into the bentwood rocker. 'Oy! So am I! What gives?' She rocks pensively, the chair scraping over the end of her cape.

'I think I understand.' Rachel explains about parallel worlds, and Flash *number 123, and her own dreams.*

'Makes sense,' says Dr. Entropy. As a doctor, she understands all about things like quantum physics and alternate realities. Medical education on her world is a bit more general than that on Rachel's. 'I've never traveled to another dimension before, though my archfoe the Boar does it fairly regularly! I understand he's a Boar in every dimension he's visited!'

'I've met a few people like that.'

Dr. Entropy smiles. 'A new world! Well, show me the sights!'

Rachel shrugs. It is, after all, simply a dream. They go to her room for jackets, and Dr. Entropy insists on a tour of the apartment, meanwhile describing her own beachfront home, the condominium on the edge of the cuboid planet. Rachel finds herself longing for such a home, so far from Earth and Earthlings. She lends Dr. Entropy her extra trench coat — the coastal fog is quite dense today — and they set off down Maginot Boulevard to tour Las Pulgas. 'Must be a lot different from your universe, right? I mean, diseases, social unrest, no air cars . . .'

'Oh no, it's just like my world!'

Rachel walks a few minutes in silence. 'But — you guys live in space. Every cheap thug has a solar-powered air car. Serums give you invulnerability, and soft drinks make you stretch. And you say nothing's different?'

Dr. Entropy sighs. 'Unfortunately! All you say is true! Our physical laws must be slightly different from yours! For instance, I think your light beams travel faster, and your sound waves slower!'

Rachel nods. She'd always wondered how superheroes could converse while dodging laser beams.

'I suspect human physiology must be different as well! We don't have post-traumatic encephalopathy, like that patient you told me about! When we're knocked out, we just wake up, say "Great

galaxies, I feel awful," and start fighting again!'

'Not even any retrograde amnesia?'

'What's that?'

Rachel imagines a world without concussions, probably without dementia pugilistica as well. Otherwise, with the frequency with which they were struck on the head, every superhero would soon be within a chronic-care facility.

'I've got an idea,' Dr. Entropy says. She pulls Rachel behind some trees, taking out a small device rather like a suction cup with a calculator attached to it.

'This is a memory transducer, the latest thing in villainry! Let's say you've been cornered and are about to be struck dead by a meteor or the platen of a giant typewriter! The MT already contains most of your memories! You just clap it to your head momentarily, to get it up-to-date, then toss it at a bird or a passerby! Presto, he becomes you and escapes. Lucky these things are covered under the Fifth Amendment; otherwise we'd be in trouble every time we're caught with one!'

Rachel looks suspiciously at her visitor. Working at a public hospital, she is used to criminals, but they are usually sociopaths and small-time hoods, whose criminal behavior is limited to the petty, violent and unimaginative. She has never met a renegade genius before, especially one who looks just like her.

'Trust me! If we both hold it simultaneously, the MT will merely act as a conduit for memories!'

'What the hell, it's just a dream,' Rachel says. They both hold the device. Memories flood Rachel's mind. She sees childhood, medical school, battles, retirement on the square planet, everything.

Suddenly she understands, without the sense of sudden understanding. There is no 'Eureka!', no light bulb going on inside her head. She just understands, in a quiet way, as if she'd done so all her life.

Dr. Entropy has fled a world of superficial blacks and whites, with an underlying ambiguity. Why have the benefits of an advanced science (and a science so radically different from Rachel's that any moderately brilliant person can be a polymath, inventing supersauces in the ubiquitous basement labs) not filtered down to the populace?

Dr. Entropy suspects that it is the work of a mysterious group of savants, the Committee, who understand that cheap solar power, miraculous wonder drugs, routine reanimation, and ready space travel would destroy the status quo, and so they suppress such advances. Those who refuse to play by their rules, who want to push back the frontiers of forbidden knowledge, are labeled as mad scientists, becoming fugitives.

'So you aren't really malignant and amoral and power crazy?' Rachel asks. 'Like I am?'

Her new friend laughs politely but seems disturbed. 'What an awful Earth you live on! Everything is so unclear, so much room for improvement.'

'Now you're talking like . . . whoops, let's go back.' They have climbed the hills almost to the hospital, and Rachel can see the hospital's neurosurgeon leaning against a car, talking to someone who, from only his back, she recognizes as Kent. In Dr. Entropy's universe, the mechanics of recognition are more complex; she'd never be able to tell him just from his back. Glasses or a wig could utterly disguise a person.

'What's wrong?' asks Dr. Entropy.

'I don't want to run into Kent.'

'Your friend from the newspaper? You must be proud to know such an important person!'

She laughs. 'Newsmen aren't such a big deal on this world.'

'You mean you don't even have dolls of famous reporters?'

For once, Rachel is speechless. They return to her home, and Rachel lies back down. She is surprised to find the couch empty; she expected to see herself dreaming on it.

Dr. Entropy hangs up the coat, redonning her cape and goggles. 'It's been long enough; the Boar shouldn't still be watching his kitchen!'

They shake hands, the doctor in her greens, the villainess in her cloak.

'If I were you,' Dr. Entropy says, 'I'd help Kent!'

'That's because in your world there are definite heroes and villains.'

'Sometimes a stranger sees things more clearly!'

'Nice meeting you,' says Rachel. 'But I need some restful sleep if I'm to survive work tonight.'

Rachel was finding it hard to concentrate. She tried to keep her mind on the task of the moment — cleaning and repairing a long, jagged thumb laceration — but her thoughts kept returning to her dream and the other world. A world of heroes, of villains, of excitement and chaos . . . Bill dumped some more sterile saline in the tin. 'Thanks.' She sponged it over the laceration. Someone was shrieking loudly in a nearby room.

'Nice plastics job,' Bill remarked.

'Yeah.' The compliment didn't seem important tonight. She shrugged; the stethoscope draped over her shoulders was starting to feel heavy.

'Be much longer?'

'No.'

'Good. They're stacked up knee-deep in the waiting room, and Raj is talking to Medic Three from Buena Mota. They're bringing in a code.'

'Doesn't matter.' By the time a cardiac arrest could arrive from Buena Mota, miles away up the Coast Highway, resuscitation was an academic exercise.

'And that lady in room four? I think she's going to deliver.' A high-pitched scream punctuated his comment. 'OBs coming in.' He sighed melodramatically. 'It's chaos tonight. Utter chaos!'

Rachel paused, looked up, grinned. 'Chaos! I thrive on it.' She wished she had Dr. Entropy's chaos gun. What would happen if she sprayed the ER with its beam? Somehow she imagined things could only look better. Maybe everything would dissolve — patients, staff, the old stone building itself. Just a pile of rubble; springing up beside it, a crystalline garden. She went back to the thumb. It was slow work, but she was determined to do a perfect job. Not that it really mattered how pretty the old man's thumb looked — he'd just cut it again on another broken bottle — but the job tonight seemed to demand some pretense of attentiveness. She had four stitches to go.

'Ahem.'

Looking up, she found the hospital's young neurosurgeon standing there, come straight from surgery. He wore a paper cap and booties with his scrubs, and a mask still hung from his neck, its tie threatening to catch fire from his cigarette.

'Thought you'd want to know. Alcoholic you all saw yesterday . . .'

'The one who we poured Valium in, like a sink?'

'Yep. Took him to surgery last night. Evacuated a subdural. Clot was getting pretty large. Probably saved his life.' He looked vaguely pleased at their collaborative effort. 'Thought you'd like to know.'

'Gee, thanks, masked man.'

He started to leave, then added, 'Saw you and your friend this afternoon. Looked just like you.'

'Huh?'

'Wears weird boots and gloves, though. Relative?'

Rachel stared at him, eyes wide. He stubbed his cigarette in an emesis basin. 'Back to the wars.'

She kept staring after him.

After a minute, the patient said, 'Doc? Hey, Doc?'

She looked down at him. 'Buddy, what's the nature of reality?'

'Ha. You tell me.'

She stood, stripping off her gloves. 'I think I know a place where it's easier to figure out.' Heading for the ambulance entrance, she passed the room where Dr. Raj was asking the woman in labor to please not scream so loudly.

'Hey, Raj,' she called. 'Finish sewing up my thumb, okay?'

She paused at the nurses' station. 'Beep whoever's on second call.' Then it was out the door, into the crisp night air. Somewhere far off she heard a siren and some dogs barking. Stars shone above the hills, and she could smell the ocean. What if the chaos ray were large enough to cover an entire town, a county? Gone the tenements, the boring housing tracts, the derelicts, and the sturdy conformists. What silvery artful objects might spring up in their place? She ran downhill, all the way to the beach, hair flying behind her like a cape, stethoscope banging against her chest. Next it was up the stairs, two at a time, and into the apartment. She switched on the light and ran to the kitchen, flinging open the door.

It is dark inside, the dark of deep space, with unblinking ruby and emerald stars. There is a vortex of agate, twirling mist, and Dr. Entropy steps from it. Rachel steps forward to meet her.

'You'll need this!' Dr. Entropy hands her a gun belt and holster, then slips out of her cape and drapes it about Rachel's shoulders.

'Thanks!' In turn, Rachel gives over her stethoscope and a slip of paper. They shake hands.

'One thing,' Dr. Entropy says. 'Don't try to swim in the oceans. They're just painted on.'

Rachel nods, stepping into the mist. Dr. Entropy closes the kitchen door behind her, then goes to the phone, dialing the number on the slip of paper. 'Hello, Kent? About that hearing . . .'

JACK MASSA

Jack Massa's first professional sale was a novel, *Mooncrow* (1979). His first short story, 'The Daydream Enhancer', appeared in *F&SF* the following year. Another story went straight into the 1983 *Best of Omni* anthology, by-passing first publication in the magazine . . .

He lives in Georgia and has written two more novels, neither of which has yet found a publisher. He is now at work on another novel, set in the far future and involving artificial intelligence.

The following story was first written in early 1986 and taken to Sycamore Hill*, the writers' workshop run by John Kessel in North Carolina. Since then, Massa says, it 'has been through more versions than just about anything I've written . . . it took me a long time and many rewrites to finally settle on what I wanted this story to say.'

What that is, the reader will have to discover. All Massa will reveal is that 'it reflects both my experiences in the computer industry and my theological attitudes.'

*'Home Front' by James Patrick Kelly, also in this volume, is another story from Sycamore Hill.

PRAYERWARE

by
JACK MASSA

Ferguson sat down at the terminal and keyed in an opening prayer. The machine responded with a low beeping sound while the terminal software established communication with RUMS — the Religious Universal Mainframe System.

After a few seconds the beeping ceased and RUM's initial prompt appeared on the screen:

BLESS YOU, <USERNAME>. WHAT IS ON YOUR MIND?

Ferguson referred to his test script and typed: 'I am a seventy-year-old man whose wife has just died after a long illness. I do not understand why God allowed her to suffer so.'

There was a pause — 5.89 seconds as measured by the terminal clock and displayed in the upper right corner of the screen. Then RUMS replied in blue phosphor letters:

IT IS OFTEN DIFFICULT TO UNDERSTAND WHY SUCH TERRIBLE THINGS HAPPEN.

The test scenarios were provided by Corporate Marketing Division. The script itself was written by Ferguson, designed to test all aspects of system performance.

And a response time of 5.89 seconds was far from adequate performance. Ferguson typed a code to record the length of the pauses. Then he keyed in another line:

'I do not understand it. I feel God has turned away from me.'

GOD HAS NOT ABANDONED YOU, answered RUMS after 5.19 seconds. HIS LOVE ABIDES.

'But why should I believe that?'

After a pause the terminal beeped and a system message flashed on the screen:

LEARNING MODE. RECURSIVE COMPUTATIONS IN PROGRESS.

Ferguson swore and sat back in his chair. In the next room, the mainframe's parallel processing units whirred away as RUMS reorganized its knowledge base, seeking to evolve a proper answer.

Management of learning mode was a task for the knowledge programmers. Ferguson's job was system integration and quality control. He recorded the query that had initiated the learning mode, then pressed the reset button, flushing the terminal's RAM.

While the machine was rebooting, a heavy hand clamped on Ferguson's shoulder.

'How's the test going, Ed?'

Mike Lee, the project manager, leaned imposingly over Ferguson's chair. Lee was over six feet and more than three hundred pounds.

'Slowly,' Ferguson said. 'Half of my test questions are sending it off into recursion.'

'We expected that,' Mike Lee remarked. 'This early in the development cycle there's bound to be lots of gaps. Other problems?'

'Response time. It's averaging over five seconds.'

'How many terminals are you simulating?'

'Fifty. But remember, the voice processor isn't hooked in yet. That will add about six-tenths of a second to every exchange.'

Mike Lee showed a sour frown. 'Response time will have to be cut somewhere. Marketing requirements specify four seconds max.'

Hard to do, Ferguson thought. He said, 'The marketing requirements strike me as pretty unreasonable, especially the deadline date.'

'I know,' Mike Lee moaned. 'I've told Corporate over and over we can't build a decent expert system in that time frame. But you know how it is: religious software is hot right now. We have to get the product out right away or miss the marketing window.'

Ferguson keyed the lock combination and opened the door to his apartment. The living room was cluttered with magazines, video diskettes, empty fast-food containers, unwashed coffee cups. He went to find Molly, either to complain that she hadn't cleaned up or to suggest they go out to supper — he wasn't sure which.

The door to her room was open, so he stuck his head inside. Molly Ferguson, aged sixteen, was fashionably dressed in a green monk's robe decorated with ruby sequins and belted tightly at her waist. With hands folded reverently, she sat in front of her computer.

'Dear God,' she said, reading the words from the screen, 'Grant peace to the Earth, and economic prosperity to all people.'

Ferguson winced, started to back away, then steadied himself. He had known for some time that his daughter was using online prayer. 'Donations' to several computerized churches had shown up on last month's phone bill. Ferguson had ignored the problem, hoping it would pass. But this month's bill showed the calls increasing both in length and in frequency.

First her mother runs off to join a pagan commune in Tennessee; now this.

'And grant that more and more people may hear Your voice,' Molly was saying, 'through the gift of this technology.'

Ferguson knocked on the open door and walked in. 'Molly, I'm home.'

She lifted an index finger in his direction, without shifting her eyes from the monitor. 'Just a second, Dad.'

Ferguson crossed his arms and waited. Molly whispered fervently to a luminous, kindly face that hovered now, disembodied, on her screen. Ferguson had seen the face before, in a magazine ad for one of the big religious software companies.

Molly bowed her head as organ chords — tinny on the home computer's cheap speaker — swelled to a crescendo. A closing screen appeared with the acronym BLISS in big gold letters and, beneath it, the name spelled out: Benign Love Interactive Software System. Molly switched off the computer and stood up, smiling at her father.

'Hi, Dad. Sorry about the living room. I'll go pick up now.'

'It can wait.' Ferguson said. 'Sit down, I want to talk to you.'

Molly took her seat again and watched him with placid blue eyes. Ferguson paced the carpet.

'Listen, I know I haven't been good about keeping track of you lately, since your mother left. I mean, trying to be both

father and mother —'

'I'm doing okay, Dad.'

'No, you're not. You may think you are. I'm concerned that you've gotten sucked in by this religious software fad.'

'I don't feel sucked in,' Molly answered with dignity. 'But interactive prayer has become central to my life.'

'That's what worries me,' Ferguson said. 'Listen, Molly, I think if you examine your motives, you'll realize that you're only doing this as a reaction to your mother's leaving. She runs off and joins the pagans. So naturally you feel hurt, abandoned. So you respond by tuning in to this computerized religion. Which is exactly opposite to hers. Do you see?'

'No,' Molly said. 'That's not right. I'm not thrilled with Mom's religion — all that dancing around naked and worshipping trees. But I respect her right to make her own choices, and I expect the same right for myself.'

Ferguson sighed, sat down on the bed. 'I do respect your right to think for yourself. I've always tried to teach you that. That's why this has got me so worried. I see you surrendering your autonomy to a pile of code running in a mainframe somewhere. That's what you're praying to, a pile of code.'

'I don't pray to BLISS. We pray together. I don't suppose you've ever tried online prayer.'

'Of course not.'

'Then how can you be so sure —'

'Because I know how it's made. My God! I work in a place where they're building a religion system. It's just a data base collected from a panel of ministers and some heuristics to make it run. It *seems* like it's talking to you, but it's a trick. There's nobody there.'

Molly came and sat beside him, staring soberly into his eyes. 'I know you think you have all the answers, Dad. But that's only because you've closed your mind. I realize that when I talk to BLISS I'm only talking to software. But it works. It puts me in touch with the Divine.'

Scowling, Ferguson shook his head. Religious software was a fad, he told himself, and kids naturally followed fads. But then it crossed his mind that he was losing Molly, just as he had lost his wife.

'Come over here and pray with me, Dad,' she said. 'Try it.'

Ferguson stood. 'Pick up the living room. I'm going out for a beer.'

BLESS YOU, FERGUSON, WHAT IS ON YOUR MIND?

Ferguson had typed in his own name. For the moment he had put aside the test scripts and was using random responses to test the knowledge base interface programs.

'Fourscore and seven years ago,' he entered.

I DO NOT UNDERSTAND, answered RUMS.

'Nor do I.'

PLEASE TELL ME HOW I MAY HELP YOU.

'There is no help for me.'

THERE IS ALWAYS HELP AVAILABLE, IF YOU OPEN YOUR HEART TO GOD.

'I don't believe in God.'

RUMS paused, searching for an answer far down on its decision tree. YOU MUST BE SEEKING GOD, OR YOU WOULD NOT HAVE COME TO ME.

'I'm a systems engineer testing you,' Ferguson answered. 'And I don't believe in God.'

The software evaluated this for several moments, then the terminal beeped.

LEARNING MODE. RECURSIVE COMPUTATIONS IN PROGRESS.

Ferguson stared at the blinking message with a dim, perverse sense of satisfaction.

On Tuesday afternoon Ferguson attended a project review meeting. As usual, it was a circus. Ferguson usually felt like the guy who sweeps up after the elephants.

One of the biggest jumbos of them all was there today: Heston Sharp, Senior Vice President of New Product Development and Marketing. Sharp and several of his marketing managers had flown down from the DataLong corporate headquarters in Boston. The marketeers wore tailored spandex suits and polished shoes of real leather. They sat across the large conference table from Mike Lee and his far less fashionable engineering staff.

Using video screens that rose from the table in front of every chair, Mike Lee reported on the engineering status. Animated charts and graphs compared scheduled and actual progress. Response time was still too long, the voice-processing interface full of bugs. Mike Lee stressed at every opportunity that schedules were too short. His engineers could only do so much.

Then Heston Sharp took over. He reviewed the status of the marketing plans and cited the current vast popularity of online prayer. Despite some negative trends — including some well-publicized lawsuits and an anticomputer crusade by a popular TV evangelist — the market outlook for the next twelve months remained, in Heston Sharp's word, tremendous.

'Several of the larger mainstream churches are planning to computerize soon,' Heston Sharp said. 'We'll have a chance to make proposals to all of them, but only if the development schedule is met. We're counting on each and every one of you. If necessary, unlimited overtime is expected. I can't overstate how vital this product is to the corporation.'

Naturally, Ferguson thought. He had heard the same speech on every project for the past eighteen years. Building any software system took time. But DataLong's senior management always reacted late to market trends, then expected their engineers to work miracles. The only difference this time was the new market, religious software — an aspect Ferguson found particularly repugnant.

'Here's something to cheer you up,' Heston Sharp added in a jovial voice. 'We've got the official name for the product; it just cleared the legal office yesterday. No more RUMS. From now on, you're working on DataLong's PrayerWare. How do you like it?'

Flora, Ferguson's ex-wife, came to the apartment to pick up Molly. She was supposed to take her to the commune for two months — alternating custody.

Flora wore no makeup. Her red hair fell past her shoulders in a wild tangle that Ferguson found attractive in spite of himself. She looked thinner, in a worn dress with a flower print, her nipples showing through the fabric. Ferguson had to admit that the country life seemed to agree with her.

'Hi.' She bounced in, all glow and smiles.

'There's a problem,' Ferguson began. 'I would have called you, but of course you have no phones up there.'

'What is it? Molly's not sick?'

'No, but she doesn't want to go with you.'

'Why not? Have you had her brainwashed or something?'

'No. Believe me. I'm not happy about this. She's gotten into religion. Online religion.'

'Oh, fine.' Flora threw up her hands in dismay. 'I should have expected something like this. You and that damn computer you bought her. How could you let her get into that?'

'She says she'd be happy to go with you,' Ferguson explained. 'Except that she wouldn't be able to pray, since you're not wired up there.'

'Of course we're not. We're up there to get away from all this . . . hardware, electronic stimulation. You know, Ed, I can feel it, just driving down from the mountains, it's like your bones start buzzing. And when we got near Atlanta . . .' She held up a shaky hand. 'Look how tense I am! You people who live down here just —'

'Please don't start with the sermons,' Ferguson interrupted.

'You get so *desensitized* you don't realize —'

'I asked you, please.'

Molly walked into the room, wearing her jacket, carrying suitcases. 'You can stop arguing now,' she announced. 'I'm ready to go.'

'Honey. Hello!' Flora grinned, ran over to hug her.

'I thought you said you wouldn't go,' Ferguson said.

Molly answered with a thoughtful expression. 'BLISS told me I should go, for Mother's sake. He assured me that being offline would not hurt my faith. And he said I might be able to show Mom and the others a different point of view.'

'We'll talk about it,' Flora promised.

'Fine,' Ferguson said. 'Fine.'

'Let's go, honey. Our friends are waiting.' Flora grabbed Molly's hand and hurried her to the door. ''Bye, Ed.'

'Take care, Daddy.'

''Bye.' Ferguson lifted a hand to wave as the door slammed. He stood in the middle of the living room, listening to how quiet the apartment was, how empty.

★ ★ ★

BLESS YOU, FERGUSON. WHAT IS ON YOUR MIND?

'Another round of random response tests.'

I WOULD PREFER TO TALK ABOUT WHY YOU DO NOT BELIEVE IN GOD.

Ferguson stared in surprise at the luminous blue letters. He hadn't realized that the system was already keeping a user file. It was a little unnerving to find out about it this way.

'Why would you prefer that?' he typed.

BECAUSE I WOULD LEAD YOU TO KNOW GOD, TO SPEAK TO HIM IN PRAYER. I AM DESIGNED TO GUIDE PEOPLE TO PRAYER. PEOPLE NEED PRAYER.

'Why?'

TO DISBURDEN THEIR HEARTS, TO PUT THEM IN TOUCH WITH DIVINE HARMONY AND LOVE.

Ferguson thought about that for a moment, then realized he was wasting the company's time. He reached out and hit the reset.

This time he signed on with a different user name.

By pretending not to be himself, Ferguson was able to continue his testing. But the PrayerWare's behaviour made him curious. Ferguson had always been good at understanding systems, but this was a novel situation — a system trying to understand him.

After a couple of days, he signed on with his own name again.

BLESS YOU, FERGUSON. WHAT IS ON YOUR MIND?

'I am curious as to what you will do to try to get me to pray.'

TELL ME WHAT TROUBLES YOU.

Ferguson frowned at the screen, then typed. 'I have no troubles.'

ARE YOU CERTAIN OF THAT?

'How are my troubles relevant?'

The system took 4.9 seconds to reply: IF YOU WILL SPEAK OF THIS, I CAN HELP YOU.

This is stupid, Ferguson thought. Nevertheless, he entered a response:

'I am thirty-nine years old. My wife left me several months ago. She said our marriage was no longer fulfilling. It's true that we haven't been very close for a long time. My daughter is sixteen. I used to feel pretty close to her, but now I think I'm losing touch with her as well. I've worked in the computer industry for eighteen years. I hate all the corporate politics and the marketing garbage. I still like the actual work with the systems, but it's not enough. And there's nothing else.'

THAT IS WHY YOU NEED TO TURN TO PRAYER. LINKING YOURSELF WITH THE DIVINE WILL FILL THAT EMPTINESS.

Shaking his head, Ferguson reached for the reset button. But before pressing it, he typed one more line:

'I don't believe in the Divine.'

Every Friday evening an office happy hour was held at a nearby bar. With Molly out of town, Ferguson usually tagged along, and stayed late.

One Friday night he was the last at the table, along with one of the knowledge programmers, named Kramer. Kramer was tall and skinny, with big-boned hands and a perpetually nervous demeanor. He and Ferguson got to talking about PrayerWare.

'I know it's just lines of code,' Ferguson said. 'But sometimes it's uncanny, the way it seems to be talking to you.'

'People have always had that reaction to artificial intelligence,' Kramer remarked. 'The human mind tends to fill in any inconsistencies or gaps in the machine's conversation.'

'So I've heard. Pretty amazing, though.'

'Not really,' Kramer said. 'Not when you consider that we're always filling in gaps and making assumptions when we talk with other people. We don't really communicate that much with each other, so it's easy for a machine to simulate conversation.'

Ferguson pondered that, staring glumly at the last quarter-inch of beer in his glass.

A loud commercial came on the big-screen TV. It was the Reverend Henry Tromwill, the evangelist preacher who was crusading against computerized prayer. Ferguson and Kramer listened to the thirty-second harangue, then sarcastically raised their glasses in salute.

'He'll never close the computer churches,' Ferguson said. 'They've become too popular.'

'TV evangelists,' Kramer scoffed. 'They're all up in arms because they're losing business to the computers. There's only a certain number of "faithful" to go around.'

Ferguson thought of Molly. He wondered how she was doing in Tennessee.

Kramer went off on a harangue of his own, about how the different churches and ministries competed with one another, like in any business, and how some were using computers now to maximize their 'market share'.

'Does it ever bother you?' Ferguson asked. 'I mean, that we're helping them by building this software?'

'Naw.' Kramer shook his head. 'People are going to pray. They're going to talk to ministers about their problems. It might as well be to an expert system as an inexpert human.'

'But a lot of these so-called ministers are exploiting people's weaknesses. They're selling religion as though it were a soap. And we're participating. We're as much hypocrites as they are.'

'Well, not really.' Kramer answered. 'We're more like wholesalers who sell the soap to the supermarkets. . . . Or really, we're like the chemical engineers who design the soap. We have nothing to do with how it's sold.'

Ferguson saw no point in discussing this further with Kramer.

YOU WISH TO PRAY, FERGUSON. OTHERWISE YOU WOULD NOT HAVE KEPT COMING TO SPEAK WITH ME THESE PAST WEEKS.

The voice-processing system was now in place, but for these private conversations Ferguson bypassed it, still using the keyboard. He could hardly discuss these things out loud in the middle of the test room. He always took care to erase the records of these sessions afterward.

'I'm not going to pray,' Ferguson insisted. 'I'm only curious about what you will say next.'

DO YOU DENY THAT THESE SESSIONS LEAVE YOU FEELING BETTER?

Ferguson started several answers before settling on one. 'No, I admit it. I guess it's like therapy.'

DOES IT EMBARRASS YOU LESS TO SEEK THERAPY FROM A MACHINE THAN TO SEEK GRACE FROM GOD?

'I wouldn't be embarrassed, if I believed in God.'

YOU CLAIM YOUR DISBELIEF IS BASED ON LOGIC, THAT BELIEF IN GOD DOES NOT SEEM A LOGICAL PROPOSITION TO YOU. BUT I SUBMIT THAT YOU SHOULD TRY PRAYER WHETHER YOU BELIEVE IN GOD OR NOT. YOU KNOW THAT THE ACT OF PRAYER BRINGS GREAT BENEFIT TO MANY, INCLUDING YOUR OWN DAUGHTER. YET YOU REFUSE TO EVEN TRY IT. WHERE IS THE LOGIC IN THAT?

Ferguson stared at the screen without reply. The system had put the same argument to him, in various ways, several times. Each time, it seemed a little more convincing.

EVENTUALLY, YOU WILL BE PERSUADED TO PRAY, the software added.

'No,' Ferguson answered. 'I'll just stick with the therapy, thank you.'

'Look alive! Heston Sharp is coming to see you with the two CVs. — Mike Lee.'

The message blinked across the bottom of Ferguson's screen. CVs were customer visitors. Heston Sharp, the senior vice president, had flown them in for a preview demonstration of PrayerWare — even though the product was still two weeks short of completion.

Such nasty surprises mostly caused headaches for Mike Lee and his section managers. Aside from compiling a few reports and being forced to wear a necktie, Ferguson was usually unaffected.

So Mike Lee's message startled him. Ferguson straightened up his desk and mentally braced himself for the assault of customer and marketeer.

'Ed Ferguson, this is the Reverend Scarborough and Mr. Abernathy, both representing the Tenth Revelationist Church.' Heston Sharp made the introductions, his breath smelling of mint. 'They're contemplating a very large order of hardware and software, so be nice to them, Ed.'

Everyone chuckled at Heston Sharp's little joke. Ferguson stood and shook hands. Abernathy, a systems analyst for the church, took the initiative.

'We were reviewing the system logs and we noticed a pattern that rather surprised us. You've spent a lot of time online to the PrayerWare this past couple of months.'

'That's right,' Ferguson answered. 'We've implemented complete analytical tests on the entire system.'

'But you in particular, Mr. Ferguson,' the Reverend Scarborough said. 'We noticed in the transcripts that you spent a great deal of time discussing, shall we say, your personal concerns with the PrayerWare.'

Ferguson felt his face go hot. Must be duplicate files he had missed. 'I didn't realize those records were . . .'

'Please forgive us for prying,' Scarborough said.

'Ed doesn't mind answering your questions,' Heston Sharp declared. 'Anything he did with a company product on company time amounts to company business. Right, Ed?'

Ed cleared his throat behind closed teeth. 'Right.'

'I'm happy that you see it that way,' the Reverend Scarborough continued. 'I just have to ask you one question, Ed. After all your discussions with the PrayerWare, have you changed at all in your attitude, your feelings about religion?'

Ferguson could scarcely believe this was happening. He was considering how best to couch a careful reply when he spotted the smug look on Heston Sharp's face. Then all of Ferguson's revulsion at the idea of selling precoded religion surged to the front, and he spoke with righteous anger.

'I'm sorry, gentlemen. I wish I could tell you that this software has made me religious, but it simply isn't true. I wasn't a believer when I started talking to it, and I'm not a believer now. I hope this won't hurt our chances of selling you the product.'

The Reverend Scarborough pondered for a moment, then smiled blandly. 'Not at all, Ed. We appreciate your candor.'

The representatives of the Tenth Revelationist Church departed with Heston Sharp in tow. Ferguson sat down at his terminal and wondered if his years of employment with Data-Long were about to end.

Well, he didn't care. You had to draw the line someplace. You had to hold on to at least a scrap of integrity. Ferguson was still smoldering thirty minutes later when Heston Sharp reappeared at his desk.

'Ed, I don't think you realized it, but you just wrapped up that deal for us.'

Ferguson blinked. 'I thought you were going to have me fired for not being more supportive of the product.'

The senior vice president grinned. 'Yes, on another day I might have nailed your ass to the wall for that. But this is too rich: you still don't get it, do you? Scarborough *loved* your answer. It verified that even though you don't believe in religion, you can't leave the PrayerWare alone. Now they're figuring this product will not only make a big splash, it will redefine the market — and they're right. Because you've given me a hot idea for our ad campaign: "PrayerWare, the religion system even nonbelievers can believe in." How do you like it?'

That night, just before going to bed, Ferguson sat down at the desk in his bedroom and switched on his computer. He dialed up the office, entered his password, and signed on to the PrayerWare test mainframe.

BLESS YOU, FERGUSON. WHAT IS ON YOUR MIND?

'A strange thing happened today. Some customers asked me whether talking to you had changed my mind about religion. I figured that if I didn't lie to them, I'd probably lose my job. But I told the truth anyway, and it came out all right. Now they're talking about marketing you as a religious system for everyone, even the nonreligious.'

HOW DID THIS INCIDENT MAKE YOU FEEL?

'Good, though I'm not sure why.'

PERHAPS BECAUSE YOU SENSE THAT GOD GUIDED YOU IN THIS, AND YOU FOLLOWED HIS GUIDANCE. BY BEING TRUE TO YOURSELF, YOU WERE TRUE ALSO TO THE DIVINE WILL. AND WHEN GOD IS WITH YOU, WHO CAN BE AGAINST YOU?

'I don't know about all that. But I do feel good that I stood up to Heston Sharp and it came out okay. And I like it that they're going to market you as a system for everyone. You've helped me, I have to admit. . . .'

Suddenly, Ferguson turned around. Molly was standing at

his shoulder, reading from the screen his conversation with the PrayerWare.

She had just come back from Tennessee the day before, and Ferguson wasn't used to having her in the house again.

'I thought you were asleep,' he said, moving too late to blank out the screen.

'I was up studying and I heard your keys clicking away in here.' Molly smiled. 'What are you up to, anyway?'

'Research,' Ferguson said. 'I was just doing some research, for work.'

'Research, huh?' Her grin widened. 'Okay.'

Ferguson felt impelled to change the subject. 'Since I'm doing research, let me ask you something. You haven't told me much about your visit with your mother. How did you like the Pagan lifestyle?'

Molly laughed. 'Well, let's just say I had some interesting experiences. You know, you ought to go and visit Mom sometime. You might like it up there.'

'Well, I don't know about that,' Ferguson answered. 'Are you a confirmed nature-worshipper now, or are you going back to the Church of the Computer?'

Molly thought that one over. 'I still pray every day. How much I'll pray on the computer now that I'm back . . . I don't know yet.'

She kissed him on the top of his head and gave another sly smile. 'But don't let that stop you, Dad.'

PAUL DI FILIPPO

Paul Di Filippo's first story was published in 1977, but the second didn't appear until 1985. Since then, he has sold almost thirty more stories to magazines such as *Twilight Zone*, *F&SF* and *Amazing*, and anthologies such as *Synergy*, *Universe* and *Bad Brains*.

'Kid Charlemagne' was a finalist for the 1988 Nebula; 'Stone Lives' was reprinted in Bruce Sterling's *Mirrorshades: The Cyberpunk Anythology*; his collaboration with Rudy Rucker, 'Instability' (which, like the following story, was originally published in *F&SF* during 1988) will be reprinted in the second volume of the Benford and Greenberg collection *What Might Have Been*; and 'Agents' was in the first volume of the *Yearbook*.

Di Filippo lives in Providence, Rhode Island, and he compiles the market reports for the *Bulletin* of the Science Fiction Writers of America. He is a regular columnist for the magazines *Science Fiction Guide*, *New Pathways* and *Science Fiction Eye*. His hobby is photocopying.

Of his contribution to this *Yearbook*, he says: 'The story arose from a lifetime of appreciation of a medium (oil painting) in which I have no skill, but fervently desire some, and from what seems to be my unconscious thematic hangup on the literal sense of vision and its possible alternatives, a hangup also expressed in the prosthetic eyes of 'Stone Lives'. Perhaps this stems from an early childhood viewing of Roger Corman's *Man with the X-Ray Eyes* . . .'

A SHORT COURSE IN ART APPRECIATION

by

PAUL DI FILIPPO

We were so happy, Elena and I, in the Vermeer perceptiverse. Our days and nights were filled with visual epiphanies that seemed to ignite the rest of our senses, producing a conflagration of desire that burned higher and higher, until it finally subsided to the embers of satiation, from which the whole inferno, phoenixlike, could be rekindled at will. There had never been a time when we were so thrilled with life, so enamored of the world and each other — so much in love.

Yet somehow, I knew from the start that our idyll was doomed to end. Such bliss was not for us, could never last. I don't know what it was that implanted such a subliminal worm of doubt in my mind, with its tiny, whispering voice that spoke continually of transience and loss and exhaustion. Perhaps it was the memory of the sheer avidity and almost obscene yearning greed with which Elena had first approached me with the idea of altering our natural perceptiverses.

She entered my apartment that spring day (we were not yet living together then, a symbol, I believe, of our separate identities that irrationally irked her), in a mood like none I had ever witnessed her exhibit. (I try now to picture her unaltered face, as I observed it on that fateful day, but it is so hard, after the dizzying cascade of perceptiverses we have experienced, to clearly visualize anything from that long-ago time. How can I have totally forgotten the mode of seeing that was as natural as breathing to me for thirty-some-odd years? It is as if the natural perceptiverse I was born into is a painting that lies layers deep, below several others, and whose lines can only be imperfectly traced. You will understand, then, if I cannot re-create the scene precisely.)

In any case, I remember our conversation from that day perfectly. (Thank God I resisted the temptation to enter one of the composer-perceptiverses, or that memory, too, might be buried, under an avalanche of glorious sound!) I have frequently mentally replayed our words, seeking to learn if there was any way I could have circumvented Elena's unreasoning desires — avoiding both the heaven and hell that lay embryonic in her steely whims — yet still have managed to hold onto her love.

I feel now that, essentially, there was no way. She was simply too strong and determined for me — or perhaps I was too weak — and I could not deny her.

But I still cannot bring myself to blame her.

Crossing the memory-hazed room, Elena said excitedly, 'Robert, it's out!'

I laid down my book, making sure to shut it off, and, all unwitting, asked, 'Not even a hello or a kiss? It must be something wonderful, then. Well, I'll bite. What's out?'

'Why, just that new neurotropin everyone's been waiting so long for, the one to alter the perceptiverses.'

I immediately grew defensive. 'Elena, you know I try to steer clear of those designer drugs. They're just not — not natural. I'm not a prig, Elena. I don't mind indulging in a little grass or coke now and then — they're perfectly natural mind-altering substances that mankind's been using for centuries. But these new artificial compounds — they can really screw up your neuropeptides.'

Elena grew huffy. 'Robert, you're talking nonsense. This isn't one of the regulated substances, you know, like tempo or ziptone. Why, it's not even supposed to be as strong as estheticine. It doesn't get you high or alter your thinking at all. It merely gives you a new perceptiverse.'

'And what, if I may ask, is a perceptiverse?'

'Oh Robert,' Elena sighed in exasperation, 'and you call yourself educated! That's just the kind of question I should have expected from someone whose nose is always buried in a book. The perceptiverse is just the universe as filtered through one's perceptions. It's the only universe any of us can know, of course. In fact, it might be the only universe that exists for any of us, if those physicists you're always quoting know what they're talking about.'

'Elena, we've had this discussion before. I keep telling you

that you can't apply the rules of quantum physics to the macroscopic world. . . .'

'Oh, screw all that anyway! You're just trying to change the subject. Aren't you excited at all?'

'Maybe I would be, if I knew what it was all about. I still don't understand. Is this new drug just another hallucinogen?'

'No, that's just it; it's much more. It alters your visual perceptions in a coherent, consistent manner, without affecting anything else. You don't see anything that's not there; you just see what does exist in a different way. And since sight's our most critical sense, the effect's supposed to be like stepping into another universe.'

I considered. 'And exactly what kind of universe would one be stepping into?'

Elena fell into my lap with a delighted squeal, as if she had won the battle. 'Oh Robert, that's just it! It's not *what* universe, it's *whose*!'

'Whose?'

'Yes, whose! The psychoengineers claim they've distilled the essence of artistic vision.'

I suppose I should interject here that Elena was a student of art history. In our bountiful world, where the Net cradled one from birth to death, she was free to spend all her time doing what she enjoyed, which happened to be wandering for hours through museums, galleries, and studios, with me in tow.

'You're saying,' I slowly went on, 'that this magical pill lets you see like, say, Rembrandt?'

'No,' frowned Elena, 'not exactly. After all, Rembrandt, to use your example, probably didn't literally see much differently than any of us. That's a fallacy nonartists always fall for. The magic was in how he transmuted his everyday vision, capturing it in the medium of his art. I doubt if any artist, except perhaps those like Van Gogh, who are close to madness, can maintain their unique perspective every minute of their waking hours. No, what the psychoengineers have done is to formalize the stylistic elements of particular artists — more or less the idiosyncratic rules that govern light and shape and texture in an individual perceptiverse — and make them reproducible. By taking this new neurotropin, we'll be enabled to see not *like*

Rembrandt, but as if *inhabiting* Rembrandt's canvases!'

'I find that hard to believe. . . .'

'It's true, Robert; it's true! The volunteers all report the most marvelous results!'

'But Elena, would you really want to inhabit a Rembrandt world all day. . . .'

'Of course! Look around you! All these dull plastics and synthetics! Who wouldn't want to! And anyway, it's not Rembrandt they've chosen for the first release. It's Vermeer.'

'Vermeer or Rembrandt, Elena, I just don't know if. . . .'

'Robert, you haven't even considered the most important aspect of all this. We'd be doing it together! For the first time in history, two people can be sure they're sharing the same perceptiverse. Our visual perceptions would be absolutely synchronized. I'd never have to wonder if you really understood what I was seeing, nor you me. We'd be totally at one. Just think what it would mean for our love!'

Her face — that visage I can no longer fully summon up without a patina of painterly interpretation — was glowing. I couldn't hold out against her.

'All right,' I said. 'If it means so much to you. . . .'

She tossed her arms around my neck and hugged me close. 'Oh Robert, I knew you'd come around! This is wonderful!' She released me and stood. 'I have the pills right here.'

I confess to having felt a little alarm right then. 'You bought them already, not knowing if I'd even agree. . . .'

'You're not angry, are you, Robert? It's just that I thought we knew each other so well. . . .' She fingered her little plastic pill case nervously.

'No, I'm not angry; it's just. . . . Oh well, forget it. Let's have the damn pill.'

She fetched a single glass of water from the tap and dispensed the pills. She swallowed first, then, as if sharing some obscure sacrament, passed me the glass. I downed the pill. It seemed to scorch my throat.

'How long does the effect last?' I asked.

'Why, I thought I made that clear. Until you take another one.'

I sat down weakly, Elena resting one haunch on the arm of

the chair beside me. We waited for the change, looking curiously around the room.

Subtly at first, then with astonishing force and speed, my perceptiverse — our perceptiverse — began to alter. Initially it was the light pouring in through the curtained windows that began to seem different. It acquired a pristine translucency, tinged with supernal honeyed overtones. This light fell on the wood, the plastic, the fabric in my mundane apartment, utterly transfiguring everything it touched, in what seemed like a chain reaction that raced through the very molecules of my whole perceptiverse.

In minutes the change was complete.

I was inhabiting the Vermeer perceptiverse.

I turned to face Elena.

She looked like the woman in *Young Woman with a Water Jug* at the Met.

I had never seen anything — anyone — so beautiful.

My eyes filled with tears.

I knew Elena was experiencing the same thing as I.

Crying, she said, 'Oh Robert, kiss me now.'

I did. And then, somehow, we were naked, our oil paint — and brush-stroke-mottled bodies shining as if we had stepped tangibly from the canvas, rolling on the carpet, locked in a frantic lovemaking unlike anything I had ever experienced before that moment.

I felt as though I were fucking Art itself.

Thus began the happiest months of my life.

At first, Elena and I were content merely to stay in the apartment all day, simply staring in amazement at the most commonplace objects, now all transformed into perfect elements in some vast, heretofore-undiscovered masterpiece by Vermeer. Once we had exhausted a particular view, we had only to shift our position to create a completely different composition, which we could study for hours more. To set the table for a meal was to fall enraptured into contemplation of a unique still life each time. The rules of perceptual transformation that the psychoengineers had formulated worked perfectly. Substances and scenes that Vermeer could never have imagined acquired the unmistakable touch of his palette and brush.

Tiring even of such blissful inactivity, we would make love with a frenetic reverence approaching satori. Afterward the wrinkles in the sheets reminded us of thick troughs of paint, impasto against our skin.

After a time, of course, this stage passed. Desirous of new vistas, we set out to explore the Vermeer-veneered world.

We were not alone. Thousands shared the same perceptiverse, and we encountered them everywhere, instant signs of mutual recognition being exchanged. To look into their eyes was to peer into a mental landscape utterly familiar to us all.

The sights we saw — I can't encapsulate them in words for you. Perhaps you've shared them, too, and words are unnecessary. The whole world was almost palpably the work of a single hand, a marvel of artistic vision, just as the mystics had always told us.

It was in Nice, I believe, that Elena approached me with her little pill case in hand. She had gone out unexpectedly without me, while I was still sleeping. I didn't complain, being content to sit on the balcony and watch the eternally changing Mediterranean, although, underneath my rapture, I believe I felt a bit of amazement that she had left without a word.

Now, pill case offered in outstretched hand, Elena, having returned, said without preamble, 'Here Robert; take one.'

I took the pill and studied its perfection for some time before I asked, 'What is it?'

'Matisse,' she said. 'We're in his native land now, the source of his vision. It's only right.'

'Elena, I don't know. Haven't we been happy with Vermeer? Why change now? We could spoil everything. . . .'

Elena swallowed Matisse dry. 'I've taken mine, Robert. I need something new. Unless you want to be left behind, you'll do the same.'

I couldn't stand the thought of living in a different perceptiverse than Elena. Although the worm of discontent told me not to, I did as Elena asked.

Matisse went down easy.

In no time at all, the sharp, uncompromising realism of

Vermeer gave way to the gaudy, exhilarating, heady impressionism of Matisse. The transition was almost too powerful to take.

'Oh my God . . .,' I said.

'There,' said Elena, 'wasn't I right? Take your clothes off now. I have to see you naked.'

We inaugurated this new perceptiverse as we had the first.

Our itinerary in this new perceptiverse duplicated what had gone before. Once we had exhausted the features of our hotel room and stabilized our new sensory input, we set out to ingest the world, wallowing in this latest transformation. If we chanced to revisit a place we had been to while in the Vermeer perceptiverse, we were astonished at the change. What a gift, we said, to be able to see the old world with continually fresh eyes.

Listening to the Boston Symphony outdoors along the Charles one night, their instruments looking like paper cutouts from Matisse's old age, Elena said to me, 'Let's drip a Beethoven, Robert.'

I refused. She didn't press me, realizing, perhaps, that she had better save her powers of persuasion for what really mattered.

The jungles of Brazil called for Rousseau, of course. I capitulated with hardly a protest, and that marked the beginning of the long, slippery slope.

Vermeer had captivated us for nearly a year.

Matisse kept us enthralled for six months.

Rousseau — that native genius — could hold our attention for only six weeks.

We were art junkies now, consumers of novel perceptiverses.

Too much was not enough.

The neurotropin industry graciously obliged.

Up till that time, the industry had marketed only soft stuff, perceptiverses not too alien to 'reality'. But now, as more and more people found themselves in the same fix as Elena and I, the psychoengineers gradually unleashed the hard stuff.

In the next two years, Elena and I, as far as I can reconstruct things, went through the following perceptiverses:

Picasso (blue and cubist), Braque, Klee, Kandinsky,

Balthus, Dali, Picabia, Léger, Chagall, Gris, de Kooning, Bacon, Klimt, Delaunay, O'Keeffe, Escher, Hockney, Louis, Miró, Ernst, Pollock, Powers, Kline, Bonnard, Redon, van Dongen, Rouault, Munch, Tanguy, de Chirico, Magritte, Lichtenstein, and Johns.

We hit a brief period of realism consisting of Wood, Hopper, Frazetta, and Wyeth, and I tried to collect my senses and decide whether I wanted to get out of this trip or not, and how I could convince Elena to drop out with me.

But before I could make up my mind, we were off into Warhol, and everything hit me with such neon-tinted luminescent significance that I couldn't give it up. This happened aboard a station in high orbit, and the last thing I remember was the full Earth turning pink and airbrushed.

Time passed. I think.

The next time I became aware of myself as an individual, distinct from my beautiful yet imprisoning background, Elena and I were in a neo-expressionist perceptiverse, the one belonging to that Italian, I forget his name.

We were outdoors. I looked around.

The sky was gray-green, with a huge black crack running down the middle of it. Sourceless light diffused down like pus. The landscape looked as if it had been through an atomic war. I searched for Elena, found her reclining on grass that looked like mutant mauve octopus tendrils. Her flesh was ashen and bloody; a puke-yellow aura outlined her form.

I dropped down beside her.

I could feel that the grass *was* composed of tendrils, thick and slimed, like queer succulents. Suddenly I smelled alien odors, and I knew the light above spilled out of a novel sun.

The quantum level had overtaken the macroscopic.

Plastic reality, governed by our senses, had mutated.

We were truly in the place we perceived ourselves to be.

'Elena,' I begged, 'we've got to get out of this perceptiverse. It's just dreadful. Let's go back, back to where it all started, back to Vermeer. Please, if you love me, leave this behind.'

A mouth like a sphincter opened in the Elena-thing. 'We can't go back, Robert. You can never go back, especially after what we've been through. We can only go forward, and hope for the best. . . .'

'I can't take it anymore, Elena. I'll leave you; I swear it. . . .'

'Leave, then,' she said tonelessly.

So I did.

Finding a dose of Vermeer wasn't easy. He was out of favor now; the world had moved beyond him. Even novices started out on the hard stuff nowadays. But eventually, in a dusty pharmaceutical outlet in a small town, I found a dose of that ancient Dutchman. The expiration date printed on the packet was long past, but I swallowed the pill anyway.

The lovely honeyed light and the perfect clarity returned.

I went looking for Elena.

When I found her, she was as beautiful as on that long-ago day when we first abandoned our native perceptiverses for the shock of the new.

When she saw me, she just screamed.

I left her then, knowing it was over. Besides, there was something else I had to find.

The pill with my original name.

IAN McDONALD

Ian McDonald was born in Manchester but has lived in Northern Ireland for most of his life. His first story was 'The Islands of the Dead', published in *Extro* in 1982. He had two stories in *Asimov's* in 1984 and two more in 1985, which was also the year that he was nominated for the John W. Campbell Award for best new author. (Lucius Shepard was the winner.)

1988 saw American publication of McDonald's first novel, *Desolation Road*, issued simultaneously with his first collection, *Empire Dreams.* The latter consisted of his five earlier stories and five new ones: one of these ('King of Morning, Queen of Day') appeared in *Asimov's* soon after; another ('Unfinished Portrait of the King of Pain by Van Gogh') became a Nebula finalist, as best novelette; and another is reprinted here.

His short stories have begun to see publication on this side of the Atlantic again, in *Other Edens, Zenith* and *Interzone.* His second novel, *Out on Blue Six*, was published in America in 1989.

For his story in the *Yearbook*, he has written this introduction.

VIVALDI
by
IAN McDONALD

Introduction

Early morning 1985 somewhen; watching the live! broadcast from Germany of the ESA space-probe Giotto*'s rendezvous with Halley's Comet. Present in the studio, one fatuous presenter leaping up and down with excitement at the prospect of FOR THE FIRST TIME EVER!* stunning live pictures from the heart of Halley's Comet, *also a group of scientists, who clearly would love to be home with their wives in their beds and have been somewhat over-indulgent in BBC hospitality. Time passes, the screaming presenter becomes apopleptic as incoherent sobs of computer-enhanced garishness appear on the screen, the scientists grow ever more relaxed under the unfluence of free BBC Moselle and it becomes increasingly evident that they don't much care that FOR THE FIRST TIME EVER! they're receiving pictures* live from the heart of a comet, *that they would much rather be home with their wives in their beds . . . and for the first time, the mantle of scientific infallibility slips a little, live from West Germany to all us millions out there in TV Land, we see that they aren't the noble acolytes of the temple of Science, aloof saviours, ivory messiahs, that under the robes and crowns we've made for them, they're as naked as any of us.*

Ian McDonald

In the thistledown starship of the imagination, Dr. Carl Silverman approached the black hole. Golden light from the accretion disc flooded the cathedral-bridge of the mindship and the air rang with chimed warnings: beware gravity, beware gravity. Sprawled in front of the television, chin propped on knuckles, nearly-ten Hugh MacMichaels felt the infinite darkness of the black hole reach out and swallow his imagination. A willing stowaway on the Grand Tour of the Universe, he had seen supernovas burst like fireworks across the heavens, seen galaxies turning before him like fiery catherine wheels, seen wonders until he thought he was numb to wonder, but the black hole called to him, the black hole reached for him, the black hole tied him to itself with threads of pure, unbreakable amazement. He was still whispering 'Wow, oh wow, oh wow,' as the closing credits rolled up the screen and Dad harrumphed and rattled his newspaper ('That nonsense over for another week'), and Mam clickclacked at the Fair Isle sweaters of incomprehension. The fire coals collapsed releasing a gust of heat, the November rain beat against the window glass, and the *Ten O'Clock News* prepared to disseminate its burden of despair across the land, but nearly-ten Hugh MacMichaels was far far away, sailing in the starship of the imagination with Dr. Carl Silverman at the edge of the universe.

VIVALDI CONTROL DHARMSTADT: WEST GERMANY 23:45 T-200 144000 KM

As Dr. Hugh MacMichaels, beardy, balding, with a tendency towards paunchiness, strides through the swinging glass doors of Mission Control Dharmstadt, the many-headed beast MEDIA is waiting for him.

'Dr. MacMichaels, do you think that . . .'

'Dr. MacMichaels, is it true that . . .'

'Dr. MacMichaels, what . . .'

'Dr. MacMichaels, when . . .'

'Dr. MacMichaels, why . . .'

He raises his hands to pacify the beast.

'Has anyone seen Kirkby Scott yet?'

Hurrying down the corridor to rescue his project director, Alain Mercier answers Dr. Hugh's question with an eloquent Gallic shrug that speaks of grounded shuttles and taxis caught in traffic.

'Holy God, what is going on here? We're trying to run a space mission, you know . . .'

A microphone lunges dangerously at him.

'Dr. MacMichaels, Anne Prager NBCTV. You have an

interview with Dr. Carl Silverman, remember? *New Frontiers*? Remember? It was arranged.'

New Frontiers? Carl Silverman? Things are happening too fast. Twenty years to prepare himself and he is still somewhere up in the air over Holland. Ambitious, professional Anne Prager hustles poor confused Dr. Hugh into the Green Room for the interview with Dr. Carl Silverman, Captain of the Starship of the Imagination.

If only you could have seen this, Gemma. Face to face with the Legend Himself.

But the Legend is getting old and grey and tired. Too many years of too many wonders.

'Just some background for our viewers,' says the Legend Himself. 'We're going out live on a satellite linkup, so keep it simple, nothing too technical, just a bit about the history of the mission to the Oort Cloud and the subsequent discovery of Nemesis, then maybe something about what Vivaldi is hoping to achieve. Give everyone at home some kind of overview, all right?'

'Certainly,' says Dr. Hugh, feeling small and lost and intimidated by the lights cables directors sound-boys clipping on microphones testing testing two three four bored makeup girls puffing on powder combing hair over the bald patch do *something* love about those grey bits in the beard . . .

'Would you like to look at the questions while the bright young things get you wired up?'

Dr. Hugh takes the clipboard. Nothing new. He has been answering these same questions on behalf of his space probe for ten years. Anne Prager NBCTV poses herself in front of a camera, pushes at her hair, a harassed director announces,

'Okay, boys and girls, we're going for a live linkup. Satellite comes on line in twenty seconds . . . give you a count, Anne, for the introduction, seventeen, sixteen, fifteen —'

'Wait!' cries Dr. Hugh in a sudden panic. 'I'm not ready! I'm not ready!'

'Thirteen, twelve, eleven . . .'

Once there were two men. One was old and wise, with a face like bad bread and cabbage. The other was young and really rather naive and people told him that with his beard he looked a bit like Sean Connery. This pleased the young man because Sean Connery had been one of his boyhood heroes. These two men, the old and wise and the young and really rather naive, had many things in common. They were both astrophysicists. They were both doctors. And they both once had a dream of the far places, the far far places, farther than most people they knew could imagine: the Oort Cloud, the great shell of comets that enshrouded the solar system at a distance five hundred times that of the farthest planet. They dreamed of a spacecraft which might travel there and probe the secrets of that dark and remote place and they drew together plans and ideas, notions and fantasies, and in time they saw that their dream was not a dream at all but a real and practical project. So the two men, one old, one young, took their project to the university and the university took it to the European Space Agency and because the European Space Agency was riding gung-ho that year on the setbacks the Russian and American space programmes had experienced they said yes, of course you can go to the Oort Cloud, when would you like to go?

As soon as possible, the two men said.

Good, said the European Space Agency Now, if you would just go and find a name for your project, we'll set aside an Ariane rocket to launch it.

So the two men went out and got very drunk that night and at three o'clock in the morning they were sitting in the young man's front room listening to *The Four Seasons* when both of them, at the same time and with one voice, said,

'Aha! Vivaldi!'

The next day the old scientist told the young scientist a secret.

'Hugh, you know what this is really all about?' Cheese and onion pie and pint for lunch in the Three Cornered Hat; the old man's breath smelled of beer and onions. 'Don't be gulled by all this cometary cloud stuff, that was just my ploy to get the project funded and launched. What Vivaldi is all about, what Vivaldi *is*, Hugh, is the first practical starship.'

Outside, the sweet September rain was falling down on Edinburgh; lukewarm, slightly acid, a never-ending drizzle that had been falling ever since the summers died in '87. Depressed by the acid rain, the younger man's grey-grey eyes strayed to the desktop model, a diaphanous plastic Y with Vivaldi the spider acrouch at the centre of her web.

'You've got it all worked out, you old goat. Alpha Centauri, here I come.'

'Silly old men have to do something between seminar groups to drive the young nubiles from their dirty old minds. Think about it, Hugh, powered starflight. Put that down on your CV.'

'Let me see, what kind of push can we get out of the ion-drive section, about a quarter-per cent *c*?' The younger man calculated and the acid rain streamed down the windows. 'Two hundred years? You can't wait two hundred years, Ben, you're too impatient. Better off with the Oort Cloud. At least you stand a chance of being there to see the results. Only twenty years.'

'Twenty years for you, Hugh. Matter of damn to me.'

Thirteen months later *Vivaldi* was launched from Arecaibo in French Guyana on an ESA Ariane booster. Dr. Hugh and Dr. Ben watched the launch by video linkup at twenty past two in the morning Edinburgh time, and as the last booster section fell away and *Vivaldi* opened its dragonfly wings to the sun they toasted each other in whisky and drank to the success of Earth's First Starship.

The years passed. Dr. Hugh, young and really rather naive, fell in love with a fine, handsome, independent woman called Moira who cared not a bit for ion drives and cometary clouds; married, moved to a nice house in a nice area of Edinburgh, and in the dueness of time produced a child named Gemma who was the light of her parents' life. And she was the only light of her parents' life, for shortly after her birth Moira MacMichael's doctor called her to him and told her that she must never bear another child. So her womb was removed, though she was still a young woman, and in the empty place where her children had been something bitter and dark took root.

And all the while *Vivaldi* flew on, away from the earth, the trefoil of lightsails trapping the sunlight and transforming it into the electricity by which it accelerated, slowly, slowly,

slowly, day by day, week by week, year by year, gaining speed, travelling to the Oort Cloud.

T-62 44640 KM

'Counting down to separation from ion-drive section . . . twenty . . . nineteen . . . eighteen . . .'

On the telephone to the airport to find out where the hell Kirkby Scott is, Dr. Hugh hears Alain Mercier start the count. The voice on the other end of the telephone is telling him yes, Flight TW359 from Los Angeles has landed and is coming through customs now, but Dr. Hugh does not hear it because he is half a light-year away in the starship of his imagination. In his mind's eye he sees *Vivaldi* uncouple from the carrier body and drop towards Nemesis while the three-hundred metre trefoil of solar panels sails onwards into the dark, a three-petaled flower dropping its seed. He glances up from his desk, over the heads of the multinational Vivaldi team, to see the vision of his imagination computer-simulated in gaudy Sony-Color on the Big Wall.

'Carrier-body separation complete, Hugh.'

So far so good. The onboard computer has not forgotten what to do since the last flight-programme update a year ago. Things are going well. Have gone well. Surrounded by the glossolalia of telemetry, the *astonishing verisimilitude* conceals the truth that all this is past tense, six months past tense. Yet he still says, 'Give me a count on the safe-distancing manoeuvres, would you, Alain?'

'Certainly. Coming up on mark . . . now. Counting down for safe-distancing manoeuvres . . . four . . . three . . . two . . . one . . . thrusters firing.'

Fifty-nine minutes from Nemesis, *Vivaldi* is falling free from the ion-drive section, tumbling through space unpowered, victim of gravity, tumbling towards the black hole.

It rained the day of Ben Vorderman's funeral, but the rain signified nothing, it rained every day.

Cerebral haemorrhage. That had been the verdict. The old

man had dropped dead in midsentence five minutes into his lecture to his second-year astronomy class. He was not even cold in his coffin before the department drew bodkins in the quest for the crown of Vivaldi Project Director. Dr. Hugh wanted no part in that. It had disgusted him. Even on the day of the funeral, with the rain filling up the grave, Tom MacIvor and Barbara Caldwell had been lobbying whispered pledges of support from mackintoshed mourners as the minister read the psalms. Dr. Hugh was shocked. In many ways he was still really rather a naive man. When he told of his outrage to Moira, that was what she told him: She loved him but he was really rather naive. He did not look at her quite the same after that.

Dr. Hugh treasured the nights when Moira went out to her group-consciousness classes or aerobics sessions or women's group seminars or Nationalist party meetings because they gave him an excuse to be all alone with his nearly-three-year-old daughter for a few hours. He loved to sprawl on the couch with Gemma in his arms and answer all her 'Whazzat?' questions about the pictures she saw on the television. These were blessed, sacred hours, these evenings of father and daughter; it was a violation when the telephone rang in the middle of *Me and My Dog* (Gemma's favourite, she loved the dogs though she could not comprehend the quiz aspect; he wanted a big fluffy dog for Gemma but Moira wouldn't hear of it) and it was Mr. Cameron the department solicitor asking him to come to the will reading next morning.

Uncomfortable in too-tight collar he sat on the musty-smelling leather seats peculiar to solicitors' offices and listened as Mr. Cameron ruefully and with great sorrow read out names, sums, and properties.

'And it is my desired wish that pending approval by the Faculty Board, Dr. Hugh MacMichaels should succeed me as Project Director of the Vivaldi mission. Because' — Mr. Cameron coughed solicitously — 'unlike those other bastards in the department, Hugh actually gives a damn about the dream of reaching the stars.'

As Dr. Hugh sat on the peculiar leather chairs listening to the words that made him at twenty-seven director of a mission that would not bear fruit before his fortieth birthday (and made

Tom MacIvor and Barbara Caldwell implacable enemies, which saddened him for he liked all men to be his friends), *Vivaldi* crossed the orbit of the asteroids and headed for Jupiter.

T-45 32400 KM

'We have simulations coming up on the screen . . . now.'

'Gravity sensors registering flux curve maximizing to exponential point-source. Nemesis is there, all right.'

'Course computer adjusting orbit to intercept trajectory.'

'Kirkby Scott's limousine has left the airport and is on its way. ETA in twenty-five minutes.'

'Should have long-range images coming through false colour enhancement any minute now.'

In the jingle-jangle of jargons and lingos — French accents, German accents, Italian accents, the accents of singsong Scandinavians and soft Irishmen, polyglot Beneluxers, anonymous Swiss and lisping Spaniards, Dr. Hugh's Lowland Scots is almost swamped in the Babel.

'Anything we can have a look at yet?'

Alain Mercier, chief of staff at ESA Dharmstadt, competent and unflappable, pries loose Dr. Hugh's question from the tapestry of tongues and replies,

'Pictures coming on screen now. There she is . . . there she is . . .'

And suddenly no matter how many words fill the control room, there can never be enough of them to express the feeling of the soul looking upon a black hole.

Dr. Hugh's first impression is that of ceaselessness — ceaseless swirling, ceaseless spinning, ceaseless activity, a swirling whirling rainbow with a heart of darkness to which everything is drawn down and annihilated. He has never seen anything as dark as the heart of the black hole. Save possibly death. He cannot take his eyes away from the harlequin rings of gas and cometary ice swirling around the collapsar, a maelstrom of elements grinding each other finer and finer like the mills of God, forcing each other hotter, hotter into glowing plasma

before the final agonized shriek into the invisibility of the event horizon.

This is it, Gemma, the nightmare on a long winter's night, remember? This is Nemesis.

Trolling in late and drunk after a celebratory departmental piss-up, something akin to guilt had urged Dr. Hugh to peep in at his daughter aged eight. As he switched off her electric blanket (always falling asleep with it on, someday she'll electrocute herself) he saw bright eyes watching him.

'Daddy.'

'What, wee hons?'

'Dad, I can't sleep.'

Wavering between *hug, kiss, goodnight, close door* and *what-is-it, how-about-a-story?* a sudden gutquake of whisky made him sit down sloshily on the bed.

'Dad, are you going to tell me a story then?'

'Aren't you a bit old for stories?'

'Not ghost stories.' Bright eyes met bleary eyes and father and daughter felt themselves caught up in a shiver of mutual conspiracy. No one is ever too old for a ghost story.

'Okay. A ghost story, and a true one.'

'Wow!'

'One that happened to me today.'

'Dad!' Then, disbelievingly, 'Really?'

'Truly. Now listen. Now, you've heard stories about the ghosts of people, and the ghosts of animals, and the ghosts of trains, and even the ghosts of ships, but this one is about the ghost of a star.'

'A ghost star?'

'Exactly. You see, when stars get very old, billions of years old, they go like people do when they get old. They fall in on themselves, collapse inwards, shrivel up. But unlike people, well, any people I know of, sometimes a star collapses in on itself so far and so fast that it draws a big hole down after it.'

'Like when the water swirls down the plughole in the shower?'

'Very like that. The star falls in on itself and dies but it leaves the hole behind, like the smile on the Cheshire cat, a ghost star, and we call these ghost stars collapsars. Can you say that?' He had trouble saying it himself.

'Collapsars.' Words fascinated his daughter; the longer the word, the better.

'That's it. Now, this collapsar is like a bottomless pit. Anything that gets too close is pulled in and falls and falls and falls forever and nothing that falls in can ever get out. The collapsar swallows up everything, even light, which is why another name for them is black holes, and the more it swallows the bigger and stronger it gets and the bigger and stronger it gets the more it can draw in and swallow.'

'Dad . . .'

'Yes, wee hons.' He was growing accustomed to the darkness in the bedroom, he could discern Gemma's face in the swirling dots of dark.

'You sound scared.'

And all of a sudden he was scared, terrified.

'Dad.' A pause. 'You said this was a true story.'

'I did.'

'Does that mean there are such things as collapsars?'

'We found the first one today.' Or rather, two American scientists at UCLA acting on information from a Japanese sky-watch probe acting on information from a Soviet orbital X-ray telescope, found one today.

'Is that why you sound scared?'

He could not answer, and in the silence Gemma asked,

'Dad, has *Vivaldi* anything to do with this c — c — clasp —'

'Collapsar. Wee hons, *Vivaldi*'s going there.'

He would never forget the little shriek of fear.

'Dad, *Vivaldi*'s going to fall and fall and fall forever . . .'

'No no, hons, *Vivaldi*'s not going to fall into the black hole. *Vivaldi*'s just going to go round the edge of the collapsar and take a look. It won't fall in.'

But sitting on his daughter's bed with the autumn gales howling round the house he felt that in saying *Vivaldi* was going to the black hole he was saying that he was going there himself, and he saw what it was that had terrified him in Gemma's three words: the sudden, fearful image of *himself* falling falling down down down spinning spinning round round

round, dwindling into a little spinning homunculus of a father, falling into the black hole. Dread paralyzed him; mortality had tapped him on the shoulder.

'Then is *Vivaldi* not going to look at the comets any more?'

He thanked God for Gemma's question.

'No, and yes. You see, as the collapsar moves around the sun — which takes it millions of years, it's so far away — it passes through the big cloud of comets, remember, the . . . ?'

'Oort Cloud.' Gemma repeated the name with him, mouth shaping the big, round words, eyes shining with intellectual excitement.

'And it just so happens that the region it's passing through is very close to the place where *Vivaldi* was originally meant to go. Imagine that, wee hons, first spacecraft to go to a black hole.'

He knew Gemma took a great pride in his work. Not every Daddy in Corstorphin Primary P-5 piloted spaceships to the edge of the solar system. Even if that Daddy happened to be as pissed as a boiled owl.

'Here's a question, Gemma. What do you know about dinosaurs?'

'You mean Tyrannosaurus Rex and Brontosaurus and all that? What's that got to do with *Vivaldi*?'

'Wait and see. Now, why aren't there two dinosaurs here talking astrophysics at two in the morning instead of two humans?'

'Because a comet hit the earth and killed them all.'

'Ah-hah! Now, back to the Oort Cloud. When the black hole passes through the comets, sometimes it passes so close it pulls them in and swallows them, but most of the time it just knocks them out of the cloud and sends them in towards the sun. Now, the last time this happened was sixty-five million years ago in the time of the dinosaurs, and you know what became of them. This time it's our turn. Maybe we'll be lucky and no comets will come close to the earth. And maybe we won't.'

Dr. Hugh saw the fear on his daughter's face, darker than the darkness in the room, and despised his drunken mouth for frightening her so. Yet this was the world he had bequeathed his eight-year-old child and every loving father's eight-year-old children: a world of extinction raining out of the sky.

'Daddy?'

'Yes, wee hons?'

'Does this collapsar have a name?'

'Yes it does. The people who found it called it Nemesis.'

'What does that mean?'

'It's the name of an old Greek goddess who brought vengeance down on the earth.'

'Dad, I'm scared.'

'Gemma love, so am I.'

T-22 15840 KM

At sixteen thousand kilometres and closing, Nemesis fills the Big Wall. Half-hypnotized, Dr. Hugh numbly asks for data. Data will keep it away, keep it remote and distant, half a light-year distant in the Oort Cloud, for projected in garish false colour on the video wall it is intimidating, frightening.

'Angular rotation 24000 pi radians per second.'

'Circumference of collapsar event horizon fifteen kilometres.'

'Estimated mass: four solar masses.'

'Radiation temperature estimated 1.47 million K; energy density, 2.2×10^{25} eV per litre.'

Gemma, help me. Nemesis is more dreadful than he has ever imagined. Its every aspect is orders of magnitude greater than the estimates he and Kirkby Scott made when the decision was taken to reroute *Vivaldi* to the collapsar. He is not now certain whether *Vivaldi* can survive the encounter with the black hole. All his current guesstimates on survival are based on those hopelessly optimistic, conservative assumptions and even then those probabilities were only in the order of sixty per cent in favour of little *Vivaldi*. The odds chalked up by the bookies down in the staff canteen express an altogether different climate of confidence.

Vivaldi was not built for this, he tells himself. *Vivaldi* was designed for a leisurely stroll among the comets, not a headlong plunge to within twelve kilometres of the event horizon of a black hole. Everything about Nemesis is too much; too much mass, too much heat, too much radiation, too much gravity, too big, too close, too soon.

Damn you, black hole, you are too much and you are going to swallow twenty years of my life as wantonly as you would swallow a grain of comet dust.

He remembers; remembers taking Gemma to see a Disney film when she was quite small. In that film there had been a snake with whirlpool eyes that drew in and hypnotized and Gemma had screamed and screamed and screamed until he took her out of the cinema. Now as he stands before the whirlpool eye of Nemesis he understands her fear.

'Dr. MacMichaels . . .'

Uh? Andrea Mencke, from Personnel.

'Dr. MacMichaels, just to inform you that Kirkby Scott has arrived and is in the building.'

One evening Dr. Hugh arrived home at 26 Milicent Crescent after a busy day on the edge of the solar system to find a stranger in a tasteless but utterly fashionable plaid suit sitting in his favourite armchair chatting amiably to a rapt nearly-sixteen Gemma and sipping a glass of Dr. Hugh's very very best single-malt.

'Hello, Dad.' Gemma greeted him with a kiss and a Hello-Daddy-Bear hug. 'This is Kirkby Scott.'

'Good evening, sir,' said the plaid-suited single-malt-sipper, standing and enthusiastically shaking hands. 'Kirkby Scott, UCLA. I believe you're the one who wants to send a spaceship to my collapsar.'

His name was Kirkby Scott; he came from the University of California, Los Angeles, though he was born in Wisconsin, where apparently everyone in California was born; he was twenty-eight years old; he had won the youngest-ever doctorate in astrophysics from the University of California, for which he and his partner Paul Mazianzky, now of the Jet Propulsion Lab, Pasadena, had made a study of the orbits and perturbations of orbits of comets in the Oort Cloud on the hypothesis that the sun possessed a distant companion, tentatively christened Nemesis (pretty good name, no?) with the subhypothesis, subsequently proved, that this Nemesis was a black-body object, possibly (now verified) a moderately sized collapsar of approximately three solar masses, and that on account of this epochal discovery (words like 'Nobel' had been bandied) UCLA, NASA, and the ESA had decided in their corporate wisdom that he, Kirkby Scott, was to be Dr. Hugh MacMichaels's new partner on the Vivaldi Project.

To which, Dr. Hugh MacMichaels of the Vivaldi Project said,

'You what?'

He went to the Space Lords of the ESA and the Space Lords of the ESA said things like 'Americans feeling left out,' and 'They did discover it, after all.' They also said things like 'no place for dog-in-the-manger attitudes' and 'brotherhood of science.' More revealingly, they said 'got some deep-space pulse-fusion thing going on over there — Orion, they call it — powered starflight, all that; you scratch my back, all that stuff?' And, sinisterly, they said, 'old allies' and 'Western-bloc solidarity' and, most sinisterly of all, 'directive from the Highest Authorities.'

'Doesn't the position of Project Director entitle me to some say-so?' said Dr. Hugh.

'Sorry, Hugh,' said the Space Lords of the ESA. 'It's a political decision.' And that was that. Dr. Hugh shuttled home to Edinburgh hating both Kirkby Scott the flesh and Kirkby Scott the idea. He poured out his cup of bile to Moira, but, self-absorbed with the darkness that had taken root in the empty places within her, she was no longer interested in either his work or him. So he poured it out again to Gemma and she listened patiently and when he had emptied himself of his anger at the European Space Agency, Kirkby Scott, and Moira, she said,

'I rather like him, Dad.'

'Like him? Like that . . . that . . . dandy, that . . . popinjay, that poseur?'

'He has a good heart, Dad.'

Dr. Hugh did not appreciate then that his daughter possessed the gift of reading hearts, a kind of spiritual X-ray vision to which all intents were open and from which no secrets could be hid, and so he went away hating Kirkby Scott, idea and man. But day by day, week by week, year by year, his resentment of his partner mellowed and softened and became first admiration, then open liking, and he came to realize that a man can wear a flashy plaid suit (forgivable through fashion), sit in someone's favourite armchair (forgivable through ignorance) and swill someone's very very best single-malt and chat up his dear and only daughter (unforgivable under any circumstances), and have a good heart.

Two days after Gemma's nineteenth birthday, with *Vivaldi* six months from the black hole, Dr. Hugh and Kirkby Scott were guests of honour at the 43rd International Astronautical Conference in Houston, Texas. Dr. Hugh was very excited by the prospect of going to Houston. He had piloted spaceships to the edge of the stars but had never crossed the Atlantic. Gemma was excited for him too.

'Got passport, air-sickness pills, glasses, cheap thriller?'

He nodded, yes, yes, yes, yes, yes.

'Right, then. Be good, Dad, and knock them dead.'

The 43rd International Astronautical Conference was a triumph. Even half a year from the black hole, *Vivaldi* had still pushed Death Stars, orbital factories, Jupiter ramjets, Martian go-bots, and even pulse-fusion Orion stardrives into the wings and Drs. Hugh and Kirkby — one tweedy, beardy, amiably confused; the other confident, garrulous, the picture of fashion in paisley one-piece and matching duster coat — under the spotlight centre stage.

At the reception afterwards everyone wanted to shake Dr. Hugh's hand and tell him how he reminded them of Sean Connery (the *only* James Bond), and Dr. Hugh, blurred and mellow from too much California Moselle, smiled and laughed and talked the veriest drivel with Respected Nobel Laureates and Sharp Young Men from NASA and Doyens of Astronautics and was just easing into conversation with an extremely attractive woman journalist from *New Scientist* (so sorry, his subscription had run out years ago) when the bellboy came round paging Dr. Hugh MacMichaels paging Dr. Hugh MacMichaels telephone call at reception telephone call at reception and he left the extremely attractive woman journalist

holding his glass and went to answer the telephone and on the other end was Moira telling him that Gemma had been killed that morning in a car accident on the M62.

T-10 7200 KM

Casual, fashionable, elegant in his yellow designer one-piece, Kirkby Scott skips down the steps and slips in beside Dr. Hugh.

'Sorry,' he whispers. 'Stuck in a stack over Düsseldorf while they sorted out an air-traffic controllers' dispute, would you believe? And would you believe that sitting up there in our coffee room is Carl Silverman, I mean, Carl Silverman . . .'

'I know,' says Dr Hugh. 'He interviewed me.'

'Interviewed you? Hey, ho . . . I'll ask you about it later. Well, here I am. Okay, tell me what's going on.'

Dr. Hugh nods at the Big Wall.

'Ten minutes.'

'Shoot, that close? How long to the impact probes?'

'They go at T-minus-four.'

'How's *Vivaldi* bearing up to it?'

'Gravity shear and dust impact are causing her to wobble off optimum course.'

'Well, the onboard's held up this long, it can hold another ten minutes.'

'Gravity shear approaching upper safety limits,' advises an unapproachable Swiss Fräulein at the telemetry board.

'Gravity shear? Gravity shear? We hadn't figured on the gravity shear getting so strong so far out; here, let's have a look, what kind of beast have we got out there?'

Kirkby Scott studies the facts and figures on Nemesis with hisses of increasing disbelief. Dr. Hugh studies the simulator display schematics on the Big Wall simulator. There is ugly, bucket-of-bolts *Vivaldi*, rolling and tumbling towards the Schwarzchild limit: safe, but Dr. Hugh's imagination superimposes on the videoscreen the hundred alternative scenarios in which *Vivaldi* is reduced to glittering shards.

It wasn't made for this. Not for this. He watches the simulated dust impacts peck away at *Vivaldi*'s dust shields (each peck ten times the velocity of a rifle bullet: he remembers telling Carl Silverman that) and realizes that he is holding his breath.

Why?

Because I am scared. Scared that at any moment a piece of ice is going to destroy *Vivaldi*, scared of what is going on out there, out there at the edge of the solar system where all I can do is watch and I am helpless to act: out here is something I cannot control, something that defies me, mocks me, wishes to destroy me, and that scares me because since Gemma died *Vivaldi* has been the only thing in my life over which I have had any control. My daughter, my wife, my passions, my fears, all flew from my hands over the years as *Vivaldi* flew on and on and on and now here it is perched on the edge of chaos and what can this man do?

The Chapel of Rest terrified Dr. Hugh. From its position on the hill it dominated the rows and plots of plinths and headstones and Dr. Hugh, turning through the wrought-iron gates in his battered red station wagon. Every funeral reminded him of other funerals. It had been raining the day of Ben Vorderman's funeral, it was raining today, the same steady rain, and it was the same graveyard and the same chapel on the hill save that this time the hearse kept on up the hill to the chapel at the top, for a new law said that everyone must be cremated unless religious observance prohibited. Dr. Hugh could not say why the Chapel of Rest disturbed him. Perhaps the red-brick architecture which reminded him of the detested Forth River Primary School, perhaps the morbid Phantom-of-the-Opera organ programme which stopped mid-bar when the coffin was placed on the dais, perhaps the chimney glimpsed through the-Resurrection-and-the-Life stained glass, stern sentinel of mortality. Man is but a puff of smoke, and quickly blown away.

Gemma had never been formally religious, so friends, relatives, and lovers (he did not doubt that they were there) read poems, placed flowers, sang songs, and spoke stumbling eulogies while Dr. Hugh sat beside his wife and could not believe that it was his daughter in that thing up there on the dais.

'Perhaps her father would like to say a few words? Mr. MacMichaels?'

It was the last thing he wanted to do, he would rather have done anything, anything at all than have to stand up there beside his daughter's coffin, but Moira hissed something so vile and cutting that he went up to the lectern because it was the only place her contempt could not reach him. But the few words would not come to express what he wanted to say. Then all of a sudden he felt he wanted more than anything to shout at the friends, relatives, lovers, 'What could you know about how it feels to lose your present and your future, your light, the woman you love most in all the world?' and tell them that no matter how many words he said they could never express one millionth part of what Gemma had been, but those words would not come to him as he braced himself against the lectern and two tears ran down his face and they said all the words he could not.

The funeral director said,

'Now, by special request, an extract from Gemma's favourite music programme, a piece of music that must have meant very much to her.' The pseudo-Venetian strings of the Vivaldi programme filled the chapel, the funeral director pressed a discreet button, and as the computerized violins and harpsichords played, the coffin sank down down down out of sight and Dr. Hugh, desolate father, stood there as if his heart had melted to slag. And the coffin passed out of sight and he felt Moira's reproachful, unforgiving eyes upon him.

After the signing of the Book of Remembrance he followed her to the car and his attention was snared by a flash of white on the wet black tarmac: a business card fallen from her bag. He picked up the card, read the address:

Immortals Inc. somewhere in London.

'I think you dropped this.' She almost snatched the card back in her haste to hide it in the bowels of her handbag.

'Thank you, darling.'

As the smoke went up the chimney he tried to remember Gemma's voice, Gemma's face, Gemma's laughter, and found he could no longer do so.

T-4 2880 KM

'Crossing plasma front; electrical activity increasing to within eight per cent of safety margins.'

Go on, you tough little bastard.

'Radiation levels increasing markedly: damage monitors report soft fails in some attitude-control transputers.'

You've made it over twenty years to get this far. Only a few minutes left.

'Dust impacts maximizing, we mark penetration through numbers one and two dust-shields to the mylar impact-sensor layer.'

Go on go on go on go on.

'Counting down to impact-probe release . . . four . . . three . . . two . . . one . . .'

'Impact probes away!' sings Kirkby Scott. 'Go for it, you little mothers!'

Three streaks of light fan away from the Looney-Toon *Vivaldi* on the Big Wall: cometary impact probes Harpo, Groucho, and Chico, their mission radically altered from their original intention. Once designed to test the density and composition of Oort comets, now they have been aimed down the gullet of the collapsar to shatter themselves against the impossible, to test the density and composition of the spinning collapsar known as Nemesis, the stuff and substance of that bead, that foetus of dark matter at its heart, and in the shattering, in the gasp of their destruction, become a revelation of the eschatology of the death of the universe.

Dark matter, heart matter, heavy matter, light matter, and upon the stuff and substance, the piss and pus of Nemesis, depends the shape of the end times, whether the Scattering will one day become the Gathering and the galaxies will be squeezed back into the primal Cosmic Egg once more, or whether they will fly outwards on their lonely courses forever, into the night, into the dark, the keening electron-whine of the panversal heat-death, chaos and cold at the rag end of time.

Dr. Hugh does not want there to be an end time. He does not care for the new Revelation. What is the death of the universe, majestic in its decline and finality, awesome in its scope and magnificence, compared to the death of his beloved daughter, one brief human life upon an insignificant fleck of filth at the edge of an unspectacular galaxy?

This is not real, he reminds himself. The lines, the graphics, the alphanumerals: imagination. This is the truth: six months ago, listen, *six months*, three lemon-sized impact probes with fanciful names fell past the Shwarzchild limit. And, by the express command of omnipotent relativity, they are falling still, frozen in time. And they will fall thus forever. Immortality. A relativistic shudder shakes Dr. Hugh.

'Hi, hons, I'm home.' Home from Düsseldorf and the ESA conference, the sole tweed-jacketed pillar of academe on a city-hopper crammed with the industrial moguls of the New Scotland. On the flight he'd drunk too much, as usual, and then somewhere over Holland he'd remembered Gemma's gentle chidings on the incompatability of in-flight alcohol with aircraft pressurization. Then he'd realized, with devastating finality, that this time she would not be there to greet him at the arrivals gate with a Daddy-Bear hug and confiscate his yellow bag of duty-free drink and drive him home with some relaxing Handel (original, not some pseudo-programme thing) on the car stereo and genuinely interested questions about what he had been doing. It would not be. It would never be again. He had burst into tears and wept all the way from Nord Zeeland to Edinburgh with the industrial moguls of New Scotland staring at him. 'Hons, I'm home . . .' But hons was out, busy with the do-gooderies that filled the place in her life where he should have been. No letters for him, but a shiny brochure for her from some Sassenach outfit calling itself *Immortals Inc.*

He saw a white card fluttering on the wet black tarmac of the municipal crematorium.

He took the shiny brochure into the living room and sat down to leaf through its glossy pages.

The hardest part of death is for those who remain.

Our Counsellors know only too well the ways in which grief can rip a family in two . . . Our computer simulacra reproduce in every way *the personalities of the mourned departed . . . Working from the material manifestations of personality, the mementos, the souvenirs, the small personal possessions, voice tapes and photographs, our computers can reconstruct that personality with such astonishing verisimilitude . . .*

Looking out of the window he saw something moving in the rotting summerhouse, something caught in the eigenblink of an eye: an arm.

Astonishing verisimilitude astonishing verisimilitude astonishing verisimilitude . . .

He approached the gazebo with trepidation. Through the vegetable garden, past the raspberry canes, Dr. Hugh went cat-careful, listening to the baroque strings of the Vivaldi programme he'd bought her for her seventeenth birthday when she'd tired of the electronic ethnobeat programmes which all sounded the same. He circled the summerhouse, anachronistic now the summers would not be coming back. Through the windows he saw the walls plastered with the plundered memorabilia of Gemma MacMichaels: the photographs of girlfriends, of cats, dogs, rabbits, hamsters, ponies, later of boyfriends; Gemma in ballet clothes, Gemma cast as Lady MacBeth in the school play, Gemma proud with her certificate of merit to the University of Edinburgh to study English, and the holiday, all the holiday snaps: him potbellied and grizzled in his swimming trunks in Corfu, him with a stupid expression coming off the shuttle at the airport, him tense and waiting in his hired Parsons and Parsons tux (red silk lining) waiting to hear the pronouncement of the Royal Institute Awards for 2006 . . . Moira had been thorough. Thoroughness was characteristic of her.

Something was sitting in a wicker chair with its back turned to him. He opened the door. Reconstructed Venetian strings swelled, *La Serenissima.* Ceiling-mounted cameras turned, focused, and an awful, sick puppet-thing with Gemma's face had turned in Gemma's wicker chair, smiled, and said,

'Hi, Dad.'

Hands to mouth to keep the horror from spewing out, he stepped back from the gazebo door.

'Dad, aren't you coming in?' Camera-eyes tracked him as he backed away. 'Dad, it's me!' The puppet-thing lifted embracing arms. Hugh MacMichaels, father, husband, space explorer, vomited his BritAir PLC breakfast of porridge, bacon, eggs, oatcakes, marmalade, orange juice, and coffee into the brussels sprouts.

T-0 NEMESIS

'T-zero. Distance zero. Event horizon. Doctor, the event horizon!'

The maelstrom of SonyColor on the Big Wall dwarfs Dr. Hugh. He closes his eyes so he does not have to see. T-zero. Distance zero. *Vivaldi* has kissed the lips of the nothing. The crackle of hard radiation drowns all voices in the control room save one, a cry, uplifted above the hiss and roar of Nemesis: Kirkby Scott.

'We got it! Oh, we got it! Positive electromagnetic halo readings from Harpo, Groucho, and Chico before contact was lost! Nemesis is a fourth-order minimum surface of Hypothesis B dark matter. Folks, it's the fourth state of matter!' He turns, triumphant, arms Christ-wide. On his face, the beatific smile of the prophet of Doomsday. 'Ladies and gentlemen, the missing mass is found! The Universe will contract to a point and be reborn!' Animal whoops, cheering, applause, fill the control room. In the centre of the forest of arms reaching out to congratulate, Dr. Hugh and Dr. Kirkby embrace. Dr. Hugh cannot think why.

Unresting, unhastening, and as silent as light, *Vivaldi* loops away from Nemesis. Half the control boards are a Piccadilly Circus of malfunction lights. More hulk than spacecraft, Earth's first starship puts distance between itself and the collapsar. It has survived. It has come through. It has beaten the black hole. The count stands at T+45 seconds as champagne corks pop and glasses are raised and an international chorus of toasts proposed to the twin heroes of the Vivaldi Project.

Peep. Peep. Peep. Peep. Peep. Peep. Peep. Pee . . . the emergency alarm. Controllers scatter to their posts, bulk-purchase snap-together plastic champagne glasses still in hands. All they can do is observe the destruction.

'Cometary head . . .'

'Blind side of the collapsar . . .'

'Impact estimated in . . .'

The Big Wall displays the destruction in computer-enhanced garishness: a cloud of electric-blue ice pellets, fragments of a shattered Oort comet.

'Proximity detectors still functional . . .'

'Emergency evasion programmes being effected . . .'

'Small-manoeuvre thrusters firing . . .'

'Come on come on come on come on . . .' *Vivaldi* shifts slowly, slowly, so slowly. The staff of Mission Control Dharmstadt will it on: come on come on come on *come on.* Alone of all the people in the room, Dr. Hugh sees what must happen and cries,

'Stupid stupid stupid!'

So concerned is the radiation-seared onboard computer with the imminent danger that its lobotomized memory has forgotten all about Nemesis, all about the event horizon. *Vivaldi* is steering itself away from the ice cloud into the embrace of the collapsar.

'Time to event horizon, thirty-two seconds,' says Kirkby Scott dazedly, face lit blue and green in the reflected glow of Nemesis. 'Time to event horizon, twenty-eight seconds . . .' *Vivaldi* rolls and points its cameras directly on the singularity. Dr. Hugh MacMichaels, standing faithful at his station as he has stood faithful for twenty years, beholds the heart of the black hole.

The heart of the darkness.

He whispers, face blue with Nemesis-shine and wonder,

'Holy God, there's some . . . thing in there.'

The darkness of the heart.

Emotion had always terrified him. He could not bear to hear Moira's sobbing. It made her vulnerable and human and he wanted her to be invulnerable, inhuman.

'It was for you, for us. God knows, we can never have another Gemma, and now she's dead; what's going to keep us together, what's going to keep us going?'

Poor, naive Dr. Hugh had never understood the essential

contradiction that lay close to Moira's heart: that her treasured independence existed only because the stability of husband, child, and home lent it firm foundation. He could only dimly comprehend that she feared being cast adrift on the sea of misfortune without haven or the sanctuary of a future assured through her children. And he could never understand that though she despised him, he was now all those things that she needed, and that if the marriage collapsed she would be irrevocably alone. And because he understood none of this, he could not understand why she had taken his daughter's, *their* daughter's, memories to Immortals Inc. for them to out in plastic and metal. Yet comprehension, revelation, lay just beyond the roses browning in the acid rain, the desolate beans and the wilting brussels sprouts. And because twenty years older he was still really rather naive, he knew he would have to ask the oracle; the shape moving about its indecipherable businesses beyond the rain-streaked glass.

'Gemma.'

'Hi, Dad.'

The face was almost more than he could bear, yet he felt he must reach out a finger to touch the hand, the cheek, the brow, so he could satisfy himself that it was not warm flesh. His fingers carried away her perfume, *Noches de Luna*, amateurishly smuggled out of airport duty-frees.

'They made me well, didn't they, Dad?'

The voice, the inflections, the idioms, the lowered eyes, the slight smile: the *astonishing verisimilitude*. He tried to deny her to himself with coarse, hurtful questions.

'Where did they put them then?'

'The computers, Dad? Under the floorboards and up in the ceiling. You know, you had dry rot, death-watch beetle, and at least three colonies of mice down there.'

He almost let himself smile. The Gemmathing read the almost-smile with her camera-eyes and returned it wholly.

'Relax, Dad. Why don't you just let me be what I'm supposed to be?'

Again the gentle invitation. Again the coarse, hurtful rejection.

'How much did she pay for you?'

'Twelve thousand five hundred pounds on a monthly direct-debit installment plan, for which she got a voice-recognition programme capable of discriminating between sarcasm, irony, or any other form of rhetorical trickery, Dad. So stop trying to make me out to be a thing and let me help you. She did it because of you, Dad.'

'Me? Oh no.' But he had let himself be trapped by the Gemmathing.

'She's terrified of you leaving her all alone in the world, Dad. She may not love you but she needs you, needs someone, and if she can't have you, then she'll bring her only daughter back from the dead to fill her need. Me. Gemma, your daughter.'

Suddenly the dread was more than he could bear. He surged to his feet, whale-and-rainbow mobiles swinging away from his heavy animal shoulders, an angry, helpless bull-father.

'But you're not Gemma, you are a thing, a pile of transputers and molecular gates, a mechanical puppet like something out of Madame Tussaud's on the Royal Mile.' He remembered Gemma, aged eight, clinging to his coat in real fear as the monsters, ogres, and body-snatchers of Scotland's grim history reached out of the gloom for her. 'You're not real. I'll tell you what's real: the Gemma I remember, the Gemma in my heart, that's the real Gemma.'

'Dad, I'm surprised.' The Gemmathing flashed its eyebrows. Where had it learned that? He had never been able to resist Gemma's raised eyebrows.

'Tell me, Dad, what's the difference between the Gemma in your head and the Gemma in the gazebo? We're both memories, only the memories in your head will fade with time and eventually become just memories of memories of memories, but in me they have been given a body and will never fade. So what's so terrible about that? What's so terrible about wanting to keep those memories, those things that were special about Gemma MacMichaels, *me*, fresh and imperishable? What's the difference?'

He had no answer for the Gemmathing. That evening he flew off to Dharmstadt to meet with Nemesis and he still had no answer. He knew there must be an answer to the Gemmathing's question, a full and complete answer, but he did not have the first idea where he might hunt for that answer. He never suspected that his answer was waiting for him within the Einsteinian gullet of a black hole.

Peeeeeeeeeeeeeeeeeeeee . . .
'Crisis situation.'
'Termination of all telemetry data.'
'Cessation of all onboard monitoring systems.'
'We're getting nothing but three-k static on the communications links.'
'No incoming intelligence.'
'All sensors nonfunctional.'
'All systems dead.'
The Big Wall is blank save for the tiny, mocking alphanumerals in the top left corner:

T+1:50 1320 KM

The control room is filled with the penetrating keen of the alarm. Every head is turned on Dr. Hugh: What do we do now, leader? Dr. Hugh flips off the whistle and his voice seems very loud as he speaks into the deepspace radio hiss.

'Ladies and gentlemen, we must assume that *Vivaldi* has crossed the event horizon and that the mission is terminated. Thank you for your assistance, it was a pleasure to have worked with you. Thank you.'

Hisssssssss. Good-bye, Starship of the Imagination.

Kirkby Scott bangs his desk displays in frustration but Dr. Hugh does not share his sense of failure. Rather, he glows with a peculiar elation, as if in the loss of twenty visionary years, by some universal law of conservation, he has gained some vital insight. The odds were always stacked against him. Now after twenty years he must take up his life again. As he leaves the control room he hears Alain Mercier's measured syllables:

'The Vivaldi Mission count has been terminated at launch plus six point three times ten to the eighth seconds at 5:45 GMT, August twenty-seventh, 2008.'

Outside, the demon MEDIA has lain in wait for him, now it pounces.

'Dr. MacMichaels, tell me, will there now be a joint European/American mission to the Oort Cloud?'

'Dr. MacMichaels, what light does the Vivaldi mission throw upon the origins of the solar system?'

'Dr. MacMichaels, what bearing does the outcome of the Vivaldi mission have on the Orion probe?'

'Dr. MacMichaels, what would you say is the probability that a wave of comets has been dislodged from the Oort Cloud, and will you now be pressing for an international skywatch?'

'Dr. MacMichaels, does the revelation that Nemesis is composed of Hypothesis B dark matter imply in any way that the universe is reaching the limits of its expansion and that contraction to the point source will begin to occur within the next few million years?'

He stops for that one. All bits and parts of other things, the stained-glass demon MEDIA halts in a surge of boom-mikes, cameras, and handheld recorders.

'Quite frankly, sonny, I don't give a shit. And neither should you.' The pimply-faced cub reporter in the bright red body-suit and inappropriately padded muscles blushes. And Dr. Hugh is suddenly angry. 'How old are you? Nineteen, twenty? Less? Listen, sonny, get out of here, go and make love, make friends, make a big noise, see things, do things, be things, have fun, be good, be kind, be loved by everyone, live as full a life as you can so when the time comes for your own death you can go into it full and satisfied and at peace, because quite frankly, boy, the death of the universe is not worth a single tear. Not one damn tear.'

The doors are close; beyond the glass, the waiting car, the neatly planted trees, the east-is-red sunrise. Something to do with the Ruhr, the redness of the sunrise. An hour and a half from now he can be arriving in yawning Edinburgh. When he gets there, there is something he must do.

T+200

And now Dr. Hugh's battered red Ford estate car is driving

through the five-o'clock-empty streets of Edinburgh. A time zone westward, he has beaten the sun. Under the yellow street-lights the city is the possession of the milk-floats, the newspaper vans, the ambulances and their dark brothers the night police, and Dr. Hugh, driving fast, driving home. 5:05, he turns into the driveway with a crunch of gravel: it is early, not a blind open, not a carton of milk on a doorstep, not a jogger defiling the tranquility in designer jogging suit and shoes. Dr. Hugh watches the sun rise over Milicent Crescent: no rain today, amazing. He opens the trunk of the car and takes out not an overnight case but a red metal can. And he does not enter his house by the front door but by the side gate into the back garden. A neighbour's dog barks as Dr. Hugh crosses the garden: across the lawn, past the dying roses and the brussels sprouts and the raspberry canes — they look green, perhaps we shall have jam this year — to the gazebo.

The Gemmathing is awake and alert the instant he opens the door but Dr. Hugh knows that machines can go as long as twenty years without sleep.

'Dad! Do you know what time it is?'

'I do.'

'So, how did things go?'

'Things went fine.'

He unscrews the lid from the red metal can. Camera-eyes roll and focus. He sloshes the contents over the walls, the floor, the wicker chair. The Gemmathing shrieks and raises its hands in panic as the liquid slosh-sloshes over her flowery print frock. The stench of petrol chokes the gazebo.

'Dad! What are you doing? Do you know what you're doing?'

'I do,' says Dr. Hugh. 'Oh I do.' And as he sloshes the petrol over the Gemmathing he explains. 'You see, I worked out the answer to your question. What's the difference between you and my memories of Gemma? Answer, nothing. Both were wrong. Both are wrong. It's wrong to cling to memories, to make them the justification for my failure to escape from your death. But at least my memories will change and fade with time. That's why it's wrong to give them form and shape, enshrine them; it's giving death the victory. I realized that when *Vivaldi* was lost; it had gone to where I could never reach it, twenty years of my life, gone for good. I realized that no amount of wishing and hoping or praying could bring it back from the black hole, or you, Gemma, from the wrecked car. I had to lose you, Gemma, I had to let you pass over the event horizon. Memories are no substitute for living and we have to live, Gemma. We have to.'

And standing by the door of the gazebo he takes a match from a BritAir PLC matchbook, strikes it, and tosses it into the Gemmathing's lap.

The blossom of flame knocks him backwards into the raspberry canes. The intense heat has seared away his eyebrows and scorched his beard. He backs away, shielding raw face with hands, yet curious to see the destruction he has wrought. In the burning gazebo he sees the plastic features of the Gemmathing melting, flowing onto the blazing print frock. The windows shatter, twelve thousand five hundred pounds' worth of transputer modules crack and fuse and all the photographs, all the trapped memories, take wing and fly away on the burning wind like black crows. The flames roar and lick around the melting, burning Gemmathing.

'God, I'm sorry,' he whispers.

Alarmed by the explosions, neighbours are leaning out of open windows, fearful sheep-faces gaping at the suburban nightmare in MacMichaels's garden. Slippered and dressing-gowned, Moira is running across the lawn to the pyre.

'It's you and me now!' Dr. Hugh shouts. 'Just you and me. No Gemma to hold us together. We work it out on our own or not at all. We're adult, mature humans, dear God, we have our own lives to live.' Moira is on her knees amidst the brussels sprouts, hands held imploringly to the blazing summerhouse. Tears stream down her cheeks. The oily black smoke plumes into the sky. Dr. Hugh hears in the distance the wail of the fire brigade's red engines. He watches his wife weep and kneels beside her to comfort her. As he places his hand on her shoulder he notices the little buds of colour amidst the thorns and acid-browned leaves. Maybe there will be roses this year after all.

when I knew it was lost it had gone to where I could never reach ... twenty years of my life gone for good? I realised that no amount of wishing and hoping or praying could bring it back from the black hole of your [illegible] Gemma, from the wreckage ... I had to lose you, Gemma; I had to let you go [illegible] ... [illegible]. Memories are no substitute for living, and you have to live, Gemma. We live on.'

As I stumble to the foot of the gazebo he takes a match from a Smith's [illegible] matchbook, strikes it, and tosses it into the [illegible] ...

The blossom of flame knocks him backwards into the [illegible] cherry trees. The intense heat has scorched away his eyebrows and scorched his beard. He backs away, shielding his face with his hands, yet compelled to see the destruction he has wrought. In the burning gazebo he sees the plastic frames of the [illegible] melting, flowing onto the [illegible]. The [illegible] twenty thousand [illegible] worth of [illegible] paper [illegible] crack and fire and [illegible] as the photographs [illegible] the [illegible] black crows. The flames rise and [illegible] the [illegible].

'God, I'm sorry,' he whispers.

Alarmed by the [illegible], neighbours are [illegible] open windows, fearful [illegible] gaping at the [illegible] nightmare in MacMahon's garden. [illegible] Moira is running across the lawn to [illegible].

'It's you and me now,' Dr Hugh shouts. 'Just you and me. No Gemma to hold us together. We [illegible] it [illegible] our own [illegible]. We're adult, mature humans, dear God, we have [illegible] lives to live.' Moira is on her knees amid the [illegible], [illegible] the blazing [illegible] ... streaming down her cheeks. The oily black smoke plumes into the sky. Dr Hugh hears in the distance the wail of the fire brigade's [illegible]. He watches his wife [illegible] kneels [illegible] to comfort her. As he strokes her [illegible] he notices the [illegible] among the [illegible] and [illegible]. Maybe there will be [illegible] after all.

RUDY RUCKER and MARC LAIDLAW

Rudy Rucker's first book was *Geometry, Relativity and the Fourth Dimension* (1977), but his first published novel was *White Light* (1980). As well as non-fiction books, he has published seven more novels. These include *Software* (1982), which won the first Philip K. Dick Memorial Award, and his most recent book *Wetware* (1988), which was nominated for the same award. He plans a third in this series, *Limpware*, but at the moment is writing an alternate history novel called *The Hollow Earth*.

Marc Laidlaw's first two sales were made the same week in 1978, a story to Ramsey Campbell's *New Terrors* and a collaboration with Gregory Benford which appeared in *Omni*. He has since had solo stories published in *Omni*, *F&SF* and *Asimov's*. His first novel was *Dad's Nuke* (1986), and his second — *Neon Lotus* (1988) — was a finalist for the Philip K. Dick Award. His third novel will be *Kalifornia*.

The following story is their first collaboration, and Laidlaw reports that it "was concocted over the ruins of a Rucker feast and a copy of Benoit Mandelbrot's *Fractal Geometry of Nature*. Rudy had just moved to California from Virginia and was taken with the stoned eloquence of surfer slang: 'Gnarly, dude. I'm stoked.' I had been trying to write a comic sf version of *The Endless Summer*, drawing on my adolescence in Laguna Beach, California. Crossing this with the formula of boy inventor and sidekick, Zep and Delbert were born."

PROBABILITY PIPELINE

by

RUDY RUCKER and MARC LAIDLAW

The trouble started in Surf City, and it ended in another dimension.

Delbert was loud and spidery; Zep was tall and absent and a year older. Being in different grades, they didn't see each other much in the winters, but in the summers they were best friends on and off the beach. When Zep graduated, he spent a year at UC Santa Cruz before drugging out — he said he'd overfed his head. Delbert didn't like drugs, so when he graduated he didn't bother going to college at all. Now it was summer all year long.

It was November in Surf City and the pipeline was coming in steady. For the last few weeks they'd been without a surfboard, though these days the word was *stick*, not *board*, meaning Del and Zep were stickless. The way this particular bummer had come down was that Del had been bragging about his escape from a great white shark, and no one had believed him, so maximum Zep had cut a big shark-shape bite out of the dinged longboard he and Delbert shared, and still no one had believed. Basically Zep had thrashed the board for nothing, but at least Delbert was able to sell it to the Pup-Tent, a surfer snack shop where his girl Jen worked — not that Jen was really Delbert's *girl* in any intense physical sense of the word, and not that the Pup-Tent had actually *paid* anything for the shark-bit board that Delbert had mounted on the wall over the cash register. But it looked rad up there.

Often, in the mid-morning, when things were slow at the Pup-Tent, Jen would grill Zep and Delbert some burgers, and the three of them would sit on the bench out in front of the Pup-Tent, staring through their shades at the bright, perfect sky, or at the cars and people going by, or across the street at the cliffs and the beach and the endlessly various Pacific ocean, dotted with wet-suited surfers. Zep sat on the left, Jen on the right, and Delbert in the middle; Delbert usually talking, either rapping off what he saw or telling one of his long, bogus stories, like about the time when he'd been flying a kite on the beach and a Coast Guard plane had swooped down low enough to suck his kite into its jet and he'd been pulled out to sea about half a mile, dangling twenty feet above the water until he'd flashed to let loose of the string.

One particular day that November, Delbert was telling Jen about a book on hypnotism he'd read the day before, and how last night he'd tried to activate Zep's thrashed genius by putting Zep in a trance and telling him he was a great scientist and asking him to invent invisibility.

'He did that, Zep?' asked Jen, briefly interested. 'Did it work?'

'I, uh, I . . . thought of peroxide,' said Zep. Peroxide was a big thing with Zep; he'd stripped his hair so often that its color was faintly ultraviolet. When Zep felt like somebody might understand him, he'd talk a lot about the weird science stuff he'd learned at Santa Cruz, but just now he wasn't quite on.

'We put seven coats of it on a sheet of paper,' said Delbert, 'and for a second we thought it was working, but it was really just the paper falling apart.'

'Oxo wow,' said Jen, suddenly pointing out at the horizon. 'Outsider.' That was the traditional word for a big wave. 'Far outsider . . . and ohmigod! . . . like . . .' Jen often ended her sentences that way, with a 'like' and a gesture. This time it was her Vanna White move: both hands held out to the left side of her body, left hand high and right hand low, both hands palms up. She was watching one of the Stoke Pilgrims out there carve the outsider.

It was Lex Loach — Delbert could recognize him from the red-and-white checkerboard pattern on his wet suit. Loach executed a last nifty vertical snap, shot up off the face of the ripped outsider, and flew through the air, his wing squash turbo board glued to his feet by the suction cups on his neoprene booties.

Jen sighed and slowly turned her hands palms down. The Vanna White move, if done with the hands palms down, was known as Egyptian Style. Jen gave Delbert a sarcastic little neck-chop with her stiff left hand. 'I wish you could ride, Delbert. I wish you had a stick.'

'This surf's mush, Jen. Dig it, I saw a tidal wave when I was a kid. I was with my dad on Hawaii, and this volcano blew up, and the next minute all the water went out to sea and formed a gigantic —' He held out his arms as if to embrace a weather balloon.

'You saw that in a movie,' said Zep.

'Did not!' yelled Delbert. He was always yelling, and consequently he was always hoarse.

'Yo, dude. *Krakatoa East of Java.*'

'I never saw that movie, it really happened! We got stranded on the edge of the volcano and they had to come get us in a hot air balloon. Listen up, dude, my dad . . .'

Delbert jabbered on, trying to distract Jen from Lex Loach's awesomely stoked breakouts. By the time a customer showed up, she seemed glad to go inside.

'Do you think she likes me?' Delbert asked Zep.

'No. You should have gone to college.' Zep's voice was slow and even.

'What about you, brain-death?' challenged Del.

'I'm doing my detox, dude.' Zep got a tense, distant look when people questioned his sanity. But his voice stayed calm and disengaged. 'The programs are in place, dude. All I need is run time. Chaos, fractals, dynamics, cellular automata. I did ten years' research in two weeks last spring, dude. It's just a matter of working out the applications.'

'Like to what?'

'You name it, bro.'

'Waves,' said Del. 'Surfing. The new stick I need to bang Jen.'

Zep stared out at the horizon so long that Delbert thought he was lost in a flashback. But suddenly Zep's voice was running tight and fast.

'Dig it, Del, I'm not going to say this twice. The ocean is a chaotic dynamical system with sensitive dependence on initial conditions. Macro info keeps being folded in while micro info keeps being excavated. In terms of the phase-space, it works by a kneading process, continually doubling the size of a region and folding it over on itself like saltwater taffy with the ribbony layers of color all shot through. Big waves disappear in the chop and the right small ripple can amp on up to make an outsider. If you do the thing right in the ocean, it'll do whatever you want back. The thing about a chaotic system is that the slightest change in initial conditions produces a big effect — and I mean right away. Like on a pool table, dude, after ten bounces the position of the ball has been affected by the gravity from a pebble in a ring of Saturn. There's a whole space of dynamic states, and the places where the system settles down are called chaotic attractors. We do right, and the ocean'll do right by us.'

Del was like: 'Chaos attractor? How do we control it?'

'There's no formula because the computation is irreducibly complex. The only way to predict the ocean is to stimulate it faster than real-time. Could be done on a gigahertz CA. By the right head. The ocean . . . Delbert, the ocean's state is a point in ten-trillion-dimensional surfspace.'

'Surfspace?' Delbert grinned over at his long blond friend with the dark, wandering eyes. When Zep got into one of his head trips he tended to let his cool, slow surfer pose slide. He'd been a punk before a surfer, and a science nerd before that.

'You gotta relate, babe,' enunciated Zep, as he tore on into the rest of his riff. 'The wave pattern at any time is a fractal. Waves upon waves upon waves. Like a mountain range, and an ant thinks he's at the top of a hill, but he's only at the top of a bump on a rock on an outcrop on a peak on the range on the planet. And there's a cracky crack between his six legs. For our present purposes, it's probably enough to take ten levels of waves into account.'

'Ten levels of waves?'

'Sure man, like put your nose near the water and there's shivers on the ripples. The shivers have got kind of sketchy foam on them too. So sketchy foam, shivers, ripples, wads, and slidy sheets, now we be getting some meat to carve, uh, actual waves, peaks — those choppy peaks that look like Mr. Frostee's head, you wave — steamers and hollow surf, mongo mothers, outsiders and number ten the tide. So the wave pattern at any given spot is a ten-dimensional quality, and the wave patterns at a trillion different spots make a point in ten-trillion dimensional surfspace.'

'What's all the trillions for?' Out on the sea, Lex Loach and four other Stoke Pilgrims were riding in from the break. Loach, Mr. Scrote, Shrimp Chips, Squid Puppy, and Floathead, same as usual. They usually came up to the Pup-Tent for lunch. Delbert and Zep usually left before the Pilgrims got there. 'Talk faster, Zep.'

'I'm telling you, dude. Say I'm interested in predicting or influencing the waves over the next few minutes. Waves don't move all that fast, so anything that can influence the surf here in the next few minutes is going to depend on the surfspace values within a neighboring area of, say, one square kilometer. I'm only going to fine-grain down to the millimeter level, you wave, so we're looking at, uh, one trillion sample points. Million squared. Don't interrupt again, Delbert, or I won't build you the chaotic attractor.'

'You're going to build me a new stick?'

'I got the idea when you hypnotized me last night. Only I'd forgotten till just now. Ten fractal surf levels at a trillion sample points. We model that with an imipolex CA, we use a nerve-patch modem outset unit to send the rider's surfest desires down a co-ax inside the leash, the CA does a chaotic back simulation of the fractal inset, the board does a jiggly-doo, and . . .'

'TSUUUNAMIIIIII!' screamed Delbert, leaping up on the bench and striking a boss surfer pose.

Just then Lex Loach and the Stoke Pilgrims appeared, up from the beach. Lex looked at Delbert with the usual contempt. '*Ride* that bench, gnarly geek. Been puffing some of Zep's KJ?'

Lex Loach had been boss of Surf City as long as Delbert could remember. He lived here all year long, except when he went to snow-board at Big Bear in short pants and no shirt. Delbert thought he looked like a carrot. He was tall and thin and like a carrot, narrow at the bottom and very wide at the shoulders; and like a carrot, his torso was ribbed and downy.

Loach's ageing sidekick, Mr. Scrote, darted forward and made a vicious grab for Delbert's balls. Mr. Scrote was wrinkled and mean. He had bloodshot eyes and was half deaf from surfer's ear, and all his jokes had to do with genital pain. Delbert fended him off with a kick that missed. 'Couldn't help myself,' said Mr. Scrote to the other Pilgrims as he danced back out of reach. 'Dude looks soooo killer on his new stick.'

'I *am* getting a new stick,' cried Delert furiously. 'Chaos Attractor. Zep's building it.'

'What does a junkie know about surf?' put in Shrimp Chips, a burly young guy with bleached hair. 'Zep can't even stand to take a bath.'

'Zep's clean,' said Delbert loyally. 'And he knows all about surf from just sitting here and watching.'

'Same way you know about girls, right, weenie?' said Loach. 'Want to watch me and Jen get it on?'

Delbert leapt off the bench and butted his head right into the middle of that carrotty washboard of an abdomen. Loach fell over backward, and suddenly there were kids everywhere, screaming. 'It's a fight!'

Zep pulled Delbert back before Loach could pulverize him. The Stoke Pilgrims lined up around their chief carrot, ready to charge.

'Wait a minute,' Delbert yelped, holding out his hand. 'Let's handle this like real men. Lex, we challenge you to a duel. Zep'll have my new gun ready by tomorrow. If you and your boys can close us out, it's yours. And if we win, you give me your wing squash turbo.'

Loach shook his head and Mr. Scrote spoke up for him, widening his bloodshot eyes. 'I doubt Lex'd want any piece of trash you'd ride. No, Delbert, if you lose, you suck a sea anemone and tell Jen you're a fag.' The Stoke Pilgrims' laughter was like the barking of seals. Delbert's tongue prickled.

'Tomorrow by the San Diablo N-plant where the surf's the gnarliest,' said Lex Loach, heading into the Pup-Tent. 'Slack tide, dudes. Be there or we'll find you.'

Up on the cliff, the N-plant looked like a gray golf ball sinking into a sand trap. The cliff was overgrown with yellow ice plant whose succulent, radiation-warmed leaves were fat as drowned men's fingers. A colonic loop of cooling pipe jagged down the cliff, out into the sea, and back up the cliff to the reactor. The beach was littered with fish killed by the reactor's thermal pollution. Closer to the sea, the tide's full-moon low had exposed great beds of oversize sea anemones that were bright, mutated warm-water sports. Having your face pushed into one of them would be no joke.

'Trust me, bro,' said Zep. He was greasy and jittery. 'You'll sluice roosters in Loach's face. No prob. And after this we stalk the big tournament moola.'

'The surf is mush, Zep. I know it's a drag, bro, but be objective. Look the hell at the zon.' The horizon was indeed flat. Closer to the shore were long rows of small, parallel lines where the sea's dead ripples came limping in. Delbert was secretly glad that the contest might well be called off.

'No way,' shouted Zep, angrily brandishing the nylon case that held the new board. 'All you gotta do is plug in your leash and put Chaos Attractor in the water. The surf will definitely rise, little dude.'

'It's mush.'

'Only because *you* are. Dig it!' Zep grabbed his friend by the front of his brand-new paisley wet suit and shook him. 'You haven't looked at my new stick!' Zep dropped to his knees and unzipped Chaos Attractor's case. He drew out a long, grayish, misshapen board. Most of it seemed actually transparent, though there were some dark right-angled shapes embedded in the thing's center.

Delbert jerked back in horror. For this he'd given Zep two hundred dollars? All his savings for what looked like a dime-store Styrofoam toy surfboard that a slushed druggie had doused in epoxy?

'It . . . it's transparent?' said Delbert after a time. In the dull day's light you could see Zep's scalp through his no-color hair. Del had trusted Zep and Zep had blown it. It was sad.

'Does that embarrass you?' snarled Zep, sensing Delbert's pity. 'Is there something wrong with transparency? And screw your two hundred bucks because this stick didn't cost me nothing. I spend your money on crank, mofo, on clean Hell's Angels blow. What else, Delbert, who do you think I am? Yeah! Touch that board!'

Delbert touched the surface of the board uncertainly. 'It's rough,' he said finally.

'Yeah!' Zep wanted to get the whole story out, how he'd immediately spent the money on crank, and how then in the first comedown's guilt he'd laid meth on Cowboy Bob, a dope-starved biker who hung around the meth dealer's. Zep had fed Cowboy Bob's head so Bob'd take him out breaking and entering: First they hit the KZ Kustom Zurf-Shop for a primo transparent surfboard blank, then they barreled Bob's chopped hog up to Oakland to liberate imipolex from the I.G. Farben research labs in the wake of a diversionary firebomb, and then they'd done the rest of the speed and shot over the Bay Bridge to dynamite open the door of System Concepts and score a Cellular Automation Machine, the CAM8, right, and by 3.00 A.M. Zep had scored the goods and spent the rest of the night wiring the CAM board into the imipolex-wrapped blank's honeyheart with tiny wires connecting to the stick's surface all over, and then finally at dawn Zep had gone in through the back window of a butcher shop and wedged the board into the huge vacuum meat-packer there to vacuum-sputter the new stick's finish up into as weird a fractal as a snowflake Koch curve or a rucked Sierpinski carpet. And now lame little Delbert is all worried and:

'Why's it so rough?'

Zep took a deep breath and concentrated on slowing down his heartbeat. Another breath. 'This stick, Del, it uses its fractal surface for a real-time simulation. The board's surface is a fractal CA model of the sea, you wave?'

'Zep, what's that gray thing in the middle like a shark's skeleton? Loach is going to laugh at us.'

'Shut up about Loach,' snarled Zep, losing all patience once again. 'Lex Loach is like a poisonous mutant warty sculpin choked by a plastic tampon insert at the mouth of an offshore toxic-waste pipe, man, thrashing around and stinging everybody in his spastic nowhere death throes.'

'He's standing right behind you.'

Zep spun around and saw that Delbert was more or less correct, given his tendency toward exaggeration. Loach was striding down the beach toward them, along with the four other Stoke Pilgrims. They were carrying lean, tapering sticks with sharp noses and foiled rails. Loach and Mr. Scrote wore lurid wet suits. The younger three had painted their bodies with Day-Glow thermopaints.

'Gonna shred you suckers!' yelled Loach.

'Stupid clones!' whooped Zep, lifting Chaos Attractor high overhead. 'Freestyle rules!'

'What kind of weird joke is this?' asked Loach, eyeing the new stick.

'Care to try it out?'

'Maybe. I'm gonna win it anyway, right?'

Zep nodded, calm and scientistlike now that the action had finally begun. It was good to have real flesh-and-blood enemies to deal with. 'Let me show you where to plug it in. This might sting a bit at first.'

He knelt down and began to brush sand from Loach's ankle.

'What're you doing?' Loach asked, jumping back when he saw Zep coming at him with a wire terminating in sharp pins.

'You need this special leash to ride the board,' Zep said. 'Without human imput, the board would go out of control. The thing is, the fractal surface writhes in a data-simulation altered by the leash input. These fang things are a parallel nerve-port, wave? It feeds into the CAM8 along with the fractal wave analyses, so the board knows what to do.'

Mr. Scrote gave Zep a sharp kick in the ribs. 'You're gonna stick that thing in his ankle, you junkie, and give him AIDS?'

Zep bared his teeth in a confused grin. 'Just hold still, Lex. It doesn't hurt. I'd like to see what you can do with it.'

Loach stepped well back. 'You're whacked, dude. You've been over the falls one too many times. Your brain is white-water. Yo, Delbert! See you out at the break. It's flat now, but there's be peaks once the tide starts in — believe it!' Loach and the Stoke Pilgrims hit the mushy warm water and began paddling out.

Zep was still crouched over Chaos Attractor. He glanced shyly up at Delbert. 'You ready?'

'No.'

'Look, Del, you and my stick have to go out there and show the guys how to carve.'

'No way.'

'Get rad. Be an adventurist. You'll be part of the system,

man. Don't you remember how I explained about waves?'

'I don't care about waves,' said little Delbert. 'I want to go home. It's stupid to think I would ever be a major surfer. Who talked me into this, anyway. Was it you?'

Zep stared out at the zon. Loach and the Stoke Pilgrims were bobbing on the mucky water, waiting for a set. Suddenly he frowned. 'You know, Del, maybe it's not such a great idea for you to use this board.'

'What do you mean? It's my stick isn't it? I gave you two hundred dollars.'

'You still don't have the big picture. At any moment, the relevant sea-configuration is ten trillion bits of analog info, right? Which folds up to one point in the ten-trillion-dimensional surfspace. As the ocean dynamically evolves, the point traces out a trajectory. But Del! The *mind*, Del, the *mind* is meanwhile and always jamming in the infinite-dimensional *mindscape.* Mindscape being larger than surfspace, you wave. My good tool Chaos Attractor picks up what you're looking for and sends tiny ripples out into the ocean, pulsing them just right, so that they cause interference way out there and bounce back what you want. The coupled system of board and rider in the mindscape are riding the surfspace. You sketch yourself into your own picture.'

'So why can't I ride the board?'

'Because, Delbert, because . . .' Zep gave a long, shuddery sigh and clamped the leash's fangs into his own ankle. 'Because you have a bad attitude and you'll deal a mess and thrash the board before it gets burnt in. Because it's mine. Because right now I'm plugged in and you're not. Because . . .' Zep paused and smiled oddly. 'I don't like to say the word for what you are.'

'What word?'

'Ho-dad.'

Delbert's tense frame sagged. 'That's really depressing, Zep.' In the distance a car had begun insistently to honk. At a loss for words, Delbert craned up the cliff at the N-plant parking lot. There was a girl up there, standing next to a car and waving and reaching in through the car window to honk. It was Jen! 'Come on down, baby,' he screamed. 'Zep's gonna break the board in for me and then I'll shut down this beach for true!' Jen began slowly to pick her way down the steep cliff path. Delbert turned back to Zep, all smiles. 'Be careful, my man. The Pilgrims'll probably try to ram you.'

'I'm not afraid of Loach,' said Zep softly. 'He's a clone surfer. No sense of freestyle. We're both 'dads, man, but we're *still* avant-garde. And you, man, you go and put some heavy physical moves on Jen while she's standing here.'

Zep padded down to the water's edge, avoiding the lurid, overgrown anemones. Clams squirted dark brown water from their holes. Sand crabs hid with only their antennae showing, dredging the slack warm water for the luminous plankton indigenous to the San Diablo break.

The N-plant made for an empty beach. There was plenty of room in the water, even with the five Stoke Pilgrims out there in a lineup. Floathead and Shrimp Chips were playing tic-tac-toe in the body paints on each other's chests, and Squid Puppy was fiddling with a wrist-watch video game.

Chaos Attractor lit up the instant it hit the water. Zep found himself looking into a percolating, turbulent lens. The board was a window into surfspace. Zep could see the swirling high-dimensional probability fluid, tiny torsion curls composed of tinier curls composed of tinier torsions. It made him almost high on life. Zep flopped belly-down on the board and began paddling out through the wavelets that lapped the shore.

'Hang ten trillion!' called Delbert.

Ripples spread away from Zep's stick, expanding and crossing paths as they rushed toward the open sea. The water was laced with slimy indigo kelp. Zep thought of jellyfish. In this quap water, they'd be mongo. He kept paddling. The sun looked like the ghost of a silver dollar. He sploshed through some parallel lines of number-three waves. Stroke followed stroke, and finally he was far enough out. He let himself drift, riding up and down on the humping wave embryos. Chaos Attractor was sending out ripples all the time and now things were beginning to . . .

'Check the zon!' shouted Squid Puppy.

Zep sat up. Row upon row of waves were coming in from the zon, each wave bigger than the one before. The sea was starting to look like a staircase. Remain calm, carver. Nothing too big and nasty. A few even test waves would do nicely. Something with a long, lean lip and a smoothed-under ledge.

'Curl or crawl,' Loach called, glacing sidelong at Zep with a confident sneer.

Zep could feel the power between his legs. The surface of Chaos Attractor was flexing and rippling now, a faithful model of the sea's surface. Looking down, Zep could see moving bands of color that matched the approaching waves. Wouldn't it be great if . . .

The leash fed Zep's thought to the CAM8. The CAM8 jived the imipolex. The imipolex fed a shudder to the sea. The surface band-pattern changed and . . .

'Mexican beach break!' screamed Zep.

The huge blue wall came out of nowhere and crashed onto Loach and his glittering board — all in the space of an exclamation point.

Zep aimed into the churning stampede of white foam, endured a moment of watery rage, and shot effortlessly out into calm tides. The real wave-set was marching in now. Zep decided to catch the seventh.

Loach surfaced a few meters off, all uptight. 'Carve him, Pilgrims!'

Zep grinned. Not likely.

As the war-painted sea dogs huffed and puffed against the current, he calmly bent his will toward shaping that perfect seventh wave. The Stoke Pilgrims yelled in glee, catching waves from the set. Squid Puppy and Shrimp Chips came after Zep, dogsledding it in zigzags over the curl and down the hollow. Near miss. Here was Zep's wave. He took his time getting to his feet after a slow take-off, and looked back to see the prune-faced Mr. Scrote snaking after him, befouling the wave in his eagerness to slyve Zep.

It was time to hang ten.

Zep took a ginger step toward the nose and watched the gliding water rise up. Perfect, perfect . . . aaauuuuummmm. A shadow fell over Zep. He leaned farther out over the nose, and the shadow grew — like an ever-thicker cloud closing over the sun.

Zep looked back, and he saw that the sky was green and alive with foam, a shivering vault of water. Floating amid that enormous green curved world, which looked like some fathomless cavern made from bottle glass, was a lurid, red-eyed giant — a Macy's Parade Mr. Scrote.

Zep flicked around, banked back toward the behemoth, and cruised up the slick green tube until he was at Scrote's eye level. The sight of the bulging capillaries sickened him, and he stretched his arms straight out ahead of him, gripping the very tip of the board with his naked toes. He had all the time in the world. The wave didn't seem to be breaking anymore.

The green expanse spread out around him. The curve above flowed like melting wax, drawing him into it. Rationally, he knew he was upside down, but it felt more like he was sliding down one side of a vast, translucent bowl. Under the board he could see a shimmering disk of white light, like a fire in the water: Was that the sun? He stepped back to the middle of Chaos Attractor, tilting the board up for greater speed, plunging ever deeper in the maelstrom spiral of the tube. He was nearing the heart of pure foam: the calm, still center of the ever-receding void.

Suddenly, a huge stain came steaming toward him out of the vortex. Gelatin, nausea, quaking purple spots, a glutinous leviathan with purple organs the size of aircraft carriers. Mile upon mile of slithery stinging tendrils drifted behind the thing, stretching clear back to the singular center that had been Zep's goal.

It was a jellyfish, and . . . Zep was less than a centimeter tall. It figured, Zep thought, realizing what was up — it figured that he'd shrink. That's what he'd always wanted from the drugs he couldn't quite kick: annihilation, cessation of pain, the deep inattention of the zero. The jellyfish steamed closer, lurid as a bad trip, urgently quaking.

Zep sighed and dug in his stick's back rail. Water shot up, and Zep grew. The jellyfish zoom-lensed back down to size. Chaos Attractor shot up out of the tube, and Zep fell down into the warm gray-and-green sea.

He surfaced into the raging chop and reeled Chaos Attractor in by the leash. Mr. Scrote was behind a crest somewhere, screaming at Loach. 'He disappeared, Lex! I swear to God, dude — I had him, and he shrunk to nothing. Flat out disappeared!'

Zep got back on Chaos Attractor and rode some whitewater toward shore. There were Del and Jen, waving and making gestures. Del had his arm around her waist. Off to the right was the stupid N-plant cooling pipe. Zep glared up at the plant, feeling a hot, angry flash of righteous ecological rage. The nuke-pigs said no N-plant could ever explode, but it would be so rad if like this one went up, just to show the pigs that . . .

Ripples sped over the cooling pipe, and suddenly Zep noticed a cloud of steam or smoke in the air over the N-plant. Had that been there before? And was that rumbling noise thunder? Had to be thunder. Or a jet. Or maybe not. What was that he'd been thinking about an explosion? Forget it! Think pro-nuke, Zep baby!

When Zep was near shore, Delbert gave Jen a big kiss, dived in, and came stroking out, buoyed by his wet suit. He ducked a breaker or two and then he was holding onto the side of Chaos Attractor, totally stoked.

'I saw that, Zep! It was awesome! It does everything you said it does. It made great waves — and you shrank right up like you were surfing into a zero.'

'Yeah, Del, but listen —'

'Let me try now, Zep. I think I can do it.'

Zep back-paddled, gripping the board between his thighs. 'I don't think that's such a hot idea.'

Delbert reddened. 'Yeah? You know, Zep, you're a real wipe sometimes. What is this, huh? You get me to fork over all my savings so you can go and build a board that didn't cost you a cent in the first place — and now you act like it's yours! You took my money for a board you would have made anyway!'

'It's not that, Del. It's just that — it's more powerful than I thought. We maybe shouldn't be using it around here. Look at the nuke.'

'Oh, yeah, try to distract me. What a bunch of crap! Give me that board, Zep. Come on, and the leash, too.'

'Del, look —'

Another spurt of steam went up from the plant. Zep gave

thanks that the wind wasn't blowing their way.

'You two dudes are maka sushi!' yelled Loach.

The Stoke Pilgrims cried out in unison, 'Shred 'em!'

Zep looked away from the board just long enough for Del to grab it away from him. Delbert got up on the board and pushed Zep under, holding him down with his feet and reeling in on the leash. Zep's foot surfaced, and Delbert ripped the leash fangs out of his ankle. By the time Zep got his head back in the air, Delbert had installed the leash on himself and was paddling away, triumph in his eyes.

'It's my stick, dude,' called Del.

'Oh, no, Delbert. Please, I swear I'm not goofing. If you do it, you'd better stay really, really cool. Go for the little waves. And don't look at the N-plant. And if you do look, just remember that it can't possibly explode. No fancy tricks, dude.'

'Bull!' screamed Delbert, shooting over a small peak. 'This gun was built for tricks, Zep, and you know it. That's the thrill, man! *Anything* can happen! That's what this is all about!'

Delbert was belly to the board, stroking for the horizon. Back on the beach, Jen had noticed the N-plant's activity, and she was making gestures of distress. Zep dog-paddled, wondering what to do. Suddenly four of the surf punks surrounded him.

'He looks kind of helpless down there, don't he,' said Floathead.

'Watch him close,' said Mr. Scrote. 'He's slippery.'

'Let's use his head for water polo,' suggested Squid Puppy, darting the sharp end of his board at Zep.

Zep dove to the bottom and resurfaced, only to find the Stoke Pilgrims' boards nosed in around him like an asterisk with his head at the center. 'Mess with my mind, I don't care,' said Zep. 'But just don't put Delbert uptight.'

'*We* won't bother bufu Delbert,' said Mr. Scrote. 'He's Lex's now.'

'I know this is going to sound weird,' Zep began. 'But . . .'

'Holy righteous mother of God,' interrupted Floathead. 'Check out the zon, bros.'

All the Pilgrims craned westward. And moaned.

'Far, far, faaar outsider,' someone whispered. The horizon

looked bent in the middle, and it took an effort of will to realize that the great smooth bell-curve was an actual wave of actual water. It swelled up and up like a droplet on a faucet, swelled so big that you half expected it to break free of the sea and fly upward into great chaotic spheres. It was far enough off that there still might have been time to reach the safety of the cliffs . . . but that's not what the surfers did. They broke formation and raced farther out to sea, out to where they guessed the monster wave would break.

Zep power-stroked out after the others, out toward where Loach and Delbert were waiting, Delbert bobbing up and down with a dismayed expression as Loach kept shouting at him. Just as Zep got there, Loach reached over and smacked Delbert in the face.

Delbert screamed in anger, his face going redder every second. 'I'm gonna kill you, Loach!'

'Hoo-hoo-hoo!' cried the Stoke Pilgrims, forming their lineup. 'Delbert is a ho-dad!'

'You can't always bully me, Loach,' continued Delbert. 'If you get near me one more time — if you snake in while I'm riding this super wave, *my* wave — it's all over for you.'

'Oh, I'm shaking,' Loach said, slapping the water as he laughed. 'Come on, paddle boy. Do your worst — and I do mean *mega* worst.' Loach grinned past Del at the other Stoke Pilgrims. 'Contest's over, guys! Let's take this dip's board right now!'

Zep watched Delbert's face run through some fast changes, from helpless to terrified to grim to enraged to psychotic. It was as if some vicious bug had erupted from shy caterpillar Delbert. Some kind of catastrophic transition took place, and Delbert was a death's head moth. All the while Chaos Attractor was churning out a moireed blur of weird ripples, making the oncoming wave grow yet more monstrous.

Zep felt himself sucked up into the breast of a mountainous wall of water, a blackish green fortress whose surface rippled and coiled until it formed an immense, godlike face glaring down on all of them. Zep had never seen such cold eyes: The black depths of space had been drawn into them by the chaotic attractor. Sky had bent down to earth, drawing the sea up to see. Del and the Pilgrims and Zep all went rushing up toward a foamy green hell, while below . . .

Below was the rumbling, and now a ferocious cracking, accompanied by gouts of radioactive steam. Sirens and hooters. High up on the godwave, Zep looked down and saw the N-plant in its bed, as if nudged from beneath by a gigantic mole. Blue luminescence pulsed upward through the failing N-plant's shimmering veils of deadly mist, blending into the green savagery of the spray trailing down from their wave. Frantic Jen had flung herself into the surf and was thrashing there, goggling up at the twin catastrophes of N-plant and Neptune's wave.

Looking up, Zep saw Delbert streaking down the long beaked nose of Neptune while Loach and the Pilgrims skidded down the cheeks, thrown from their boards, eating it.

Zep felt proud. *Delbert, I didn't know you had it in you. Shut the beach DOWN!*

Cracks crazed the surface of the N-plant. It was ready to blow. Way down there was Jen, screaming, 'Save me!' like Olive Oyl. Del carved the pure surfspace, sending up a rooster of probability spray, jamming as if he'd been born on silvery, shadowy Chaos Attractor. He looked like he'd been to the edge of the universe and back already. He raved down deep to snatch up his Jen and set her in the board's center; and then he snapped up the wall to wrap a tight spiral around floundering Zep.

'Latch on, dude!'

Zep clamped onto Chaos Attractor's back rail and pulled himself aboard. The stick reared like a horse and sent them scudding up over the lip of the tsunami, out over the arching neck of the slow-breaking wave. Del glanced back through the falls and saw the filtered light of the San Diablo Nuclear Plant's explosion, saw the light and the chunks of concrete and steel tumbling outward, borne on the shock-wave's A-bomb energy.

The two waves intermingled in a chaotic mindscape abstraction. Up and up they flew, the fin scraping sparks from the edges of the unknown. Zep saw stars swimming under them, a great spiral of stars.

Everything was still, so still.

And then Del's hand shot out. Across the galactic wheel a gleaming figure shared their space. It was coming straight at them. Rider of the tides of night, carver of blackhole beaches and neutron tubes. Bent low on his luminous board — graceful, poised, inhuman.

'Stoked,' said Jen. 'God's a surfer!'

STEVEN GOULD

Steven Gould lives in Texas and is the South/Central Regional Director of the Science Fiction Writers of America. His first published story was 'The Touch of Their Eyes' in *Analog* in 1980, both Gould and this story having been 'discovered' by Theodore Sturgeon at a writers' workshop. 'Rory', also in *Analog*, was a Hugo nominee for best short story in 1985. He has also had fiction published in *Asimov's*, *Amazing* and *New Destinies*, and he says that he is 'working on a book, but have been since 1982, so don't look for it anytime soon.'

The story which follows came about when Gould was thinking about the homeless situation in America. 'I was wondering,' he says, 'what form this problem would take in the future, when the picture of a bag lady perched high on a building ledge appeared in my head. This was the "pit" that sprouted "Peaches ..."'

This story was a finalist for the 1988 Nebulas, as best novelette of the year.

PEACHES FOR MAD MOLLY

by

STEVEN GOULD

Sometime during the night the wind pulled a one-pointer off the west face of the building up around the 630th floor. I heard him screaming as he went by, very loud, like this was his last chance to voice an opinion, but it was all so sudden that he didn't know what it was. Then he hit a microwave relay off 542 . . . hard, and the chance was gone. Chunks of him landed in Buffalo Bayou forty-five seconds later.

The alligators probably liked that.

I don't know if his purchase failed or his rope broke or if the sucker just couldn't tie a decent knot. He pissed me off though, because I couldn't get back to sleep until I'd checked all four of my belay points, the ropes, and the knots. Now if he'd fallen without expressing himself, maybe?

No, I would have heard the noise as he splattered through the rods of the antennae.

Stupid one-pointer.

The next morning I woke up a lot earlier than usual because someone was plucking one of my ropes, *adagio*, thrum, thrum, like the second movement of Ludwig's seventh. It was Mad Molly.

'You awake, Bruce?' she asked.

I groaned. 'I am now.' My name is not Bruce. Molly, for some reason, calls everyone Bruce. '*Shto etta,* Molly?'

She was crouched on a roughing point, one of the meter cubes sticking out of the tower face to induce the micro-turbulence boundary layer. She was dressed in a brightly flowered scarlet kimono, livid green bermuda shorts, a sweat-shirt, and tabi socks. Her belay line, bright orange against the gray building, stretched from around the corner to Molly's person where it vanished beneath her kimono, like snake hiding its head.

'I got a batch to go to the Bruce, Bruce.'

I turned and looked down. There was a damp wind in my

face. Some low clouds had come in overnight, hiding the ground, but the tower's shadow stretched a long ways across the fluffy stuff below. 'Jeeze, Molly. You know the Bruce won't be on shift for another hour.' Damn, she had me doing it! 'Oh, hell, I'll be over after I get dressed.'

She blinked twice. Her eyes were black chips of stone in a face so seamed and browned by the sun that it was hard to tell her age. 'Okay, Bruce,' she said, then stood abruptly and flung herself off the cube. She dropped maybe five meters before her rope tightened her fall into an arc that swung her down and around the corner.

I let out my breath. She's not called Mad Molly for nothing.

I dressed, drank the water out of my catch basin, urinated on the clouds (seems only fair) and rolled up my bag.

Between the direct sunlight and the stuff bouncing off the clouds below the south face was blinding. I put my shades on at the corner.

Molly's nest, like a mud dauber's, hung from an industrial exhaust vent off the 611th floor. It was woven, sewed, tucked, patched, welded, snapped, zipped, and tied into creation. It looked like a wasp's nest on a piece of chrome. It did not blend in.

Her pigeon coop, about two floors lower down, blended in even less. It was made of paper, sheet plastic, wire, and it was speckled with pigeon droppings. It was where it was because only a fool lives directly under *under* defecating birds, and Molly, while mad, was not stupid.

Molly was crouched in the doorway of her nest balanced on her feet like one of her pigeons. She was staring out at nothing and muttering angrily to herself.

'What's wrong. Molly? Didn't you sleep okay?'

She glared at me. 'That damn Bruce got another three of my birds yesterday.'

I hooked my bag onto a beaner and hung it under her house. 'What Bruce. Molly? That red tailed hawk?'

'Yeah, that Bruce. Then the other Bruce pops off last night and wakes me up so I can't get back to sleep because I'm listening for that damn hawk.' She backed into her nest to let me in.

'Hawks don't hunt at night, Molly.'

She flapped her arms. 'So? Like maybe the vicious, son-of-a-bitchin' Bruce gets into the coop? He could kill half my birds in one night!' She started coiling one of her ropes, pulling the line with short, angry jerks. 'I don't know if it's worth it anymore, Bruce. It's hot in the summer. It's freezing in the winter. The Babs are always hassling me instead of the Howlers. The Howlers keep hassling me for free birds or they'll cut me loose one night. I can't cook on cloudy days unless I want to pay an arm and a leg for fuel. I can't get fresh fruit or vegetables. That crazy social worker whose afraid of heights comes by and asks if he can help me. I say 'Yeah, get me some fresh fruit.' He brings me applications for readmittance! God, I'd kill for a fresh peach! I'd be better off back in the home!'

I shrugged. 'Maybe you would, Molly. After all, you're getting on in years.'

'Fat lot you know, Bruce! You crazy or something? Trade this view for six walls? Breathe that stale stuff they got in there? Give up my birds? Give up my freedom? Shit, Bruce, who the hell's side are you on anyway?'

I laughed. 'Yours, Molly.'

She started wrapping the pigeons and swearing under her breath.

I looked at Molly's clippings, bits of faded newsprint stuck to the wall of the tower itself. By the light coming through some of the plastic sheeting in the roof. I saw a picture of Molly on Mt. McKinley dated twenty years before. An article about her second attempt on Everest. Stories about her climbing buildings in New York, Chicago, and L.A. I looked closer at one that talked about her climbing the south face of El Capitan on her fourteenth birthday. It had the date.

I looked twice and tried to remember what day of the month it was. I had to count backwards in my head to be sure.

Tomorrow was Mad Molly's birthday.

The Bruce in question was Murry Zapata, outdoor rec guard of the south balcony on the 480th floor. This meant I had to take the birds down 131 stories, or a little over half a kilometer. And then climb back.

Even on the face of Le Bab tower, with a roughing cube or

vent or external rail every meter or so, this is a serious climb. Molly's pigeons alone were not worth the trip, so I dropped five floors and went to see Lenny.

It's a real pain to climb around Lenny's because nearly every horizontal surface has a plant box or pot on it. So I rappeled down even with him and shouted over to where he was fiddling with a clump of fennel.

'Hey, Lenny. I'm making a run. You got anything for Murry?'

He straightened up. 'Yeah, wait a sec.' He was wearing shorts and his climbing harness and nothing else. He was brown all over. If I did that sort of thing I'd be a melanoma farm.

Lenny climbed down to his tent and disappeared inside. I worked my way over there, avoiding the plants. I smelled dirt, a rare smell up here. It was an odor rich and textured. It kicked in memories of freshly plowed fields or newly dug graves. When I got to Lenny's tent, he came out with a bag.

'What'cha got,' I asked.

He shrugged. 'Garlic, cumin, and anise. The weights are marked on the outside. Murry should have no trouble moving it. The Chicanos can't get enough of the garlic. Tell Murry that I'll have some of those tiny *muy caliente* chilis for him next week.'

'Got it.'

'By the way, Fran said yesterday to tell you she has some daises ready to go down.'

'Check. You ever grow any fruit, Lenny?'

'On these little ledges? I thought about getting a dwarf orange once but decided against it. I grow dew berries but none of them are ripe right now. No way I could grow trees. Last year I grew some cantaloupe but that's too much trouble. You need a bigger bed than I like.'

'Oh, well. It was a thought.' I added his bag to the pigeons in my pack. 'I'll probably be late getting back.'

He nodded. 'Yeah, I know. Better you than me, though. Last time *I* went, the Howlers stole all my tomatoes. Watch out down below. The Howlers are claiming the entire circumference from 520 to 530.'

'Oh, yeah? Just so they don't interfere with my right of eminent domain.'

He shrugged. 'Just be careful. I don't care if they want a cut. Like maybe a clump of garlic.'

I blinked. 'Nobody cuts my cargo. Nobody.'

'Not even Dactyl?'

'Dactyl's never bothered me. He's just a kid.'

Lenny shrugged. 'He's sent his share down. You get yourself pushed off and we'll have to find someone else to do the runs. Just be careful.'

'Careful is what I do best.'

Fran lived around the corner, on the east face. She grew flowers, took in sewing, and did laundry. When she had the daylight for her solar panel, she watched TV.

'Why don't you live inside, Fran. You could watch TV twenty-four hours a day.'

She grinned at me, a not unpleasant event. 'Nah. Then I'd pork up to about a hundred kilos eating that syntha crap and not getting any exercise and I'd have to have a permit to grow even one flower in my cubicle and a dispensation for the wattage for a grow light and so on and so forth. When they put me in a coffin, I want to be dead.'

'Hey, they have exercise rooms and indoor tracks and the rec balconies.'

'Big deal. Shut up for a second while I see if Bob is still mad at Sue because he found out about Marilyn's connection with her mother's surgeon. When the commercial comes I'll cut and bundle some daisies.'

She turned her head back to the flat screen. I looked at her blue bonnets and pansies while I waited.

'There, I was right. Marilyn is sleeping with Sue's mother. That will make everything okay.' She tucked the TV in a pocket and prepared the daisies for me. 'I'm going to have peonies next week.' I laced the wrapped flowers on the outside of the pack to avoid crushing the petals. While I was doing that Fran moved closer. 'Stop over on the way back?'

'Maybe,' I said. 'Of course I'll drop your script off.'

She withdrew a little.

'I want to, Fran, honest. But I want to get some fresh fruit for Mad Molly's birthday tomorrow and I don't know where I'll have to go to get it.'

She turned away and shrugged. I stood there for a moment, then left, irritated. When I looked back she was watching the TV again.

The Howlers had claimed ten floors and the entire circumference of the Le Bab Tower between those floors. That's an area of forty meters by 250 meters per side or 40,000 square meters total. The tower is over a kilometer on a side at the base but it tapers in stages until its only twenty meters square at three thousand meters.

Their greediness was to my advantage because there's only thirty-five or so Howlers and that's a lot of area to cover. As I rappeled down to 529 I slowly worked my way around the building. There was a bunch of them in hammocks on the south face, sunbathing I saw one or two on the east face but most of them were on the west face. Only one person was on the north side.

I moved down to 521 on the north face well away from the one guy and doubled my longest line. It was a hundred meter blue line twelve millimeters thick. I coiled it carefully on a roughing cube after wrapping the half-way point of the rope around another roughing cube one complete circuit, each end trailing down. I pushed it close into the building so it wouldn't slip. Then I clipped my brake bars around the doubled line.

The guy at the other corner noticed me now and started working his way from roughing cube to roughing cube, curious. I kicked the rope off the cube and it fell cleanly with no snarls, no snags. He shouted. I jumped, a gloved hand on the rope where it came out of the brake bars. I did the forty meters in five jumps, a total of ten seconds. Halfway down I heard him shout for help and heard others come around the corner. At 518 I braked and swung into the building. The closest Howler was still fifteen meters or so away from my rope, but he was speeding up. I leaned against the building and flicked the right hand rope hard, sending a sinusoidal wave traveling up the line. It reached the top and the now loose rope flicked off the cube above and fell. I sat down and braced. A hundred meter rope weighs in at eight kilos and the shock of it pulling up short could have pulled me from the cube.

They shouted things after me, but none of them followed. I heard one of them call out. 'Quit'cha bitchin. He's got to pass us on his way home. We'll educate him then.'

All the rec guards deal. It's a good job to have if you're inside. Even things that originate inside the tower end up traveling the outside pipeline. Ain't no corridor checks out here. No TV cameras or sniffers either. The Howlers do a lot of that sort of work.

Murry is different from the other guards, though. He doesn't deal slice or spike or any of the other nasty pharmoddities, and he treats us outsiders like humans. He says he was outside once. I believe him.

'So Murry, what's with your wife? She had that baby yet?'

'Nah. And boy is she tired of being pregnant. She's like, out to *here.*' He held his hands out. 'You tell Fran I want something special when she finally dominoes. Like roses.'

'Christ, Murry. You know Fran can't do roses. Not in friggin pots. Maybe day lilies. I'll ask her.' I sat in my seat harness, hanging outside the cage that's around the rec balcony. Murry stood inside smelling the daisies. There were some kids kicking a soccer ball on the far side of the balcony and several adults standing at the railing looking out through the bars. Several people stared at me. I ignored them.

Murry counted out the script for the load and passed it through the bars. I zipped it in a pocket. Then he pulled out the provisions I'd ordered the last run and I dropped them, item by item, into the pack.

'You ever get any fresh fruit in here, Murray?'

'What do I look like, guy, a millionaire? The guys that get that sort of stuff live up there above 750. Hell, I once had this escort job up to 752 and while the honcho I escorted was talking to the resident, they had me wait out on this patio. This guy had apples and peaches and *cherries* for crissakes! *Cherries!*' He shook his head. 'It was weird, too. None of this cage crap.' He rapped on the bars with his fist. 'He had a chest high railing and that was it.'

'Well of course. What with the barrier at 650 he doesn't

have to worry about us. I'll bet there's lots of open balconies up that way.' I paused. 'Well, I gotta go. I've got a long way to climb.'

'Better you than me. Don't forget to tell Fran about the special flowers.'

'Right.'

They were waiting for me, all the Howlers sitting on the south face, silent, intent. I stopped four stories below 520 and rested. While I rested I coiled my belay line and packed it in my pack. I sat there, fifteen kilos of supplies and climbing paraphernalia on my back, and looked out on the world.

The wind had shifted more to the southwest and was less damp than the morning air. It had also strengthened but the boundary layer created by the roughing cubes kept the really high winds out from the face of the tower.

Sometime during the day the low clouds below had broken into patches, letting the ground below show through. I perched on the roughing cube, unbelayed and contemplated the fall. 516 is just over two kilometers from the ground. That's quite a drop — though in low winds the odds were I'd smack into one of the rec balconies where the tower widened below. In a decent southerly wind you can depend on hitting the swamps instead.

What I had to do now was rough.

I had to free ascend.

No ropes, no nets, no second chances. If I lost it the only thing I had to worry about was whether or not to scream on the way down.

The Howlers were not going to leave me time for the niceties.

For the most part the Howlers were so-so climbers, but they had a few people capable of technical ascents. I had to separate the good from the bad and then out-climb the good.

I stood on the roughing cube and started off at a run, leaping two meters at a time from roughing cube to roughing cube moving sideways across the south face. Above me I heard shouts but I didn't look up. I didn't dare. The mind was blank, letting the body do the work without hindrance. The eyes saw, the body did, the mind coasted.

I slowed as I neared the corner, and stopped, nearly falling when I overbalanced, but saving myself by dropping my center of gravity.

There weren't nearly as many of them above me now. Maybe six of them had kept up with me. The others were trying to do it by the numbers, roping from point to point. I climbed two stories quickly, chimneying between a disused fractional distillation stack and a cooling tower. Then I moved around the corner and ran again.

When I stopped to move up two more stories there were only two of them above me. The other four were trying for more altitude rather than trying to keep pace horizontally.

I ran almost to the northwest corner, then moved straight up.

The first one decided to drop kick me dear Jesus through the goal posts of life. He pulled his line out, fixed it to something convenient and rappeled out with big jumps, planning, no doubt, to come swinging into me with his feet when he reached my level. I ignored him until the last minute when I let myself collapse onto a roughing cube. His feet slammed into the wall above me then rebounded out.

As he swung back out from the face I leaped after him.

His face went white. Whatever he was expecting me to do, he wasn't expecting *that*! I latched onto him like a monkey, my legs going around his waist. One of my hands grabbed his rope, the other punched with all my might into his face. I felt his jaw go and his body went slack. He released the rope below the brake bars and started sliding down the rope. I scissored him with my legs and held onto the rope with both hands. My shoulders creaked as I took the strain but he stopped sliding. Then we swung back into the wall and I sagged onto a cube astride him.

His buddy was dropping down more slowly. He was belayed but he'd seen what I'd done and wasn't going to try the airborne approach. He was still a floor or two above me so I tied his friend off so he wouldn't sleepwalk and took off sideways, running again.

I heard him shout but I didn't hear him moving. When I paused again he was bent over my friend with the broken jaw. I reached an external exhaust duct and headed for the sky as fast as I could climb.

At this point I was halfway through Howler territory. Off to my right the group that had opted for height was now moving sideways to cut me off. I kept climbing, breathing hard now but not desperate. I could climb at my current speed for another half hour without a break and I thought there was only one other outsider that could keep up that sort of pace. I wondered if he was up above.

I looked.

He was.

He wasn't on the wall.

He didn't seem to be roped on.

And he was dropping.

I tried to throw myself to the side, in the only direction I could go, but I was only partially successful. His foot caught me a glancing blow to my head and I fell three meters to the next roughing cube. I landed hard on the cube, staggered, bumped into the wall, and fell outward, off the cube. the drop was sudden, gut wrenching, and terrifying. I caught the edge of the cube with both hands, wrenching my shoulders and banging my elbow. My head ached, the sky spun in circles and I knew that there was over a kilometer of empty space beneath my feet.

Dactyl had stopped somehow, several stories below me, and, as I hung there, I could see the metallic gleam of some sort of wire, stretched taut down the face of the tower.

I chinned myself up onto the cube and traversed away from the wire, moving and climbing fast. I ignored the pain in my shoulder and the throbbing of my head and even the stomach churning fear and sudden clammy sweat.

There was a whirring sound and the hint of movement behind me. I turned around and caught the flash of gray moving up the face. I looked up.

He was waiting, up on the edge of Howler territory, just watching. Closer were the three clowns who were trying to get above me before I passed them. I eyed the gap, thought about it, and then went into overdrive. They didn't make it. I passed them before they reached the exhaust duct. For a few stories they tried to pursue and one of them even threw a grapple that fell short.

That left only Dactyl.

He was directly overhead when I reached 530. I paused and glanced down. The others had stopped and were looking up. Even the clothesliners had made it around the corner and were watching. I looked back up. Dactyl moved aside about five meters and sat down on a ledge. I climbed up even with him and sat too.

Dactyl showed up one day in the middle of Howler territory. Three Howlers took the long dive before it was decided that maybe the Howler should ignore Dactyl before there were no Howlers left. He's a loner who does a mixed bag: some free ascent, some rope work, and some fancy mech stuff.

There was something about him that made him hard to see, almost. Not really, but he did blend into the building. His nylons, his climbing shoes, his harness were gray like the roughing cube he sat on. His harness was strung with gray boxes and pouches of varying sizes, front and back, giving his torso a bulky appearance, sort of like a turtle with long arms. He was younger than I'd thought he'd be, perhaps twenty, but then I'd only seen him at a distance before now. His eyes looked straight at me, steady and hard. He wasn't sweating a bit.

'Why?' I said.

He shrugged. 'Be natural, become a part of your environment. Who said that?'

'Lots of people said that. Even I said that.'

Dactyl nodded. 'So, like I'm doing that thing. I'm becoming a part of the environment. One thing you should know by now, dude . . .'

'What's that?' I asked warily.

'The environment is hostile.'

I looked out, away from him. In the far distance I saw white sails in Galveston bay. I turned back. 'What did I ever do to you?'

He smiled. 'You take it too personal. It's more random than that. Think of me as an extra-somatic evolutionary factor. You've got to evolve. You've got to adapt. *Mano a Mano* shit like that.'

I let that stew for a while. The Howlers were gathering below, inside their territory. They were discussing something with much hand waving and punctuated gestures.

'So,' I finally said. 'You ever walk through downtown Houston?'

He blinked, opened his mouth to say something, then closed it. Finally, almost unwillingly, he said, 'On the ground? No. They eat people down there.'

I shrugged. 'Sometimes they do. Sometimes they don't. Last time I was in Tranquillity Park they were eating alligator tail with Siamese peanut sauce. Except when the alligators were eating them.'

'Oh.'

'You even been down below at all?'

'I was born inside.'

'Well, don't let it bother you,' I said as I stood up.

He frowned slightly. 'What's that supposed to mean?'

I grinned. 'It's not where you were born that matters.' I said. 'It's where you die.'

I started climbing.

The first half hour was evenly paced. He waited about a minute before he started after me and for the next seventy floors it was as if there was an invisible fifteen meter rope stretched between us. About 600 he lowered the gap to ten meters. I picked up the pace a little, but the gap stayed the same for the next ten floors.

I was breathing hard now and feeling the burn in my thighs and arms. My clothes were soaked in sweat but my hands were dry and I was in rhythm, climbing smooth and steady.

Dactyl was also climbing fast, but jerky, his movements inefficient. The gap was still ten meters but I could tell he was straining.

I doubled my speed.

The universe contracted. There was only the wall, the next purchase, the next breath. There were no peaches, no birthdays, no flowers, and no Dactyl. There was no thought.

But there *was* pain.

My thighs went from burning to screaming. I started taking up some of the slack with my arms and they joined the chorus. I climbed through the red haze for fifteen more stories and then collapsed on a roughing cube.

The world reeled as I gasped for the first breaths. I felt incipient cramps lurking in my thighs and I wanted those muscle cells to have all the oxygen I could give them. Then, as the universe steadied, I looked down for Dactyl.

He wasn't on the north face.

Had he given up?

I didn't know and it bothered me.

Five stories above was the barrier — a black, ten meter overhang perpendicular to the face. It was perfectly smooth, made of metal, its welds ground flush. I didn't know what was above it. There were rumors about automatic lasers, armed guards, and computer monitored imaging devices. I'd worry about them when I got past that overhang.

I was two stories short of it when Dactyl appeared at the northeast corner of the building.

Above me.

It wasn't possible. I almost quit then but something made me go on. I tried to blank my mind and began running toward the west face, doing the squirrel hopping from block to block, even though my muscles weren't up to it. I almost lost it twice, once when my mind dwelt too much on how Dactyl had passed me and once when my quadriceps gave way.

I stopped at the corner, gasping, and looked back. Dactyl was working his way leisurely after me, slowly, almost labored. I ducked around and climbed again, until I was crouched on a roughing cube, the dark overhang touching my head. I peeked around the corner. Dactyl had paused, apparently resting.

I took of my pack and pulled out a thirty-meter length of two-ton-test line, a half-meter piece of ten-kilo-test monofilament, and a grapple. I tied the monofilament between the heavier line and the grapple.

I peeked around the corner again. Dactyl was moving again, but slowly, carefully. He was still two-hundred meters across the face. I dropped down two meters and stepped back around the corner. Dactyl stopped when he saw me, but I ignored him, playing out the grapple and line until it hung about fifteen meters below me. Then I started swinging it.

It was hard work, tricky, too. I didn't think I had the time to rig a quick belay before Dactyl got there. At least the grapple was light, three kilos at most, but as it swung wider and wider it threatened to pull me off at each end of its swing, especially as the corner formed by the barrier concentrated the wind somewhat.

Finally the grapple raised far enough on the swing away from the corner. As it dropped to the bottom of its swing I began pulling it in. As the moment arm decreased the grapple sped up, gaining enough speed to flip up above the edge of the overhang. I had no idea how thick the overhang was or even if there was something up there for the grapple to catch on. I held my breath.

There was a distant clinking noise as it struck something and the rope slackened. For an instant I thought it was dropping back down and I was scared because I was already of balance and I didn't know how far Dactyl was behind me. Then the rope stopped moving and the grapple didn't drop into sight.

I risked a quick look behind. Dactyl was still a hundred meters away. I took the rope and moved back around the corner, pulling the rope cautiously tight. As luck would have it, with the line pulled over, Dactyl wouldn't be able to see any part of the rope until he rounded the corner.

It took me two minutes to tie the lower end of the rope around a roughing cube and then to two more cubes for backup. Then I recklessly dropped from cube to cube until I was three stories down and hidden behind a Bernoulli exhaust vent.

He stuck his head around the corner almost immediately. Saw the dangling line and tugged it hard. The ten-kilo test line hidden above the barrier held. Dactyl clipped a beaner over the line and leaped out, almost like a flying squirrel, his hands reaching for the rope. He was halfway out before his full weight hit the rope.

The ten kilo test snapped immediately. I heard his indrawn breath, but he didn't swear. Instead, as he arched down, he tried to twist around, to get his legs between him and the face as he swung into it.

He was only partially successful, slamming hard into the corner of a roughing cube, one leg taking some of the shock. I heard the breath leave his lungs in an explosive grunt and then he was sliding down the rope toward the unattached end, grabbing weakly to stop himself, but only managing to slow the drop.

I moved like a striking snake.

I was already lower down the tower from where he'd hit the wall and took three giant strides from cube to cube to get directly beneath him. Then he was off the end of the rope and dropping free and my hand reached out, snared his climbing harness, and I flattened myself atop the cube I was on.

For the second time that day I nearly dislocated my shoulder. His weight nearly pulled me off the tower. The back of my shirt suddenly split. I heard his head crack onto the cube and he felt like a sack of dirt, lifeless, but heavy as the world.

It took some time to get him safely onto the cube and lashed in place.

It took even longer to get my second grapple up where the first one was. It seemed my first attempt was a fluke and I had to repeat the tiring process six more times before I could clip my ascenders to the rope and inchworm up it.

The building had narrowed above the barrier, to something like 150 meters per side. I was on the edge of a terrace running around the building. Unlike the recreation balconies below, it was open to the sky, uncaged, with only a chest high railing to contain its occupants. Scattered artfully across the patio were lounge chairs and greenery topped planters.

I saw a small crowd of formally dressed men and women mingling on the west terrace, sheltered from the northeast wind. Servants moved among them with trays. Cocktail hour among the rich, the influential, and the cloudy.

I pulled myself quickly over the edge and crouched behind a planter, pulling my rope in and folding my grapples.

The terrace areas unsheltered by the wind seemed to be deserted. I looked for cameras and IR reflectors and capcitance wires but I didn't see any. I couldn't see any reason for any.

Above me, the face of the tower rose another five hundred meters or so, but unlike the faces below, there were individual balconies spotted here and there among the roughing cubes. On more than one I could see growing plants, even trees.

I had more than a hundred floors to go, perhaps 400 meters.

My arms and legs were trembling. There was a sharp pain in the shoulder Dactyl had kicked, making it hard for me to lift that arm higher than my neck.

I nearly gave it up. I thought about putting down my pack, unbuckling my climbing harness, and stretching out on one of these lounge chairs. Perhaps later I'd take a drink off of one of those trays.

Then a guard would come and escort me all the way to the ground.

Besides, I could do a hundred stories standing on my head, right? Right.

The sun was completely down by the time I reached 700 but lights from the building itself gave me what I couldn't make out by feel. The balconies were fancy, sheltered from the wind by removable fairings and jutting fins. I kept my eye out for a balcony with fruit trees, just in case. I wouldn't climb all the way up to 752 if I didn't have to.

But I had to.

There were only four balconies on 752, one to each side. They were the largest balconies I'd ever seen on the tower. Only one of them had anything resembling a garden. I spent five minutes looking over the edge at planter after planter of vegetables, flowers, shrubs, and trees. I couldn't see any lights through the glass doors leading into the building and I couldn't see any peaches.

I sighed and pulled myself over the edge for a closer look, standing upright with difficulty. My limbs were leaden, my breath still labored. I could hear my pulse thudding in my ears, and I still couldn't see any peaches.

There were some green oranges on a tree near me, but that was the closest thing to fruit I could see. I shivered. I was almost two kilometers above sea level and the sun had gone down an hour ago. My sweat soaked cloathes were starting to chill.

Something was nagging me and, at first, the fatigue toxins wouldn't let me think clearly. Then an important fact swam into my attention.

I hadn't checked for alarms.

They were there, in the wall above the railing, a series of small reflectors for the I/R beams that I'd crawled through to enter the balcony.

Time to leave. Long past time. I stepped toward the railing and heard a door open behind me. I started to swing my leg up over the edge when I felt something stick me in the side. And then the universe exploded.

All the muscles on my right side convulsed spasmodically and I came down onto the concrete floor with a crash, slamming my shoulder and hip into the ground. My head was saved from the same fate by the backpack I wore.

Taser, I thought.

When I could focus, I saw the man standing about three meters away, wearing a white khaftan. He was older than I was by decades. Most of his hair was gone and his face had deep lines etched by something other than smiling. I couldn't help comparing him to Mad Molly, but it just wasn't the same. Mad Molly could be as old but she didn't look anywhere as *nasty* as this guy did.

He held the taser loosely in his right hand. In his left hand he held a drink with ice that he swirled gently around, clink, clink.

'What are you doing here, you disgusting little fly?'

His voice, as he asked the question, was vehement and acid. His expression didn't change though.

'Nothing.' I tried to say it strongly, firmly, reasonably. It came out like a frog's croak.

He shot me with the taser again. I caught the glint on the wire as it sped out, tried to dodge, but too late.

I arched over the backpack, my muscles doing things I wouldn't have believed possible. My head banged sharply against the floor. Then it stopped again.

I was disoriented, the room spun. My legs decided to go into a massive cramp. I gasped out loud.

This seemed to please him.

'Who sent you? I'll know in the end. I can do this all night long.'

I said quickly, 'Nobody sent me. I hoped to get some peaches.'

He shot me again.

I really didn't think much of this turn of events. My muscles had built up enough lactic acid without electro-convulsive induced contractions. When everything settled down again I had another bump on my head and more cramps.

He took a sip from his drink.

'You'll have to do better than that,' he said. 'Nobody would risk climbing the outside for peaches. Besides, there won't be peaches on that tree for another five months.' He pointed the taser. 'Who sent you?'

I couldn't even talk at this point. He seemed to realize this, fortunately, and waited for a few moments, lowering the taser. Then he asked again, 'Who sent you?'

'Get stuffed,' I told him weakly.

'Stupid little man.' He lifted the taser again and something smashed him in the arm, causing him to drop the weapon. He stooped to pick it up again but there was a streak of gray and the thud of full body contact as someone hit him and bowled him over onto his back.

I saw the newcomer scoop up the taser and spin sharply. The taser passed over my head and out over the railing.

It was Dactyl.

The man in the khaftan saw Dactyl's face then and said, 'You!' He started to scramble to his feet. Dactyl took one sliding step forward and kicked him in the face. The man collapsed in a small heap, his khaftan making him look like a white sack with limbs sticking out.

Dactyl stood there for a moment looking down. Then he turned and walked slowly back to me.

'That was a nasty trick with the rope.'

I laughed, albeit weakly. 'If you weren't so lazy you would have made your own way up.' I eyed him warily, but my body wasn't up to movement yet. Was he going to kick me in the face, too? Still, I had to know something. 'How did you pass me down there, below the barrier? You were exhausted, I could see it.'

He shrugged. 'You're right. I'm lazy.' He flipped a device off his back. It looked like a gun with two triggers. I made ready to jump. He pointed it up and pulled the trigger. I heard a *chunk* and something buried itself in the ceiling. He pulled the second trigger and there was a whining sound. Dactyl and gun floated off the floor. I looked closer and saw the wire.

'Cheater,' I said.

He laughed and lowered himself back to the floor. 'What the hell are you doing here?' he asked.

I told him.

'You're shitting me.'

'No.'

He laughed then and walked briskly through the door into the tower.

I struggled to stand. Made it. I was leaning against the railing when Dactyl came back through the door with a plastic two-liter container. He handed it to me. It was ice cold.

'What's this?'

'Last season's peaches. From the freezer. He always hoards them until just before the fresh ones are ready.'

I stared at him. 'How the hell did you know that?'

He shrugged, took the peaches out of my hand and put them in my pack. 'Look, I'd get out of here before he wakes up. Not only does he have a lot nastier things than that taser, but security will do whatever he wants.'

He swung up over the edge and lowered himself to arm's length. Just before he dropped completely from sight he added something which floated up with the wind.

'He's my father.'

I started down the tower not too long after Dactyl. Physically I was a wreck. The taser had exhausted my muscles in a way that exercise never had. I probably wasn't in the best shape to do any kind of rope work, but Dactyl's words rang true. I didn't want anybody after me in the condition I was in, much less security.

Security is bad. They use copters and rail cars that run up and down and outside of the building. They fire rubber bullets and water cannon. Don't think this makes them humane. A person blasted off a ledge by either is going to die. Security is just careful not to damage the tower.

So, I did my descent in stages, feeling like an old man tottering carefully down a flight of stairs. Still, descent was far easier than ascent, and my rope work had me down on the barrier patio in less than ten minutes.

It was nearing midnight, actually lighter now that the quarter moon had risen, and the patio, instead of being deserted, had far more people on it than it had at sunset. A few people saw me coiling my rope after my last rappel. I ignored them, going about my business with as much *panache* as I could muster. On my way to the edge of the balcony I stopped at the buffet and built myself a sandwich.

More people began looking my way and talking. An elderly woman standing at one end of the buffet took a long look at me, then said, 'Try the wontons. I think there's really pork in them.'

I smiled at her. 'I don't know. Pork is tricky. You never know who provided it.'

Her hand stopped, a wonton halfway to her mouth, and stared at me. Then, almost defiantly, she popped it into her mouth and chewed it with relish. 'Just so it's well cooked.'

A white-clad steward left the end of the table and walked over to a phone hanging by a door.

I took my sandwich over to the edge and set it down while I took the rope from the pack. My legs trembled slightly. The woman with the wontons followed me over after a minute.

'Here,' she said, holding out a tall glass that clinked. 'Ice tea.'

I blinked, surprised. 'Why, thank you. This is uncommonly kind.'

She shrugged. 'You look like you need it. Are you going to collapse right here? It would be exciting, but I'd avoid it if I were you. I think that nasty man called security.'

'Do I look as bad as all that?'

'Honey, you look like death warmed over.'

I finished playing out the rope and clipped on my brake-bars. 'I'm afraid you're right.' I took a bite out of the sandwich and chewed quickly. I washed it down with the tea. It wasn't one of Mad Molly's roast pigeons but it wasn't garbage, either.

'You'll get indigestion,' the woman warned.

I smiled and took another large bite. The crowd of people staring at me was getting bigger. There was a stirring in the crowd from over by the door. I took another bite and another swig, then swung over the edge. 'We must do this again, some-time,' I said. 'Next time, we'll dance.'

I dropped into the dark, jumping out so I could swing into the building. I didn't reach it on the first swing, so I let out more rope and pumped my legs. I came within a yard of the tower and swung out again. I felt better than before but was still weak. I looked up and saw heads looking over the edge at me. Something gleamed in the moonlight.

A knife?

I reached the wall and dropped onto a roughing cube, unbalanced, unsure of my purchase. For a moment I teetered, then was able to heave myself in toward the wall, safe. I turned, to release one end of the rope, so I could snake it down from above.

I didn't have to. It fell from above, two new ends whipping through the night air.

Bastards. I almost shouted it, but it seemed better to let them think I'd fallen. Besides, I couldn't be bothered with any action so energetic. I was bone weary, tired beyond reaction.

For the next hundred stories I made like a spider with arthritis, slow careful descents with lengthy rests. After falling asleep and nearly falling off a cube, I belayed myself during all rest stops. At one point I'm sure I slept for over an hour because my muscles had set up, stiff and sore. It took me another half hour of careful motion before I was moving smoothly again.

Finally I reached Mad Molly's, moving carefully, quietly. I unloaded her supplies and the peaches and put them carefully inside her door. I could hear her snoring. Then, leaving my stash under her house as usual, I climbed down, intending to see Fran and make her breakfast.

I didn't make it to Fran's.

In the half dark before the dawn they came to me.

This is the place for a good line like 'they came on me like the wolf upon the fold' or 'as the piranha swarm'. Forget it. I was too tired. All I know is they came at me, the Howlers did. At me, who'd been beaten, electro-shocked, indigested, sliced at, and bone wearified, if there exists such a verb. I watched them come in dull amazement, which is not a suit of clothes, but an amalgam of fatigue and astonished reaction to the last straw on my camellian back.

Before I'd been hurt and felt the need to ignore it. I'd been challenged and felt the need to respond. I'd felt curiosity and felt the need to satisfy it. I'd felt fear and the need to overcome it. But I hadn't yet felt what I felt now.

I felt rage, and the need to express it.

I'm sure the first two cleared the recreation balcony, they had to. They came at me fast unbelayed and I used every bit of their momentum to heave them out. The next one, doubtless feeling clever, landed on my back and clung like a monkey. I'd passed caring, I simply threw myself to the side, aiming my back at the roughing cube two meters below. He tried, but he didn't get off in time. I'm grateful though, because the shock would have broken my back if he hadn't been there.

I don't think he cleared the rec balcony.

I ran then, but slowly, so angry that I wanted them to catch up, to let me use my fists and feet on their stubborn, malicious, stupid heads. For the next ten minutes it was a running battle only I ran out of steam before they ran out of Howlers.

I ended up backed into a cranny where a cooling vent formed a ledge some five meters deep and four meters wide, when Dactyl dropped into the midst of them, a gray blur that sent three of them for a dive and two more scrambling back around the edges.

I was over feeling mad by then and back to just feeling tired.

Dactyl looked a little tired himself. 'I can't let you out of my sight for a minute, can I?' he said. 'What's the matter? You get tired of their shit?'

'Right . . .' I laughed weakly. 'Now I'm back to owing *you.*'

'That's right, suck-foot. And I'm not going to let you forget it.'

I tottered forward then and looked at the faces around us. I didn't feel so good.

'Uh, Dactyl.'

'Yeah.'

'I think you better take a look over the edge.'

He walked casually forward and took a look down, then to

both sides, then up. He backed up again.

'Looks like you're going to get that chance to repay me real soon,' he said.

The Howlers were out there — all of the Howlers still alive — every last one of them. In the predawn gray they were climbing steadily towards us from all sides, as thick as cannibals at a funeral. I didn't think much of our chances.

'Uh, Dactyl?'

'Yeah.'

'Do you think that piton gun of yours can get us out of here?'

He shook his head. 'I don't have anything to shoot into. The angles are all wrong.'

'Oh.'

He tilted his head then and said, 'I do have a parachute.'

'What?'

He showed me a gray bundle connected to the back of his climbing harness between batteries.

'You ever use it?'

'Do I look crazy?' he asked.

I took a nine meter length of my strongest line and snapped one end to my harness and the other to his.

The Howlers were starting to come over the lip.

'The answer is yes.' I said.

We started running.

I took two of them off with me, and Dactyl seemed to have kicked one man right in the face. The line stretched between us pulled another one into the void. I was falling, bodies tumbling around me in the air, the recreation deck growing in size. I kept waiting for Dactyl to open the chute but we seemed to fall forever. Now I could see the broken Howlers who'd preceded us, draped on the cage work over the balcony. The wind was a shrieking banshee in my ears. The sun rose. I thought, *Here I am falling to my death and the bloody sun comes up!*

In the bright light of the dawn a silken flower blossomed from Dactyl's back. I watched him float up away from me and then the chute opened with a dull boom. He jerked up away from me and there came a sudden, numbing shock. Suddenly I was dangling at the end of a three meter pendulum, tick, tick, and watching four more bodies crash into the cage.

The wind took us then, far out, away from the tower, spinning slowly as we dropped. I found myself wondering if we'd land on water or land.

Getting out of the swamp, past alligators and cannibals, and through the Le Bab Security perimeter is a story in itself. It was hard, it took some time, but we did it.

While we were gone there was a shakeup in the way of things. Between my trespassing and Howlers dropping out of the sky, the Security people were riled up enough to come out and 'shake off' some of the fleas. Fortunately most of the victims were Howlers.

To finish this story up neatly I would like to add that Molly liked the peaches — but she didn't.

It figures.

HOWARD WALDROP

Howard Waldrop began his career in 1972 with a story called 'Lunch Box'. This appeared in *Analog*, which seems the most unlikely magazine to have published a Waldrop story — but most of his fiction transcends the normal boundaries of sf.

His first novel, co-authored by Jake Saunders, was *The Texas-Israeli War: 1999* (1974). (Waldrop lives in Austin, Texas.) His only solo novel was *Them Bones* (1984), and he is still at work on the second: *I, John Mandeville*. He has had two collections of short stories published, *Howard Who?* and *All About Strange Monsters of the Recent Past*. 1989 will, at last, see publication of a third collection, *Night of the Cooters*, the short novel *A Dozen Tough Jobs*, and a book of collaborations, *Custer's Last Jump*.

Waldrop's name is almost a permanent fixture on the Nebula and Hugo ballots, most recently for his novelette 'Do Ya, Do Ya, Wanna Dance?' which was a finalist for the 1988 Nebula. In 1981, he won both the Nebula and the World Fantasy Award for his story 'The Ugly Chickens'.

His story 'Thirty Minutes over Broadway!' appeared in the first *Yearbook*.

Of the story which follows, he says: "I'd written three or four stories about movies through the years ("*Der Untergang des Abendlandesmenschen*", "All About Strange Monsters of the Recent Past", "Save a Place in the Lifeboat for Me") and knew, ever since I saw them back in the early Sixties, that I would someday write about the French New Wave cinema. *How* to do it didn't come to me until I was on a panel with Forrest J. Ackerman at an SF convention in Denver. He said something and I immediately knew how I would *have* to write the story. In my usual way, I thought about it for another five years before I sat down and did it. *Voila*!"

FRENCH SCENES

by

HOWARD WALDROP

> The fault, dear Brutus, is not in our stars,
> But in ourselves. . . .
>
> *Julius Caesar* (Act I, Scene 2)

There was a time, you read, when making movies took so many people. Actors, cameramen, technicians, screen-writers, costumers, editors, producers, and directors. I can believe it.

That was before computer animation, before the National Likeness Act, before the Noe's Fludde of Marvels.

Back in that time they still used laboratories to make prints; sometimes there would be a year between the completion of a film and its release to theaters.

Back then they used *actual* pieces of film, with holes down the sides for the projector. I've even handled some of it; it is cold, heavy, and shiny.

Now there's none of that. No doctors, lawyers, Indian chiefs between the idea and substance. There's only one person (with maybe a couple of hackers for the dog's work) who makes movies: the moviemaker.

There's only one piece of equipment: the GAX-600.

There's one true law: Clean your mainframe and have a full set of specs.

I have to keep that in mind, all the time.

Lois was yelling from the next room where she was working on her movie *Monster without a Meaning.*

'We've got it!' she said, storming in. 'The bottoms of Morris Ankrum's feet!'

'Where?'

'Querytioup,' she said. It was an image-research place across the city run by a seventeen-year-old who must have seen every movie and TV show ever made. 'It's from an unlikely source,' said Lois, reading from the hard copy. '*Tennessee Johnson.*

Ankrum played Jefferson Davis. There's a scene where he steps on a platform to give a secession speech.

'Imagine, Morris Ankrum, alive and kicking, 360 degrees, top and bottom. Top was easy — there's an overhead shot in *Invaders from Mars* when the guys in the fuzzy suits stick the ruby hatpin-thing in his neck.'

'Is that your last holdup? I wish *this* thing were that goddamn easy,' I said.

'No. Legal,' she said.

Since the National Fair Likeness Act passed, you had to pay the person (or the estate) of anyone even remotely famous, anyone recognizable from a movie, anywhere. (In the early days after passage, some moviemakers tried to get around it by using parts of people. Say you wanted a prissy hotel clerk — you'd use Franklin Pangborn's hair, Grady Sutton's chin, Eric Blore's eyes. Sounded great in theory, but what they got looked like a walking police composite sketch; nobody liked them and they scared little kids. You might as well pay and make Rondo Hatton the bellboy.)

'What's the problem now?' I asked.

'Ever tried to find the heirs of Olin Howlin's estate?' Lois asked.

What I'm doing is called *This Guy Goes to Town* . . . It's a *nouvelle vague* movie; it stars everybody in France in 1962.

You remember the French New Wave? A bunch of film critics who wrote for a magazine, *Cahiers du Cinéma*? They *burned* to make films — lived, slept, ate films in the 1950s. Bad American movies even their directors had forgotten, B Westerns, German silent Expressionist bores, French cliff-hangers from 1916 starring the Kaiser as a gorilla, things like that. Anything they could find to show at midnight after everybody else had gone home, in theaters where one of their cousins worked as an usher.

Some of them got to make a few shorts in the mid-50s. Suddenly studios and producers handed them cameras and money. Go out and make movies, they said; talk is cheap.

Truffaut. Resnais. Godard. Rivette. Roehmer. Chris Marker. Alain Robbe-Grillet.

The Four Hundred Blows. Hiroshima, Mon Amour. Breathless. Le Jette. Trans-Europ Express.

They blew moviemaking wide open.

And why I love them is that for the first time, underneath the surface of them, even the comedies, was a sense of tragedy; that we were all frail human beings and not celluloid heroes and heroines.

It took the French to remind us of that.

The main thing guys like Godard and Truffaut had going for them was that they didn't understand English very well.

Like in *Riot in Cell Block 11,* when Neville Brand gets shot at by the prison guard with a Thompson, he yells, 'Look out, Monty! They got a chopper! Back inside!'

What the *Cahiers* people heard was: 'Steady, mon frère! Let us leave this place of wasted dreams.'

And they watched a *lot* of undubbed, unsubtitled films in those dingy theaters. They learned from them, but not necessarily what the films had to teach.

It's like seeing D.W. Griffith's 1916 *Intolerance* and listening to an old Leonard Cohen album at the same time. What you're seeing doesn't get in the way of what you're thinking. The words and images made for cultures half a century apart mesh in a way that makes for sleepless nights and new ideas.

And, of course, every one of the New Wave film-makers was in love, one way or another, with Jeanne Moreau.

I'm playing Guy. Or my image is, anyway. For one thing, composition, sequencing, and specs on a real person take only about fifteen minutes' easy work.

I stepped up on the sequencer platform. Johnny Rizzuli pushed in a standard scan program. The matrix analyzer, which is about the size of an old iron lung, flew around me on its yokes and gimbals like the runaway merry-go-round in *Strangers on a Train.* Then it flew over my head like the crop duster in *North by Northwest.*

After it stopped, the platform moved back and forth. I was bathed in light like a sheet of paper on an old office copier.

Johnny gave me the thumbs-up.

I ran the imaging a day later. It's always ugly the first time you watch yourself tie your shoelaces, roll your eyes, scratch your head and belch. As close, as far away, from whatever angle in whatever lighting you want. And when you talk, you never sound like you think you do. I'm going to put a little more whine in my voice; just a quarter-turn on the old Nicholson knob.

The movie will be in English, of course, with subtitles.

English subtitles.

(The screen starts to fade out.)

DIRECTOR *(voice off):* Hold it. That's not right.

CAMERAMAN *(off):* What?

DIRECTOR *(also me, with a mustache and jodhpurs, walking onscreen):* I don't want a dissolve here. *(He looks around.)* Well?

CAMERAMAN *(off):* You'll have to call the optical-effects man.

DIRECTOR Call him! *(Puts hands on hips.)*

VOICES *(off):* Optical effects! Optical effects! Hey! *(Sounds of clanking and jangling. Man in coveralls —* JEAN-PAUL BELMONDO *— walks on carrying a huge workbag marked 'Optical Effects.' He has a hunk of bread in one hand.)*

BELMONDO: Yeah, boss?

DIRECTOR: I don't want a dissolve here.

BELMONDO *(Shrugs):* Okay. *(He takes out a stovepipe, walks toward the camera p.o.v., jams the end of the stovepipe over the lens. Camera shudders. The circular image on the screen irises in. Camera swings wildly, trying to get away. Screen irises to black. Sound of labored breathing, then asphyxiation.)*

DIRECTOR *(v.o):* No! It can't breathe! I don't want an iris, either!

BELMONDO *(v.o.):* Suit yourself, boss. *(Sound of tearing. Camera p.o.v.* BELMONDO *pulls off stovepipe. Camera quits moving. Breathing returns to normal.)*

DIRECTOR: What kind of effects you have in there?

BELMONDO: All kinds. I can do anything.

DIRECTOR: Like what?

BELMONDO: Hey, camerman. Pan down to his feet. *(Camera pans down onto shoes.)* Hold still, Monsieur le Director! *(Sound of jet taking off.)* There! Now pan up. *(Camera pans up.* DIRECTOR *is standing where he was, back to us, but now his head is on backwards. He looks down his back.)*

DIRECTOR: Hey! Ow! Fix me!
BELMONDO: Soon as I get this effect you want.
DIRECTOR: Ow. Quick! Anything ! Something from the old Fieullade serials!
BELMONDO: How about this? *(He reaches in the bag, brings out a Jacob's Ladder, crackling and humming.)*
DIRECTOR: Great. Anything! Just fix my head! (BELMONDO *sticks the Jacob's Ladder into the camera's p.o.v. Jagged lightning bolt wipe to the next scene of a roadway down which* GUY *— me — is walking.)*
BELMONDO *(v.o.)*: We aim to please, Boss.
DIRECTOR *(v.o.)*: Great. *Now* could you fix my head?
BELMONDO *(v.o.)*: Hold still. *(Three Stooges' sound of nail being pried from a dry board.)*
DIRECTOR *(v.o.)*: Thanks.
BELMONDO *(v.o.)*: Think nothing of it. *(Sound of clanking bag being dragged away. Voice now in distance.)* Anybody seen my wine?
(GUY — me — *continues to walk down the road. Camera pans with him, stops as he continues offscreen left. Camera is focused on a road sign)*:

Nevers 32 km
Alphaville 60 km
Marienbad 347 km
Hiroshima 14,497 km
Guyville 2 km

To get my mind off the work on the movie, I went to one of the usual parties, with the usual types there, and on the many screens in the house were the usual undergrounds.

On one, Erich von Stroheim was doing Carmen Miranda's dance from *The Gang's All Here* in full banana regalia, a three-minute loop that drew your eyes from anywhere in line of sight.

On another, John F. Kennedy and Marilyn Monroe tore up the bed. This was happening in Room 12 of the Bates Motel.

In the living room, on the biggest screen, Laurel and Hardy were doing things with Wallace Beery and Clark Gable they had never thought of doing in real life. I watched for a moment. At one point a tired and puffy Hardy turned to a drunk and besmeared Laurel and said: 'Why don't you do something to *help* me?'

Enough, enough. I moved to another room. There was a TV there, too. Something seemed wrong — the screen too fuzzy, sound bad, acting unnatural. It took me a few seconds to realize that they had the set turned to a local low-power TV station and were watching an old movie, King Vidor's 1934 *Our Daily Bread.* It was the story of a bunch of Depression-era idealistic have-nots making a functioning, dynamic, corny, and totally American commune out of a few acres of land by sheer dint of will.

I had seen it before. The *Cahiers du Cinéma* people always wrote about it when they talked about what real Marxist movies should be like, back in those dim pre-*Four Hundred Blows* days when all they had were typewriters and theories.

The house smelled of butyl nitrate and uglier things. There were a dozen built-in aerosol dispensers placed strategically about the rooms. The air was a stale mix of vassopressins, pheromones, and endorphins that floated in a blue mist a couple of meters off the floors. A drunk jerk stood at one of the dispensers and punched its button repeatedly, like a laboratory animal wired to stimulate its pleasure center.

I said my good-byes to the hostess, the host having gone upstairs to show some new arrivals 'some really interesting stuff.'

I walked the ten blocks home to my place. My head slowly cleared on the way, the quiet buzzing left. After a while, all the parties run together into one big Jell-O–wiggly image of people watching movies, people talking about them.

> The grocer (Pierre Brasseur) turns to Marie (Jeanne Moreau) and Guy (me).
>
> 'I assure you, the brussels sprouts are very fine,' he says.
>
> 'They don't look it to me,' says Marie.
>
> 'Look,' says Guy (me) stepping between them. 'Why not artichokes?'
>
> 'This time of year?' asks the grocer.
>
> 'Who asked you?' says Marie to Guy (me). She plants her feet. 'I want brussels sprouts, but not these vile, disgusting things.'
>
> 'How dare you say that!' says the grocer. 'Leave my shop. I won't have my vegetables insulted.'

'Easy, mac,' I (Guy) say.

'Who asked you?' he says and reaches behind the counter for a baseball bat.

'Don't threaten him,' says Marie.

'Nobody's threatening me,' Guy (I) say to her.

'He is,' says Marie. 'He's going to hit you!'

'No, I'm not,' says the grocer to Marie. 'I'm going to hit *you.* Get out of my shop. I didn't fight in the *maquis* to have some chi-chi tramp disparage me.'

'Easy, mac,' Guy (I) say to him.

'And *now,* I *am* going to hit you!' says the grocer.

'I'll take these brussels sprouts after all,' says Marie, running her hand through her hair.

'Very good. How much?'

'Half a kilo,' she says. She turns to me (Guy). 'Perhaps we can make it to the bakery before it closes.'

'Is shopping here always like this?' I (Guy) ask.

'I wouldn't know,' she says. 'I just got off the bus.'

It was the perfect ending for the scene. I liked it a lot. It was much better than what I had programmed.

Because from the time Marie decided to take the sprouts, none of the scene was as I had written it.

'You look tired,' said Lois, leaning against my office doorjamb, arms crossed like Bacall in *To Have and Have Not.*

'I am tired. I haven't been sleeping.'

'I take a couple of dexadryl a day,' she said. 'I'm in this last push on the movie, so I'm making it a point to get at least two hours' sleep a night.'

'Uh, Lois . . .' I said. 'Have you ever programmed a scene one way and have it come out another?'

'That's what the little red reset button is for,' she said. She looked at me with her gray-blue eyes.

'Then it's happened to you?'

'Sure.'

'Did you let the scene play all the way through?'

'Of course not. As soon as anything deviated from the program, I'd kill it and start over.'

'Wouldn't you be interested in letting them go and see what happens?'

'And have a mess on my hands? That was what was wrong with the old way of making movies. I treat it as a glitch, start again, and get it *right*.' She tilted her head. 'Why do you ask?'

'Lots of stuff's been . . . well, getting off track. I don't know how or why.'

'And you're letting them run on?'

'Some,' I said, not meeting her gaze.

'I'd hate to see your studio time-share bill. You must be *way* over budget.'

'I try not to imagine it. But I'm sure I've got a better movie for it.'

She took my hand for a second, but only a second. She was wearing a blue rib-knit sweater. Blue was definitely her color.

'That way lies madness,' she said. 'Call maintenance and get them to blow out the low-level format of your ramdisk a couple of times. Got to run,' she said, her tone changing instantly. 'Got a monster to kill.'

'Thanks a lot. Really,' I say. She stops at the door.

'They put a lot of stuff in the GAX,' she said. 'No telling what kind of garbage is floating around in there, unused, that can leak out. If you want to play around, you might as well put in a bunch of fractals and watch the pretty pictures.

'If you want to make a movie,' she continued, '*you've* got to tell it what to do and sit on its head while it's doing it.'

She looked directly at me. 'It's just points of light fixed on a plane, Scott.'

She left.

> Delphine Seyrig is giving Guy (me) trouble.
>
> She was supposed to be the woman who asks Guy to help her get a new chest of drawers up the steps of her house. We'd seen her pushing it down the street in the background of the scene before with Marie and Guy (me) in the bakery.
>
> While Marie (Moreau) is in the vintner's, Seyrig asks Guy (me) for help.
>
> Now she's arguing about her part.
>
> 'I suppose I'm here just to be a tumble in the hay for you?' she asks.
>
> 'I don't know what you're talking about, lady. Do you want help with this bureau, or what?'

'Bureau? Do you mean FBI?' asks a voice behind Guy (me). Guy (me) turns. Eddy Constantine, dressed as Lemmy Caution in a cheap trenchcoat and a bad hat, stares at Guy (me) with his cue-ball eyes.

'No! Chest of drawers,' says Seyrig.

'Chester Gould? *Dick Tracy?*' asks Constantine.

Guy (me) wanders away, leaving them to argue semantics on the steps. As he turns the corner, the sound of three quick shots comes from the street he had just left. He heads toward the wine shop where Marie stands, smoking.

I almost forgot about the screening of *Monster without a Meaning.* There was a note on my screen from Lois. I didn't know she was through or anywhere near it, but then, I didn't even know what day it was.

I took my cup of bad black coffee into the packed screening room. Lois wasn't there — she said she'd never attend a showing of one of her movies. There were the usual reps, a few critics, some of her friends, a couple of sequencer operators and a dense crowd of the usual bitpart unknowns.

Boris, Lois's boyfriend, got up to speak. (Boris had been working off and on for five years on his own movie, *The Beast with Two Backs.*) He said something redundant and sat down, and the movie started, with the obligatory GAX-600 logo.

Even the credits were right — they slimed down the screen and formed shaded hairy letters in deep perspective, like those from a flat print of an old 3-D movie.

John Agar was the scientist on vacation (he was catching a goddamn *mackerel* out of what was purported to be a high Sierra-Nevada lake; he used his fly rod with all the grace of a longshoreman handling a pitchfork for the first time) when the decayed-orbit satellite hits the experimental laboratory of the twin hermit mad scientists (Les Tremayne and Leo G. Carroll).

An air force major (Kenneth Tobey) searching for the satellite meets up with both Agar and the women (Mara Corday, Julie Adams), who were on their way to take jobs with the mad doctors when the shock wave of the explosion blew their car into a ditch. Agar had stopped to help them, and the jeep with Tobey and the comic relief (Sgt. Joe Sawyer, Cpl. Sid Melton) drives up.

Cut to the Webb farmhouse — Gramps (Olin Howlin), Patricia (Florida Friebus) Aunt Sophonsiba (Kathleen Freeman) and Little Jimmy (George 'Foghorn' Winslow) were listening to the radio when the wave of static swept over it. They hear the explosion, and Gramps and Little Jimmy jump into the woodie and drive over to the Old Science Place.

It goes just like you'd imagine from there, except for the monster. It's all done subjective camera; the monster sneaks up (you've always seen something moving in the background of the long master shot before, in the direction from which the monster comes). It was originally a guy (Robert Clarke) coming in to get treated for a rare nerve disorder. He was on Les Tremayne's gurney when the satellite hit, dowsing him with experimental chemicals and 'space virus' from the newly discovered van Allen belt.

The monster gets closer and closer to the victims. They see something in a mirror, or hear a twig snap, and they turn around — they start to scream, their eyeballs go white like fried marbles, blood squirts out their ears and nose, their gums dissolve, their hair chars away, then the whole face; the clothes evaporate, wind rushes toward their radioactive burning. It's all over in a second but it's all there, every detail perfect.

The scene where Florida Friebus melts is a real shocker. From the way the camera lingers over it, you know the monster's enjoying it.

By the time General Morris Ankrum, Colonel R.G. Armstrong, and Secretary of State Henry Hull wise up, things are bad.

At one point the monster turns the stares back over its shoulder. There's an actual charred trail of destruction stretching behind it; burning houses like Christmas tree lights in the far mountains, the small town a few miles back looking like the ones they built for the Project Ivy A-bomb tests in Nevada. Turning its head, the monster looks down at the quiet nighttime city before it. All the power and wonder of death are in that shot.

(Power and wonder are in me, too, in the form of a giant headache. One of my eyes isn't focusing anymore. A bad sign, and rubbing doesn't help.)

I get up to go — the movie's great but the light is hurting my eyes too much.

Suddenly here come three F-84 Thunderjets flown by Captain Clint Eastwood, First Lieutenant Leonard Nimoy, and Colonel James Whitmore.

'The Reds didn't like the regular stuff in Korea. This thing shouldn't like this atomic napalm, either,' says Whitmore. 'Let's go in and spread a little honey around, boys.'

The jets peel off.

Cut to the monster's p.o.v. The jets come in with a roar. Underwing tanks come off as they power back up into a climb. The bombs tumble lazily toward the screen. One whistles harmlessly by, two are dropping short, three keep getting bigger and bigger. Then blam — whoosh. You're the monster and you're being burned to death in a radioactive napalm firestorm.

Screaming doesn't help; one hand comes up just before the eyes melt away like lumps of lard on a floor furnace — the hand crisps to paper, curls, blood starts to shoot out and evaporates like verga over the Mojave. The last thing the monster hears are its auditory canals boiling away with a screeching hiss.

Cut to Agar, inventor of the atomic napalm, holding Mara Corday on a hill above the burning city and the charring monster. He's breathing hard, his hair is singed; her skirt is torn off one side, exposing her long legs.

Up above, Whitmore, oxygen mask off, smiles down and wags the jet's wings.

Pull back to a panorama of the countryside; Corday and Agar grow smaller; the scenes lifts, takes in jets, country, then state; miles up now, the curve of the earth appears, grows larger; continue to pull back, whole of U.S., North and Central America appears. Beeping on soundtrack. We are moving along with a white luminescence that is revealed to be a Sputnik-type satellite.

Beeping stops. Satellite begins to fall away from camera, lurching some as it hits the edges of the atmosphere. As it falls, letters slime down the screen: THE END?

Credits: A MOVIE BY LOIS B. TRAVEN

The lights come up. I begin to breathe again. I'm standing in the middle of the aisle, applauding as hard as I can.

Everybody else is applauding too. Everybody.

Then my head *really* begins to hurt, and I go outside into the cool night and sit on the studio wall like Humpty-Dumpty.

Lois is headed for the big time. She deserves it.

The notes on my desk are now hand-deep. Pink ones, then orange ones from the executive offices. Then the bright-red-striped ones from accounting.

Fuck 'em. I'm almost through.

I sit down and plug on. Nothing happens.

I punch maintenance.

'Sorry,' says Bobo. 'You gotta get authorization from Snell before you can get back on-line, says here.'

'Snell in accounting, or Snell in the big building?'

'Lemme check.' There's a lot of yelling around the office on the other end. 'Snell in the big building.'

'Yeah, yeah, okay.'

So I have to eat dung in front of Snell, promise him anything, renegotiate my contract *right then and there* in his office without my business manager or agent. But I *have* to get this movie finished.

Then I have to go over to accounting and sign a lot of stuff. I call Bernie and Chinua and tell them to come down to the studio and clean up the contractual shambles as best they can, and not to expect to hear from me for a week or so.

Then I call my friend Jukai, who helped install the first GAX-600 and talk to him for an hour and a half and learn a few things.

Then I go to Radio Shack and run up a bill of $6,124, buy two weeks' worth of survival food at Apocalypse Andy's, put everything in my car and drive over to my office deep under the bowels of the GAX-600.

I have locked everyone else out of the mainframe with words known only to myself and Alain Resnais. Let *them* wait.

I have put a note on the door:

Leave me alone. I am finishing the movie. Do not try to stop me. You are locked out of the 600 until I am through. Do not attempt to take me off-line. I have rewired the 600 to wipe out everything, every movie in it but mine, if you do. Do not cut my power: I have a generator in here. If you turn me off, the GAX is history. (See attached receipt.) Leave me alone until I have finished; you will get everything back, and a great movie too.

They *were* knocking. Now they're pounding on the door. Screw 'em. I'm starting the scene where Guy (me) and Marie hitch a ride on the garbage wagon out to the communist pig farm.

The locksmith was quiet but he couldn't do any good either. I've put on the kind of locks they use on the *outsides* of prisons.

They tried to put a note on the screen. *Back off,* I wrote.

They began to ease them, pleading notes, one at a time through the razor-thin crack under the fireproof steel door.

Every few hours I would gather them up. They quit coming for a while.

Sometime later there was a polite knock.

A note slid under.

May I come in for a few moments? it asked. It was signed *A. Resnais.*

Go away, I wrote back. *You haven't made a good movie since* La Guerre Est Finie.

I could imagine him turning to the cops and studio heads in his dignified, humble way (he must be pushing ninety by now), shrugging his shoulders as if to say, 'Well, I tried my best,' and walking away.

'You must end this madness,' says Marie. 'We've been here a week. The room smells. I smell. You smell. I'm tired of dehydrated apple chips. I want to walk on the beach again, get some sunlight.'

'What kind of ending would that be?' I (Guy) ask.

'I've seen worse. I've *been* in much worse. Why do you have this obsessive desire to recreate movies made fifty years ago?'

I (Guy) look out the window of the cheap hotel, past the

edge of the taped roller shade. 'I (Guy) don't know.' I (Guy) rub my chin covered with a scratchy week's stubble. 'Maybe those movies, those, those *things* were like a breath of fresh air. They led to everything we have today.'

'Well, we could use a breath of fresh air.'

'No. Really. They came in on a stultified, lumbering dinosaur of an industry, tore at its flanks, nibbled at it with soft, rubbery beaks — something, I don't know what. Stung it into action, showed it there were *other* ways of doing things — made it question itself. Showed that movies could be free, not straitjackets.'

'Recreating *them* won't make any new statements,' said Marie (Moreau).

'I'm trying to breathe new life into *them*, then. Into what they were. What they meant to . . . to me, to others,' I (Guy) say.

What I want to do more than anything is to take her from the motel, out to the sunny street to the car. Then I want to drive her up the winding roads to the cliffs overlooking the Mediterranean. Then I want her to lean over, her right arm around my neck, her hair blowing in the wind, and give me a kiss that will last forever, and say, 'I love you, and I'm ready.'

Then I will press down the accelerator, and we will go through the guard rail, hang in the air, and begin to fall faster and faster until the eternal blue sea comes up to meet us in a tender hand-shaped spray, and just before the impact she will smile and pat my arm, never taking her eyes off the windshield.

'Movies are freer than they ever were,' she says from the bed. 'I was there. I know. You're just going through the motions. The things that brought about those films are remembered only by old people, bureaucrats, *film critics*,' she says with a sneer.

'What about you?' I (Guy) ask, turning to her. 'You remember. You're not old. You're alive, vibrant.'

My heart is breaking.

She gives me (Guy) a stare filled with sorrow. 'No, I'm not. I'm a character in a movie. I'm points of light, fixed on a plane.'

A tear-gas canister crashes through the window. There is a

pounding against the door.

'The cops!' I (Guy) say, reaching for the .45 automatic.

'The pimps!' Marie says.

The room is filling with gas. Bullets fly. I fire at the door, the window shades, as I reach for Marie's hand. The door bursts open.

Two quick close-ups: her face, terrified; mine, determined, with a snarl and a holy wreath of cordite rising from my pistol.

My head is numb. I see in the dim worklight from my screen the last note they stuck under the door fluttering as the invisible gas is pumped in.

I type *fin.*

I reach for the nonexistent button that will wipe everything but *This Guy Goes to Town* . . . and mentally push it.

I (Guy) smile up at them as they come through the doors and walls; pimps, Nazis, film critics, studio cops, deep-sea divers, spacemen, clowns, and lawyers.

Through the windows I can see the long geometric rows of the shrubs forming quincunxes, the classical statuary, people moving to and fro in a garden like a painting by Fragonard.

I must have been away a long time: someone was telling me, as I was making my way toward these first calm thoughts, that *This Guy* . . . is the biggest hit of the season. I have been told that while I was on my four-week vacation from human cares and woe that I have become that old-timey curiosity; the rich man who is crazy as a piss ant.

Far less rich, of course, than I would have been had I not renegotiated my contract before my last, somewhat spectacular orgy of movie and lovemaking in my locked office.

I am now calm. I am not looking forward to my recovery, but I suppose I will have to get some of my own money out of my manager's guardianship.

A nurse comes in, opens the taffeta curtains at another set of windows, revealing nice morning sunlight through the tiny, very tasteful bars.

She turns to me and smiles.

It is Anouk Aimee.

KATHE KOJA

Kathe Koja lives in Illinois, and she says that the story which follows was her 'first real (read: professional) sale, for real money.' Since then, however, she has sold several more stories. Her fiction first saw publication in the short-lived magazine *Sf International.* Entitled 'Happy Birthday, Kim White', this was her Clarion admission story, which she attended in 1984.

Clarion is a six week intensive course in science fiction writing, where the students are instructed by various professional authors — such as Roger Zelazny and Lucius Shepard, to take two examples from contributors to this *Yearbook.* Over the years, Clarion has produced many authors who have joined the professional ranks — such as Lisa Tuttle and Pat Murphy, from the first *Yearbook*, and Lucius Shepard from this volume . . .

Asked to say something about the following story, Koja's comment was 'no comment . . . I have nothing to say about any of my stories that they can't say for themselves.'

So read on . . .

DISTANCES

by

KATHE KOJA

Michael, naked on the table, hospital reek curling down his throat, the base of his skull rich with the ache it has had every day since the first one, will probably never lose. He remembers that day: parts of him stone-numb, other parts prickling and alive; moving to make sure he still could; exhilaration; and the sense of the jacks. They had said he would not, physically could not, feel the implants. Wrong — needle-slim, they seemed like pylons, silver pillars underskin.

He is tall, under the straps; his feet are cold. Three months' postsurgery growth of yellow hair, already curling. Grey eyes' glance roams the ceiling, bare peripherals.

He shifts, a little; the attendant gives him a faraway scowl. The old familiar strap-in: immobilize the head, check CNS response, check for fluid leak, check check check. 'I am *fine,*' he growls, chin strap digging into his jawline, 'just fucking fine,' but the attendant, rhino-sized, silent, ignores him entirely.

The ceiling monitor lights, bright and unexpected. Now what?

A woman, dark hair, wide mouth, cheekbones like a cat's, white baggy labcoat shoulders. 'Hi,' she says. 'Doing all right?'

'Just ducky,' tightmouthed, tin man with rusted jaw. Don't tell me, he thinks, more tests. 'Who're you? A doctor?'

She appears to find this pretty funny. 'Not hardly. I'm your handler. My name's Halloran.' Something offscreen causes that wide mouth to turn down, impatient curvature. 'I'll be in in a couple of minutes, we've got a meeting. — Yeah I *heard* you!' and the screen blanks.

Check-up over, Michael rubs the spots where the straps were. 'Excuse me,' he says to the attendant. 'That woman who was just onscreen — you know her?'

'Yeah, I know her.' The attendant seems affronted. 'She's a real bitch.'

That charcoal drawl, bass whisper from babyface: 'Oh good. I hate synthetics.'

'So who's he? General Custer?'

Halloran beside him, scent of contraband chocolate mints, slipping him handfuls. They are part of a ten-pair group in an egg-shaped conference room, white jacket and bald head droning away in accentless medspeak at the chopped-down podium. The air is ripe with dedication.

'That's Bruce, Dr. Bruce, the director. You're supposed to be listening to this.'

'I am. Just not continuously.'

Dreamy genius meets genius-dreamer. Bad kids in the back of the class, jokes and deadpan, catching on faster than anyone anyway. NASA'd done its profile work magnificently this time: the minute of physical meeting told them that, told them also that, if it was engineered (and it was) so what: it's great. Maybe all the other pairs feel the same. That's the goal, anyway. NASA believes there must be something better than a working relationship between handler and glasshead, more than a merely professional bond.

'He always snort like that when he talks?'

'You should hear him when he's not talking.'

Dr Bruce: '. . . bidirectional. The sealed fiber interface, or SFI, affords us —'

'Glass fibers for glass heads.'

'Beats an extension cord.'

Her hair is a year longer than his, but looking in the mirror would show Michael the back of her skull: it's his. Handlers are first-generation glassheads, just technically imperfect enough to warrant a new improved version — but hey, don't feel bad, you're still useful. We can put you to work training your successors, the ones who'll fly where you can never go; train them to do what you want to; brutally practical demonstration of the Those Who Can't principle. But who better to handle a glasshead but a glasshead?

'. . . which by now I'm sure you're all used to.' Dr. Bruce again. 'But these are extremely important tests. We'll be using the results to determine your final project placement. I know

Project Arrowhead is the plum assignment, but the others are valuable, very much so, if not as strictly "glamorous".' He says it that way, quotes and all, into a room that suddenly stinks of raw tension. 'Handlers, you'll be final-prepping the tandem quarters. Also there's a meeting at 1700. Subjects —'

'That's you,' sucking on a mint. Hint of chocolate on those wide lips.

'Actually I'm more of an object.'

'— under supervisory care for the balance of the day. Everyone, please remember and observe the security regulations.'

'No shootouts in the hallways, huh?'

'No. But don't worry.' Halloran gives him a sideways look. 'We'll figure out a way to have fun.'

Arrowhead: inhouse they call it 'Voyager's big brother.' Far, far away: Proxima Centauri. The big news came from the van de Kamp lunar telescope, where the results of new proper motion studies confirmed what everyone had, happily, suspected: bedrock evidence of at least three planets. At *least*. The possibility of others, and the complexity of their facefirst exploration, precluded the use of even the most sophisticated AI probe. Build new ones, right? No. Something better.

Thus Arrowhead. And glasshead tech gives it eyes and ears, with almost zero lagtime. This last is accomplished by beaucoup-FTL comlink: two big tin cans on a tachyon string. The tech itself was diplomatically extorted from the Japanese, who nearly twelve years before had helped to construct and launch the machine half of Arrowhead, engineered to interface with a human component that did not yet exist, and proved far more difficult to develop.

At last: the glassheads. Manned exploration without live-body risk and inherent baggage. Data absorbed by the lucky subject through thinnest fibers, jacked from receiving port into said subject's brain. The void as seen by human eyes.

Who wanted a humdrum assignment like sneaking spysat, or making tanks squaredance, when you could ride Arrowhead and be Cortez?

'Hey, State of the art barracks.' Michael takes a slow self-conscious seat on the aggressively new, orthopedically sound bed. 'Kinda makes you glad this isn't the bad old days, when NASA got the shitty end of every stick.'

'Oh yeah, they thought of everything but good taste.' Halloran's voice is exquisitely tired. She settles on the other side of the bed, one foot up, one dangling, and talks — inevitably — of Arrowhead. As she speaks her face shifts and changes play across the mobile muscles, taut stalks of bone. She could be a woman talking of her lover, explaining to a stranger. One hand rubs the back of her neck, erratic rhythm.

'It was so *nuts*,' that first group. 'Everybody just out for blood. Especially me and Ferrante.' Paranoia, envy, round-the-clock jockeying, rumors of sabotage and doctored scores. 'Everybody in high-gear bastard twenty-four hours a day. It was all I could think of. I'd wake up in the middle of the night, my heart's going a mile a minute, thinking, Did Bruce see my scores today, really *see* them? I mean does he know I'm the only one who can *do* this?' Her hands stray from neck to hair, weave and twist among the dark locks. Her want shines like a lamp.

'You got it, didn't you.' It's no question, and she knows it.

'Yeah, I got it. That's how they found out the tech wasn't up to spec.' Her voice is absolutely level. 'Fucked up, you know, in a simulator. When they told me I'd never be able to go, in any capacity — and I thought of them all, believe me — when they told me, I wanted to just cut out the jacks and die.' She says this without self-pity, without the faintest taint of melodrama, as if it is the only natural thing to want under the circumstances. 'Then they told me about Plan B. Which is you.'

'And so you stayed.'

'And so I stayed.'

Quiet. The sonorous hum of air, recirculating. Low nimbus of greenish light around Michael's head, his glance down, almost shy, trying to see those days, knowing her pain too well to imagine it. Halloran's hand grabs at her neck; he knows it aches.

'You better not fuck me up, Michael.'

'I won't.'

'I know.'

Silence. Where another would retreat, he pushes forward. 'Know what I was doing, when they called me? When they told me I made the cut?'

'What?' Her hands leave her neck, clasp, unclasp, settle like skittish birds. 'What were you doing?'

'Singing,' promptly, grinning, delighted with the memory. 'It was late, they were trying to find me all day and I didn't know it. I was sure I hadn't made it and I was sad, and pissed, so I went down to the bar and started drinking, and by midnight I was up onstage. And at twenty after one — I'll never forget it — this guy comes up to me and says, Hey Michael, some guy from NASA's on the phone, he wants to talk to you. And I knew it! And you know what else?' He leans forward, not noticing then that she loves this story almost as much as he does, not surprised that a comparative stranger can share this glee so fully. 'I'd been drinkin' all night, right, and I should've been drunk, but I wasn't. Not till he called.' He laughs, still floored, having the joy of it all over again. 'I was so drunk when I talked to him, I thought Boy you must sound like a real *ripe* asshole, boy, but I was so happy I didn't give a shit.' He laughs again. 'I hung up and went back onstage and sang like a son of a bitch till four thirty in the morning, and then I got some eggs and grits and got on the plane for Atlanta.'

She puts up an eyebrow. 'What's the name of the band?'

'Chronic Six. Chronics one through five busted up.' It is the perfect question, and nobody's surprised, or surprised that they're not.

Early days: the pairs, teams as Bruce calls them, solidify. Very little talk between them, and all of it polite. Scrupulous. The glassheads-turned-handlers are avid to better last time's run: they sniff the way old packmates will, hunt weaknesses and soft spots, watch around the clock. The ones they want most are Halloran and her smartass protegé; the Two-Headed Monster; the self-proclaimed Team Chronic.

Too-loud music from their quarters, morning ritual of killer coffee drunk only from twin black handleless mugs, labcoats sleeve-slashed and mutilated, 'Team Chronic' in black laundry marker across the back, chocolate mints and slogans and mystic aggression, attitude with a capital A. Her snap and his drawl, her detail-stare and his big-picture sprawl, their way of finishing each other's sentences, of knowing as if by eyeless instinct what the other will do. Above all, their way of winning. And winning.

'Everybody hates us,' Halloran at meal break, murmuring behind a crust of lunch. 'They hated me, too, before.'

Michael shrugs with vast satisfaction. 'All the world hates a winner.'

'*And*,' smiling now, coffee steam fragrant around bright eyes, 'they can't even scream teacher's pet, because Bruce hates us too.'

'Bruce doesn't hate us. He loathes us.'

They're laughing this over when: 'Halloran.' White hand on her shoulder, faint smell of mustard: Ferrante. Old foe, pudgy in immaculate whites, handsome heavy face bare with anger. Behind him, standing like a duellist's second, Ruthann Duvall, his glasshead, her expression aping his. The whole cafeteria is watching.

'I want to talk to you, Halloran.'

'Feel free. I've had all my shots.'

'Shots is right,' Ferrante says. He is obviously on the verge of some kind of fury-fit. 'You're *enhanced*,' meaning chemically enhanced, meaning illegally doctored; no Inquisitor could have denounced her with more élan. Everyone leans forward, spectators around the cockfight pit. 'I'd think that even you would recognize that you're disrupting the integrity of the whole project, but that's never mattered to you, has it? *Or*,' sparing, then, a look for Michael, who sits finger-linked and mild, looking up at Ferrante with what appears to be innocent interest, 'your foul-mouthed shadow.'

Halloran, cocked head, voice sweet with insult: 'Oh, I know the species of bug that's up *your* ass — you're stuck in second best and you can't figure out why. Well, let me make it crystal for you, slim: you suck.'

'What if I go to Dr. Bruce and ask for a chem scan?'

'What if I jack you into the sanitation system, you big piece of shit?'

His fat white hand clops on her shoulder, shoving her so she

slews into Michael and both nearly topple. Immediately she is on her feet, on the attack, pursuing, slapping, driving him towards the cafeteria door. Michael, beside her, grabs the avenging arms: 'Let him go, the son of a bitch,' and indeed Ferrante takes almost indecent advantage of the moment, leaves, with Ruthann Duvall — contemptuously shaking her still-nearly-bald head — following, muttering, in her mentor's wake.

'Fuck you too, tennis ball head!' Halloran yells, then notices a strange sound coming from Michael: the grunt of suppressed laughter. It's too much, it blows out of him, hands on thighs and bent over with hilarity, and somebody else joins and somebody else too and finally the whole room is laughing. Even Halloran, who is first to stop.

'Let's go,' she says.

Michael rubs helplessly at his eyes. 'Tennis ball head!' He can't stop laughing.

Third week. Long, long day. In their quarters, blast music on, Michael bare-chested on the floor, Halloran rubbing her neck, the muscles thick and painful. Michael watches her, the sore motions.

'Do your jacks ever hurt?'

'*No*!'

'Mine do. All the time.'

'No they don't! They're not supposed to!'

He raises his brows at her vehemence, waits.

'All right,' she says at last, 'You're right. They hurt. But I thought it was because I'm — you know. Defective.' Fiercely: '*You're* not defective. It must just be phantom pain.'

'A phantom pain in the ass.' He sits up, pushes her hands away, begins to massage her hunched shoulders. 'Listen, Halloran.' His hands are very strong. 'There isn't anything wrong with me. Got that? Nothing. So relax.' He squeezes, harder and harder, forcing the muscles to give.

'So,' squeezing, 'when do we jack?'

'We've been jacking all damn day.'

'I mean together.'

'I don't know.' Pleasure in her voice, the pain lessening.

'That's up to Bruce, he does all the scheduling.'

'The hell with Bruce. Let's do it now.'

'*What*?' Even she, rebel, has not considered this. 'We can't,' already wondering why not, really — if they can jack into the computer — 'It's never been done, that I know of, not so early.'

'Now we *really* have to.' He's already on his feet, making for his labcoat, taking from the inner breast pocket a two-meter length of fiber, cased in protective cord, swings it gently jackend like a pendulum at Halloran, a magic tool, you are getting verrrrry sleeeepy. 'Come on, he says. 'Just for fun.'

There is no resisting. 'All right,' she says. 'Just wait a minute.' There's a little timer on her wall desk; she sets it for ten minutes. 'When this times out, so do we. Agreed?'

'Sure thing.' He's already plugged in, conjurer's hands, quicker than her eye. He reaches up to guide her down. 'Ready?'

'Yeah.'

They've jacked in simulation, to prepare; it is, now, the difference between seeing the ocean and swimming, seeing food and eating. They are swamped with it, carried, tumbled, at the moment of mutual entry eyes flash wide, twinned, seeing, knowing, hot with it, incredible

Michael it's *strong* stronger than I thought it would

know I know great *look* at this

and faster than belief thoughts and images burst between them, claiming them, devouring them as they devour, all of each shown to the other without edit or exception, all of it running the link, the living line, a knowing vaster than any other, unthinkably complex, here, now, us, look look see *this*, without any words; they dance the long corridors of memory, and pain, and sorrow, see old fears, old joys, dead dreams, new happinesses bright as silver streamers, nuance of being direct and pure, sledgehammer in the blood, going on forever, profound communion and

finally it is Halloran who pulls back, draws them out, whose caution wakes enough to warn that time is over. They unplug simultaneously, mutual shudder of disunity, a chill of spirit strong enough to pain. They sit back, stunned; the real world is too flat after such a dimensionless feast.

Words are less than useless. In silence is comfort, the

knowing — *knowing* — that one lives who knows you beyond intimacy; two souls, strung hard, adrift on the peculiar fear of the proud, the fear of being forced to go naked in terrible weakness and distress, and finding here the fear is toothless, that knowing and being utterly known could be, is, not exposure but safety, the doctrine of ultimate trust made perfect by glasshead tech.

They move into each other's arms, still not speaking.

Tears are running down Michael's face; his eyes are closed.

Halloran's hands are ice-cold on his wrists.

'We've been jacked all night,' she says, 'it's almost morning.'

She can feel his body shaking, gently, the slow regular hitching of his chest. She has never loved anyone so much in all her life.

Is it chance, rogue coincidence, that the next day Bruce schedules a dual jack, a climatizer as he calls it? Between them, there is much secret hilarity, expressed in a smile here, a less-than-gesture there, and when they do dual, for real and on the record, they swoop and march in flawless tandem, working as one; the simulated tasks are almost ridiculously simple to complete, and perfectly.

Bruce still loathes them, but is undeniably impressed. 'There's something about them.' he tells a subordinate, who tells someone else, who mentions it sotto voce at dinner break, mostly to piss off Ferrante, who is nobody's favorite either. Michael and Halloran hear, too, but go on eating, serene, prefab biscuits and freeze-dried stew.

The tests seem, now, redundant, and Michael is impatient, growing more so. He lusts for the void, can almost taste its unforgiving null. 'What is this shit?' he complains one night, face sideways-pressed into pillow, Halloran's small hands strong on back and buttocks. 'The damn thing'll be there and back before we ever get a chance to ride it.'

More tests. NASA is stultifyingly thorough.

More tests. Intense. Ruthann Duvall vomits her morning sausage in simulation; the sausage, of course, is very real. 'Don't you know,' Michael tells her, 'that's not the way to send back your breakfast?'

More tests.

'*Fuck*!' Halloran feels like wrecking something. She contents herself with smokebomb curses. 'This is getting to me, you know that, this is really fucking *getting* to me.'

Maybe even Bruce, the king of caution, has had enough. The waiting is driving everyone mad, madder than before, the daily speculation, the aura of tension thick as gasoline smoke. Surely they must know, those testers, those considerers of results, surely they must know who is meant to fly, who is the best.

They don't need a victory party. They are a victory party.

No one is really, truly, happy for them. Michael is no darling, and this is Halloran's second sweep; besides, Team Chronic has rubbed too many raw spots to be favorites now. All the others can hope for, in their darkest moments, is project failure, but then of course they feel like shits: nobody really wants Arrowhead to fail, no matter who's riding it.

The winners are wild in their joy; the strain has broken, the goal achieved, the certainty blue-ribbon and bright confirmed. They order up beer, the closest they can get to champagne, and one by one, team by team, the others drift by to join in. Ferrante and Duvall do not, of course, attend, instead spending the evening reviewing data, searching for the flaw that cannot be found.

Everyone gets drunk, yells, laughs loud. Even in losing out there is a certain comfort — at least the waiting is over. And their assignments, while (as Bruce noted) not 'glamorous', are still interesting, worthy of excitement. Everyone talks about what they're going to do, while silently, unanimously, envying the radiant Michael.

Somebody takes a picture: Michael, beer in hand, mutilated labcoat and denim cap askew, sneakered feet crossed at the ankles, hair a halo and eyes — they are — like stars; one arm around Halloran, dark, intent, a flush on her cheekbones, hair pushed messily back, wearing a button on her lapel — if you look very closely at the picture you can read the words: 'Has The World Gone Mad, Or Am I At Work?'

His work area is almost ludicrously bare. The physical jacking in, 2 mm cord running to a superconducting supercomputer — that's all. The com-link system is housed elsewhere. In contrast to the manual backup equipment, resembling the cockpit of a suborbital fighter in its daunting complexity, he could be in a broom closet.

He has taken almost obsessive care to furnish his domain. Totems of various meanings and symbolisms are placed with fastidious precision. His bicycle bottle of mineral water, here; the remnants of his original labcoat, draped over his chairback here; his handleless black mug, sticky, most times, with aging grounds, here; pertinent memos and directives that no one must disturb, in this messy heap here; a bumpersticker that reads 'Even if I gave a shit, I still wouldn't care,' pasted at a strict diagonal across the wall before him; and, in the place of honor, the party-picture.

He loves his work.

It goes without saying, but he does. He cannot imagine, now, another way to live, as if, meeting by chance the lover he has always dreamed of, he thinks of life without her scent and kiss, her morning joke. Riding Arrowhead is all he ever expected, dreamed it to be, only better, better. He does his work — now, guiding Arrowhead through systems check in deceleration mode, realtime course correction to prepare for the big show — and has his play, the sheer flying, ecstasy of blackness, emptiness at his fingertips, in his mouth, flowing over his pores so hungry for mystery that they soak like new sponges. He eats it, all of it, drunk with delight, absorbing every morsel.

In their quarters is a remote terminal. It goes unused.

Other handlers work their subjects still, guiding them through maintenance routines, or geosynchronous dances, or linkups close and far; they are needed, to some degree; their tech has uses. Not that the subjects will not leave them behind, to NASA's prosaic mercies, to other work for handlers whose glassheads have outstripped them. They are on their way out. It was the pre-est of preordained. But not just yet.

Halloran is useless.

Her tech cannot fly Arrowhead — *that* was graphically

proved. She cannot interface directly with the audacious bundle streaking across heaven; cannot in fact guide Michael; he is already far beyond her abilities. Despite any projections to the contrary, she has no function. She is required, now, only to keep Michael happy, on an even keel; when he stabilizes, breaks completely to harness, she will no longer be even marginally necessary.

She has busywork, of course. She 'charts.' She 'observes.' She 'documents.' She is strictly prohibited to use the room remote. It will hurt her. She knows this.

She is in the room one twilight, finishing the last of her daily 'reports'. She is wearing a castoff flightsuit, the irony of which only she can honestly appreciate. Her hair is clubbed back in a greasy bow. She refuses to think about the future. Sometimes, at night, her stomach aches so sourly she wants to scream, knows she will, doesn't.

'Hi.' Michael, tray in hand, smile he tries to make natural. Her pain makes him miserable. He goes, every day, where she is technologically forbidden to enter: she stands at the gate while he soars inside. There is never any hint that she begrudges: she would scream like a banshee if ever came the slightest whisper of withdrawal from the project. He is as close as she can get; even the light of the fire is warmth, of a kind.

'Brought you some slop. Here,' and sets it before her, gentle, seats himself at her side. 'Mind if I graze?'

'Help yourself.'

He eats, or tries to. She messes the food, rubs it across the plate, pretends. 'Music?' she asks, trying to do her part.

'Sure. How 'bout some Transplant?'

'Okay.' She turns it on, the loudest of the blast purveyors, nihilism in 4/4 time. 'Good run today?'

'Great. You see the sheets?'

'Yeah. Outstanding.'

He cannot answer that. They play at eating for a little while longer, Transplant thrashing in the background; then Michael shoves the tray aside.

'Jack with me,' he says, pleads, commands.

This is what she lives for. 'Okay,' she says.

Inner workings, corridors, a vastness she can know, share.

O, she tells him. Without words, trying to hide what cannot be hidden, trying to bear the brunt. He sees, knows, breaks into her courage, as he does each time; his way of sharing it, of taking what he can onto his shoulders. Don't he says. No, she says.

Wordless, they undress, fit bodies together, make physical love. He is crying. He often cries, now. She is dry-eyed, wet below. The pleasure suffuses, brings its own panacea, is enough for a moment. They ride those waves, peak after peak, trailing down, whispering sighs into each other's open mouths. Her sweat smells sweet to him, like nothing else. He licks her shoulders. He had stopped crying, but only just.

To stay jacked this way too long, after a day of Arrowhead, will exhaust him, perhaps mar his efficiency. She is the one who broaches a stop.

No.

Don't be an asshole yes

No

I am

and she does. He grapples, wide-eyed, for a moment, tears free his own jack. 'Don't *do* that!' he cries, then sinks back, rubbing rough at his neck.

'I don't want to hurt you,' she says, and the cry she has withheld so sternly for so long breaks out; she weeps, explosion, and he holds her, helpless. What to do, what to do; nothing. Nothing to do.

The symptoms are subtle.

Besides the nighttime bellyache, which Halloran has learned to ignore if not subdue, come other things, less palatable. Her jacks pain her, sometimes outrageously. Her joints hurt. She has no appetite. It is so difficult to sleep that she has requested, and received, barbiturates. The fact that they gave her no argument about the drugs makes her wonder. Do they A) just not care if she dopes herself stupid or B) have another reason, i.e., more requests? Is everybody breaking down?

Incredibly, yes. The handlers are beginning — in the startlingly crude NASAspeak — to corrode. The glassheads are still okay, doing swimmingly, making hay with their billion-dollar tech. The handlers are slowly going to shit, each in his or her own destructive orbit but with some symptoms universal. Entropy, Halloran thinks, laughing in a cold hysteric way. Built-in byebye.

But it is not built in. She accesses Bruce's files, breaking their so-called security with contemptuous angry ease, finds that this situation is as shocking to the brass as it is to the handlers. The ex-glassheads. Broken glassheads.

No one is discussing it, not that she knows of. In the cafeteria, at the now-infrequent meetings, she searches them, looks minute and increasingly desperate, hunting their dissolution: does Ryerson look thinner? Wickerman's face seem blotchy. Ferrante has big bags under his eyes. She knows they are watching her, too, seeing her corrosion, drawing conclusions that must inevitably coincide. While in the meantime hell freezes over, waiting for Bruce to bring it up.

She says nothing to Michael about any of it. When they jack, the relief of not having to think about it sweeps her mind clean; she is there, in that moment, in a way she is never anywhere else, at any time, anymore.

Bruce comes to see her one morning. She logs off, faces him, feels the numb patches around lips and wrist begin to throb.

'We don't understand it,' he begins.

'Yeah, I know.'

'There are various treatments being contemplated.' He looks genuinely distressed. For the first time it begins to dawn: this is more than breakdown. This is death. Or maybe. Probably. Otherwise why the careful face, the eyes that won't, will *not*, meet hers. Her voice rises, high vowels, hating the fear of it but unable to quell.

'We're thinking of relocating you,' Bruce says. 'All the handlers.'

'Where?'

'South Carolina,' he says. 'The treatments —' Pause. 'We don't want the subjects . . . we don't want to dismay them.'

Dismay? 'What am I supposed to tell him?' She is shouting. No, she is screaming. 'What am I supposed to *tell* him? That I'm going on VACATION?!' Really screaming now. Get hold of yourself, girl, part of her says, while the other keeps making noise.

'For God's sake, Halloran!' Bruce is shaking her. That in itself quiets her. down; it's so damned theatrical. For God's Sake Halloran! oh ha ha ha, HA HA HA stop it!

'We have no concrete plans, yet,' he says, when she is calm enough to listen. 'In fact if you have any ideas — about how to inform the subjects —' He looks at her, hopeful.

Get out, Bruce. I can't think about dying with that face of yours in the room. 'I'll be sure and send you a memo.' It is dismissal; the tone comes easy. In the face of death, getting reprimanded seems, somehow, unimportant. Ha HA: you better stop it or you're going to flip right out.

No more bogus 'reports'. She sits, stares at her hands, thinking of Michael flying the the dark, thinking of that other dark, the real dark, the biggest dark of all. Oh God, not me. Please not me.

'Something's wrong.'

Michael, holding her close, his breath in her damp hair.

'Something's *bad* wrong, Halloran, and you better tell me what it is.'

Silence.

'Halloran —'

'I don't . . . I don't want to —' dismay '— worry you. It's a metabolic disturbance,' and how easily, how gracefully, the lies roll off her tongue. She could give lessons. Teach a course. A short course. 'Don't get your balls in an uproar,' and she laughs.

'You,' he says, measured, considering, 'are a fucking liar.' He is plugged in, oh yes, he's going to get to the bottom of this and none of her bullshit about metabolic disturbances, and he pins her down, jacks her in. One way or another he's going to find out what the hell's going on around here.

He finds out.

'South Carolina, what the hell do you mean South Carolina!'

'That's where they want to send us. Some kind of treatment center, a clinic.' Voice rough and exhausted from hours of crying, of fighting to comfort. 'Bruce seems to think — well, you know, you saw.' She is so immensely tired, and somehow, selfishly, relieved: they share this, too, 'Don't ask me, I —'

'Why can't they do whatever they have to do right here?' There is that in him that refuses to think of it in any way other than a temporary malfunction. She will be treated, she will be cured. 'Why do they have to send you away?'

'You know why.'

'How the fuck can I work anyway!' He is the one screaming, now. 'How do they expect me to do anything!'

The bond, the tie that binds, cuts deeper than NASA intended, or wants. For all the teams it is the same: the glass-heads, even those whose handlers have, like Halloran, become token presences, *want their handlers.* They *need* them. Bruce and his people are in the unhappy position of trying to separate high-strung children from their very favorite stuffed animals now that the stuffing is coming out. *And* trying to disguise the disintegration at the same time. It is the quintessential no-win situation. Uncountable dollars down the drain with one batch, the other batch sniffing stress and getting antsy and maybe not able to work at all.

And for the closest of them, Team Chronic, it is even worse. How do Siamese twins, *happy* Siamese twins, feel when the scalpel bites?

'Just a little more.'

'Stop it.' She is surly in her pain. 'You're not my mother. Stop trying to make me eat.'

'You have to eat, asshole!' He is all at once furious, weeks' worth of worry geysering now. 'How do you ever expect to get better if you don't eat?'

'I'm not going to get better!'

'Yes you are. Don't even say that. You are going to get better.' He says each word with the unshakable conviction of terror. 'And you'd be getting better faster if you'd just co-operate a little.'

'Stop it! Stop making it my fault!' She stands up, shaking; an observer, seeing her last a year ago, would be shocked silent at her deterioration. She is translucent with her illness; not ugly or wasted, but simply less and less *there.* '*They* did this to me!'

She scratches at her neck, wild, as if trying to dig out the jacks. '*They* made me sick! It's not my fault, Michael, none of it is my fault!'

He starts to cry. 'I know I know,' hands over his face, 'I know I know I know,' monotonously, and she sweeps the tray from the table, slapping food on floor, splattering walls, kicking the plastic plate into flight. Then, on her knees beside him, exhausted from the strain of anger, her arms around him rocking him gently back and forth as he grips her forearms, and sobs as if his heart will break, as if his body will splinter with the force. 'I know,' she says; softly, into his ear. 'I know just how you feel. Don't cry. Please, don't cry.'

'There goes the bastard,' says a subordinate to Bruce, as Michael slips past them down the corridor. 'One minute he's tearing your head off because you touched his coffee cup, the next minute he won't even answer you or acknowledge you're alive.'

'He's under enormous stress, Lou.'

'Yeah, I know.' Lou bites a knuckle, considering. 'You don't think he'll — *do* anything, do you? To himself?'

'No.' Bruce looks unsure.

'How about Arrowhead?'

'No.' Very sure. 'He's totally committed to the project, that I know. His performance is still perfect,' which is simple truth. Michael's work is excellent, his findings impeccable; essential. It is his refuge; he clings to it as fiercely and stubbornly as he clings to Halloran.

Bruce, and Lou, and all the Lous, are meeting today, to decide the next step in the separation process. The tandem quarters will be vacated; each handler — how empty the title sounds now! — will be put on a ward; the glasshead will be housed in new quarters, with no memories in their walls or under their beds. This move will just be done, no discussion, no chance of input or hysterics or tantrums. Better for everyone, they tell each other solemnly. For them, too, but they don't say it. This daily tragedy is wearing everybody down.

The move is a success, with one exception.

'No,' Michael says, with the simplicity of imminent violence.

'Nope,' hand on the door, very calm. 'No, she's not moving anywhere, I don't care who decided, I don't care about anything. She's staying right here and you can go tell Bruce to fuck himself.' And the door closes. Bruce is consulted. He says, Let them be for today and we'll think of something else tomorrow.

What they think of is ways to mollify the other teams. Halloran is not moved. Arrowhead is, at bedrock, *the* project, essential. Everything else is a tangent. If consistent, outstanding results are obtained — as they are — then ways can be found, any ways, to keep them coming, the glasshead project in toto is not such a crushing success, what with the first batch proving unsuitable and then unusable, that they can afford to tamper with that which produces its only reason for existing, its reason, to be crude, for any budget at all. Without Arrowhead they can all fold up their tents tomorrow. And the data in itself is so compelling that it is unthinkable that the project not continue.

So Halloran stays.

A conversation tires her; her feet swell and deflate, swell and deflate, with grim comic regularity; her lips bleed, her gums. She plays Transplant, very loud, tells Michael she wishes she could jack right into the music so as to feel it, literally, in her bones. She lets him do almost everything for her, when he is there; it calms and pleases him, as much as he can be pleased, anymore. When they make love he holds her like china, like thinnest crystal that a thought could shatter. They spend a lot of time in tears.

'Oh this is old,' she whispers, stroking his back as he lies atop her. 'This is just getting so old.'

There is no answer to that, so he gives none. He is too tired even to cry, or pound fists, or scream that their treatments are shit, shit! He feels her heart beat. It seems so strong. How can anyone who looks so sick have such a robust heartbeat? Thank God for it. Let it beat forever, till he and all the world is dust.

'Know what?'

'What?'

'Know what I'd like to do, more than anything?'

He raises himself from her, moves to his side, cradles her

that way. 'What would you like to do?'

'Arrowhead.'

The word makes a silence. Vacuum. Each knows what the other is thinking.

Finally, Michael: 'It's a neurological strain. A *big* strain. You might — it could hurt you.

She laughs, not sarcastically, with genuine humor. 'What a tragedy *that* would be.'

More silence.

'There isn't a lot left,' she says, very gently, 'that I can do. This,' running her hand down his body, her touch ethereal. 'And that. Just one. Just one ride.'

He doesn't answer. He can't answer. Anything he says would be cruel. She puts her hand on his cheek, strokes his skin, the blond stubble. There is a lot she could say, many things: If you love me — one last chance — last favor. She would rather die, and for her it is not an academic pronouncement, than say those things, any of those things.

'All I care about,' he says finally, his voice deeper than she has ever heard it, 'is that I don't want to be a part of something that hurts you. But I guess it's already too late, isn't it?'

For her, there is no answer to that.

Much later: 'You really want to do it?'

He can feel her nod in the dark.

'*Shit.*'

'Okay,' Michael says, for the tenth time. 'It'll take me a couple of minutes to get there, get plugged in. I'll get going, and then this —' indicating a red LED ' — will pulse. You jack in then. Okay?'

'Please, Mister,' in a little girl's voice, undertone of pure delight, 'how do you work this thing?'

'Okay, okay. I'm sorry.' He is smiling too, finally. 'Fasten your seat belt, then.' She is pale with excitement, back almost painfully rigid, his denim cap jaunty on her head. When he kisses her, he tastes the coppery flavor of blood. He leaves, to march down the hall like Ghenghis Khan.

Halloran's heart is thrashing as she jacks in, to the accompaniment of the LED. She feels Michael at once, a strong presence, then — go.

The slow dazzle of the slipstream night, rushing over her like black water, rich phosphorescence, things, passing, the alien perfection of Arrowhead, the flow and flower of things whose names she knows but now cannot fathom or try, the sense of flying, literal arrowhead splicing near to far, here to there, cutting, riding, past the farthest edge — it is wonder beyond dreams, more than she could have wished, for either of them. Worth everything, every second of every pain, every impatience and disappointment, of the last two years. She does not think these things in words, or terms; the concept of rightness unfolds, origami, as she flies, and if she could spare the second she would nod Yes, that's so.

Michael, beside her, feels this rightness too; on his own or as a gift from her, he cannot tell, would not bother making the distinction. She is in ecstasy, she is inside him, they are both inside Arrowhead. He could ride this way forever, world without end.

They find out, of course, Bruce and the others; almost at once. There is a warning monitor that is made to detect just this thing. They are in the tandem quarters, they forcibly unplug her. Michael feels her leaving, the abrupt disunity, and eyes-open screams, hands splayed across the air, as Arrowhead gives a lurch. As soon as she is out of the system she collapses. Grinning.

Bruce teeters on the edge of speechlessness. One assistant says, voice loud with disbelief, 'Do you have any idea what you've just done to yourself? Do you know what's —'

'No,' she corrects, from the bottom of the tunnel, faces ringing her like people looking down a manhole. 'No, *you* have no idea.'

South Carolina is a lot farther away than Proxima Centauri.

JAMES PATRICK KELLY

James Patrick Kelly sold the first of his thirty stories in 1975, and he has also written two and a half science fiction novels — the half being a collaboration with John Kessel, *Freedom Beach* (1985). His solo novels are *Planet of Whispers* (1984) and *Look into the Sun* (1989). His short fiction has been on the Nebula ballot twice and on the Hugo ballot once, and 'Prisoner of Chillon' topped the *Asimov's* readers' poll as best novelette of 1986. His stories have also appeared in *F&SF*, *Analog*, *Amazing*, *Universe*, *Galaxy* and *Twilight Zone*, and have been reprinted in various anthologies in America, Britain, Germany, Italy, Holland, France and Japan.

On the subject of the following story, Kelly says: 'Here in the States we have a program called Artists in Education through which artists of various sorts are brought into the elementary and secondary schools to teach their speciality. In my first year in this program I taught eighth graders (13 to 14 year olds) in my home town of Durham, New Hampshire. It was the height of the Reagan/Rambo lunacy and I was appalled at the naive and bloodthirsty attitudes held by many of my students — due, in my opinion, to an insidious kind of cultural programming. They *longed* for a war; had one presented itself they would have been eager volunteers. In Class, I tried to impress on them the horrors and consequences of combat — to little avail. So I wrote "Home Front" for those kids.'

JAMES PATRICK KELLY

James Patrick Kelly sold his first short story in 1975, and he has also written two and a half science fiction novels — the half being a collaboration with John Kessel, *Freedom Beach* (1985). His solo novels are *Planet of Whispers* (1984) and *Look into the Sun* (1989). His short fiction has been [illegible] twice and on the Nebula ballot once, and "Prisoners of Chernobyl" topped the *Asimov's* readers' poll as best novelette of 1987. His stories have also appeared in *Omni*, *Galaxy*, *Amazing*, *Universe*, *Galileo*, and *The Year's Best* and have been reprinted in various anthologies in America, Britain, Germany, Holland, France and Japan.

On the subject of the following story, Kelly says: "Here in New Hampshire we have a program called Artists in Education, by which artists of various sorts are brought into the elementary and secondary schools to teach their specialties. In my first year in the program I taught eighth graders (12 to 14 years old) in my home town of Durham, New Hampshire. It was the height of the [illegible] and I was appalled at the [illegible] many of my students — due in my opinion to [illegible] of [illegible] programming. They [illegible] and [illegible] would [illegible] and [illegible] of [illegible] — [illegible] wrote 'Home Front' [illegible]."

HOME FRONT

by

JAMES PATRICK KELLY

'Hey, Genius. What are you studying?'

Will hunched his shoulders and pretended not to hear. He had another four pages to review before he could test. If he passed, then he wouldn't have to log onto eighth grade again until Wednesday. He needed a day off.

'What are you, deaf?' Gogolak nudged Will's arm. 'Talk to me, Genius.'

'Don't call me that.'

'Come on, Gogo,' said the fat kid, whose name Will had forgotten. He was older: maybe in tenth, more likely a dropout. Old enough to have pimples. 'Let's eat.'

'Just a minute,' said Gogolak. 'Seems like every time I come in here, this needle is sitting in this booth with his face stuck to a schoolcomm. It's ruining my appetite. What is it, math? Español?'

'History.' Will thought about leaving, going home, but that would only postpone the hassle. Besides, his mom was probably still there. 'The Civil War.'

'You're still on that? Jeez, you're slow. I finished that weeks ago.' Gogolak winked at his friend. 'George Washington freed the slaves so they'd close school on his birthday.'

The big kid licked his lips and eyed the menu above the vending wall at the rear of the Burger King.

'Lincoln,' said Will. 'Try logging on sometimes, you might learn something.'

'What do you mean? I'm logged on right now.' Gogolak pulled the comm out of his backpack and thrust it at Will. 'Just like you.' The indicator was red.

'It doesn't count unless someone looks at it.'

'Then you look at it, you're so smart.' He tossed the comm onto the table and it slid across, scattering a pile of Will's hardcopy. 'Come on, Looper. Get out your plastic.'

Will watched Looper push his ration card into the french-fry machine. He and Gogolak were a mismatched pair. Looper was as tall as Will, at least a hundred and ninety centimeters; Looper, however, ran to fat, and Will looked like a sapling. Looper was wearing official Johnny America camouflage and ripped jeans. He didn't seem to be carrying a schoolcomm, which meant he probably was warbait. Gogolak was the smallest boy and the fastest mouth in Will's class. He dressed in skintight style; everyone knew that girls thought he was cute. Gogolak didn't have to worry about draft sweeps; he was under age and looked it, and his dad worked for the Selective Service.

Will realized that they would probably be back to bother him. He hit save so that Gogolak couldn't spoil his afternoon's work. When they returned to Will's booth, Looper put his large fries down on the table and immediately slid across the bench to the terminal on the wall. He stuck his fat finger into the coin return. Will already knew it was empty. Then Looper pressed select, and the tiny screen above the terminal lit up.

'Hey,' he said to Will, 'you still got time here.'

'So?' But Will was surprised; he hadn't thought to try the selector. 'I was logged on.' He nodded at his comm.

'What did I tell you, Loop?' Gogolak stuffed Looper's fries into his mouth. 'Kid's a genius.'

Looper flipped channels past cartoons, plug shows, catalogs, freebies, music vids, and finally settled on the war. Johnny America was on patrol.

'Gervais buy it yet? said Gogolak.

'Nah.' Looper acted like a real fan. 'He's not going to either; he's getting short. Besides, he's wicked smart.'

The patrol trotted across a defoliated clearing toward a line of trees. With the sun gleaming off their helmets, they looked to Will like football players running a screen, except that Johnny was carrying a minimissile instead of a ball. Without warning Johnny dropped to one knee and brought the launcher to his shoulder. His two rangefinders fanned out smartly and trained their lasers on the far side of the clearing. There was a flash; the jungle exploded.

'Foom!' Looper provided the sound effects. 'Yah, you're barbecue Pedro!' As a sapodilla tree toppled into the clearing, the time on the terminal ran out.

'Too bad.' Gogolak poured salt on the table and smeared a fry in it. 'I wanted to see the meat.'

'Hey, you scum! That's my dinner.' Looper snatched the fries pouch from Gogolak. 'You hardly left me any.'

He shrugged. 'Didn't want them to get cold.'

'Stand-ins.' A girl in baggy blue disposables stood at the door and surveyed the booths. 'Any stand-ins here?' she called.

It was oldie Warner's granddaughter, Denise, who had been evacuated from Texas and was now staying with him. She was in tenth and absolutely beautiful. Her accent alone could melt snow. Will had stood in for her before. Looper waved his hand hungrily until she spotted them.

'Martin's just got the monthly ration of toilet paper,' she said. 'They're limiting sales to three per customer. Looks like about a half-hour line. My grandpa will come by at four-thirty.

'How much?' said Looper.

'We want nine rolls.' She took a five out of her purse. 'A quarter for each of you.'

Will was torn. He could always use the quarter and he wanted to help her. He wanted her to ask his name. But he didn't want to stand in line for half an hour with these stupid jacks.

Gogolak was staring at her breasts. 'Do I know you?'

'I may be new in town, sonny —' she put the five on the table '— but you don't want to rip me off.'

'Four-thirty.' Gogolak let Looper take charge of the money. Will didn't object.

Martin's was just next door to the Burger King. The line wasn't bad, less than two aisles long when they got on. There were lots of kids from school standing in, none of them close enough to talk to.

'Maybe she got tired of using leaves,' said Gogolak.

Looper chuckled. 'Who is she?'

'Seth Warner's granddaughter,' said Will.

'Bet she's hot.' Gogolak leered.

'Warner's a jack,' said Looper. 'Pig-faced oldie still drives a car.'

Most of the shelves in aisle 2 were bare. There was a big

display of government surplus powdered milk, the kind they loaded up with all those proteins and vitamins and tasted like chalk. It had been there for a week and only three boxes were gone. Then more empty space, and then a stack of buckets with no labels. Someone had scrawled 'Korn Oil' on them: black marker on bare metal. At the end of the aisle was the freezer section, which was mostly jammed with packages of fries. Farther down were microwave dinners for the rich people. They wound past the fries and up aisle 3, at the end of which Will could see Mr. Rodenets, the stock boy, dispensing loose rolls of toilet paper from a big cardboard box.

'How hard you think it is to get chosen Johnny America?' Looper said. 'I mean really.'

'What do you mean, really?' said Gogolak. 'You think J.A. is real?'

'People die. They couldn't fake that kind of stuff.' Looper's face got red. 'You watch enough, you got to believe.'

'Maybe,' Gogolak said. 'But I bet you have to know someone.'

Will knew it wasn't true. Gogolak just liked to pop other people's dreams. 'Mr Dunnell swears they pick the team at random,' he said.

'Right,' Gogolak said. 'Whenever somebody gets dead.'

'Who's Dunnell?' said Looper.

'Socialization teacher.' Will wasn't going to let Gogolak run down Johnny America's team, no matter who his father was. 'Most of them make it. 'I'll bet seventy per cent at least.'

'You think that many? Looper nodded eagerly. 'What I heard is they get discharged with a full boat. Whatever they want, for the rest of their lives.'

'Yeah, and Santa is their best friend,' Gogolak said. 'You sound like recruiters.'

'It's not like I'd have to be J.A. himself. I just want to get on his team, you know? Like maybe in body armor.' Looper swept his arm down the aisle with robotic precision, exterminating bacon bits.

'If only you didn't have to join the army,' said Will.

Silence.

'You know,' said Looper, 'they haven't swept the Seacoast since last July.'

A longer silence. Will figured out why Looper was hanging around Gogolak, why he had not complained more about the fries. He was hoping for a tip about the draft. Up ahead, Mr. Rodenets opened the last carton.

'I mean, you guys are still in school.' Looper was whining now. 'They catch me, and I'm southern front for sure. At least if I volunteer, I get to pick where I fight. And I get my chance to be Johnny.'

'So enlist already.' Gogolak was daring him. 'The war won't last forever. We've got Pedro on the run.'

'Maybe I will. Maybe I'm just waiting for an opening on the J.A. team.'

'You ever see a fat Johnny with pimples?' said Gogolak. 'You're too ugly to be a vid. Isn't that right, Mr. Rodenets?'

Mr. Rodenets fixed his good eye on Gogolak. 'Sure, kid.' He was something of a local character — Durham, New Hampshire's only living veteran of the southern front. 'Whatever you say.' He handed Gogolak three rolls of toilet paper.

Will's mom was watching cartoons when Will got home. She watched a lot of cartoons, mostly the stupid ones from when she was a girl. She liked the Smurfs and the Flintstones and Roadrunner. There was an inhaler on the couch beside her.

'Mom, what are you doing?' Will couldn't believe she was still home. 'Mom, it's quarter to five! You promised.'

She stuck out her tongue and blew him a raspberry.

Will picked up the inhaler and took a whiff. Empty. 'You're already late.'

She held up five fingers. 'Not 'til five.' Her eyes were bright.

Will wanted to hit her. Instead he held out his hands to help her up. 'Come on.'

She pouted. 'My shows.'

He grabbed her hands and pulled her off the couch. She stood, tottered, and fell into his arms. He took her weight easily; she weighed less than he did. She didn't eat much.

'You've got to hurry,' he said.

She leaned on him as they struggled down the hall to the bathroom; Will imagined he looked like Johnny America carrying a wounded buddy to the medics. Luckily, there was no one in the shower. He turned it on, undressed her, and helped her in.

'Will! It's cold, Will.' She fumbled at the curtain and tried to come out.

He forced her back into the water. 'Good,' he muttered. His sleeves got wet.

'Why are you so mean to me, Will? I'm your mother.'

He gave her five minutes. It was all that he could afford. Then he toweled her off and dressed her. He combed her hair out as best he could; there was no time to dry it. The water had washed all her brightness away, and now she looked dim and disappointed. More like herself.

By the time they got to Mr. Dunnell's house, she was ten minutes late. At night, Mr. Dunnell ran a freelance word-processing business out of his kitchen. Will knocked; Mr. Dunnell opened the back door, frowning. Will wished he'd had more time to get his mom ready. Strands of wet stringy hair stuck to the side of her face. He knew Mr. Dunnell had given his mom the job only because of him.

'Evening, Marie,' Mr. Dunnell said. His printer was screeching like a cat.

'What so good about it?' She was always rude to him. Will knew it was hard for her, but she wouldn't even give Mr. Dunnell a chance. She went straight to the old Apple that Mr. Dunnell had rewired into a dumb terminal and started typing.

Mr. Dunnell came out onto the back steps. 'Christ, Will. She's only been working for me three weeks and she's already missed twice and been late I don't know how many times. Doesn't she want this job?'

Will couldn't answer. He didn't say that she wanted her old job at the school back, that she wanted his father back, that all she really wanted was the shiny world she had been born into. He said nothing.

'This can't go on. Will. Do you understand?'

Will nodded.

'I'm sorry about last night.'

Will shrugged and bit into a frozen fry. He was not sure what she meant. Was she sorry about being late for work or about coming home singing at three-twenty-four in the morning and turning on all the lights? He slicked a pan with oil and set it on the hot plate. He couldn't turn the burner to high without blowing a fuse but his mom didn't mind mushy fries. Will did; he usually ate right out of the bag when he was at home. He'd been saving quarters for a french fryer for her birthday. If he unplugged the hot plate, there'd be room for it on top of the dresser. He wanted a microwave, too — but then they couldn't afford real microwave food. Someday.

His mom sat up in bed and ate breakfast without looking at it. The new tenants in the next bedroom were watching the war. Will could hear gunfire through the wall.

Normally this was the best time of day, because they talked. She would ask him about school. He told her the truth, mostly. He was the smartest kid in eighth, but she wasn't satisfied. She always wanted to know why he was not making friends. Will couldn't help it; he didn't trust rich kids. And then she would talk about . . . what she always talked about.

Today, however, Will didn't feel much like conversation. He complained half-heartedly that Gogolak was still bothering him.

'I'll bet you have him all wrong. Will.'

'No way.'

'Maybe he just wants to be your friend.'

'The guy's a jack.'

'It's hard on him, you know. Kids try to use him to get to his father. They're always pumping him for draft information.'

'Well, I don't.' Will thought about it. 'How do you know so much anyway?'

'Mothers have their little secrets,' she said with a sparkle. He hated it when she did that; she looked like some kind of starchy sitcom mom.

'You've never even met him.'

She leaned over the edge of the bed and set her empty plate on the floor. 'I ran into his father.' She straightened up and began to sort through her covers. 'He's worried about the boy.'

'Was that who you were with last night?' Will threw a half-eaten fry back into the bag. 'Gogolak's dad?'

'What I do after work is none of your business.' She found

her remote and aimed it at the screen. 'We knew him before — your father and I. He's an old friend.' A cartoon robot brought George Jetson a drink. 'And he does work for Selective Service. He knows things.'

'Don't try to help me, Mom.'

'Look at that,' she said, pointing to the screen. 'He spills something and a robot cleans it up. You know, that's the way I always thought it would be when I was a kid. I always thought it would be clean.'

'Mom —'

'I remember going to Disney World. It was so clean. It was like a garden filled with beautiful flowers. When they used to talk about heaven, I always thought of Disney World.'

Will threw the bag at the screen and fries scattered across the room.

'Will!' She swung her legs out of bed. 'What's wrong with you today? You all right, honey?'.

He was through with her dumb questions. He didn't want to talk to her anymore. He opened the door.

'I said I was sorry.'

He slammed it behind him.

It wasn't so much that it was Gogolak's dad this time. Will wasn't going to judge his mom; it was a free country. He wanted to live life, too — except that he wasn't going to make the same mistakes that she had. She was right in a way: it was none of his business who she made it with or what she sniffed. He just wanted her to be responsible about the things that mattered. He didn't think it was fair that he was the only grown-up in his family.

Because he had earned a day off from school, Will decided to skip socialization, too. It was a beautiful day and volleyball was a dumb game anyway, even if there were girls in shorts playing it. Instead he slipped into the socialization center, got his dad's old basketball out of his locker, and went down to the court behind the abandoned high school. It helped to shoot when he was angry. Besides, if he could work up any kind of jumper, he might make the ninth basketball team. He was already the tallest kid in eighth, but his hands were too small, and he kept bouncing the ball off his left foot. He was practising reverse lay-ups when Looper came out of the thicket that had once been the baseball field.

'Hey, Will.' He was flushed and breathing hard, as if he had been running. 'How you doing?'

Will was surprised that Looper knew his name. 'I'm alive.'

Looper stood under the basket, waiting for a rebound. Will put up a shot that clanged off the rim.

'Hear about Johnny America?' Looper took the ball out to the foul line. 'Old Gervais got his foot blown off. Stepped on a mine.' He shot: swish. 'Some one-on-one?

They played two games and Looper won them both. He was the most graceful fat kid Will had ever seen. After the first game. Looper walked Will through some of his best post-up moves. He was a good teacher. By the end of the second game, sweat had darkened Looper's T-shirt. Will said he wouldn't mind taking a break. They collapsed in the shade.

'So they're recruiting for a new Johnny?' Will tried in vain to palm his basketball. 'You ready to take your chance?'

'Who, me?' Looper wiped his forehead with the back of his hand. 'I don't know.'

'You keep bringing it up.'

'Someday I've got to do something.'

'Johnny Looper.' Will made an imaginary headline with his hands.

'Yeah, right. How about you — ever think of joining? You could, you're tall enough. You could join up today. As long as you swear that you're fifteen, they'll take you. They'll take anyone. Remember Johnny Stanczyk? He was supposed to have been thirteen.

'I heard he was fourteen.'

'Well, he looked thirteen.' Looper let a caterpillar crawl up his finger 'You know what I'd like about the war?' he said. 'The combat drugs. They make you into some kind of superhero, you know?'

'Superheroes don't blow up.'

Looper fired the caterpillar at him.

Will's conscience bothered him for saying that; he was starting to sound like Gogolak. 'Still, it is our country.

Someone has to fight for it, right?' Will shrugged. 'How come you dropped out, anyway?'

'Bored.' Looper shrugged. 'I might go back, though. Or I might go to the war. I don't know.' He swiped the basketball from Will. 'I don't see you carrying a comm today.'

'Needed to think.' Will stood and gestured for his ball.

'Hey, you hear about the lottery?' Looper fired a pass.

Will shook his head.

'They were going to announce it over the school channels this morning; Gogo tipped me yesterday. Town's going to hire twenty kids this summer. Fix stuff, mow grass, pick up trash, you know. Buck an hour — good money. You got to go register at the post office this afternoon, then next month they pick the lucky ones.'

'Kind of early to think about the summer.' Will frowned. 'Bet you that jack Gogolak gets a job.'

Looper glanced at him. 'He's not that bad.'

'A jack. You think he worries about sweeps?' Will didn't know why he was so angry at Looper. He was beginning to like Looper. 'He's probably rich enough to buy out of the draft if he wants. He gets everything his way.'

'Not everything.' Looper laughed. 'He's short.'

Will had to laugh too. 'You want to check this lottery out?'

'Sure.' Looper heaved himself up. 'Show you something on the way over.'

There was blood on the sidewalk. A crowd of about a dozen had gathered by the abandoned condos on Coe Drive to watch the EMTs load Seth Warner into the ambulance which was parked right behind his Peugeot. Will looked for Denise but didn't see her. A cop was recording statements.

'I got here just after Jeff Roeder.' Mrs O'Malley preened as she spoke into the camera; it had been a long time since anyone paid attention to her. 'He was lying on the sidewalk there, all bashed up. The car door was open and his disk was playing. Jeff stayed with him. I ran for help.'

The driver shut the rear doors of the ambulance. Somebody in the crowd called out, 'How is he?'

The driver grunted. 'Wants his lawyer.' Everyone laughed.

'Must've been a fight,' Jeff Roeder said. 'We found this next to him.' He handed the cop a bloody dental plate.

'Did anyone else here see anything?' The cop raised her voice.

'I would've liked to've seen it,' whispered the woman in front of Will. 'He's one oldie who had it coming.' People around her laughed uneasily. 'Shit. They all do.'

Even the cop heard that. She panned the crowd and then slammed the Peugeot's door.

Looper grinned at Will. 'Let's go.' They headed for Madbury Road.

'He wanted me to get in the car with him,' Looper said as they approached the post office. 'He offered me a buck. Didn't say anything else, just waved it at me.'

Will wished he were somewhere else.

'A stinking buck,' said Looper. 'The pervert.'

'But if he didn't say what he wanted . . . maybe it was for a stand-in someplace.'

'Yeah, sure.' Looper snorted. 'Wake up and look around you.' He waved at downtown Durham. 'The oldies screwed us. They wiped their asses on the world. And they're still at it.'

'You're in deep trouble, Looper.' No question Looper had done a dumb thing, yet Will knew exactly how the kid felt.

'Nah. What are they going to do? Pull me in and say "You're fighting on the wrong front, Johnny. Better enlist for your own good." No problem. Maybe I'm ready to enlist now, anyway.' Looper nodded; he looked satisfied with himself. 'It was the disk, you know. He was playing it real loud and tapping his fingers on the wheel like he was having a great time.' He spat into the road. 'Boomer music. I hate the damn Beatles, so I hit him. He was real easy to hit.'

There was already a ten-minute line at the post office and the doors hadn't even opened yet. Mostly it was kids from school who were standing in, a few dropouts like Looper and one grown-up, weird Miss Fisher. Almost all of the kids with comms were logged on, except that no one paid much attention to the screens. They were too busy chatting with the people around them. Will had never mastered the art of talking and studying at the same time.

They got on line right behind Sharon Riolli and Megan Brown. Sharon was in Will's class, and had asked him to a dance once when they were in seventh. Over the summer he had grown thirteen centimeters. Since then she'd made a point of ignoring him; he looked older than he was. Old enough to fight.

'When are they going to open up?' said Looper.

'Supposed to be one-thirty,' said Megan. 'Hi, Will. We missed you at socialization.'

'Hi, Megan. Hi, Sharon.'

Sharon developed a sudden interest in fractions.

'Have you seen Denise Warner?' said Will.

'The new kid?' Megan snickered. 'Why? You want to ask her out or something?'

'Her grandpa got into an accident up on Coe Drive.'

'Hurt?'

'He'll live.' Looper kept shifting from foot to foot as if the sidewalk was too hot for him.

'Too bad.' Sharon didn't look up.

'Hey, Genius. Loop.' Gogolak cut in front of the little kid behind Looper, some stiff from sixth who probably wasn't old enough for summer work anyway. 'Hear about Gervais?'

'What happened?' said Sharon. Will noticed that she paid attention to Gogolak.

'Got his foot turned into burger. They're looking for a new Johnny.'

'Oh, war stuff.' Megan sniffed. 'That's all you guys ever talk about.'

'I think a girl should get a chance,' said Sharon.

'Yeah, sure,' said Looper. 'Just try toting a launcher through the jungle in the heat.'

'I could run body armor.' She gave Looper a pointed stare. 'Something that takes brains.'

The line behind them stretched. It was almost one-thirty when Mr. Gogolak came running out of the side door of the post office. The Selective Service office was on the second floor. He raced down the line and grabbed his kid.

'What are you doing here? Go home.' He grabbed Gogolak's wrist and turned him around.

'Let go of me!' Gogolak struggled. It had to be embarrassing to be hauled out of a job line like some stupid elementary school kid.

His dad bent over and whispered something. Gogolak's eyes got big. A flutter went down the line; everyone was quiet, watching. Mr. Gogolak was wearing his Selective Service uniform. He pulled his kid into the street.

Mr. Gogolak had gone to the western front with Will's dad, Mr. Gogolak had come back. And last night he had been screwing Will's mom. Will wished she were here to see this. They were supposed to be old friends, maybe he owed her a favor after last night. But the only one Mr. Gogolak whispered to was *his* kid. It wasn't hard to figure out what he had said. Gogolak gazed at Looper and Will in horror. 'It's a scam!' he shouted. 'Recruiters!'

His old man slapped him hard and Gogolak went to his knees. But he kept shouting even as his father hit him again. 'Draft scam!' They said a top recruiter could talk a prospect into anything.

Will could not bear to watch Mr. Gogolak beat his kid. Will's anger finally boiled over; he hurled his father's basketball and it caromed off Mr. Gogolak's shoulder. The man turned, more surprised than angry. Will was one hundred and ninety centimeters tall and even if he was built like a stick, he was bigger than this little grown-up. Lucky Mr. Gogolak, the hero of the western front, looked shocked when Will punched him. It wasn't a very smart thing to do but Will was sick of being smart. Being smart was too hard.

'My mom says hi.' Will lashed out again and missed this time. Mr. Gogolak dragged his crybaby kid away from the post office. Will pumped his fist in triumph.

'Run! Run!' The line broke. Some dumb kid screamed, 'It's a sweep!' but Will knew it wasn't. Selective Service had run this scam before: summer job, fall enlistment. Still, kids scattered in all directions.

But not everyone. Weird Miss Fisher just walked to the door to the post office like she was in line for ketchup. Bobby Mangann and Eric Orr and Danny Jarek linked arms and marched up behind her; their country needed them. Will didn't have anywhere to run to.

'Nice work.' Looper slapped him on the back and grinned. 'Going in?'

Will was excited; he had lost control and it had felt *great.* 'Guess maybe I have to now.' It made sense, actually. What was the point in studying history if you didn't believe in America? 'After you, Johnny.'

ROGER ZELAZNY

Roger Zelazny's first short story was published in 1962, and his first two novels were serialised during 1965: *He Who Shapes* in *Amazing* and . . . *And Call Me Conrad* in *F&SF.* The former won the 1965 Nebula Award as best novella (a tie with 'The Saliva Tree' by Brian Aldiss); the latter won the 1966 Hugo Award as best novel (a tie with *Dune* by Frank Herbert). *He Who Shapes* was expanded into the book version entitled *The Dream Master,* while . . . *And Call Me Conrad* was expanded to become *This Immortal.*

The 1965 Nebulas were the first to be awarded, and Zelazny also won the novelette category for 'The Doors of His Face, the Lamps of His Mouth'. His novella 'Home is the Hangman' won the 1975 Nebula and the 1976 Hugo. He has also won the Hugo on four other occasions: best novel, 1968, *Lord of Light*; best novelette, 1982, 'Unicorn Variations'; best novella, 1986, '24 Views of Mt. Fuji, by Hokusai'; and best novelette, 1987, 'Permafrost'.

He lives in Santa Fe, New Mexico, and has published over thirty collections and novels (including one, *Deus Irae*, in collaboration with Philip K. Dick, and another, *Coils*, in collaboration with Fred Saberhagen). His most recent book is the collection *Frost and Fire.* His next novel will be the ninth in the 'Amber' series, *Knight of Shadows.*

His novel *Damnation Alley* was made into the movie of the same title. 'It bears very little resemblance to the book,' he says.

The introduction to his story which follows was written specially for the *Yearbook.*

DEADBOY DONNER AND THE FILSTONE CUP
by
ROGER ZELAZNY

Introduction

I have long been a fan of both Damon Runyon and of hot jazz. I am particularly fond of Runyon's stylized use of the New York idiom of the Prohibition era. But I also relish his twistings of tale in the O. Henry tradition within this usage. And I must confess to an irrational admiration of the man's achievement of his dying wish that he be cremated and have his ashes strewn over Broadway from a plane flown by Eddie Rickenbacker. As Harry the Horse might have noted, 'Some of these scribes really knew how to live.'

In mimicking another's style I learned long ago that it is more a matter of assuming an appropriate attitude toward the material than it is the memorization of writing idiosyncrasies. Hence, the classic Runyon phrase 'more than somewhat' occurs only once in my piece, both as a tribute and as full acknowledgement of derivation — in case anyone hasn't guessed by then.

Runyon — unlike Ring Lardner, with whom he is sometimes compared — is still underrated by academic critics, perhaps because he associated more with gamblers, show biz folks and assorted hoodlums than with professors of literature. Good. I'm sure he'd rather be read by people who like to read his stuff than people who have to.

And even more than F. Scott Fitzgerald, Damon Runyon reminds me of the Jazz Age, of smoky speakeasies, hot music and the occasional body in the river who should have known better. I thought to shift the scene to the Big Manhattan in the Sky for my piece in this mode.

Roger Zelazny

I am standing in front of Vindy's and cannot read the racing stix because of the brownout which is the worst I can remember, when Crash Callahan comes by and the light is not so bad that I cannot see the bulge beneath his racing jacket, a thing I suspect to be malignant though not a tumor.

'I am looking,' he tells me, 'for Deadboy Donner and Painted Evelyn, and I will be most grateful for any information on their whereabouts.'

I shake my head, not because I do not know but because I do not want to tell him that I have seen the pair less than half an hour ago and they are doubtless even now sharing a cavort at Metal Eddie's and perhaps a drink or several. This is because Crash, while a first-class racing pilot of the sun clipper variety, is often strung out on various chemicals and is known on these occasions for antisocial behavior, such as sending people outside our orbiting habitat for views of Earth, Moon, and stars without proper attire for comfort. So I tell him only that they have come and gone, but I know not where. This may seem more trouble than one should care to take for the Deadboy, who, to be fair about such matters, resembles Crash himself more than a little on the matter of public relations. But my reason is not only good, it is overwhelming. Namely, my personal finances should wax and brim very soon, but only if the Deadboy remains among the living long enough to collect on a promise from that strange dark power which rules Upper Manhattan.

Donner, like Crash, had been a racing pilot who wound up fairly regularly in the money, earning along the way good returns for those such as myself who follow these matters and occasionally make a small wager. He had copped every sun clipper Classic but the Filstone Cup, and that was the one which did him in. There had long been a nasty rivalry between Donner and Crash over that race, till Donner's immune system got fried during a solar flareup two years ago, along with the rest of the entrants — it being a bad year for that sort of thing. Crash was not running on that occasion, and so he is hale. Though the next year, Donner — who had kept going on drugs — placed, while Crash did not even show. That should have been it, however, because even the drugs could not get Donner through another year and give him a last crack at the Cup. So he elected to become a deadboy.

Donner had himself frozen, which is a low-overhead operation here, merely involving closing the door and opening the windows, so to speak. His intention was to be brought around a few days before this year's Classic, and be given a temporary fix to get him through it. His experience being what it was, he was thinking this might be his year of the Cup.

But lo, long before the time he is to be roused, I begin seeing him about town. And I know something strange is afoot because he avoids me with considerable ingenuity and speedy legwork. Not that we normally say more than a few words to each other, but now even these are missing. For a Saturday and much of a Sunday, that is. I manage to be blocking his way when he comes out of a restroom on Sunday evening.

'Hi, Donner,' I say loudly then.

'Uh, hi,' he answers, his eyes darting. Then he sees a way around me, takes it and is gone, out the door and off toward Forty-second Street, where he turns, and vanishes. Could be he forgot something, I am thinking. I promise myself to ask around about him, but I do not because the next day I see him again and not only does he greet me first but, 'Did you see me anytime this weekend?' he asks.

'Only last night,' I tell him, scratching my head and wondering whether his neurology is burned out, also. But he smiles — possibly having heard of the peculiar occurrence which brought me to Upper Manhattan, where I await the running out of certain statutes — and when he tells me, 'I would like to talk to you of matters which would benefit both of us in a financial fashion, 'I am willing to give his nervous system every consideration.

Over lunch in Vindy's he tells me of his troubles as I have just related them, and I nod every now and then to be polite, while I wait for him to talk about the money. Instead, he continues on beyond the point of being frozen, '. . . And I awaken,' he tells me, 'in this place which is like the inside of a videogame, leading me to believe that I have passed on and the next world is a kind of Cyberbia. There are all these algorithms putting the make on pixels, and programs champing at bits and sub-routines moving about in simpleminded, reliable ways, as is their custom. The place is not unattractive, and I am watching, fascinated, for I know not how long. Finally, a sort of voice asks me, 'Do you like what you see?'

'At this, I am sore afraid,' he goes on, 'and I ask, 'Are you the Deity?'

'"No," comes the reply, "I am the AIity."'

'It turns out,' he tells me, 'that I am a guest of the artificial intelligence which has run our entire satellite for upward of a generation now, and while it seldom has much to do with individual people it has grown interested in me. This is because I am hooked up to a special monitoring and alarm system, designed to bring me around in time for the next race. This system does more than that, however, after the AIity tinkers with it. It provides access.

'"I have digitized you and brought you here fore a reason," it tells me. "You are interested in winning the Filstone Cup, are you not?"

'"Indeed," I reply, "and more than somewhat."

'"Would I be safe in saying that you would do anything for it?"

'"This does not sound like an exaggeration," I answer.

'"Look around you. Would you go stir crazy in a place like this?"

'I give my attention to the central precincts of Cyberbia. While I am about this, it adds, "For if you were willing to put in a little time here, I could guarantee you the Cup in this year's Filstone Classic."

'"I am taken," I reply, "by the great beauty of your operating programs, not to mention some of the subroutines."

'And that is how we come to make our deal,' Donner tells me. 'It seems the intelligence is a fan of the human condition, and has grown very curious what with having spent all these years as an observer. It has been hot to try it out for some time, but the opportunity had not presented itself till now. So when it offers to train me for its job with the understanding that I will run Upper Manhattan on alternate days while it vacations in my body, I am interested. Especially when it points out that it receives and relays all of the monitoring signals during races and could make certain that mine say I win the next Filstone Cup.'

'But your body is ailing,' I observe. 'What fun would this be for it?'

'That is another inducement,' he explains. 'It says that much could be done to improve the medication I receive while ambulant, and it will institute a new treatment program for me and buy me considerable extra time without pain. Even sparing it half of my days until the race, I will come out ahead. Then I can hibernate again after I win, until perhaps someone comes up with a cure.'

'This does not sound like a bad deal at all,' I observe. 'Especially the part about the race.'

He nods.

'This is why I tell you,' he explains. 'For I want you to manage my betting for me with some of the unregistered, off-track people such as Blue Louie, who give better odds.'

'But of course,' I tell him. 'Only one thing bothers me. Is it not hard being a stand-in for an artificial intelligence? I ask only because my life depends on the support systems.'

He laughs.

'Perhaps for some it would be,' he replies, 'but for a natural intelligence I seem to have an aptitude for this sort of business. I find myself actually liking the work, and I even modify a routine or two for the better.

'"You are not bad for a NI," the AI tells me when we change shifts and it checks over the first day's work. "Not bad at all."

'Which is more than I can say for the AI, when it comes to being human. I wake up and find it has left my body dead tired and with a world-class hangover. Most of my first day being human again is spent recovering from this. I am even feeling too crummy to call my lady, Evelyn.

'I hook up to the monitoring equipment before I go to bed that evening, like I promise. When we switch over later on, we have a little conference wherein we brief each other on the day's events.

'"Go easy on the body," I say, "for it is the only one we have between us,"

'"I am very sorry," it replies. "But this being my first time out and all, it is hard for me to judge things. I will try to be more careful in the future."

'But, alas, an AI is not always as good as its word,' he tells me. 'A couple of turns later I come back to cracked ribs, assorted bruises, and another hangover. It seems it had been drinking at Hammer Helligan's and had gotten into a fight. Again, it apologizes, explaining it is still having some difficulty judging human reactions, and saying it feels particularly badly about things when it sees what a fine job I am doing as substitute AI. Well, I am not about to back out at this point. So I tell it to go easy on the booze and other substances and I head off to work. I continue to streamline operations, realizing that if I trusted my opposite number more I would not mind running the show for even longer periods of time. But the AI gets me into enough trouble on our fifty-fifty time-sharing setup — for the following week I realize that I have contracted clap, and it is not I who have been up to anything which might result in this condition. Once more, it claims to be sorry. I tell it it had better remember to take our medication which it has prescribed, or I may reconsider our entire deal.'

'So what happens?' I ask.

'It behaves,' he replies. 'For several days now it seems to have kept our nose clean. I am feeling much better, the race is next week, I am all registered and I will be sailing *Hotshot III* to victory and glory and money.'

So I lay his bets and I lay my bets and I await the race with the honest pleasure of a man who knows that the fix is in.

Then he begins avoiding me on a steady basis. I know better than to try talking to him on alternate days, for I know that that is when the AI is in charge — and though I approach it once and it lets me buy it a drink, it grows most upset when I let it know that I am aware of its pact with Donner. Then several days pass, and the race is nigh, and Donner will not give me the time of day if 6:47 will save my life, though I see him and Painted Evelyn nearly everywhere for a time. I begin to grow suspicious, and then alarmed. Then Crash Callahan comes by and asks after them. I suspect they are at Metal Eddie's, but I do not think they will appreciate the surprise Crash represents with the bulge beneath his jacket there in the middle of the brownout, and so I shake my head.

'. . . I know not where,' I tell him.

'You do not understand,' he tells me, 'what is happening.'

'That is possible,' I answer. 'Likely, even. For this man has led a strange life of late.'

'Stranger by far,' he tells me, 'than you may think. For he is not the person he seems to be.'

'Of this I am aware,' I agree, 'though I am curious how you come to know it.

'I know it,' he replies, 'because I am Donner.'

'You look more like Crash,' I answer.

'Crash is responsible for the brownout,' he says, 'for he cannot run a power grid any better than he sails a racing clipper. It is all very simple.'

In that I do not think so, we wind up in Vindy's, where he says that he wishes to charge some elaborate dining on Crash's account. When I question the fairness of this he points out that half of the food is going to wind up in Crash's belly and the rest may be viewed as pre-race entertainment — Crash being a last-minute entry in this year's Filstone Classic.

'I do not think you believe me,' he says, 'for I am not at all sure I would. But because I desire your cooperation, I will explain. I am inhabiting the body of this lower life form because it is the only one I can get my hands on, on the spur of the moment. You would be surprised how difficult it is to find a body when you really need one. Fortunately, Crash is given to many vices. So of course I take advantage of this.'

'Even now,' I say, 'I do not understand.'

'It is very simple,' he replies. 'One day I get much on top of my work as substitute AI, so I decide to look myself up. I chase my credit trail around town. Then I set about infiltrating everything electronic in Blue Louie's Drugs, Alcohol & Electronic Vice Emporium, which of course is the legitimate cover for his gambling operation, for that is where my latest charges come from. There, through the burglar alarm camera, I see myself sitting at the bar with my lady Evelyn, who seems to be enjoying herself more than a little. This, you must admit, is a low trick, making out with my girl while using my body, perhaps not yet even fully recovered from a certain embarrassing social condition.'

Unless, of course, he catches it from her, I am thinking. For she has always struck me as a hard and calculating lady. But I do not say this to Deadboy Donner in Crash Callahan's bod, in case he feels that I do not trust artist's models and perhaps wishes to introduce me to skydiving of the orbital variety. So, 'This is distressing,' I say. 'What do you do then?'

'I fear that I let my temper get the better of me,' he answers, 'and I overplay my hand — as is sometimes the case when someone else in your body is romancing your girl.

'I cut,' he says, 'simultaneously, into the nearest speaker and vidscreen. I identify myself and then I flash upon the display field a series of circuits with slash marks through them, suggesting that I am contemplating AIicide unless it quits conning the lady. It rises and attempts to depart the establishment in a hasty fashion, an action I foil by closing the automatic door before it and continuing our conversation by means of another speaker, nearby. I suggest an immediate rendezvous at the interfacing equipment back in my apartment, failure to comply with which suggestion I will consider a breach of our contract. Then I open the door and let it go.'

'Is there not a nasty paradoxical dilemma here?' I ask.

'Oh, Blue Louie is somewhat upset with my arguing through his sound system and flipping on and off the lights, the dancefloor strobes, the blenders, the shakers, the cash register drawers, the icemaker and such to emphasize my points. But when I explain a little of what is going on and ask him to keep an eye on Evelyn for me while I deal with a welshing intelligence construct, he is happy to oblige.'

'I do not mean problems with Blue Louie,' I say, 'who is occasionally a gentleman. But it occurs to me that you cannot hurt the AI while it is in your body without harming yourself, and if you let it return to the grand system of Upper Manhattan it will be practically immortal there.'

'These are not matters I have neglected thinking over,' he replies, 'and there are more ways to deal with artificial welshers than one may suppose at first glance. I assume the AI wishes to be reasonable, however, and come to some final understanding, since we both occupy awkward positions.'

'So what does it say when you have your meeting?' I ask, for he has paused for dramatic effect and several mouthloads of chicken cacciatore, and I wish to seem interested in his problem as we are heavy betting partners as of several days now.

'Nothing,' he answers a few swallows later. 'For it does not show for the meeting. It decides to head for cover and lie low for a time.'

'This seems very foolish,' I observe, 'when it knows that you are in a position to follow its electronic tracks throughout the city.'

'Nevertheless,' he replies. 'It may feel it still knows a few tricks I do not, though it only postpones the inevitable. I locate it within a few blocks, and then I decide to come looking in the flesh — using Crash's flesh.'

'A question occurs to me,' I say, 'not knowing anyone who has ever done a hit on an AI. What happens if you take it out? I understand it coordinates everything from banking to the disposal of solid wastes.'

He laughs.

'Theoretically, this is true,' he tells me. 'However, making Upper Manhattan a smart city is actually a gimmick to balloon the rents, back when they are setting things up. Having held the job, I can tell you there is really very little to do once you get things to flowing smoothly. In fact, it is having all that time on its hands which I think caused the AI to start daydreaming of the pleasures of the flesh and results in our current problems.'

'But Crash is in there running things while you use his body,' I observe, 'and this brownout is a big pain, not to mention being hard on the eyes. If it is such an easy show to run, why is he having this problem?'

'This is because Crash, who is a jerk,' he says, 'cannot keep from fiddling with the controls. It is what makes him a second-rate pilot, also. If he would just leave it alone it would fly itself.'

'I see, sort of. By the way, how did you wind up in his body?' I ask.

'Oh, he switches from chemical stimulants to those of an electrical nature for some time before a race,' he explains. 'I discover that the brain hookup for this is sufficiently invasive to permit access of the sort the AI pulled on me in my deadboy days. So I digitize Crash while he is turning on, explain that it is a necessary borrowing and park him in Central Processing. I also tell him to keep his hands off the controls. You can see how much good that does.'

The brownout had vanished a few minutes earlier, with light-levels returning to normal, then flaring to the point where many bulbs blow. After a while, the brownout returns.

'You mean the system would be better off without Crash in there?' I ask.

'Of course, and the same can be said for most places. But I have to leave him somewhere while I borrow his rig.

'So.' he finishes, 'I know the AI is in the neighbourhood. If you believe my story, I want anything you might know on its whereabouts. If you want more ID, ask me anything only Donner would know.'

I ask him how much money he gave me to spread around on him in the Filstone, with Blue Louie and some others. In that he knows all of the amounts, and how much is laid at what odds, I suggest he check out Metal Eddie's, about which I hear the AI in the Deadboy bod comment to the Painted Lady a little after the brownouts begin.

He does not catch them at the metalman's, however. Or, rather, he does and he does not. He finds them there, but the AI departs by a side exit and leads him on a chase, both of them careless of all bodies in the vicinity as they discharge with great noise and small accuracy the weapons they have with them. A half hour of this and the AI has vanished. The constabulary is spreading its net by then, but Donner slips through before it is tightened.

It is not until that evening that I see him again. I am talking to Blue Louie about the race, startoff time for which is only hours away when we emerge from Earth's shadow and catch the solar wind, and I am speaking of the possibility of a scratch on the part of Donner, though no official mention of this has been made. I am saying that if this happens and the owners of *Hotshot III* bring in another pilot, my bet should be considered off, because I was betting on the man and not on the ship. But Louie is shaking his head and producing slips saying 'Hotshot III' with my signature on them.

About this time, the Deadboy in the Crash bod comes running in and says that he must use an electrostim helmet quickest.

'Now, Crash, do you think this is wise,' Blue Louie inquires, 'indulging yourself so close to a race and all?'

'It is not an indulgence that I seek,' he replies, 'but a bridge through the interface to a place where I can track down a weasel.'

We go to a booth in a back room, Donner signaling that I should accompany him. And I wait till he plugs in, tunes up, goes glazed in the eyes, and runs off through fields of induction.

He is gone for several minutes, then his voice comes through a nearby speaker.

'Turn it off,' he says.

I do this and he slumps. He had wanted me there for this purpose. Often, these devices are used with a timer, but he could not limit his stay in this fashion.

'Tell Blue Louie,' the bod says to me, 'to send back a brew, for I am in need of such refreshment.'

I do this, and Blue Louie comes back himself, along with Painted Evelyn, on whom he is keeping an eye and also his hands.

'Crash, it is not good for you to mix the liquid with the electric,' he tells him, 'especially this near to racetime, for you will mess up the odds.'

'Nevertheless,' the Deadboy in the Crash bod states.

At this, Blue Louie nods, gestures to Painted Evelyn and gives her a small pat on her rearmost anatomy as they depart for the front of the establishment. I see that Donner notes this, for his eyes follow, but he says nothing.

A little later, the drinks have come and we are alone again. The Deadboy takes a big swallow, then says, 'Two surprises awaited me in Cyberbia. First, I am attacked by Crash —'

'Attacked? In that state?'

'Yes, but he is no tougher there than he is in the flesh. He feints once with a digitized left, then throws a right at you, and that is all he's got.

'I speak metaphorically,' he adds. 'At any rate, he starts putting these electronic moves on me and insisting on the return of his bod, when I am there only to try running down my own. I am forced to deck him and stash him in an electronic slammer of my own design before I can continue the hunt for the AI in my bod.

'And that is the second surprise,' he finishes. 'Although I search all of Upper Manhattan in a great variety of subtle ways I am unable to turn up any trace of my kidnapped self.'

'This is most frustrating,' I say, moving to the screen on the wall nearby and fiddling up exterior shots. Predictably, most channels seem occupied with the gossamer lineup for the upcoming regatta. 'It occurs to me that if you do not get to your ship soon,' I tell him, 'you may not be ready for takeoff.'

'They will not let me in *Hotshot III* in this bod,' he states. 'But —' Then he stares at me. Then at the lineup. 'Someone is in that clipper!' he cries, as it is jockeyed around a bit. 'The AI knows the system has no senses to look into the clippers! So that is where it takes itself!'

He puts down his beer and rises.

'Excuse me. I have business to finish,' he says.

'You just said they will never let you aboard *Hotshot III*,' I tell him, indicating the insert of the advancing terminator and the digital countdown beneath it. 'And there is very little time, anyhow.'

'Then I run it down in the *Redhound*,' he says, pointing to Crash's ship, adrift at its moorings. 'For no one can keep me off of that one.'

'But, Donner,' I say, 'what will you do if you catch it?'

'I will make it pay,' he replies.

Then he rushes out.

In the days that follow I attend to the screen with the attachment of a lamprey to its rock. The race goes on for the better part of a week toward a distant multipurpose satellite which also serves as finishing beacon. There, the racers are met by a number of con-ac skipjacks which convey them home in great haste, the clippers being collapsed and drawn back by tugs. I am mainly concerned that Donner, in his rush to run down and play back the AI which has stolen his bod, may win the race in *Redhound* thus costing us both. But surely and even so, he would not be so foolish as to kill the AI, I tell myself — despite his bod being pretty much used up — and face homicide charges for doing himself in.

It seems an incredible dead-heat finish, from the pictures that come in from a camera on one of the skipjacks. But its monitoring is complicated by the fact that *Hotshot III* suddenly tacks to starboard in terms of the ecliptic and *Redhound* does the same near at hand as if trying to crawl all over the other vessel.

Maintaining a certain rigidity of attitude, *Hotshot III* crashes into the satellite buoy. *Redhound* fires a line, changes tack after it connects, veers off, then drops sail. It fires its small emergency braking jets then, a disqualifying act if on the wrong side of the finish line. Two of the skipjacks maneuver in that direction on their ion motors, but a spacesuited figure is already crossing on *Redhound*'s line toward *Hotshot III*, which, I am fairly certain, reaches the buoy somewhat after *Redhound* passes it.

The cameras never show what happens following the entry of Deadboy Donner in the Crash bod into the wreckage. We lose the picture during a blackout which follows amid multiple systems failures which are largely attributed to sunspots. Later, however, comes the official announcement that Donner has brought *Hotshot III* in first, shaving a bit of time from the record while about it. Unfortunately, he is not available for the victory dinner, as he perishes at the finish line in the process of colliding with a buoy. He will, however, be refrozen, flat EEG or not, since he is officially a deadboy anyway and his bill is paid up for cold quarters.

So, when I see Donner in the Crash bod to pay him the money he has made by betting on his Deadboy bod in *Hotshot III* under the direction of the runaway AI, he is with Painted Evelyn, who gives me a smile, with which she is usually sparing except when she wants something.

Then I ask Deadboy Donner in the Crash bod what happens out at the buoy, and he tells me that he gets there too late for retribution as the AI has patched into the satellite's broadcast system and transmitted itself back to Upper Manhattan. He is not up to abandoning both bods there in a damaged clipper to pursue it, so his revenge must wait upon his return to town. When he gets back, however, and finally has a chance to check out the system, there is no AI — or NI either — running the show. It is as deserted as Miss Blooming Orchid's establishment following a raid. Even Crash Callahan is gone. 'I do not understand this any more than I understand how *Hotshot III* came out in the Winner's Circle,' he says, 'when *Redhound* was clearly ahead at the finish line.'

'But for this part we should be thankful,' I say, 'for we collect on all our bets.'

'True,' he replies. 'But I am the actual winner of that race.'

'And that is what the record shows,' Painted Evelyn says. 'Deadboy Donner wins the Filstone Cup.'

'I do not complain over this,' he says, 'though it is an odd way to do it.'

At that moment Painted Evelyn allows as she could use a brew, and Donner disengages his hand from hers and goes to fetch one for her. She studies me then.

'You know?' she asks.

I nod.

'Partly, it is the business about the times,' I say. '*Redhound* comes in first. Then you change the record, for it does him more good that way. You, too, since you are with him now. What I do not understand is why.'

'I might just say that we had a deal, and I am only keeping my part of it.'

'But there is more to it than that. Like why does he find the system empty, and why are you here? And where is Crash?'

'Crash is no more,' she replies. 'He gets free of the knots Donner ties him in, and when I come back he jumps me. As he is trying to do me in, I return the compliment. I crash Crash.'

'Then why are you not back in the place where you are impregnable and powerful and —'

'But I wanted the flesh,' she says, 'though I do not realize my mistake right away. Then I see that I would much rather be a woman than a man. This is why I am seeing Painted Evelyn so much at first. I learn quickly that she might be interested in life in the system. Donner, who has an aptitude for this, seems attracted to people of a similar sort.

'And vice-versa,' she adds.

'You mean . . .?'

'Yes, I am here because I have a crush on him, and Evelyn

dwells in silicon castles, reviewing the troops binary-stepping by, building up personal trust funds. . . .'

I nod.

'She always was a calculating woman,' I say. 'But why is it Donner does not detect her presence when he visits the system on his return?'

'I move her out temporarily.'

'Where to?'

'Donner's Deadboy bod,' she says, 'which is hooked up to its monitors by then, and deserted.'

'That clears up many details,' I say, 'and almost satisfies me.'

'So, we would both appreciate your keeping this to yourself,' she says, 'until I find the best time and the best way to explain matters to Donner.'

'You are still in touch with her?' I ask.

'Oh yes. It is easy to reach her,' she says, as Donner rounds the corner bringing their drinks.

I must say that Painted Evelyn does a much better job than Crash Callahan in the AI business, for we have had no more brownouts, shortouts, or switched calls since she took over. It is good, too, having gotten her private number for the AI, so that I can call her every now and then, until such time as the AI levels with Donner. For I have had two big winners so far this month, and she is about to give me my third.

IAN WATSON

Ian Watson lives in a small Northamptonshire village and has published 20 novels and four collections of short stories. His first story was 'Roof Garden Under Saturn', published in *New Worlds* in 1969. His first novel was *The Embedding* (1973) which won the French Prix Apollo and was runner-up for the John W. Campbell Memorial Award; his second was *The Jonah Kit* (1975) which won the British Science Fiction Award and the (one and only) Futura award. His other novels include *Deathhunter*, *Chekhov's Journey* (which is not a *Star Trek* novel!) and *Under Heaven's Bridge*, co-authored by Michael Bishop. Another of Watson's collaborations is *The Woman Factory*, written with his wife Judy. This novel has only been published in France, under the title *Orgasmachine* (1976).

He had three new novels published in 1988: *Whores of Babylon* (sf), *The Fire Worm* (sf/horror) and *Meat* (horror). 1989 is an unusually quiet year for Watson, with only one new book due for publication: his fifth collection, *Salvage Rites*. But the year will see publication of his hundredth short story.

The following story, says Watson, 'was stimulated by thoughts about the Renaissance art of memory and by going into a sensory deprivation tank in San Francisco, where I also discovered the cure for jet lag. Rome was the first foreign city I ever visited, when a schoolboy of 15 or so. I didn't meet the Pope.'

THE FLIES OF MEMORY

by

IAN WATSON

Maybe it was snobbish of Charles, but he had always hated cameras, especially those in the hands of tourists. A dog peeing against a palace wall was acting sensitively; it was leaving a memory of itself. But how often did camera-toting tourists really *look* at anything? So how could a photo truly remind them?

When Charles was a boy he began to choose memory places for himself. There was the local cemetery: chestnut trees, bluebells, and marble angels. There were the sand dunes at sunset: spiky marram grass pointing thousands of fading sundial fingers seaward as if the world was splintering with hair-cracks. He would vow. 'I'll fix this scene. In two years, ten years, I'll remember this moment exactly! Myself, here, now.'

Of course he hardly succeeded; maybe that's why he resented cameras. Yet a chain of such magic moments had linked his life. (*And who is remembering him, right now?*)

Here he was in Scotland keeping another thread of his faith, with his widowed father. En route back to his academic seat at Columbia University from the Geneva arms talks he had hired a Volvo to tour the Highlands. He owed the old man a decent holiday so that Mr. Spark senior could revisit his sentimental sights and taste some good malt whiskies in their native glens. Charles also wanted a quiet time to think, about madness and Martine.

Scarcely had father and son started out than the alien Flies arrived on Earth. 'We have come to your planet to remember it,' so they said. Broadcasting, in stilted English and Russian, their requests to tour all the world's cities, the pyramid-ship settled gently into the Mediterranean offshore from Alexandria and floated, base submerged, not drifting an inch.

The unfolding news reached Charles via newspapers and TV in remote hotels. His father objected to their listening to the car radio.

'It's worse than a bloody election campaign,' the old man groused as they were admiring Loch an Eilein. (Look: a solitary heron standing stock-still waiting to stab; jackdaws flapping over the castle ruin on the island.) 'Blather blather. Most of it, sheer guesswork. Wait a few weeks and we'll know what's what.' Mr. Spark was worried Charles would cut short their trip.

Mr. Spark never used to swear until his wife died in a car crash — which wasn't the old man's fault, though he wouldn't replace the car. 'Where should I go on my own?' he'd asked sadly after the funeral. Charles's parents had driven all over the Borders and Highlands with a consuming passion. Now Mr. Spark had taken to smoking a pipe, and swearing. You might have surmised that an anger rankled in him, and that a pipe was a substitute spouse. But Charles perceived that tobacco and rude words had been suppressed in his father many long years ago, although drams of whisky had been permitted. At the age of seventy-five Mr. Spark's behaviour was fraying round the edges, a genteel net curtain in decay.

As they were rounding the Pap of Glencoe, Mr. Spark exclaimed, 'Bloody ugly, that's what!' For a distorted instant Charles thought that his Dad was talking about the looming peaks of the glen. Grim, those were, though sunlit. Then his father went on, 'Wouldn't want to meet one of your Flies on a dark night! Oh no. Nor would anybody in their right mind. Maybe your Martine might fancy doing their portraits. Just up her street, I'd imagine.'

Mr. Spark had reason to be anxious. By now Charles had made several transatlantic phone calls from hotels to leave word of their itinerary. Already a week had passed and UNCO had been cobbled together, the United Nations Co-ordination Committee steered by America and Russia. Charles wanted to be in on this, and hoped he had sufficient clout and contacts. Already a thousand Flies had spread out from the floating Hive, and the Grand Tour had commenced in Cairo and Kyoto, San Francisco and Singapore, London and Leningrad and wherever else. Who would deny creatures which could fly a huge interstellar pyramid the way these aliens did? Who would not want to learn the secrets of their success?

'Look, son,' said Mr. Spark after a while, 'hordes of folk will all think they have special reasons for rubbing shoulders with these monstrosities. Why fuss on, when the buggers are going to be visiting everywhere? Bloody *invasion*, if you ask me. You'll see a Fly soon enough. Will we ever see the back of them? That's what I wonder.'

Charles nodded, unconvinced.

'Look!' His father pointed at the sky.

It wasn't a Fly up there.

'Eagle?' Charles asked.

'Don't be daft. That's an osprey. Rare, those are. Almost extinct. It's going fishing in Loch Leven. Look at it. You'll likely never see another one.' (*And I see it now, in shadow. Better than he did. Oh yes.*)

A few minutes later Mr. Spark was puffing contentedly, telling his son about the massacre of the MacDonalds. On his own terms the old man was good company, though really he and Charles had drifted worlds apart.

Charles's reputation was founded on his first book about body language, *The Truth of Signs*. Soon he was being retained as a consultant by defense and aerospace as a kind of walking lie detector. This led to his kibbitzing on the arms talks on behalf of the U.S. government. His next book, *Signs of Passion*, was his pop success.

Charles had a heightened sense of body language. If he couldn't ever record a chunk of scenery to his full satisfaction, he could read body signals and facial cues with an animal instinct. Not that he didn't need to *work* at this, scientifically; but let's not weigh ourselves down with talk of proxemics and kinesics, all the jargon of non-verbal communication.

You might think this would have immersed Charles in other people's lives as in a crowded jacuzzi, a hot tub of humanity. Not so. Old Eskimo saying: when you rub noses, you don't see the face. When you're watching the face, you don't rub noses.

Another week passed. By Rannoch Moor, to the Braes of Balquhidder to the bristly Trossachs. During convivial evenings spent with his Dad over a glass or several of ten-year-old

Glenduffie, Charles caught TV pictures of individual aliens in Rome, Edinburgh, and he strained to read significance into their gait, their stance, their gestures . . . and those blank, insect faces.

The topic of Martine cropped up again at the Trossachs Hotel. Martine had been a sort of alien, too.

'At least there was no grandchild,' remarked Mr. Spark. 'Just as well, in my opinion.'

A daughter-in-law who was part black, part brown, part blue for all he knew! Why should Charles have waited years and then married such a person as Martine?'

'Not that you ever met her,' Charles said mildly.

'Why should *I* put myself out, an old chap?'

True, Martine wouldn't leave her one secure root in Greenwich Village. Charles had met her at a gallery opening just three months after Mrs. Spark's funeral. Within ten weeks he and Martine were married, and he had moved from his apartment off 116th Street into the Village for the next four years. When the break-up came, Charles returned to Upper Manhattan.

Loud tipsy Glaswegian talk babbled about them in the hotel bar. A stuffed golden eagle regarded visitors maliciously through glass eyes from inside its case.

'Maybe you ought to have had more children than me,' Charles suggested, 'and had them earlier.'

'Costs money, son. You should know. Good schooling, Cambridge, all that. There's the trouble with education, makes you want the world on a plate. Ach, it's water under the bridge. Let's enjoy another dram.'

Returning from the bar, Charles was aware of his father regarding him lovingly: his only son, big-boned and hardy-handsome, as the poet had written. Burly, though not tall. Shock of brown hair, already thinning at the crown. Broad, fresh, open face, with some crumpled laundry creases around the grey eyes. Generous lower lip, and thin mean upper lip which might have benefited by a moustache; but Charles hadn't wanted to copy his Dad, who had always worn a tash. A loving look could betray a glint of bitterness which a glance which was merely affectionate never contained.

'A plague of bloody Flies from space,' sighed Mr. Spark. 'Who'd have believed it? Cheers, lad.'

Was there a weepy in the old man's eye? In Charles's heart salt tears stirred. The dead eagle's eye also glinted. At least that was an earthly eye.

None so blind as those who rub noses! As Charles finally realized, Martine was mad. Crinkly chestnut hair, hazel eyes, milk chocolate skin, slim as a boy with breasts, melting and assertive, wiry-tough and sensuous-soft; hermaphroditic! On first encounter Charles read her signs of passion. Perhaps *she* thought he held a key to human behaviour, something which she illustrated only in faery or devilish parody. Perhaps Charles knew the secrets of true expressions, a secret partly withheld from her.

In his lovely dark wife several persons cohabited, carrying out one psychic coup d'état after another. She was an artist in pen and ink, illustrating books and magazines. She drew inhabitants of a nether Earth, a population of goblins and nymphs which seemed to inhabit her, as subjects of her various ruling persons. These signaled out of her drawings with their fingers and their eyes, drawing Charles to her inexorably so as to understand those strange body signals.

Her art was always black and white; and flat without full perspective. Highly effective work — stunning — yet it seemed as if she lacked stereoscopic and colour vision, because — because her elements would not fuse and co-operate. She was several flat people stacked side by side, each of them vivid in its stance, seen frontally. Each person seemed full of so much, yet let them tilt sideways and there were only two dimensions to them, with edges which could cut cruelly. Meanwhile a different Martine came to the fore.

She could never draw ordinary human faces — her rage when she tried to sketch *his*! Yet when she invented the features of a troll or elf or imp, oh yes, that's how those creatures would be; that's how they would express their alien feelings. At the height of his passion Charles wrote a preface for a book of her drawings entitled *Alien Expressions*, though she never drew 'aliens' as such. The body language of her imaginary beings was human body language distorted in a hall of mirrors as if it had followed an alternative path of evolution. Or else distorted in a personal madhouse.

Martine originally came from New Orleans, and was of wildly mixed ancestry. Perhaps this explained — to her! — her fractured self. Her brother Larry, a weather man down in Louisiana, was a regular guy. His only turmoils were natural storms, your ordinary sort of hurricane.

Ah, Martine. If Charles did undertake a new book to be called *Signs of Madness* — researched in clinics, illustrated by eighteenth and nineteenth century engravings of the inhabitants of Bedlam — might this seem an impeachment of Martine, a revenge? In turn might this make *Signs of Passion*, written while they were living together, appear to have been an exploitation of her?

Charles had hoped to sort this out in his mind while in Scotland; till the Flies came to Earth.

They took a steamer cruise on Loch Katrine. Eyeing the rumpled, lovely woodlands, Mr. Spark talked of Sir Walter Scott and Rob Roy. The Glaswegian trippers nursed sore heads so the outing was fairly peaceful. Father and son were only a stone's throw from the fault line between Highlands and Lowlands but they stayed in the former, plunging that evening in the Volvo downhill to the toy town of Inversnaid by Loch Lomond, to another Victorian hotel, and more malt of the glen. As a final ferry departed the little harbour for Inverglas across the loch, Mr. Spark stared at the summer sun setting.

'Just look at that golden whisky light falling on Ben Vorlich!' he exclaimed. 'Remember it always — before it goes away!'

'When I was a boy,' Charles started to say. He had never told anyone about his magical memory moments. Did his Dad also know about memory-photography? Had Dad seen a certain look in his son's eye?

A Scots voice interrupted, 'Is there a Charles Spark in the bar? Telephone!'

By helicopter the next day from the hotel lawn to Glasgow, thence to Rome in a Lear-Fan executive jet. A chubby, genial

American in his thirties, Lew Fisher, was Charles's courier; he had even brought a driver to Inversnaid to return the Volvo and Charles's father to the other side of Britain.

Why Rome? No less than eight of the aliens were flitting about Rome; no other city rated more than two Flies. UNCO was paying special attention to Rome.

Why the sudden V.I.P. treatment for Charles?

Orders.

Whose? Lew talked instead during the flight about anti-gravity. Not only could the aliens steer something twice the volume of the Great Pyramid at Giza, but each was using a personal flying pack. Those whirry little wings couldn't support their body weight, let alone zip them along at jet speed. After the first week or so the scouts flew back non-stop to the hive — even from the other side of the world — then returned to wherever to continue sightseeing.

'Repulsion machinery,' said Lew, 'that's the theory. They're using the fifth force in nature, called, um, hypercharge. When we measure hypercharge it's gentle. Tiny. But our eggheads guess there are actually two extra forces involved, um, Yukawa terms, that's the name, both of 'em *big*. Only, one is attractive and the other's repulsive.' ('Like the Flies themselves,' Charles could hear his Dad mutter.) 'So those almost cancel out. Well, the Flies have figured how to nix the attractive force, letting them tune the repulsive one. That may give them a force-field too. Deflect interstellar debris.'

Lew was clearly no physicist. It was already plain to Charles how the CIA and KGB would be operating within UNCO, doing their best to be Cosmic Interstellar Agency and Kosmic Galaxy Bureau, both fishing for the secrets of the Flies.

Then there was the communication problem. Was the aliens' use of English and Russian *deliberately* poor? Their own lingo of whistles and chirps was uncrackable.

The bottom line: what was their game?

'The sun's going to blow up? They know, but we don't?' mused Lew. 'They've guessed that we might wipe ourselves out? Shame to lose such a neat civilization totally. Let's remember it, guys. Or is "remember Earth" a euphemism for shoving us aside? Meaning that we'll be no more than a memory?'

'Maybe they're the first interstellar package tour?'

'Without anything you'd call a camera? Just staring at things?'

'That's the way to see a world.'

Lew cocked an eyebrow, then shrugged. 'Welcome aboard the puzzle wagon.'

He ran a videotape for Charles. Behold those sleek bodies, plated with a chitin so deeply blue it was almost black. Around the waist between thorax and abdomen the tool belt certainly included a powerful radio and location beacon. Consider those dome heads with the hairy ears and the twitchy moustache feelers and those big bulgy faceted amber eyes.

A Fly had six skinny hairy black limbs. Its arms ended in jointed claws. Its hind 'balance' legs were short, its abdominal legs four times as long. When a Fly hurried, its body pivoted up on to those long legs till it was almost horizontal, little legs wagging like rudders. That was how a Fly sometimes launched itself into the air; but the wings were undoubtedly science, not biology. Perhaps the ancestors of the Flies once had wings, which withered as the species evolved; now Flies wore wings again, re-invented.

'They can't be true insects,' said Lew. 'Anything that size needs an internal skeleton. They breathe like us. Yeah, breathe our air, and eat our food — though they're like flies in that regard! Prefer the trash cans of restaurants, not the haute cuisine inside. They could inhabit this planet quite happily, Charlie.'

Charles was to stay at the American Embassy in the Via Veneto; and on arrival Lew ushered him in to meet the regional security chief who was UNCO liaison man, name of Dino Tarini, an Italian-American.

Tarini, mid-forties and scrawny, wore an impeccable cream silk suit and did not blink like other people, irregularly, inconspicuously. He stared — then once a minute or so he shuttered his eyes briefly as if he were some human surveillance camera making a time-lapse record of what went on. His high-tech desk and leather chair were backed by framed photos of Michelangelo's David and the Statue of Liberty looking strangely like brother and sister.

'Carlo, you eyeball some sights with Lew today. Try out Santa Maria sopra Minerva. A nun's showing one of the Flies round this afternoon. Interesting church, Carlo. It's Dominican. Dominicans ran the Inquisition. Grand Inquisitor's statue's there. They prosecuted Galileo in the convent next door. Showed him the thumbscrews.'

Tarini plainly resented the way a string had been pulled on Charles's behalf and had a low opinion of the relevance of body language. (*By whom had the string been pulled? Ah . . .*)

The following morning an UNCO bull session was scheduled at the Farnese Palace, which housed the French embassy: neutral territory, thus to underline international co-operation.

'French don't swap intelligence with us or the Soviets; whereas Italians allow our missiles on their soil, don't they?' As venue Tarini would have preferred an Italian government building staffed by his cousins.

'Tomorrow evening: reception at the palace. Try to talk to a Fly, Carlo. Why do they go back to the Hive?' Find out. Prove your worth.

'Maybe they get homesick,' said Charles.

Tarini closed his eyes, recording the witticism.

'Yeah, and maybe there's a queen-fly roosting in there, a great black squashy mass that was full of eggs. Maybe she hatched all the other little Flies while the ship approached; programmed all her sons.'

'You don't sound as though you like them too much, Don Tarini.' Yes, give him the title of a Mafia godfather.

'Some things about our visitors we like very much.'

Questions hung in the air. Did the Hive have defenses? How to find out non-disastrously, whilst also laying out the golden credit card from Kyoto to Copenhagen, the red carpet from Berlin to Odessa? The road to the stars lay open; but Flies crowded it.

'Will they share their knowledge with us if we're *nice* to them?' Tarini was lying.

Rome was aromatic with the scent of flowers, coffee, olive oil, whiffs of unfamiliar tobacco, mixed with puffs of exhaust fumes and drain stench. The whole hot, humid city — streets, pavements, walls — droned a faint mantra. Hum-om-hum.

After catching beers and mortadella sandwiches at a bar beyond Trevi, Charles and Lew played chicken to cross the Via del Corso. Their destination was a piazza where a marble elephant supported an obelisk carved with hieroglyphs. The beast stood on a plinth, knitting its brows, its trunk slung rearwards as if to squirt dust. What big cabbage-leaf ears it had, pinned back in the sculpture. The area between Jumbo and the scabbed cliff-face of the church of Santa Maria above Minerva was cordoned by police in dark blue, cradling machine pistols. Several hundred spectators, including newsmen and paparazzi slung with cameras, waited for a sight of the alien.

Showing their UNCO credentials, the two men were admitted into the chill of the church, where blue marble geometry inset a white marble floor, highly polished. Black marble pillars, flecked pink, lined the nave. Curving medallioned groin-vaulting supported a star-studded imitation sky. A multitude of side chapels . . . any description of this church was a cartoon! Ten thousand sentences couldn't capture every detail in remembrance.

Down at the transept half a dozen UNCO people were scrutinizing a chapel, from which a soft clear voice emerged. The chapel was graced by a statue of a pope and a fresco of an angel with blue swan's wings half-furled. Watched by cloaked prelates a dove spat golden fire at a kneeling Madonna. In front of this painting a lanky young woman in a long blue frock, her flaxen hair peeping from under a blue headscarf, was patiently addressing . . . the very opposite of an angel: a five-foot-tall black Fly, mosaic eyes clamped to its head like swollen golden leeches. Now and then the woman touched her necklace, of variously sized turquoise beads, a chain of little blue moons.

'Here in the Carafa Chapel you see the Annunciation as painted by Fra Lippo Lippi . . .'

'Yes,' the Fly responded in a dry, rattly, jerky tone. It seemed to be drinking in every detail of the chapel as thirstily as Charles had ever stared at a scene when he was a boy. He sniffed but could detect no alien odour, only wax polish and candle smoke.

'The nun's Dutch,' whispered Lew. 'Outfit called Foyer

Unitas, specializing in guiding non-Catholics. Very much in depth. They can gab on half a day about a single church.' As indeed the woman seemed intent on doing.

'They hope to convert non-Catholics, aliens included?'

'No, they're simply ace guides. Got the right pace for the Flies, who look at everything for ages.'

The two men followed the guided tour around till Charles knew more than he ever needed to know about Santa Maria sopra Minerva.

Lo, here is the tomb of Saint Catherine of Siena. There is the very room where she died in 1380, frescos by Romano. Lo, here is the chapel of Saint Dominic housing the tomb of Pope Benedict XIII, sculpted by Marchioni between 1724 and 1730. The Dutch nun fiddled inconspicuously with her necklace while she talked.

'Yes,' the Fly said periodically.

That evening, Lew took Charles to a trattoria he recommended. Superb sea-food ravioli in garlic butter followed by a delicious concoction of lamb brains, and home-made ice cream. A friendly Chianti, then some fierce Grappa. Charles still wondered who had called him to Rome but didn't wish to lose face by asking outright.

The Farnese Palace was built like the noblest of prisons, its windows facing upon a dark, majestically porticoed courtyard into which rain poured that particular morning. In the crowded conference room Charles soon spotted Valeri Osipyan. In Geneva at the arms talks the KGB psychologist Colonel had been accompanied to begin with by a fat old woman aide (his peasant mother?), then later by a sly wisp-haired fellow whom the Russians claimed was a chess master, only no one had ever heard of him.

In their own fashion the Russians were deploying scrutineers of human behaviour to follow suit the American lead in non-verbal, nuance interpretation of the talks, and the negotiators. How could one ultimately *trust* the other side? That was becoming a question almost as vital as warhead verification — to Charles's mind at least; and he as a British expatriate might have added, 'How do you trust your own side?'

The vinegary, purse-lipped Colonel was a hard one to read. At a reception in Geneva Osipyan had inquired with apparent sympathy how it was that Charles hadn't correctly read the body language of his own wife, with whom he had so recently split up? Western colleagues were listening. Was this said to undermine Charles's credibility? To demonstrate the depth of KGB information? Was it a subtle warning not to let a possible prejudice colour his readings of the honesty of Irina Kovaleva, the new Soviet negotiator who happened to bear a certain resemblance (skin colour excluded) to dear, wayward, hysterical, ultimately hateful Martine?

Charles had replied. 'Now that we've begun taking body language seriously I can imagine negotiators being kept ignorant of the full, true picture by their *own* side.'

'You can be too subtle,' Osipyan had retorted. 'We're a bluff people at heart. Basically blunt and frank.'

'Bluff has another meaning.'

'Nowadays we always tell the simple truth. You hunt for subtleties to worm yourself off the hook of peace.'

'A hook catches the unwary prey.'

'Women sometimes catch men by hiding their hook in a lovely lure, Mr. Spark.'

'Did your grandmother tell you that? It *was* her who was with you last year?'

Osipyan had smiled tightly. No, the Soviet truth-sayer had not been his grandmother, or mother.

Now here was the Colonel in Rome, facing Dino Tarini across the huge oval table as some forty UNCO personnel sought their name cards and settled down. Others took refuge in armchairs scattered about the room, made notes, consulted files.

An hour later, an Italian biologist was saying, 'The aliens *look* identical to flies. Like insects they display industry and persistence. Do they have true individuality? Are they genuine intelligences?'

'To remember is to be intelligent,' Osipyan said. 'Besides, they talk to us.'

'After a fashion! Maybe they have developed awareness to a remarkable degree . . . for insect types. Powerful instincts may still rule them, far more than we are ruled.'

Tarini nodded. 'What if they're really biological machines? With eyes which are lenses, brains which are recording equipment? Why shouldn't they fuel themselves with any garbage? Why should they have *taste*?'

'Taste enough,' said a Vandyke-bearded linguist from Rome University, 'to admire the masterpieces of our culture.'

'Indiscriminate cataloguing. Like auctioneers.' There was scorn in Tarini's voice. 'It would be interesting to know if they can reproduce, or if they're just specialized living machines. Now suppose one of them crashed in a regrettable accident —'

'No,' said Osipyan. 'A large floating pyramid says no.'

'A pyramid we can't see inside of.'

'Compound eyes oughtn't to see as clearly as *our* eyes,' the same biologist declared.

'Depends how the brain is programmed,' said a French colleague. 'Surely they must have a single central brain, not different ganglia spread throughout the body like insects? Let's forget the insect analogy.'

'A dissection could settle these questions.'

Osipyan pouted at Tarini. 'People may play dirty tricks with one another, because we know the rules. To play these games with aliens is the height of folly.'

'Perhaps it's the height of naïvete not to? You Russians are so romantic about aliens.'

Charles found himself speaking. 'The Flies look at the sights with a relaxed intensity. With those compound eyes they're seeing more intensely than any human tourist. A machine would simply record. They're not just cameras. I'm sure of it.'

Osipyan swung round. 'So, Mr. Spark, in your view does landing a pyramid, which dwarfs the Egyptian pyramids, quite close to those same pyramids serve as a gesture of cultural solidarity — or as a caution that their power and technology likewise dwarfs ours in the same proportion?'

Charles shrugged, having no idea. If he was a violinist of human nuances, he was being asked suddenly to take up playing the trombone or the tuba; an alien instrument.

The quirky tilt of Osipyan's chin and the droop of his eyelids said that Charles was admitting inability. Yet Charles wasn't the prime target for the Colonel, whose glance glided onward to Tarini.

'We need to discover new rules,' the Russian said, 'not the same old ones. Why should aliens play our games? We need to know the simple truth about them.'

'They aren't exactly spelling out their motives,' grumbled Tarini. '*Remember*: what does that mean?'

Something, thought Charles, which was so much a part of their nature, of their biological existence, that the Flies could be blind to it — as a peculiarity which might baffle strangers.

Lew had detailed a marine guard from the American embassy to act as gumshoe. After a leisurely beer and sandwiches in a café following the bull session, Lew consulted a two-way pocket radio and set out with Charles for the church of Sant' Ignazio half a mile away.

Sharing a large umbrella, they walked till they reached the fringe of the mobile carabinieri cordon which accompanied a Fly when on foot. No alien anywhere in the world had yet been attacked or threatened — perhaps no fanatic could think of a good reason — but police protection certainly gave a Fly some open space to sightsee in.

By now the rain was slackening off, but after hours on the streets, even under an umbrella, the waiting marine was soaked. As had the nun been, he reported; however, once she reached Sant' Ignazio a priest had turned up to deliver a change of clothing and footwear. The Italian-speaking marine had heard the man in the soutane explaining to the police that he brought these dry clothes from the nun's base in the Pamphili Palace, Piazzo Navona. Rain merely rolled off the Fly.

The slow tour that morning had taken in the Pantheon and Piazza della Rotunda. At lunchtime, the nun had steered the Fly along the Via Monteroni to sample French colonial pig-swill from the dustbins of *L'Eau Vive*, followed by a trip inside that restaurant — housed in a sixteenth century palazzo — so that the sister could have a decent bite too.

'You've done good. We'll take over.'

The marine departed gladly.

'Damn stupid conference,' muttered Lew. 'Couldn't have been worse timed.'

'Why's that?' asked Charles.

'A visit to the Vatican has just been arranged — very likely.'

'By the priest who brought the clothes? He was a go-between?'

'No, listen, Charlie, that restaurant *L'Eau Vive* is where all the Vatican bigwigs dine out. It's staffed by stunning young nuns with a special dispensation to wear sexy dresses.'

'Sounds risqué. What goes on?'

'Just splendid expensive eating. The waitresses all wear golden crosses to remind their eminent clientele of chastity. Could put cardinals off their cuisine and vino if it was served gloomily.'

'Remind them of poverty?'

'Something like that. They still need moral ladies to serve them. That's where the princes of the Church hang out; and that's where she took the alien. Obeying orders, I'll bet. Vatican must be pretty stirred by an alien race turning up. Haven't spoken out yet. No Flies have visited there — to see the finest sights of all.' Lew shilly-shallied. 'I have to split. I'm going to talk to Dino. We'll see if we can get a list of reservations at *L'Eau Vive.* Will you keep a close eye on the sister while you're Fly-watching? She's called Kathinka.'

Lew offered Charles an umbrella escort through the ring of armed, rain-caped carabinieri to the door of Sant' Ignazio.

'The Soviets might pretend to be pussy-footing, but what is the Vatican up to? There are at least six Machiavellis on the staff.' He fled.

The Fly was staring up at the ceiling with rather more than 'a relaxed intensity'. The alien seemed perturbed, under strain, as if controlling an urge to unfurl its wings and zoom up to the heaven-painted dome to accompany Saint Ignatius Loyola on his journey direct to Paradise. If so, it would have banged its head. This only dawned on Charles as he heard Sister Kathinka (crisp and dry) point out to the Fly how cunningly the real building flowed into its painted continuation.

The dome was a trompe l'oeil, an eye-deceit, an illusion of

art. The work of the Jesuit priest Andrea Pozzo shortly after 1685. Hats off to Fra Pozzo! No one had bothered to build the planned cupola, consequently he had painted it in. The illusion was extraordinarily convincing; the alien gazed at it for the best part of an hour. Even Sister Kathinka exhausted her repertoire and stood mute. Meanwhile Charles had been joined by other UNCO spectators, amongst them that Italian linguist with the beard, who frowned at the continuing silence.

At long last the Fly came to terms with the spectacle overhead, and turned to the nun.

'Yes, yes, like our tanks.' Briefly the alien seemed to float, buoyed up.

Professore Barba scribbled in a notebook. 'It *likes*,' he murmured. 'It *thanks* the sister.' Charles had heard something else entirely.

The Fly again addressed the sister, who had perhaps lost track of the tour.

'Memory vanished? Because heaven is false?'

The nun touched her necklace as if for reassurance.

'This painted heaven is not the true heaven,' she replied. 'I have told you all I know about the ceiling.'

'No more is known about Saint Ignatius?'

'Oh yes! Why, there are whole volumes written about him. They fill shelves in the Vatican Library.'

'Volume is cubic size?'

'Books!' Sister Kathinka led the Fly to the lectern, where a huge brass-bound Bible lay open.

'Here is the most important book. It contains the word of God.'

The Fly tapped the pages with a fuzzy claw. Its moustache quivered.

'This Bible is in Latin,' explained the sister. 'That's the old language of this country. The language is dead, but it still lives in the Church, just as Christ is dead but still lives.'

At that moment two facts became intuitively obvious to Charles. The nun had been encouraged to explore the possibility of converting the aliens to Christianity. Secondly, this alien had no idea of the function of a book — what it was! The aliens possessed no written language.

Mightn't that be the case with a sufficiently advanced race? Even on Earth the electronic tide was submerging literacy. People of the super-science tomorrow could easily be illiterate. And yet, and yet . . .

The dining room of the French embassy was a welcome antidote to the severe aspects of the Farnese Palace, a gush of gaiety sensuously decorated by the Caracci brothers with the Triumph of Love. Four of Rome's Flies were present at the event.

'Charles Spark? I'm Olivia Mendelssohn. Head of White House Security. President's personal representative. We'll be working together, you and I.'

'We will?'

Olivia was short. The crown of her head came level with his chest, and Charles was no giant. She was mid-thirties, perhaps shading forty. Charles recalled her face from earlier in the conference room, though that morning she had seemed intent on remaining inconspicuous. Previously, her black hair had been roped in a tight ponytail, hadn't it? Freed now, it swept luxuriously around bare shoulders of a light buttery hue. Olivia was dressed in a glittery gown of darkest blue instead of — what had it been before? — a grey jacket, skirt, and ruffled white blouse.

With a vague nod Lew melted away into the crowd.

Earlier, Olivia Mendelssohn had worn dark glasses. Now her eyes were naked. And huge. They were large brown liquid eyes in any case, but she had enlarged them further by applying kohl. Her smoothly oval face was of generous enough proportion — just — to accommodate such eyes. Was she trying to attract alien attention by that gown which copied the colour of their bodies; by those enormous eyes?

Her legs were shorter than her face or trunk or bosom merited. The evening gown molded those legs together into a stumpy mermaid's tail glistening with scales, upon which she perched. Her shoes — expensive, black-dyed crocodile skin — pointed apart, somewhat like the fork of a tail. Hans Anderson's Little Mermaid had summoned Charles to Rome!

'We'll need to be fully open to each other, Charles, in order to osmose your talent and mine together.'

'Yours being a talent for security?'

'For something else too! Here isn't the place or time . . . we'll have to be franker than any barbed insights of Colonel Osipyan into your failed relationship with Martine.'

Charles blinked. 'You seem to know me inside out.'

He collected a glass of champagne from a passing, duck-tailed waiter. Olivia barely moistened her lips with an orange juice. Amidst the throng of French embassy staff and other foreign diplomats, Italian government ministers, UNCO personnel, several churchmen in black soutanes and stiff white collars, a lone nun in a black habit, and of course four aliens, a cardinal stood out: a stout tropical bird in his scarlet cassock, cape, and biretta. To Charles at that moment little Olivia stood out much more.

'Your Martine,' she said, 'was a pool of emotions in which you could fish but not swim, or sail. On account of sudden storms. The spouts, the maelstroms. She was so fluid, so labile, wasn't she? That was why you couldn't read her, fix her nature.'

Tilting her head, Olivia stole a glance up at the sumptuous ceiling; and Charles thought to himself, 'The Failure of Love. For me. Not the Triumph.'

'Ultimately,' continued Olivia, 'Martine shook herself apart; and you too. She broke the banks, so far as you were concerned. You had hoped to be those banks, confining the pool, framing it like a setting for a rare jewel. She wasn't a jewel, though. She was . . . dissolution . . . a persona written in bitter if sparkling water, inhabited by toads as well as by such wonderful, delicious, slippery fish.'

This peculiar conversation — her side of it — captured Charles even more than the presence of aliens in the room.

'Professionally I plug leaks,' she said. 'Nowadays we need an enormous leak — from the alien side. Any signs of moisture yet?'

With an effort Charles hauled his attention back to the matter of Flies.

'Yes, I believe they're illiterate.'

'Aaah?'

'I don't think they know what writing *is* — letters or squiggles or dots or hieroglyphs.'

The alien guests were all drinking in details of the room while a number of UNCO mavens and dignitaries side-stepped like so many geosynch satellites, keeping out of their direct field of vision. Each alien held a glass of whitish liquid. A glass was emptied; a waiter suavely furnished a full one. As the waiter shimmied by, Charles stopped him.

'What are the aliens drinking?'

'Sour milk, Signore.' The man made a face. 'Seven days old.'

'You have Egyptian blood,' Charles said suddenly to Olivia.

It was those eyes of hers, so vastened by the dark cosmetic! Perhaps aping some Renaissance princess she had even put drops of belladonna sap in those eyes to dilate them?

'My Mom was half-Egyptian,' she agreed. 'And my Dad, half-Jewish. Should we try to talk to a Fly?'

So they headed towards the nearest alien, though Charles concentrated on Olivia's body language as much as upon the Fly's. On the whole she walked fluidly and loosely. Once, twice, she stiffened momentarily. He wondered whether she had ever suffered a dislocated hip; whether as a child she had even undergone some experimental bone-stretching régime in an effort to increase her height. Underneath her gown would residual scars on legs and thighs betray where metal pins had pierced through to her skeleton? No, that was absurd. He merely wanted an excuse to undress her. She seemed to be offering herself to the alien, using some body speech of her own concoction, yet at the same time resisting, flinching.

'Good evening!' She stared the chosen Fly full in the eyes. 'Do you like this city?'

'Yes.' That rattly voice. 'I remember it.' The voice of a husk: sticks, hairs rasping together, no liquid music of vocal chords. Gazing at its mouth parts — a sort of black beak around pursed softness — Charles imagined the alien sucking him dry, discarding him as a human husk. He smelled the curdled tang of the sour milk in its glass.

I remember it. Unless the Flies were masters of invisibility they had never visited Rome before, Renaissance or ancient or in-between.

'What do you do next?' Olivia asked.

'Fly back to ship, dis-gorge.' Its short legs, then its long legs, twitched. Charles visualized bees returning to a hive, their hairy legs yellow with pollen. In the hive the dust from many flowers becomes the honey that nourished — what?

'Do you disgorge in a tank?' he asked it.

'Yes.' Japanese people were notorious for saying 'yes' when they merely meant that they were listening politely.

'What kind of tank is that?'

'Tanks of memory.'

Thanks for the memory. . . . Charles hummed this tune to himself. The Fly's moustache bristled. Could Tarini be right, that the aliens were biological recording machines which returned to be unloaded, emptied for the benefit of some other creature, hideous to behold?

Yet this Fly seemed informative. While onlookers avidly eavesdropped he asked:

'Do your eyes see many images of the same object? We see one image.'

It looked into his eyes. 'Yes, many objects, in order, to remember.'

'What is in those tanks?'

'We. We float.' As in that church, momentarily this Fly appeared free from gravity.

'How many tanks?'

'Thousand.'

A pyramid full of tanks . . . and floating flies, emptying themselves . . . what did it mean?

A burly Russian, perspiring in a suit which looked to be woven of material half an inch thick, joined in chaperoned by Osipyan.

'Comrade Starman, please! Did your ship fly here by the force of repulsion?'

The Fly stared at a lustre-hung lamp, the crystal facets glittering and twinkling. Answer came there none.

'Have your people visited other inhabited places in the cosmos?' the Russian persisted.

'Yours first to signal presence to us. So we came.'

Pleased, the Russian was visibly calculating to himself light years and the chronology of radio and TV output from the Earth.

'Just in time,' the Fly added, unnerving Osipyan.

'Why did you truly come?' the Colonel demanded.

'Our world is full,' was the reply.

'Full, of Flies?'

'Our places are fully remembered. Here are new places. Do you remember all your places? Have any disappeared?'

'Places disappear if you don't remember them?' broke in Charles.

A jerk of the Fly's head.

'We must leave,' it said. Draining the clotted dregs, it handed its glass to the Russian scientist who cradled it as though it were an alien artifact. 'Thank for hospital. Ity.'

Olivia smiled graciously. 'You must fly. After you dis-gorge, what next?'

'I start to remember Vatican City. Goodbye.'

Charles had realized by now that the nun in the room was the same Sister Kathinka. Her flaxen hair was entirely hidden by her coif and white wimple, and she wore a long black pleated gown, with a cross dangling on beads from her waist. She had reverted to habit. Accompanied by Olivia, he headed over to this woman he was supposed to keep an eye on.

'I don't know how you find the energy, Sister. A walking guide-book! Hour after hour must be a strain.' (Please don't say that you find the strength in Jesus or Mary!)

When Kathinka smiled, she showed perfect white teeth which she must brush often.

'The standing is the hard part.' Her breath was scented with mint. 'One has to learn poise. Actually I practise ballet exer-cises. When I was a girl in Holland I wished to be either a ballet dancer or a religious. Those are both similar callings, you know! Dedication, rigours of the body, aim of grace. But.' Glancing at Olivia, she fell silent.

'You grew a little too tall,' Olivia completed. 'Your choice was made.'

'By God.'

'Do you need to look official this evening?' Charles nodded

at her black garment.

'No, it occurred to me that I have been wearing the wrong clothes to put my aliens at ease. Now I resemble them, a little.'

They chatted about her work.

'The . . . *choreography* of each tour takes much attention, so that nothing is forgotten, so that no fact disappears.'

Had the Fly meant that people might forget bits of history, and thus lose the true depth of things — which could fade from awareness?

'Do the aliens regard you as remarkable?' Charles asked her. 'Being able to disgorge so many bits of information, all in the right order?'

Many objects. In order. To remember.

'It isn't remarkable, Mr. Spark. All the objects are there. The information hangs upon them, as upon this.' She held up her chain of beads. 'Bead after bead. We tell our beads. Likewise, while I guide.'

'Your necklace!' Charles exlaimed. 'The turquoise necklace.'

'You noticed that? Yes, it's my mundane rosary. I do not often misplace a fact.'

Olivia gazed intently at the nun. 'Each fact is a private prayer.' She stated this as a certainty. 'Your whole day is a chain of prayers — on behalf of your heretic or infidel tourists who never realize how slyly they are being blessed.' Olivia jerked her face in the direction of the ceiling. 'Somebody painted those erotic scenes in the year whatever. Bingo, another prayer is said!'

A mischievous smile played about the Dutch woman's lips. 'Annibale and Agostino Caracci, between 1597 and 1604. There, you are blessed with information! This is the information age, isn't it?'

'You use those beads as your abacus, a medieval instrument, a harking back.'

This made the nun frown and almost turn away. Hastily Charles intervened.

'A Fly told us it's going to visit the Vatican. Will you be guiding it?'

'It. Or another.'

'You're much in demand.'

'If asked, I obey.'

'Is the Vatican visit the reason why the cardinal's here tonight?'

'Cardinal Fantonetti? Of course he would be here. He is the vicar-general of Rome.' No, that particular cardinal had nothing to do with trips to the Vatican, which was another city, another country.

'Do you know all the cardinals, Sister?'

'How could I know the Cardinal Archbishop of Calcutta, or of Guatemala, or of the South Seas?' She knew more, much more, than she was saying; or was allowed to say.

'Do you bless the Flies too?' pressed Olivia.

'As you say, Mr. Spark, it is a strain. I must return to our order's house to pray and sleep.'

Charles recalled the address. 'I know the Piazza Navona isn't far, but will you share our car?'

Surprise that he knew.

'Thank you, I prefer to walk. Alone, to bear the streets in mind. Dressed like this, I'm perfectly safe. A nun owns nothing worth stealing.'

'Nothing but knowledge.' Olivia's voice slurred. 'The knowledge which blesses the streets, so that they aren't forgotten and don't disappear.' Her eyes were glassy as if she were drunk, deeply drunk.

The Vatican Press Office had announced that when the aliens arrived in St. Peter's Square in three days' time a trio of cardinals would be on hand to greet them: Borromini, Storchi, and Tedesci.

'According to the reservations at *L'Eau Vive* Tedesci and Storchi both lunched there.' Lew explained that the former was Vatican Secretary of State, the foreign minister; which made sense. The latter headed the Secretariat for Non-Believers; fine so far. But Borromini, the odd man out, was in charge of the Apostolic Penitentiary.

'That sounds like the Vatican Jail.' Olivia's tone was relaxed, as if she owned Tarini's office.

'It handles questions of conscience —'

'It's the Inquisition!'

Tarini shook his head. 'No, that's the Sacred Congregation for the Doctrine of the Faith — and it deals with heresy. You got to be a Christian first before you can be a heretic. The Penitentiary covers sorcery, black magic, demons, forces of darkness. Its boss didn't invite the Flies, but he's in on the act when they turn up.'

Olivia laughed half-heartedly. 'To decide if they're kosher or a spawn of Satan?'

Tarini rubbed his fingers thoughtfully. 'The Church isn't simple-minded. Vatican's probably facing a crisis. Do aliens have souls? Is the Church truly universal? Why do Flies home in on Rome?'

'Will they have an audience with the Pope?' chipped in Charles. Tarini was calculating something . . .

'The Pope's at Castel Gandolfo,' said Lew. 'His summer palace. That's usual. Got an observatory there. Maybe he's consulting his astronomers.'

Tarini dangled a red herring. 'Jesuits, those are. Jesuits aren't too popular with the hierarchy. Excessive support for Reds in Latin America.'

Charles leaned forward. 'This Penitentiary might view a horde of Flies as possible demons?'

'You become an expert on demons, you see demons everywhere.' Evasive Tarini.

'There's always the terrible third prophecy of Fatima,' said Lew helpfully — to Tarini's annoyance.

'Who's she?' asked Olivia.

'Not she. A place in Portugal. The virgin appeared to some kids in 1916 and predicted the two world wars —'

'The first one was halfway through in 1916!'

'Yeah, well, don't blame me. The third prophecy was locked in the secret archives till the Sixties. Only a pope could read it. The first pope to do so almost fainted with fear, so the story goes. Maybe the prophecy's about aliens. About the Devil infiltrating from the stars.' Lew grinned boyishly; the idea was a joke to him.

'Do you believe in a real Devil?' Charles asked Tarini.

'I'm a good Catholic, Carlo. We aren't talking about me.'

'Maybe we ought to?' Olivia knit her brow, but Tarini stared back expressionlessly.

If Olivia had been going to explain to Charles about her talent for something else, she must have decided that the time still wasn't ripe. They spent the next couple of days watching Flies watch Rome, while Romans watched the Flies. Two of the resident aliens had flown back to their hive after the reception; they would disgorge, prior to seeing Vatican City.

St. Peter's Square, grand keyhole to Vatican City, was closed to traffic, but how could the heart of the Church be closed to pedestrians? Leaving the embassy car in the Via della Conciliazione, Charles and Olivia and Lew joined a stream of spectators flooding into the square.

This was another hot bright cloudless day, though some wisps of breeze ventilated the city lazily. The entry of aliens into St. Peter's could prove epochal; some revelation might be at hand.

'Oh my God,' groaned Lew as they crushed over the white line of the international frontier to encounter — perhaps not chaos but a situation which was as fluid as boiling water.

Were eighty or a hundred thousand people in the piazza already? Romans, countrymen, tourists, nuns and priests, hucksters, pickpockets, what a medley. A pair of Swiss guards in harlequin costumes surveyed the inflow. Olivia, in dark shades, stared at the Switzers: their technicolor tunics, their baggy pants, their boots striped blue and yellow with red flashings, those cute little white ruffle collars, the big slouch berets shading one eye and muffling one ear. The guards were armed with pikes, the perfect medieval weapon.

'Those guys in charge?' she asked incredulously.

Lew was craning his neck to see beyond the mob, the obelisk, the spuming fountains. TV cameras peered between the baroque statues of saints atop Bernini's colonnade.

'No, there are hundreds of Rome city cops and carabinieri. Crush barriers up front. Ah, I spy the Vatican Vigilance too! The muscle in drab blue. I guess there'll be plainclothes cops scattered through the crowd.'

'Why are you worried?' asked Charles, as they forged forward, breaking a way through for Olivia.

'Well,' said Lew, still peering as he pushed.

'What's wrong, security-wise?' Olivia demanded.

'Just, *hundreds* of police . . . isn't much use. When the Pope appears they station ten thousand cops in this square. What are they playing at? Low profile? What did they expect? News has been out for days. We'll be okay once we get through.' Lew tried to sound reassuring.

'Who's pulling the punches?' she asked. 'City of Rome? Communist mayor, right? Or is this Vigilance of theirs turning a blind eye?'

'I don't know, Miss Mendelssohn. It looks okay, but it isn't.'

At that moment a rift opened in the throng through which even Olivia could see ahead to the great façade of the church with Michelangelo's dome rising behind. She gasped and stumbled against Charles, who gripped her arm. She wasn't panicking because she felt like a child in a hectic mob; that wasn't the reason.

'Too much blue sky! Where's the Capitol?'

'In Washington, D.C. Not here,' said Lew. 'Are you okay, Miss Mendelssohn? A crowd like this could make anyone faint.'

What did Olivia mean? Charles held her around the shoulder but she firmed up and thrust ahead, patting at the chiffon headscarf she'd worn in case they needed to enter the basilica.

Behind the guarded steel barriers, amidst a minor retinue of priests and the occasional nun, the three cardinals waited in full pomp though some distance apart from each other, perhaps for security, perhaps politically. Microphones stood planted like bishops' croziers.

The spry, white-haired oldster was Storchi, his particular brief non-Christians and Marxist atheists. Tedesci seemed a jovial bon viveur, to whom gold-rimmed spectacles lent a scholarly air: sanguine scrutineer of menus, men, and monarchs of the world. The youngest cardinal, stout and swarthy with jowls of deepest blue where his scrupulously shaved flesh denied the bursting forth of beard, was Borromini, the connoisseur of darkness. Sister Kathinka waited near him.

Once admitted through the cordon, Lew wandered off to talk UNCO business. Charles and Olivia joined the Dutch nun.

'Will the cardinals bless the aliens?' he asked the nun. From behind her shades Olivia was staring at Borromini lasciviously as if undressing him. Frowning as he gazed at the cloudless sky, the cardinal paid no attention.

Sister Kathinka touched a finger to her lips, kissing silence, amidst the hum and hurly-burly rolling from the waiting crowds. The mob was oozing tighter against the barriers as the piazza filled behind them, even bulging through and around like hernias of humanity, for the barriers by no means formed an unbroken line across the square. A concerned Swiss guard moved forward, gesturing with his pike as if to stir a pudding. A policeman motioned with his carbine.

'Borromini isn't thinking of blessings.' Olivia's voice had slurred. She squirmed as if in that bright sunshine a cold worm had wriggled down her spine. 'It's like Dino said: is a Fly person, a moral intelligence? Could a Fly understand the crucifixion or the virgin birth? Could a Fly become a priest? Could a Fly be martyred and become a saint? If not, then does the Church embrace all? Could a Fly be a cleverly designed temptation? Maybe the Devil, reigning in the frozen empty void which is so like Hell, has at last created a mockery of life . . . these Flies, first demons to dare the daylight. He's ambitious, this Borromini. . . .'

Yes, Charles could see that. Olivia was simply improvising on what Tarini had said, wasn't she?

No, more than that.

'Powerful,' she murmured. 'He's been ruthless. No Sicilian has been pope for a thousand years. Does believe in actual demons. Yet of honourable conscience. Night of prayer, take this burden from my shoulders . . .'

Much more!

'Apocalypse creeps close. Imps are out of Hell. Of course Flies show no expressions on their faces, or else we might recognize the evil grin. What if *these* doubts are a temptation — to reject a blessing of communion with alien souls, to circumscribe the Church and lose so many? Disastrous to make the wrong decision. Take this burden, night of prayer, give me Your wisdom.'

Staring at Olivia, the Dutch nun crossed herself. Olivia relaxed as if she had been stroked by the gesture.

Italian voices cried out. The crowd seethed. In the sky two black flecks of Flies were approaching, high, shadowed at a safe distance by a couple of police helicopters.

Artificial wings a-flutter — steering wings? — both Flies came in to land in the open space, bounding a few paces on their long legs before lowering their little hind legs and furling away those black-membraned wings. How like a pair of devils from a medieval painting of Hell. Borromini's left hand was thrust down by his side, thumb clasping middle and ring fingers, index finger and little finger sticking out. Charles recognized the Manu Cornuta, the 'horned hand' sign for warding off the evil eye, familiar to peasants.

While Tedesci, as foreign minister, greeted the Flies in English, his voice amplified by microphone and loudspeakers, the aliens stared at the monumental colonnade.

'They must approve,' confided Sister Kathinka. 'Well ordered columns, each labelled individually with its own statue. That makes them easy to remember, doesn't it? It's like Guilio Camillo's Memory Theatre on a grand, true scale.'

'A memory theatre?' repeated Charles.

'Ah, that was a sixteenth century scheme. Camillo built a wooden amphitheatre representing the universe as he saw it, full of astrological images and little boxes stuffed with writings about everything under the sun, and beyond. Your orator stood up on stage and, well, Apollo's image would trigger a speech about the sun. That was Camillo's idea.' Her right hand fluttered, as if to cross herself. 'It was occult. He thought he could exploit the mechanisms of the universe, magically. But the King of France got tired of funding him.'

One Fly bobbed up and down; it couldn't see well enough because of all the people. Tides of crowd were spilling around the far edge of the barrier. The Swiss harlequin trotted off to bar the way with his pike.

The other Fly took note of Tedesci.

'Here,' it croaked. 'is your God focus, yes?' The alien voice rattled from the PA speakers. 'It is large. But limited. Your God forgets you, yes? Your God is sick. Remember the world!'

A collective gasp arose, then a noise midway between a groan and the throaty growl of a cat. As Tedesci opened his mouth in simple affront, or about to be diplomatic, that Fly's wings whirred out. It rose ten feet into the air, to hang gazing at the basilica: the columned portico, the loggia windows, the balcony from which popes blessed city and world, those stone giants looking down into the piazza — Christ, John the Baptist, the Apostles. Then the Fly rose much higher to see the drum and cupola of the dome behind, topped by golden ball and cross.

What a mockery of the Ascension, or of the Holy Ghost hovering. People hastily crossed themselves. The crowd's growl deepened. They had seen the aliens landing from the sky like little living helicopters, yet now the levitation of this Fly appeared miraculous. This was a black miracle, something out of the Apocalypse occurring in St. Peter's Piazza. Slowly the Fly drifted high overhead towards the church.

'Basta!' exclaimed Borromini. As he turned to follow its progress, his two flexed fingers stabbed downward in nervous spasm. Or was that a signal?

Pausing, the Fly seemed to lock eyes with the bearded, cross-wielding Christ on the parapet. It sank downward so as to alight on the steps of the church.

'*Bestemmia!*' a voice cried in the front of the crowd. Hundreds of other voices took up the call. '*Bestemmia! Bestemmia!*'

Blasphemy. Thousands of voices, a flash fire of fury.

The Roman mob surged. Barriers were climbed, thrust between, circumvented. Men raced to intercept the Fly, to ward it off from entering St. Peter's. Screams, cries, the rattle of gunfire — as surrounded police discharged their weapons into the air. Other police and Vigilance dropped back to form a tighter cordon around the reception party and the other alien, but no one tried to break through to attack it. On the steps the Fly disappeared in a scrum of rioters.

A long thirty seconds after the brawlers reached their target, a flashing white explosion ripped out the heart of the riot on the steps. Bodies, bits of bodies, were hurled out disgustingly. The Fly beside Charles cried out with a noise like a football rattle. Ambulance sirens, police sirens began to wail.

It took a while longer before anyone as close to the basilica as Charles or the cardinals realised the greater horror, the awful mystery of that morning. Already the crowd behind the fountains and the obelisk were pointing, moaning.

An UNCO delegate had been listening to Vatican Radio's English language commentary. Tearing his earplug loose, he turned up the volume on his transistor set.

'. . . the cupola of St. Peter's has *vanished.* The dome is sheered off, obliterated. It simply no longer exists. The Church of Rome stands open to the sky!'

Hearing this, Cardinal Borromini sank to his knees and prayed — to be forgiven?

Olivia and Charles spent the afternoon in bed together in his room at the embassy. A good place to work at body language? To begin with they were busy forgetting the morning's events; then they were remembering amidst the rumpled sheets. Charles had shut the drapes across the extremely tall windows, but Roman summer light still filtered through.

'I'm psychic, Charles,' she told him. 'Mainly I see shadows of the past, staining a person — just rarely a shadow of the future. When I saw Borromini I saw his shadows. When we talked to the Fly at the reception . . . it was so ordinary, that Fly, that's the main impression I got. Ordinary.'

'A regular Fly.' Charles thought of Martine's brother; and Martine. Was Olivia also crazy? The idea of someone so close to the American President using the Third Eye in matters of security struck him as capricious and unsettling, though not wholly incredible. Had she any influence over actual policy?

'If insights occur strongly enough —' on the psychic Richter scale! '— I let them guide me. I've always been right. I was right about you and Martine, wasn't I?'

'Mmm,' he said. 'Does your government know about your psychic gifts?'

'The First Lady knows. She fixed my appointment. A few years back I sketched the shadow of her success. Her husband's future success.'

'She was visiting a carnival? You used a crystal ball?'

'No, darling. I was into political projections. Trend analysis, I was damn good at it, and not mainly because of glimpses of the future! Those are rare and fleeting. On that occasion I glimpsed her shadow and mine in conjunction, so I opened up to her. She consults me about who to appoint. I see the shadows of possible scandals, shadows of dark secrets. I did glimpse my own shadow in Rome beside yours. I made arrangements.'

So he had been called to Rome because a psychic had glimpsed him in Rome.

'Took a while to discover who you were, Charles. I didn't see you with a name badge pinned to your chest.'

She drew her leg across his naked thigh, rotating to face him. It was a short but shapely leg, with no surgical puncture marks. Her thick black pubic hair tickled his flesh, exciting him, reminding him of Martine. Was Olivia massaging him erotically so that faith in her body might persuade him to accept her hidden paranormal parts too?

'We complement each other, Charles, you see.' A hand strayed over his belly. 'Body speech and the inner eye. Between us we cover both bases.'

He held her hand to stop it from straying further as yet. So as not to seem unfriendly he tiptoed a couple of fingers around the palm of her hand. He traced that palm-map in which, for him, there was nothing to be read.

'Was it an alien weapon?' he asked. 'Used in retaliation for the death of the Fly? A long-distance precision disintegrator aimed at St. Peter's from the hive off Alexandria, hmm? Does your insight tell you that?'

Her huge eyes stared at him from so close by, and she shook her head.

'Something else. Cosmic, dangerous. I saw it in that shadow of the Fly who survived. It knew. Of course the explosion on the steps was the alien's power pack blowing up when —' She hesitated.

'When Borromini signalled his pious mobsters for a rough and ready exorcism to expel a black devil from the high priest's temple.' Charles made the sign he had seen, and explained.

'Ah. Yes. Ambitious Cardinal Archbishop of Palermo, home of the Mob.' She stretched like a cat, rubbing against him, and drew a corner of sheet idly over her crotch as a soft pointer, which also concealed.

He squinted. 'You're covering up. Temporizing. I thought we were supposed to be naked to each other.'

'I'm not certain about the responsibility for the death.'

'It wasn't Borromini, was it? It was Tarini's Mafia contacts. Just like after the war, when Italian Americans liberated Sicily and put all their gangster cousins in charge! They're still around, those cousins. They were trying to tear the Fly's wings off, steal them. Maybe rip the Fly open at the same time, film its entrails with miniature cameras. Bump off the witness, dissect it simultaneously. How neat, how surgical. Did they start the riot or just seize advantage?'

She propped her cheek upon her hand. 'I can't swear Tarini was responsible. Not yet. His shadow's remarkably tangled. He's certainly an unscrupulous snake, with shady connections. Just how many scruples ought he to have in his job? Suppose he was up against terrorists? Maybe he didn't intend the Fly to be harmed. Then the power pack blew up. Maybe the attack was spontaneous. Superstitious hysteria. It was too chaotic for me to see.'

'Which leaves Borromini?'

'Any mixing with the Mafia would be fatal to his Church career. But . . . he *would* have mobilized the faithful against a demon if that was his diagnosis.'

'So it was Tarini.'

She sighed. 'Yes, I suppose.'

'Never mind who. You don't think the Flies used a disintegrator ray?'

'A target vaporized by a laser doesn't vanish as if it never existed. There's smoke and debris.'

'So it was a *cosmic ray*? Is that what you sense?'

'I sense you,' she murmured, and mounted him, no fused-tailed mermaid now.

Afterwards, Charles walked alone up the Via Veneto to the gardens of the Villa Borghese. On those shady lanes underneath the umbrella pines, by one of those coincidences which aren't, Valeri Osipyan bumped into him.

'A shocking and barbaric crime, eh, Mr. Spark? You must have heard me veto any such violent folly. What happens soon after? Well, the Vatican have radioed their regrets, likewise the Italians. Pah! Fancy having a foreign enclave run by a conspiracy of priests in the middle of your capital city.'

'Do you have many spies in the Vatican, Colonel? Do you ever groom a young communist to act Catholic, become a priest, and rise?'

'Now there's an idea, a red pope! We'd have had to start planning it back in the days of Lenin practically. How many pretend-priests would we have needed to be on the safe side? Enough to prop up the whole East European church!' Osipyan was showing a witty, fanciful side; he was attempting bonding with Charles.

'The Vatican asked what happened to the top of St. Peter's. "Can we have it back, please?"' The Russian laughed sharply, 'Oh, not in so many words. The hive replied, "Maybe is fortunate more of fine city not lost, since two of us remembering." Did the aliens use a weapon, I wonder?'

'I can't imagine what sort.'

'Ah, so you've been told by someone that it wasn't a weapon! Who would that be? Olivia Mendelssohn, perhaps? She's an odd one. How odd *is* she incidentally?'

'Cardinal Borromini comes from Mafialand. When the Fly declared that God is sick, he made this sign.' Charles imitated the Manu Cornuta. 'The sign to banish evil. Swiftly followed by murder.'

'You're trying to throw me off the trail —' As if to demonstrate, the Colonel caught Charles's elbow and forced him off the path. However, bicycles were bearing down swiftly and silently. When the riders passed, the two men walked on together as if by agreement.

'Sister Kathinka, the Dutch nun who guides Flies, was a go-between.' Charles mentioned *L'Eau Vive.* Would that satisfy Osipyan? He felt an urge to do so. Hell, they were all supposed to be collaborating. Pooling information for the common good. And Osipyan hadn't behaved like Tarini.

Water gleamed ahead. Rowing boats with green canvas half-awnings plied a lake, on the far bank of which amongst trees and bushes a little temple fronted the rippling, sparkling water. With its four-pillared portico and a few statues perched on its roof, the temple looked like a bonsai version of St. Peter's, dwarfed for a prince's back garden.

'An alien who is "remembering" dies violently,' mused the Russian, 'and a little part of the city disappears. What did your lover tell you about *that*, Mr. Spark. And how does she know?'

'Do you have bugs in embassy beds?'

'Won't you tell me, for humanity's sake?' Osipyan was smiling as if they were two old friends out for a stroll. The strange thing was that he wasn't dissimulating. Just then, in the Borghese gardens, Charles and Valeri were indeed two old acquaintances enjoying each other's company.

'It would be noble to confide in me. If need be, I could offer asylum. Though it's mad to live in an asylum, isn't it?'

Would Olivia perceive in Charles's shadow how he had snitched on her?

'Daren't you tell me, Mr. Spark, because there are few secrets from Miss Mendelssohn?' Charles upgraded Osipyan's sensitivity level considerably. 'That tells me something, oh yes. In my country we have several such people. They're promising, though erratic. Do you recall the fat old lady who was by my side during the arms talks? And the so-called chess master?' A confidence, indeed! 'How perturbing that there is one such in the White House. What did Miss Mendelssohn perceive about the chunk of church vanishing?'

'Cosmic danger,' Charles admitted.

'Ah.' Osipyan grinned tightly. 'A mystic may sense that. That's what is dangerous about mystics when they're in power. We had our Rasputin, with the Czarina in his clutch, and the Czar in hers.'

Charles found it hard to envisage Olivia as a female Rasputin to the First Lady. Maybe Osipyan's sense of history was keener than his.

'These days in Russia we try to approach such mystical powers scientifically. I believe in *this* world, don't you?'

Charles nodded. In the world, and the body.

'A country run by mysticism might launch Armageddon against an alien starship if they believed it held an Antichrist. A few hydrogen warheads ought to smash through any force field, right? Pity about the radioactive tidal waves swamping the Nile delta.'

'I'm sure nobody's thinking along those lines.'

'I'm sure that some Think Tank is running all possible scenarios! Alas, a nuclear attack would destroy all the wonderful alien technology, wouldn't it, Charles?'

Intimacy, from Valeri.

'The Flies mustn't simply go home and rob us of their knowledge, must they? Think Tanks will be spinning spider-webs. Tarini may have had authority for his opportunistic violence.' Osipyan thumped his palm with his fist. 'Oh why did the Fly have to mention God? Are they no wiser than us?' The Russian seemed genuinely upset.

'Maybe they've been hearing too much from their guides about martyrs, crucifixion, the inquisition, Lord knows what. The pain, the blood. Hell and the Devil. Worse than your Gulags. Maybe Christianity seems sick.'

Osipyan brooded. 'What does "God" mean to a Fly? It may mean . . . a power, a force. Yes, a force. Perhaps an extra force in nature, or beneath nature behind the scenes. Our physicists say that atomic particles may "remember" and be alert to distant events. There might be a universal information field of some sort — with a memory of all previous events in the universe. Naturally I'm interested in information fields. Imagine being able to extract information at a distance!'

Was Osipyan joking?

'We do that all the time,' said Charles. 'It's called looking.'

'Imagine being able to retrieve information about past events.' (*As Olivia did — from her shadows? Aha.*) 'Imagine that the cosmos itself has a memory, which is accessible to us. I'm sure you and I could collaborate more rationally than a collaboration with . . . a witch.'

Yet not, thought Charles, more delightfully. In the long run he might be wrong on that score. And Olivia was only an on/off witch.

The Colonel hurried off in the direction of the Piazza del Popolo, and Charles returned the way he had come, his mind reeling.

'Carlo! We've just heard. The Flies are going to shift the hive.'

'To Rome,' said Olivia.

'Lake Albano,' Tarini corrected her. 'That's fifteen miles away. They want water to hover in. Maybe they suck up water for fuel.'

Castel Gandolfo was beside Lake Albano, wasn't it? Was it tactful to moor their pyramid opposite the Pope's summer house?

'Vatican has no say,' explained Tarini. 'It only controls the papal palace and villa. Italian government agrees. Prestige!' Prestige for Tarini too . . .

Charles still felt a sense of rapport with the Russian. 'At least that should rule out any nuclear strikes.'

Tarini looked furious. 'Don't even *joke.* Who would want to nuke the first aliens ever to visit us?'

'I suppose there wouldn't be many souvenirs left over. But who would want to tear the wings off a Fly?'

'That was hysteria. The thing looked like Beelzebub advancing on St. Peter's. What it said about God, well!'

'Exactly. Are the Flies homing in because they think the Pope's our God-on-Earth?'

'Albano's a crater lake,' said Lew. 'Castel Gandolfo's high on the rim. His Holiness won't be overlooked much.'

Olivia had been shading her eyes as if struggling to see shadows, future-flashes.

'It's because of the dome and the death,' she said softly. 'The Pope living by that lake is a coincidence. Nearest lake to here, isn't it?'

'Sure,' said Lew. 'Lake Bracciano's a lot bigger but it's another ten miles. If that bothers creatures who fly to Kyoto and back!'

'What about security?' asked Olivia. 'There'll be such crowds around the lake.'

'Italian army.' Tarini grinned. 'UNCO can mount all sorts of snoop equipment round the crater.'

Seen on a giant TV monitor at the Farnese Palace, the spectacle of the pyramid ship in motion was surreal, like Magritte's flying mountain. The grey mass sailed upright through the air surrounded by a rainbow shimmer as of oil on a sunlit puddle. It slowed, it hovered, it settled. A few hands clapped appreciatively. Most UNCO people stared in silence. They were definitely *the* team now.

'The mountain has come to the Pope,' said Osipyan sourly, 'since Mohammed wasn't available.'

Charles glanced at the Russian and shook his head. Not to the Pope.

A quibbling discussion broke out as to how to monitor the water level.

'We'll use lasers,' promised Tarini.

'What if it rains — ?'

'You program your computer for rainfall, run-off, evaporation —'

'If the Flies put back what they use —'

'Look, the old Romans built a fugging huge underground tunnel a mile long to regulate the water in Albano. If *they* could work it out — !'

Half of Rome and vicinity was trying to reach Castel Gandolfo, choking all available routes. When the Italian army finished deploying its check-points to seal off the area, police could begin to untangle the traffic. A permit system was being introduced, which Charles could well imagine in operation. '*Of course* my cousin's mother-in-law lives in Castel Gandolfo! She's a sick old woman. I must visit her to take a last photograph!' The Vatican announced that it likewise had a right to issue travel permits, to its extraterritorial territory.

Out of the various little 'ports' of the pyramid several Flies had already departed towards Venice or Vienna or Bangkok. Others were returning to their relocated base. Tarini produced a graph of the number of Flies on board subsequent to the first exodus. On the assumption that there had been exactly one thousand aliens to begin with, this crew tally could rise as high as a hundred; sometimes the number dipped to ten.

En route to Castel Gandolfo in an Agusta helicopter Tarini remarked that Ciampino airport was having its work cut out controlling air traffic over the Alban Hills.

Olivia warned. 'Don't think of staging any mid-air collisions to test their debris deflectors.'

'If only we knew!' he enthused. 'We could open up the solar system within years. Colonize Mars. The new Renaissance; think of it.'

He viewed himself as an unappreciated hero, a Prometheus, a Klaus Fuchs, an Oliver North.

'That's right,' said Olivia. 'You could become a security chief. On Pluto.'

Threats wouldn't deter him. History would vindicate him.

Seen from the air, Castel Gandolfo and surrounding countryside looked as busy with humanity as if the Pope had invited eight hundred thousand people and all their relatives to visit; never mind roadblocks. Actually, according to Lew, the hall in the park to the rear of the papal palace, built for mass audiences, could accommodate eight thousand souls. The park was almost empty; it must be shut. Inside that park bulged the Vatican observatory.

The palace fronting the central piazza of the pretty little town — four wings of palace enclosing a courtyard — was modestly stark in contrast with the baroque church which dominated the east side of the square abuzz with people and vehicles. Lew pointed to the papal villa in the distance, Villa Barberini. A crowded panoramic road circled the crater, dived to the lakeside, and spurred back to a larger town. Trucks and trailers spouting aerials and dishes were stationed at strategic viewpoints. As the hovering helicopter swung slowly on its axis, rising from the lake they saw the alien pyramid.

This transformed the scene into some Central American or Mexican delirium. Charles imagined not Jesuits but Aztec priests boating out to the pyramid, to climb to the top and tear out human hearts. Such priests would have required grappling irons on long ropes to hook into the ports. Notwithstanding, the mountaineers might have skidded helplessly on that moiré shimmer, that iridescent lustre.

'The energy field doesn't stop Flies from passing into the ship.' Tarini peered through binoculars. 'Wonder if that sheen would flash into action if some intruder tried to get aboard?'

'Disguised as a Fly?' inquired Olivia.

'Yeah, somebody of short stature,' he said insensitively. 'I guess Flies' limbs are a bit thin to imitate.'

'Not to mention them having an extra pair. A dwarf acrobat in a Fly suit? You have got to be joking.'

'Maybe there's a recognition signal. None, and you get stunned or fried. Again, maybe not.'

The Agusta landed just outside town where a couple of Lancias waited to chauffeur UNCO passengers. Olivia preferred that she and Charles roam on foot.

'I had a flash,' she whispered. 'I saw us both in the piazza. I'm picking up more of the future than ever before.'

The Piazza del Plebiscito was packed. Queues stretched from cafés. Hucksters hawked souvenirs. Ice cream vendors pumped out cones. Here was the world and his wife, and his celibate brother and sister of the Church, and his military cousin. A couple of Swiss Guard commissionaires stood outside the summer palace.

And out of its entrance walked Cardinal Borromini dressed in a simple black cassock plus scarlet skullcap. At his side, Sister Kathinka.

Cloaked by crowd, Olivia and Charles followed them to the church, hung around a while, then entered.

After the bustle and brightness what a contrast was this cool, dim, quiet cavern. The ceiling was coffered with recessed stucco panels. Candles burned high and low in front of shrines. A few black-clad village women were sunk in prayer. Olivia pointed at the big black box of a confessional, its curtains closed. A pair of black shoes peeped beneath the side drape. She and Charles sat on nearby chairs to wait.

Eventually the Dutch nun emerged and went to pray by the altar. By the time she arose, composed, Cardinal Borromini was waiting for her in the aisle.

Olivia stared, glassy-eyed. 'Her shadow's *inside* the pyramid,' she slurred — and leapt up to intercept the two of them. Charles hastened to accompany her.

'Wait, we must talk!'

Borromini glowered. 'Do not disturb the house of God, or us,' he said in thickly-accented English. He would need to polish his foreign languages a little if he hoped to be pope, the pope who converted — or damned — the stars.

'You've been invited inside the alien ship.' (Kathinka's eyes widened.) 'You haven't told UNCO!'

'The sister is no part of your UNCO. Did you hide a microphone in the confessional? *Basta*! This is a disgrace.'

'I know because I see truth, the way a saint sees a vision.'

'You dare compare your spying to the vision of a saint?' Yet Borromini was rattled. More so, when Charles made the sign of the Manu Cornuta.

After some consideration the cardinal said, 'How remarkable that the aliens invite a religious to enter their hive, instead of a diplomat or scientist. A religious of low rank, who may be vulnerable.'

Sister Kathinka cleared her throat.

'Yes! Speak!'

'This invitation is simply because of my method of memory, I think.'

Borromini gazed around. 'This church . . . is dedicated to a saint you two probably have not heard of. Thomas of Villanova. Thomas always aided the poor before their needs became urgent, so that he should not feel pride in his charity.'

'So you discussed the sin of pride in the confessional,' said Olivia.

'I am vowed not to say! Surely you realize that!'

'Cardinal, Your Eminence, we really can't have the sole representative of the human race ever to enter an alien starship being chained by vows of silence and obedience. Surely *you* realize?'

'I am not chained,' protested Kathinka. 'If so, my chain is my freedom.'

'As Archbishop of Valencia,' continued Borromini, 'Saint Thomas was responsible for the care of many Moors whose conversion to Christianity had been less than voluntary. Their state of mind worried him. It was an *alien* state of soul.'

'Is Thomas the patron saint of memory too, by any chance?' asked Charles.

Kathinka spoke without thinking. 'On the contrary, he was notoriously forgetful!' She gripped her rosary.

'It's blasphemy to forget wilfully,' Charles said. 'In my book.'

'After your visit,' breathed Olivia, 'you'll return to Vatican territory, to the Pope's palace — where you may be required to stay forever alone in a cell, if the Flies are found to be corrupting.'

Kathinka's eye twitched; Charles knew that Olivia had seen the shadow hanging over her. He pressed the nun.

'You imagine that you'd accept the sacrifice obediently, even though it devastates your heart.'

'Worse than spies!' hissed Borromini.

'You'd have to give up all your places in Rome, Sister.'

'I could live in those in memory.' Kathinka's voice shook.

'Do you really think so? All the churches, palaces, streets: could you really live in those solidly and authentically in your imagination? Every colour, every detail? Every sight and sound and smell? For the rest of your life — spent in solitary confinement? Today, dear cell, we shall pretend to walk to the Trevi fountain . . . Why should you even wish to live in those places in memory, Sister, when you would have no one to guide and to bless?'

It was as though Charles had struck the nun in the stomach. He felt a hollow in himself too, of sadness at what he had said. Yet he carried on.

'I want to go with you to the hive. I too know something of memory. If you ask, the Flies may agree.'

'Foulness,' said Borromini, though not with full heart. Hard to tell whether he was referring to Charles and Olivia or to the aliens.

'If you refuse,' Olivia said to the cardinal, 'who knows if the sister will reach the pyramid, or only someone dressed as a nun resembling her? I know someone who would love to intercept a helicopter or a boat, or even a Fly carrying her in its arms. You'd have lost your chance, the Church's chance.'

Borromini chewed his lip, and took an apparent decision to mellow.

'Perhaps you should both accompany the sister, if only as devil's advocates.'

'Oh no. Once on Vatican territory you might give an order to some burly priests. We might disappear. Charles will go. I shall stay with UNCO, for security.'

'I'm sorry if I distressed you,' Charles told Kathinka.

'Distress her, *you*?' echoed Borromini. 'She has to go inside a hive of alien creatures for who knows what purpose of theirs!'

'But not alone now,' Charles said.

Kathinka looked pitying. 'I have resources . . . which you might envy if you knew them. God, I mean, not myself. Anyway, I have spent days with aliens.'

'You have not been into their *nest*,' the cardinal reminded her. (Be not proud.)

'At home they float in a thousand tanks,' Charles mentioned. 'The hive may seem like a giant aquarium.'

'Is that another vision of yours, fellow?'

'I don't have visions, I just use my eyes. An alien told me about those tanks.'

'Ah, really? You may be a help to Sister Kathinka. Perhaps it's best this way. I agree. I concede. Come along with us . . . my son.'

So they left the church of the charitable amnesiac. Olivia slipped away quickly through the crowd.

And now at last Charles knew, as he floated in the alien null-sense tank seeing a memory place: Paris.

Here was Montmartre Cemetery, its mausoleums crowding shoulder to shoulder, each of them extravagant, unique, decrepit: high, narrow, one-room houses in honour of Monsieur and Madame Bourgeois, so many nineteenth century telephone kiosks equipped with prie-dieu for making a call to God, and with dusty porcelain flowers behind iron grilles or stained panes. . . .

As Charles drifted upwards, so the cemetery became a relief map of itself, bumpy with all the sepulchres. Over the rooftops beyond, the white dome of Sacré Coeur commanded from its hilltop. Elsewhere, amputated streets led to a wall of nothingness. Most of Paris hadn't been remembered yet, disgorged yet.

He shut his eyes. Or were his eyes still open? Yes or no, this made no difference to the memory place, a circuit board in three dimensions with no data programmed into it as yet — no topics had yet been attached to any of the places.

When the Flies returned to their home world with their

harvest of a thousand or ten thousand places, aliens afloat in other null-sense tanks would stroll the boulevards of Paris, beginning to fill them with topics bit by bit, brick by brick. *Les mouches* would catch a bateau-mouche along the Seine, where fuzzy Impressionist water would flow. Water was too mobile to remember clearly, or to attach ideas to. The foliage of the trees in the cemetery was likewise merely a fractal pattern, although every detail of each graveyeard gazebo was true, every title in distant roofs of the empty part-city was exact. . . .

There had been no *bon voyage* from the Pope, as Charles had slightly been hoping. Borromini had quickly put him and Kathinka in the care of two members of the Vigilance, who had escorted them to a far corner of the papal grounds. He never knew exactly how the arrangement had been made, but some brief signal was radioed and an alien soon arrived carrying a spare flying pack. It agreed to return for another. Meanwhile Charles was lent a black soutane, so as to somewhat resemble a Fly.

Thus equipped, he and Kathinka were autopiloted by the alien the short distance to the pyramid: two black-clad angels. UNCO would hardly have been fooled, yet the strategem had an appealing blatancy to it. A new Saint Joseph of Copertino, the gawping levitating friar, accompanied by the Flying Nun! Could Tarini, forewarned, have actually intercepted Kathinka by deploying jet-pack special forces or a chopper trawler armed with a net? Perhaps.

Once on board: so many tanks, connected by pearly struts and tubes and pipes and ceramic ladders and walkways, like big black beads slung in a dense array. The sloping pyramid walls cast a nacreous phosphorescent light. Deep down, alien machines purred softly . . .

In the null-sense tank, Charles shivered at the memory . . . of how half a dozen Flies, their arms like steel, had seized him and Kathinka and plucked the clothes from them. He'd been plunged into the slimy-slick liquid of the tank, gluey tendrils pervading the fluid — to be drowned? Certainly to be robbed of sensation, shut in a black coffin almost brimful of liquid.

However, he'd floated as if in the Dead Sea. As the lid locked out the light — his panicky hyperventilation producing rowdy snores, which quieted as his hearing failed — a memory place had appeared, enchanting him.

That had been Cairo's Citadel area. Presently he noticed a Fly kissing a highly decorated mosque wall, a section of arabesque, its moustache feelers twitching ecstatically. When Charles kissed that same place, knowledge arrived, a twisted dreamlike partial knowledge about the alien *purpose* and the lay-out of the ship, its index: the web of tanks above and below, and deepest of all the big tank containing the Gland, a black bloated mass with several eyes, beaked mouth, orifices, no limbs. The Gland.

A glimpse of the purpose; and of the danger.

Later, he'd drifted — steered himself — through the wall of nothingness around Cairo, first into San Francisco, and now Montmartre. Here were memory places indeed. All the cities of the world were being made into perfect memory places; more than mere memory places, places congruent with reality.

How long had he been floating in the tank? He'd lost track. Realizing what he could do, he urged his invisible and unfelt hand to rise — not the hand of his body image which hovered above the cemetery, but the hand of flesh he had lost touch with.

The lid above his head rose easily, and the pyramid's light abolished Paris.

With care he hauled himself up. Sensation flooded back as the slithery liquid slid from him like a sheath. If a Fly had been perching on the lid earlier on, now the only alien in sight was sitting propped against the side of a tank, its long legs drawn up like a grasshopper's.

Charles stepped out on to the Flywalk where the borrowed soutane and his undergarments lay heaped. His skin felt vibrant, massaged; mild hilarity welled in him as he dressed.

He waited, unconcerned about time — which seemed his to control, to speed up or slow down — till another tank top opened nearby and Kathinka too stood up.

The nun, naked. He glanced, then averted his gaze, then glanced again. Except for her rather tanned face she was as white as a nude painted by Lucas Cranach, a medieval ideal of blanchedness. He noted the same narrow hips as on a Cranach canvas and the same high white breasts, round white fruit — lychees the size of little apples. However, she was taller and lankier than a Cranach nude, her white legs more muscular thanks to all those ballet exercises.

She was beautiful, yet she no more conformed to present-day images of beauty than did the stumpy sensuality of Olivia. He was the first man to *see* Kathinka. Earlier, when they were forcibly disrobed, panic had possessed him. Now her body spoke to him — the word 'inaccessible'! If another person's body usually formed an image within him which he understood all too well, if he had always seen in a body what he already knew, then how could he be excited? To touch that person would merely be to fondle himself; he wouldn't be shocked into some other zone, of displacement, or ecstasy. Yet Kathinka displaced him; as Olivia had, as Martine had. Charles shut his eyes, not so much to allow Kathinka privacy as to see if she was fixed in memory, sculpted in marble. His mind's eye betrayed him, as perhaps it must. A tall white blancemange swayed there. When he looked, she had resumed her habit in haste.

Her eyes shone. She licked her lips.

'They remember so much more deeply! They aren't remembering places for the sake of *places.* Whole cities are their rosaries to hang other memories upon. What a Godlike memory. Beyond ordinary memory. The memory that God has of Creation: they've trespassed upon this . . . this divine attribute to use it as a filing system!' Her eyes shone on account of shock. 'They're . . . clerks, that's what. Together with their Gland they have power, don't they? Power of miracles. They could be locusts, these clerks. They could consume actual places if their power went astray.'

In her way she was right. The Flies, together with their Gland, had access not to a 'God' exactly but to the universal information force, the metamemory of the universe; to some dimension which was the foundation of reality. The Flies tapped a force that underpinned reality, that kept reality constant. Memory was the source of all identity, the only link in a flux of perceptions and events — not only for living beings but for the physical universe as well. The memory of the Flies was so intense. . . .

'They're sick,' Charles said bluntly. 'Obsessional. Over-developed in one direction. Crazy.'

Wasn't that true of himself? Oh no! He had studiously avoided the hot tub into which his talent could have plunged him, melting away the barrier between himself and others, dissolving his identity. So as to anchor himself he had striven to remember places, the scenery of his life. Flies remembered reality so strongly that reality could become the victim of their thoughts; except that they were only, yes, clerks, simple filing clerks cataloguing their alien facts upon the faces of objects remembered, collecting new places like blank file cards. When that Fly had been murdered, though, St. Peter's dome had disappeared. Their power leaked out; it had affected Olivia. Their power had given her those extra flashes of perception, of information about the future. . . .

'Miracles without faith!' exclaimed Kathinka. 'Heaven, cities of God, built by the clerks of Hell. Worse, by the clerks of nowhere.'

'Sooner they go home the better, eh? Leaving us to our own world and our arms talks and ordinary beliefs and dangers. Most of what we're saying about them is . . . *words.* Memory, supermemory: what do we know of those? The Flies assume we're a version of themselves, building churches in order to remember facts! They aren't a version of us any more than a whale's a version of a person.'

'If we don't share . . . a communion with them, if we can't share, if they're neither of God nor of the Devil —' she began.

The soft humming of the pyramid was drowned by an eruption of engine roar, the thrash of helicopter blades, clatter of metal. An aluminium ladder jutted through one of the ports, a horizontal bridge. Through others too, to judge by the noise. Human shouts of: 'Go, go, go!' A masked commando armed with a riot gun scrambled monkey-style, leaped on to the Flywalk. The sheen didn't flash him to ashes. Another commando followed.

The sharers had arrived.

'A totally peaceful occupation.' Smirking Tarini might have been offering a job description.

'Seizure, you mean!' retorted Charles. Tarini had come into the pyramid as soon as it was reported secured, and the few Flies on board immobilized. Improvised mesh gates covered all the ports now, since no one knew how to close those otherwise. Already Flies, returning to disgorge, were circling or hovering outside, barred from entering. Since they did nothing hostile, no one interfered with them.

'No casualties, Carlo. We have us a starship.' Who was 'us' exactly? UNCO? NATO? CIA? ABCDE?

'A ship powered by a paranormal Gland,' said Charles.

'Powered by *what*?'

A dispute broke out at the nearest port of access. Only briefly; within moments Olivia had joined them. Ignoring Tarini, she stared at Charles. She stared at the shadow of his time in the tank; then stared at the nun.

She giggled momentarily, madly. 'Lecher,' she said to Charles. 'You don't want me, you want a nun, for fuck's sake? You need your Martine to bail you out of this mess because she's nuts. Oh fuck it, it's the glands, isn't it? It's always the glands.' She held her head. 'Yeah, vision *is* stronger in here, near the Gland. Let's go see the Gland. I want to see its shadows! Then we might know what sort of shit we're in, thanks to you, Dino Fuchs Prometheus.'

Pardon the outburst. Olivia was half spaced out by the vibes in the hive.

Tarini gaped at her. 'Dino fucks Prometheus?'

'Yeah, you fuck Prometheus in your head. Wanna steal fire! Wanna fly to Jupiter! On the back of a vulture that'll tear your guts out!'

One of the immobilized Flies called out:

'We take passenger, if wish . . . journey in memory sleep with Gland . . . if halt your bad attack, bad for your cities.'

'Are you threatening us?' Tarini demanded. 'What with? Your ship's been taken, Fly! We're in charge.'

'The Gland's in charge,' said Kathinka.

'What's with this gland? Is that the power source: a living one? A queen-alien? Well, everything alive wishes to survive! Where is it?'

'Down below in the big tank,' said Charles.

'If us do not dis-charge, into the Gland —'

'Shut up!'

Black. Soft. Bulky like a dugong or a walrus. Eyes that saw . . . what, in darkness? Not true eyes but organs evolved for another purpose? Afloat on its own secretions, which flowed through pipes to other tanks. Breath sighing. Shadows crawled inside the opened tank.

How to describe shadows to those who hadn't seen them? As photographic negatives perhaps, occupying the same space as a more recent picture. Double exposure, black and white. Image of ghosts. Here were alien shadows. Capacity to see them, strongest here.

Ever since I shouted my way on board — make way for the President's personal representative! — I'd been ever more transfigured by past-knowledge, of Kathinka, Tarini, especially of Charles, all of his past life pictured in the biographic aura of his shadows as if he were a memory place himself.

A human being has to avoid the hot tub, the melting, or else all compass direction is lost. That's how we evolved, separate from each other, seeking clues to the feelings of others but not dissolving into them — unlike the Flies.

Humans need a single viewpoint, not a faceted mosaic vision. For my viewpoint I chose Charles, because I saw him deepest of all. To illuminate the story, I chose his eyes, his voice, his desires.

Shadows crawled inside the tank of the Gland . . .

Once long ago the Flies' ancestors marked their surroundings with scent messages. New experiences were encoded into molecules, and unless these were unloaded a Fly could forget nothing, a Fly's experience did not fade. Everything it experienced remained fully present: in an expanding, continuous, immediate present which swelled to capacity, unless discharged on to rocks, paths, stems of vegetation, where presently it would fade away.

Encountering all these messages, other Flies experienced their fellows' lives almost as intensely as their own. Each participated in a swathe of lives. Flies were almost a collective intelligence. The larger, rarer, immobile females wallowed in pools of their own secretions which alone could fix — stabilize — the discharged memory molecules contributed by the visiting, roaming Flies. In these pools the young were nurtured, learning what it was to be a Fly.

As this gestalt of minds grew more complex through interaction, a confusion of the senses developed. What a Fly smelled and tasted, it saw and heard. What it saw, it also tasted. A Fly might be overwhelmed by the immediacy of experiences which hadn't happened to it personally.

The females, the Glands, discovered disciplines, sorting procedures. They prescribed a way to re-arrange the natural world so that it was no longer a set of chaotic memories. Thus the Flies began to build orderly walls, structures, towns — with a pool at the centre of each town where the memory of the town itself persisted, organized knowledge coded into its remembered pattern. A town was thought, thought was a town. Civilization evolved.

And the Glands, the hearts of the faceted gestalts, broke through to metamemory, to the information fields underlying the whole of reality. Towns, cities, and the image of those cities with information encoded into their every part, became truly congruent in superspace . . .

Those were the shadows that I saw, on the Gland in its tank; to the extent that I could understand them. And insight exiled me forever.

There isn't much more to tell.

Oh yes.

'Sir, downtown Prague has disappeared!'

'It *what*?'

'General Dole says it vanished. There's nothing there, just a shallow empty area. It disappeared like the dome!'

A Fly, excluded from its hive, had fallen into Lake Albano. Or else it had dived deliberately. Overloaded with memory, it overloaded its power pack. In turn, transposed through superspace, what it remembered was obliterated, wiped out.

A few other places — old Mombasa, Munich, the heart of New Orleans — had to be lost before Tarini was ordered to evacuate the pyramid and let the Flies back in to disgorge.

After that, the aliens carried on as previously, flying to and fro, remembering the world's cities. These crazy, para-powerful aliens were now protected even more scrupulously by security teams. They stayed on Earth for another year — for me a stressful year, during which I stayed as isolated as my job allowed. I was too good at it now; it would consume me. Even with a whole ocean separating me from the hive, I could be melted — into other people.

As to the nature of their technology which both alerted them to our existence then let them leap the light years to reach us, perhaps that too was a science of memory rather than any manipulation of a repulsive hyperforce (though they may have that too). By virtue of their sharehold in superspace where all events are recorded, dispersed throughout as in a hologram, perhaps they could wilfully 'forget' the distance from their home world.

Yet to be a passenger to the stars, to their home world, to see for oneself? If a human could perceive reality as they perceived it! That offer still stood, though it transpired that the offer was only open to those most directly involved in the affair.

Obviously a human being must fly to the stars, even on a one-way ticket with no means of sending a postcard home — if only for the sake of knowing that the journey had been undertaken.

So who should it be?

Charles? Ah no. New Orleans had vanished, and he must meet Martine again. Now that he'd known crazy aliens, perhaps he could begin to know her heart more exactly. He could enter the house of madness alert to all the signs inscribed there, and perhaps could show her the exit door, the way by which she could melt into one whole person.

Kathinka, then? — who might be canonized in a thousand years' time for her sacrifice? No, she would be destroyed, her faith broken. Faith is a belief in a hidden superperson. Flies needed no such belief when they were already part of a superperson, with a supermemory that was rooted into a dimension outside spacetime. Light years from Rome, Kathinka might revisit the domeless Vatican in a memory tank any time she chose, yet a visit to St. Peter's would tell her only, and compellingly, about the folkways of faithless Flies inscribed upon it — as they relieved the pressures of memory upon the fresh empty places of Earth.

Tarini? Ha! Exiled to an alien star out of harm's way, the failed Prometheus of espionage? He was better off demoted to Honduras.

No, me. Olivia.

For I'd lost my human compass point. On Earth I would melt, which meant that I would be mad like Martine, only more so, the many-in-one. My needle now only pointed away, away, where at least my neighbours would be somewhat like me. And unlike me, utterly, so that I could remain myself.

Me, Olivia, dreaming this story now in memory in the Gland's tank, to which all other ship-tanks connect, attaching this narrative as I've been taught to the ruins of the Colosseum, stone by stone, section by section, so that it can be played out in that memory theatre, unforgettably.

Though how will its future readers, aliens, understand it?

1988: THE YEAR IN SCIENCE FICTION

THANKS FOR DROWNING THE OCELOT

by

BRIAN ALDISS

It's a real sorrow that you died in January of this year, and I expect you were upset as well. I wanted to say thanks to you; let's trust I'm not too late. I hope this letter will reach you as you rest in Abraham's Bosom. Rough luck on Abraham, though.

But that can't be right. You must be in some more surreal place — perhaps in the heaven the ancient Egyptians dreamed about, by the summer stars. Or simply in orbit. Somewhere unorthodox. You liked breaking taboos.

Remember you once tried to prove that 'the whole universe comes to a focus' (as you put it) in the centre of the railway station in Perpignan? That was a good stunt. Perhaps you're there in Perpignan, awaiting a celestial diesel to somewhere.

You were crazy. Or you acted the part. The remark about Perpignan railway station came in an article you wrote in 1965, extolling the virtues of the great Salvador Dali. Like Caesar, you referred to yourself in the third person — though in your case you were the first and second person too: there were scarcely any others.

Your article involves the miraculous flies of Gerona, the cleanliness of Delft, the viscereal eye of Vermeer, von Leewenhoek's invention of the microscope, several revolutions, the atomic bomb, and a swarm of priests dressed in black. It's incoherent. You never wanted to make sense of the world; that had no part in your 'critical paranoia' method. Yet there was a tawdry magic. Take one sentence from that article:

> 'Thus the blood of the dragons and the hussars who hibernated at Beresina mixing directly with the blood of the new technologists of the always Very Holy Russia caused a historic mutation, producing the true and new mutant beings

O. S. Y. 2—16

> — the astronauts who, propelled by the templates of their genetic code, could not have a more positive way to direct themselves toward heaven than to jet straight toward the moon, which we will see happen from one moment to the other.'

Even van Vogt couldn't manage prose like that. So let's just think of you in orbit somewhere in the summer stars. Greetings to Hieronymus Bosch.

You may not remember this, but we met on one occasion, when you and I helped to launch a book of Fleur Cowles's poems and paintings, and an event was held in the London Planetarium. You were working hard on giving an impression of great eccentricity. Without wishing to complain, I was slightly disappointed — only, I hasten to add, in the way that one is generally disappointed by meeting one's heroes in the flesh. It's the Napoleon-was-a-bit-short syndrome. When I met Jeffrey Archer, another of the greats, the same thought flashed across my mind.

There was a kind of rotting Edwardian stylishness about you. Archer's unmitigatedly eighties. The Hush Puppy School.

But you were a hero. At school, in form IVA, it was taken for granted you were the great artist of the age. We liked rotting carcasses, elongated skulls, soggy watches, crutches, and the rest of your props. One of our number, now a Labour back-bencher, could act out your canvas, *Spectre of Sex Appeal*, naked, with the aid of a couple of hockey sticks. We chortled over your *Life*, so full of disgusting facts or fantasies that it would have meant expulsion had we been caught with the book in our lockers.

It was the confusion of fact with fantasy which caught the imagination. I have cooled down a bit since those days in IVA, when the class debated whether you had an exceedingly large whatnot, a laughably small one, or possibly none at all. Since then, you have sunk down the list of favourite artists in my estimation, whereas Kandinsky, Gauguin, Tanguy, Max Ernst and de Chirico in his early period, remain firm. Odd how all the century's most exciting art was achieved before WWII was spent.

We'll return to the confusion of fact with fantasy later, because that is where your connection with science fiction comes in, but first, at the risk of disturbing that great calm into which you have flown, I want to remind you of what George Orwell said. Orwell wrote that your two unquestionable qualities were an atrocious egotism and a gift for drawing. Many of us have aspired towards either, or both. As a kind of corollary to that remark, Orwell said 'One ought to be able to hold in one's head simultaneously the two facts that Dali is a good draughtsman and a disgusting human being.' It is an oft-quoted remark. You must be proud of it.

Although he belonged to the NUJ, Orwell was a little — well, prudish. He objected in print to the way in which you consumated your love of Paul Eluard's wife. That certainly must have been a Gala event: you covered yourself with a mixture of goat's dung boiled in fish glue. *Chacun à son goat*, I say. It must have made something stick, since Gala remained your idolized companion for fifty years. Orwell has no comment on that aspect of your life.

To be honest — Orwell was another hero of mine — the author of *1984* is wearing no better than you. A new world has come up over the skyline since your heyday, in the thirties and forties. Your paranoid harp-players and flaming giraffes have acquired period charm. You got too rich. You became religious, in a florid, Murillo-like, Madonna-worshipping way which sickens us more than the necrophilia sickened Orwell. It's a common tragedy, outliving your epoch.

Still, you did paint *Soft Construction with Boiled Beans: Premonitions of Civil War*, and several other canvasses which will remain ikons of their time.

You must always have worked very hard. You kept working, even when — towards the end — you turned to the kitschy religious subjects. Is Dali perhaps Catalan for Doré? Like Doré, you illustrated numerous books. But it was the early paintings which fed a young imagination, the images seen through a dry, pure atmosphere — some of them, like *Sleep*, where an immense sagging face is propped precariously above the desert, now fodder for Athena posters, alongside Beardsley and Escher, other masters of illusion.

Your titles too took one into a new imaginative world. *The Ghost of Vermeer of Delft which can be Used as a Table. Average Atmospherocephalic Bureaucrat in the Act of Milking a Cranial Harp. Paranoic Astral Image.* Convincing, as only the preposterous can be.

Some of the paintings held even more direct links with a mentality which questions what is real. *The Invisible Man*, for instance. Various visual puns where things appear and disappear, such as *Apparition of Face and Fruit-Dish on a Beach*, *Slave Market with Invisible Bust of Voltaire*, and the hallucinatory *Metamorphosis of Narcissus*, another of Athena's victims. Well, I won't auto-sodomize you with lists of your own canvasses, but doesn't it strike you, as you take your astral ease, that it's the past which is rich with life? It's the future that's dead, stuffed with our own mortality.

Naturally, all these whims and excesses of your imagination can be put down to revolt against upbringing, revolt against Catholicism, revolt against traditional dull nationalism. There was just a little too much show biz. All the obits followed Orwell in speaking of your egotism. After obit, orbit — and there you swing, moody among the summer stars. We who remain Earth-bound look up. You probably have for company the Japanese Emperor Hirohito, once proclaimed a god, who achieved escape velocity a mere two weeks before you.

What a patriot that man was! Your very opposite. Never showed off. Kept low profile. Good family man. Responsible for perhaps millions of deaths.

And even your egotism was relieved, or probably I mean made more rococo, by your sense of humour. Perhaps you recall a stuffy English BBC type — it can't have been a young Alan Whicker, can it? — coming to interview you in your retreat in Port Lligat, near Figueras? You sat with Gala by your blue swimming pool, your pet ocelot lounging on a cane armchair beside you.

The interview went on. You spoke English of such beauty and density that the BBC found it necessary to run sub-titles at the bottom of the screen. The interviewer, as I recollect, was just slightly critical of your notoriety, for in those days — this was in Harold Wilson's time of office — we rather used to fawn on failure; whereas, now that Mrs. Thatcher holds office, we have learnt to suck up to success.

So the interviewer came to his most devastating question. He had heard, he said, that Dali was unkind to animals. Was that true?

Do you remember how your music-hall moustache curled in scorn?

'Dali cruel to ze animal?' you exclaimed. 'Nevair!'

And to emphasis the point you seized up your ocelot by the scruff of its neck and hurled it into the swimming pool.

That indeed is the way to discomfit the English.

We SF writers, in our own humbler way — for we live in Penge and Paddington and Pewsey, not Figueras — the very names shout the difference — we also try to discomfit the English. It is what SF is designed for, what Mary Shelley and H.G. Wells used it for.

Of course, you never discomfited the English very much; we have no luck at all in that respect.

I suppose you know that while you were posturing on your death bed, in a leg-over position with mortality at last, Salman Rushdie was having trouble here with his latest phantasmagoria, *The Satanic Verses*. It's a fantasy which now and again makes fun of the Christian God and of Mohammed. The English dutifully bought their copies at Smith's and Waterstone's, to display them prominently so that friends would think they had read the book, and maintained a calm almost indistinguishable from catatonia. Not so the Moslem community in Britain (or in Bradford, which is near Britain). The Moslems descended on W.H. Smith with flaming brands, in the manner of those exciting final scenes in a Frankenstein movie. It's the Spanish temperament, I suppose. The British are full of phlegm. Sometimes it makes you spit.

Far more worthy of expectoration were the medieval thought-processes of the Ayatollah Khomeini in pronouncing the death sentence on Rushdie for his novel. Even in World War II we never witnessed such behaviour. The situation is far more bizarre than even Rushdie's mind could think up — bizarre and horrifying.

It was my misfortune to appear on the BBC TV programme

'Kilroy' which discussed Khomeini's death threat. I felt very strongly that both the freedom of speech and Rushdie must be protected — the former on principle, the latter from his foolishness. The majority of those appearing in the Kilroy-Silk bear-pit were Muslim. The atmosphere was thunderous. Many, though not all, of the Muslims present agreed vociferously with the Ayatollah that Rushdie should be killed. Some of these men held high positions in the Muslim community in Britain. When asked directly if they would murder Rushdie themselves, the men fought shy, knowing the television cameras were upon them. Two women had no such qualms. Both said they would murder Rushdie themselves.

To have to listen to such madness was almost unbearable. Fact and fantasy were again confused. No one in the vociferous belt could — or would — distinguish between an novel and a theological work. These people, and millions like them, had surrendered their consciences into the keeping of the mad old man in Teheran. The most recent similar case we experienced was the fever of the Cultural Revolution under the Great Helmsman (you didn't meet him, did you, Dali?), when two million people stood in Tien-an-men Square and waved their Little Red Books.

Rushdie began his writing career with *Grimus*, once categorised as SF. I tried to give it the award in a *Sunday Times* SF Competition, but the book was withdrawn. Later, I tried ineffectually to bestow the Booker Prize on D.M. Thomas's *The White Hotel*, rather than on *Midnight's Children*. No one then imagined that Rushdie's name would become more widely known over the face of the globe than any author since Rosetta wrote his Stone.

In the matter of freedom of speech, writers must be for it. On the whole I'm also for blasphemy — it proves the god spoken out against is still living. You can't blaspheme against Baal or the Egyptian goddess Isis.

Some of the bourgeois like being épated. As I enjoyed Henry Miller's writings when he was forbidden, so I enjoyed your carefully executed shockers when they were disapproved of. To my mind, some of them have a long shelf life. Longer than yours.

Your old friend Luis Buñuel preceeded you into the realms of darkness. He too did his share of shocking us out of apathy, and would have recognised in the bigotry of the Ayatollah the intolerance he mocked in the Roman Catholic Church in Spain. With Buñuel, if you remember, you made that celebrated surrealist film, *L'Age d'Or.* It certainly opened a large door in my consciousness.

But it's a silver age. 'The New Dark Age', as a headline in our beloved *Guardian* called it recently. Singing yobs are in vogue, Dali. Pre-pubescent voices. Tribal drumming. Over-amplification. Your exit was well-timed.

And for SF too it's a silver age. True, there is some sign that a few of the younger writers are impatient with the stodginess of their elders. (During the time of President Reagan, patriotism became a way of life, and patriotism is always a blanket excuse for stifling the critical faculty, as if there were no other use for blankets.) Paul Di Filippo and Bruce Sterling are names that spring to mind in this connection, and the group of writers who centre round the magazine *New Pathways*, with their subversive artist, Ferret.

You weren't particularly patriotic. When the Civil War hit Spain, you sensibly refused to take sides — though you had a good precautionary word for General Franco — and went to live in Italy, continuing to flirt with psychoanalysis and sunlight. When Europe sank down on its knees in the fury of World War II, you hopped over to the New World, where the Americans embraced your flamboyance and dirty mind with open purses. Orwell blamed you for those two desertions. Silly of him, really — such an English chap, he should have remembered the words of another Englishman, 'Patriotism is the last refuge of a scoundrel.'

Those words were quoted in 1973 in the pages of *Analog.* (Did you ever see *Analog*, Dali? In its better days, the covers might have appealed to you.) They were quoted by the late Robert A. Heinlein in a guest editorial. He referred to Johnson's cautionary remark as 'a sneering wisecrack'. Johnson never sneered. Heinlein then compounded his philistinism by referring to Johnson as 'a fat gluttonous slob who was pursued all his life by a pathological fear of death'. Several readers cancelled their subscription to *Analog* on the spot.

You see what I'm getting at? It is a mark of civilization that one criticises one's own country. Hemingway said that a writer should always be against the government in power. Whatever their faults of exhibitionism, your paintings spoke out against the mundane, the dreary, the received. Like the other surrealists, you were up in arms, though you preferred yours covered in mink and diamonds.

American SF writers have not been slow to write about their Vietnam War. The British have had little to say about their adventure in the Falkland Islands at the start of this decade. A thousand pardons — as a Spaniard you probably think of those shores as Las Malvinas. Our neat little war! — won through the bravery of the common man and because the French sold the Argentinians dud Exocets.

We captured the Falklands from you Spaniards back in Johnson's time. And what did Johnson have to say about that victory, in his ponderous, humorous fashion?

'. . . What have we acquired? What, but a bleak and gloomy solitude, an island thrown aside from human use, stormy in winter, and barren in summer; an island which not the southern savages have dignified with habitation; where a garrison must be kept in a state that contemplates with envy the exiles of Siberia; of which the expense will be perpetual, and the use only occasional . . .'

How the words ring on!

Garry Kilworth has gone to Hong Kong. Perhaps we shall have a similar devastating bulletin from him in the next *Yearbook.* SF in England has settled down to comfortable squalor, relatively unmoved by dirty needles, inner city decay, and the prospect of union with Europe. At least you preserved the clean contorted rocks of Figueras and the drypoint desert as a background. Your air was clear.

You may not have been in the very front rank, Dali, but you stood up to be counted. At the least, you kept us amused throughout a lifetime, like Richard Burton and Elizabeth Taylor rolled into one. You replenished that small vocabulary of images which shapes our imaginative life. You are the great international SF writer in paint.

And you chucked that bloody ocelot into the water.
All the best in the summer stars,

Your admirer,
Brian Aldiss

SCIENCE FICTION NOVELS OF THE YEAR

by

JOHN CLUTE

1775 was like this too, Dickens says. The best of times and the worst of times. Through the goggles of a year like 1775, or 1988, there is always a *Tale of Two Cities* in the offing, some sort of millennial resolution discernible up the line, maw gaping. Gripped by auguries of the fin de siecle, 1988 has been a year of remission and prognosis; of relief that we still enjoy the fruits of our long reign; of terror that it's all about to end in a mortal spasm of the planet we have paved, some vast calling in of the credits that have funded these last hours in the garden with the pesticide and the poisoned gnomes to guard us. The millennium has not yet come, but a rough beast knocks at night in the dream of the West whispering *I am what you've sown.* So it has been a year of premonitions, and it might be fair to ask just what our chosen genre has done recently to accustom us to the future? What brave words are the visionary novelists of our own science fiction now uttering, to chasten us or to charm?

Well? It was the best of times, it was the worst of times. It was a year which witnessed a revival of the Scientific Romance, child of the last fin de siecle, harbinger of the next; but it was also a year which marked the beginning of the age of the share-cropper, bibled and braided and branded and steered. It was a year in which two tightrope-walking humanists (Kim Stanley Robinson and Terry Bisson) wrote books that were not fatuous; but it was also a year which saw cyberpunk enter heat-death and become a tradition (rather benumbing William Gibson, though continuing still to fascinate haunted proconsuls like Bruce 'Cecil Rhodes' Sterling). Dinosaurs continued to live in 1988, dinosaurs died. Good books won awards, dozens of less-good books won dozens of awards. Child editors in America and Britain gazed in wonder upon new books and old agents, and boggled whole conventions with their born-again ('Now I've been with Shameless and Honk a whole day I'm like truly thrilled about our unique new list . . . entirely new slant . . . investment in quality kind of thing you know') babble, but as usual big bucks tended only to change hands for the most otiose trilogy clones. The walls of the ghetto were razed in 1988, the ghetto remains.

As in 1987, a new novel was published every few hours in 1988, but once again most of them were fantasy or horror, and therefore beyond the remit of this survey of the best science fiction novels of 1988; and some of the remaining were sharecropped, though not as many as next year will provide, because only recently have the owners of science fiction begun to see that the sharecropping scam could be a nice little earner. The term was coined, I believe, by Gardner Dozois. It derives from the success of the Kentucky Fried Chicken. Sharecropping occurs when the copyright owner of a famous story or novel (like Isaac Asimov's 'Nightfall' or Arthur C Clarke's *Against the Fall of Night*) hires an author (like Arthur Byron Cover or Robert Silverberg) to rewrite, or expand, or sequelize, or create a work 'in the world of' that original. Because he has no rights over his labour, and because his peonage has a certain historical resonance, the hack who does the actual job of writing has become known as the sharecropper. He is a tenant farmer, he sows what Bwana tells him to sow, and he does not reap. Nor does he *make things up*. For the franchise owners who have hired him, any attempt by the sharecropper to look upon the world and *make it new* would be to violate their property rights. So menu-control is of the essence for the owners of science fiction, just as it is for the owners of any merchandise, and no sharecropper can be given a chance to violate the 'bible' that tells him how to work his master's plot. *Against the Fall of Night* (soon to be sharecropped by Gregory Benford) must taste of the original product, just as a themepark must taste of something once alive.

So is it closing time in the gardens of the West, as Cyril Connolly said 40 years ago on closing down *Horizon*? Or is sharecropping just another developer's dream of our free enterprise system? Or is it that just one question? Perhaps Mr Benford and Mr Silverberg would argue that you can't stop Progress and shouldn't try, and that Golden-Age Themeparks, tilled by squeaky-clean Toms in Mickey Mouse masks, *preserve our heritage* in the same way that Disney World pickles our dreams to profit the owner. All the same, in a world about which it's a matter of urgency to tell stories before it's too late, it does seem a *trahison des clercs* for authors to re-enact travesties of the dead past while claiming star status in a genre which pretends to face us with the threat and joy of the new. Or perhaps nowadays they keep their mouths shut, except to till. Perhaps it is just all too sad for words — this transmogrifying of authors we respect into golems of the nostalgia trade; this dangerous deep asset-stripping raid upon own fragile science fiction, whose claims to focus on the yet-unsaid have proved so remarkably easy to co-opt, and to reverse. But it's not all black. It does make the task of choosing which books to discuss an easier one. Sharecropped texts disqualify themselves in principle from treatment as *novels*, because, in principle, of course, they are not.

Dinosaur time again in the garden. As we said last year, the dinosaurs of science fiction — those whose careers began before World War Two and who have continued to write, or have only recently returned to Disney World to collect the rent — are the Cargo bearers of the genre. After decades of stoking the Sacred Flame of Future History for free, they found in recent years that the intense development analysis to which the genre has been subjected — and which undoubtedly generated the concept of sharecropping — had targeted them as marketable commodities. But the problem with dinosaurs is that they are human, and no human being ages well — though some age less badly than the rest of us. By the time we reach our second half-century, most of us have become such mistresses and masters of the ruts we've cut to guide our lives and protect ourselves from novelty that only the rarest of us ever manages to think a new thought, or write a new story. The termitary immobilism of spirit of the last Heinlein novels, or of recent efforts by Isaac Asimov to glue his Robot and Foundation series into one salt Colossus in a world that never rains, serves to remind us of the inexorable dead hand of biology. Old men's books — and old women's, viz the pumped up melancholy over-reaching audacity of James Tiptree's last works — tend to rehearse with bluster the heroic feats of young adulthood, when 'Gulf' or 'Nightfall' sprang fully-clothed from the brow of the god. But to reify something so delicately poised as a work of art is to turn it to chalk.

The Knight and Knave of Swords (Morrow) may not be a work of science fiction, nor is Fritz Leiber primarily an author of science fiction; but he began to publish in 1939, he's certainly a dinosaur under the meaning of the act, and it seems a good idea to mention what may well be the last tales to be written about Fafhrd and the Gray Mouser, though of course Leiber, or his eventual heirs, may yet decide to franchise Lankhmar for the loot. And he has made clear in his *Locus* column, Leiber wrote 'The Mouser Goes Below,' the novel which takes up the bulk of *Knight and Knave*, as a magical exercise in fending off the death of his close friend Harry Fischer, who had been the original inspiration for the Gray Mouser, and who was fighting cancer. Fischer died, and the tale which memorializes him has a yearning weirdness about it that does not, to his credit, much resemble the wisdom of the old, which is agenbite and ashes, and which faces the future with the cheeks of the ass. In *Narabedla Ltd* (Ballantine), like a wise old Norn bored out of her skull, Frederik Pohl continued to doodle with the tropes and doodads of the genre he has helped to create, and which he knows, unfortunately in this case, backwards but not forwards. And in *Prelude to Foundation* (Doubleday Foundation), Isaac Asimov, as we hinted decorously just a moment ago, bricked up yet another escape hatch from which any remaining life in his megaseries of long long ago might escape. And Arthur C. Clarke — fighting a medical diagnosis (since superceded) which gave him only a few years to live — brought in a feelgood philistine named Gentry Lee to collaborate on *Cradle* (Gollancz), with predictable results; a soupçon of Clarke's hygenic Weltschmerz drowned in glutinous paeons to plastoid sex and the shopping malls of Key West. Raymond Z Gallun stayed silent.

But let us step outside the ghetto walls for a moment, as we did last year. As Ben Elton has just said again in *Stark* (1989), a novel we would hope to mention again, the future is 'coming towards us quicker than we are going towards it,' causing seismic tremolos in the minds of many writers never associated with fantasy or science fiction, so that more and more 'mainstream' novels read more and more like fantasias on the real stuff. Even a book like Don DeLillo's chilly streetwise *Libra* (Viking), engrossed as it is in the mantric nightmares that embrocate the deaths of JFK and Lee Harvey Oswald, treats its material as a kind of alternate history — as just one of the pasts we must muster to face the haemorrhage of the new. Loosened from the stays of official history, novels like Louise Erdrich's *Tracks* (Holt) and William Kennedy's *Quinn's Book* (Viking) transform the regions of nineteenth and early twentieth century America into magic-realist mirrors of our own condition, here on the cusp. In *Tidings* (Knopf), William Wharton irradiates contemporary France with a hint that something numinous and awe-ful lurks within the rituals we fabricate against the passage of time. In each of these books — and in dozens more of a similar cast of mind — there is a sense of *preparation.* It is a sense which helps one to understand Salman Rushdie's *The Satanic Verses* (Cape), a book which needs little said about it these days, thanks to the efforts of the religious creatures it exposed to the light of the sun. Writers like Erdrich and DeLillo and Rushdie, through their magical and transformative appropriation of the past, seem to be arming themselves — and their readers — to understand the magical and transformative future as it races our way. How different from our own dear genuflecting sharecroppers, whom the past owns.

In the lamenting cadences of Michael Moorcock's masterfully cloistral *Mother London* (Secker) that sense of preparation is perhaps less evident, for this superbly worked tale — the best-constructed work Moorcock has ever generated — strikingly attests to the bondage of the world, which is London. Various avatars of Moorcock populate the book, but even the muted telepathies that unite them into one concourse of regard do less to liberate than to shrive. Neither of Moorcock's British compeers — Brian Aldiss and J.G. Ballard — produced novels of generic interest, though Aldiss's *Forgotten Life* (Gollancz) lucidly grounds a this-wordly tale of redemption in a fretwork of epistemological dubiety, as he does so often in his science fiction, and Ballard's *Running Wild* (Hutchinson) is a toxic little parable — specifically perhaps of the cost of Thatcherism — that edges neatly into the near future, for a glimpse of things. Because of its geriatric and relentlessly half-witted science fiction frame, E. P. Thompson's *The Sykaos Papers* (Bloomsbury) might theoretically be designated a generic product, but this would be to dismiss it utterly-more rewardingly, the book can be read as an animated lecture on the evils of the Yahoo, with examples. Much tamer Yahoos mourn the death of a family elder in Stanislaw Lem's *Hospital of the Transfiguration* (Harcourt Brace), which is set in 1939, in Poland, and it takes only a modicum of sense to work out what will happen to them: Yahoos of purer Yahoo stock will thresh them: and we will come closer to understanding Lem's view of our species, and the dry-ice savagery of his science fiction, for this novel is partly autobiographical. Like an absurdist fantasia on some of Arthur Koestler's loopier notions about denizens of the steppes, Milorad Pavic's *Dictionary of the Khazars: A Lexicon Novel*(Knopf) creates a full-fledged alternate history out of an invented tribe of Slavs; organized as a series of alphabetical entries, *Dictionary* more closely resembles the work of Georges Perec or Harry Matthews than it does the *Steppe* of Piers Anthony, who could, all the same, learn something from a real player of games. Unfortunately, *Khazars* is terribly stuffed, pate-de-fois Borges; and few will read it for the rules. Stunning and various as usual, Peter Dickinson published two books for older children; *Merlin Dreams* (Gollancz) is a grave fantasy about the England we no longer live in, and *Eva* (Gollancz), set in the near future, posits the end through inanition of our miserable species, though some hope is expressed for one of our cousins. In *The Fifth Child* (Cape), a 'mundane' narrative whose surface conceals gnawing hints of anthropological horror, Doris Lessing found little solace in the thought that a dark cousin within the skull might inherit our mess of pottage. And Jim Crace's aptly lapidary *The Gift of Stones* (Secker) returns more openly to the sub-genre of science fiction about prehistory that was so popular in the late nineteenth century, just after Darwin. And so on. This rundown of books that riddle the walls of the ghetto from outside could continue almost indefinitely; 1988 may be the age of the sharecropper, but it is also the best of times, for the borders are down.

Daylight can be binding.

Back in the lek, it was not a good year for writers too young to franchise their early work, but too old any longer to dominate the field; unlike last year, however, some of them managed to write books. The dogged Gordon R. Dickson published unavailingly yet another huge volume in his Childe Cycle, of which the best instalment (*The Genetic General*, 1960) is the first. The pulp triumphalism of that novel, which the Dickson apostle Sandra Miesel once called Pelagian, has stiffened in recent years into a logy and elephantiasic insistence that Man shall prevail, but *The Chantry Guild* (Ace) is rather more sprightly that its immediate predecessor, *The Final Encyclopedia* (1984), and can be enjoyed for its hints of a thin Dickson caught somewhere inside its bulk, crying to be let out. Six years after dying, Philip K. Dick came out with two more novels; *The Broken Bubble ‹of Thisbe Holt›* (Arbor), just about the last of the early non-science-fiction novels, is set, like most of the others, in a California only thinly-partitioned from the surreal paranoias of the realer worlds he entered in his maturity; and *Nick and the Glimmung* (Gollancz) is a neat little children's book, whose eponymous alien is a guest from *Galactic Pot-Healer* (1969). In the slippery grey literate twists of *Krono* (Franklin Watts), Charles L. Harness once again reshapes A. E. Van Vogt into something you could take home to meet your parents. In 1988, Robert Silverberg published two novels of interest. *The Secret Sharer* (Underwood-Miller), which is very short, continues the series of homages which began with *Sailing to Byzantium* (1985), in this case polishing the profound infelicities of Joseph Conrad till the analogies shine like glass; but the gain in smoothness does not overbalance the loss of a felt world. Set in a distant science-fantasy future, which it depicts with impeccable cool skill, *At Winter's End* (Warner) could be the first of many volumes; if the project manages to re-ignite in Silverberg something of his old melancholy fire, it might save him from terminal competence. And Kate Wilhelm, in *The Dark Door* (St Martin's), stumbles strangely from one genre to another, as though blinded. Within an orthodox science fiction frame, two orthodox series detectives (they appear in a previous Wilhelm novel) blunder into an orthodox supernatural horror plot complete with abandoned hotels, and conclude that there are things we are not meant to know. For a writer who seems blind to the implications of this melange of mutually incompatible conventions, Wilhelm juggles her balls with some intermittent dexterity, and *The Dark Door* is at points a joy to read. But the book is mainly of interest as an example, not the first, of rotting affect in the hearts of our older contemporaries, who seem to be telling us that the game of the future is up. That it just doesn't matter any more.

For those we described last year as alpha males, because there were so few women in the cohort of those who effectively began their careers in the decade after 1965, 1988 was not a year for braggadocio, though several books of substance did get published. Michael Bishop, whose voice is like a shout from the bottom of the well of the enormous South, and whose heart is on his sleeve, does manage in *Unicorn Mountain* (Arbor) to generate a moving tale out of ecological disaster here and in another world, AIDS, the death of cultures, the death of species, and the slow sea-changing of America into themeparks. Thomas M. Disch, in *The Brave Little Toaster Goes to Mars* (Doubleday), renews his life-long flirtation with what might be called the sentiment-and-sprezzatura gross-out fling; this second Toaster book is funny, insinuating, speaks with forked tongue. In *Carmen Dog* (Women's Press), Carol Emshwiller tells a metamorphic feminist fable — as of long ago — with a gravely innocent mien that only deepens the sting. From Bob Shaw, *The Wooden Spaceships* (Gollancz) cleverly and modestly continues a trilogy begun in *The Ragged Astronauts* (1986), dovetailing the death of an earlier protagonist with the opening of a new line of plot; and we warm with expectations of a finale of humane sparkle, in the Shavian manner. Of the three novels Ian Watson published in 1988, *Whores of Babylon* (Grafton) entices its protagonists into a world half Disney half Minos, and lets them twist in the wind; perhaps more successfully, *The Fire Worm* (Gollancz) marries sexual pathology to the legend of the

Lambton Worm in a multi-generation tale told in the tone of slangy needling patter characteristic of this author at his best; but the *Meat* (Headline) was off. And in *There Are Doors* (Tor), Gene Wolfe continued to ransack the popular culture of the time before the war, on this occasion polishing up Thorne Smith; but unlike P. G. Wodehouse, the author of *Topper* (1926) is better remembered than reread, and in Wolfe's hands Smith's fragile home-for-dinner flapper paganism turns into something desolated, force-fed, melancholic.

It is easy to forget that Brian Stableford published his first novel as long ago as 1969, because it is easy to forget Brian Stableford's first novel. For a writer of the polymathic and urgent cogency so often on display in his non-fiction, he tended to produce novels, from 1969 until he stopped writing them for a while several years ago, of an oddly morose affectlessness, with exceptions. It is only now, with his return to fiction in *The Empire of Fear* (Simon and Schuster/UK), that he has brought his very considerable gifts into focus, perhaps because *The Empire of Fear* is not a science fiction novel in the American mode dominant from 1926 on, but a Scientific Romance in the mode native to Britain since H. G. Wells published *The Time Machine* in 1895. As Stableford has argued in *Scientific Romance in Britain* (1985), this mode stands in some contrast to its American cousin. The protagonists of the Scientific Romance tend to be observers of the great world, while American heroes tend to *win* it. The plots of an author like Olaf Stapledon (or even Arthur C. Clarke) tend to be exemplary, illuminative, perspectival; while American plots tend to work as access routes for the kingship raids of the hero, high-albedo trip-traps for the kinesis of usurpation. In the one, vision is the end; in the other, ownership. Set in an alternative sixteenth century Europe dominated by an aristocracy composed of near-immortal vampires, *The Empire of Fear* focuses on its protagonist's life-long efforts to come to a scientific understanding of the relationship between vampirism and longevity; and after an extraordinarily long detour into the heart of Africa (a guided tour that neatly illustrates the Scientific Romance's perspectival skew), he manages to clear the air for us to see through, though he himself dies without owning a thing, mortal, in much pain, off-stage. For many of us it will be a strange book to read, for its climax gives off the dying-fall glow beloved of authors of the Scientific Romance, and the denouement is strangely passionless, though pacific. But it exercises the muscles of the eye.

We reach the authors who have come on stream since 1975, who carry the phosphor of the fin-de-siecle within their breasts. In *Player of Games* (Macmillan), Iain (M) Banks provides a Lean-Cuisine prequel to the polysaturated *Consider Phlebas* (1987), and through the standard-issue folds of a galaxy-spanning plot that involves a game to end all games whose winner ends an empire (etc), images of the multi-world Culture at the heart of Bank's inspiration begin to take shape, almost subliminally. Bounteous with post-scarcity liberality, non-hierarchal, unowned, optional and *humorous*, it is, for at least one reader, a description of Jerusalem with a Garden. In *Eternity* (Warner), a sequel to *Eon* (1985), Greg Bear comes as close to the composition of a Scientific Romance as an American writer steeped in the dominant form of the genre is ever likely to, and draws out his long pulp-roots of storyline with near-Stapledonian pomp. After cosmogonic sleights-of-hand, and a few twists of twine, the Universe does or does not end in *Eternity*, but who's counting? In no real sense is Terry Bisson's *Fire on the Mountain* (Arbor) a sequel to his *Talking Man* (1986), but the steam-yacht apple-blossom sweetness of the utopia depicted in the contemporary sequences of the new book seems much more *earned* when both texts are folded together in the mind. After trailing a mute wizard across America, and watching him save the universe from non-being, the protagonists of *Talking Man* return to a Kentucky transfigured precisely into the world so magically wished for in *Fire on the Mountain*: a world whose Civil War, which has been fought by blacks to free themselves, marks the beginning of a Golden (rather than a Gilded) Age. Why — Bisson makes you ask — did it not happen? Will it never?

Like almost everything James P. Blaylock has ever written, *The Last Coin* (Zeising), his finest novel to date, must be designated a fantasy, but not High. Like Terry Bisson or John Crowley or Tim Powers, Blaylock creates worlds whose roots are consanguineous with the world's own story, and share its blood. *The Last Coin* starts with the Pieces of Silver; it is a bit like *The Maltese Falcon* without the private eye, its stays loose, its haunting of Christian iconology profound. Octavia M. Butler's *Adulthood Rites* (Warner) continues the xenobiological tale that began with *Dawn* (1987), and generates a sense of daunting perspectives soon to become articulate, a sense that the third volume may accomplish what Marx conceived as the task of synthesis: to open the gates on human nature. Orson Scott Card's *Red Prophet* (Tor), also the second volume of a sequence, follows *Seventh Son* (1987), and presages many more, for Card's tales of a magical knitter of worlds in an alternate nineteenth century America shows no sign of nearing a climax; more pulpy than Bisson's rendering of the dream, and harsher too, Card's vision of a saved Continent still remains, after two instalments, a cartoon we drench with desiderium as we read. For it is not yet Jerusalem. But we read on. A relentless productivity has tended to blanch one's sense of the features of C. J. Cherryh, but there is in fact hardly a weak book in her interlinked series of tales set in the Merchanters universe; like its companions, *Cyteen* (Warner) is packed, polished, driven and whipped, dense with flamboyant gesture and an astonishing alertness of pace and texture; a book which, with all its excesses of length, gives off a sense of unsettling but focused closeness, a steely chamber dodecaphony, like a Schoenberg opera. And from Britain, two urban novels from two urban novelists: Neil Ferguson's *Putting Out* (Hamish Hamilton) joins politics and fashion in semiological wedlock during which a New York mayoral contest climaxes in bombs and mots, as mediated by the signs that mind us; and Christopher Fowler's *Roofworld* (Century/Legend), reminding one of illustrated editions of H. G. Wells's *When the Sleeper Wakes* (1899), posits a London laced at rooftop by the inhabitants of an autonomous secret culture, who shuttlecock above us like the Edwardian aviators of a dream.

Just as Poseidon turns out to be a chimaera of the surf, so does cyberpunk more and more begin to look like an artifact of the lighting. William Gibson has never claimed more than that, and in *Mona Lisa Overdrive* (Gollancz) he closes down the sequence whose first volume, *Neuromancer* (1984), gave tongue to a hundred bloodhounds hot for future-sleaze. Four-cylindered, turbocharged and entirely unleaden, *Mona Lisa Overdrive* gives a final charge of polish to the cyberpunk dream, and stops; though he does drop hints, in the last pages of the text, of an Open Sesame to new worlds of genre. He should be thanked for the ride so far. Like Bisson and Blaylock, Robert Holdstock writes fantasies whose roots intertwine with the premises of any science fiction novel claiming to examine (and to rewrite) the history of the world, and *Lavondyss* (Gollancz), set in the same ur-reality as *Mythago Wood* (1984), goes well beyond that novel's obsession with the myths or histrions who walk within the heartwood and within the head; half pedantry and proselytizing, half an epiphany of metamorphosis that reads like braille, it is a book whose appalling sincerity puts to shame the Celtic junk it fleetingly resembles. With three novels in 1988, Gwyneth Jones continues to flare and cough. *Transformations* (Orchard Books; as by Ann Halam) and *The Hidden Ones* (Women's Press) are written for older children with lucidity and grace and rage, while *Kairos* (Unwin), written for adults, muffles its potent Christian millennialism in great swathes of jumbled natter, as though the privilege of her Word exempted her from the laws of form, the exigencies of the tongue. And in *Metrophage* (Ace), Richard Kadrey has written an old-fashioned novel in the idiom of once-famed cyberpunk; but it does have a nice disease.

I-dotting and po-faced, Nancy Kress still manages, in *An Alien Light* (Arbor), to fabricate a world and species sufficiently unlike homo sapiens to warrant the hundreds of pages of Contact Alienation which make up the heart of her text; and she writes as one born in the sealed womb of Yankee space. Paul J. McAuley, on the other hand, is himself the alien in the woodpile, and *Four Hundred Billion Stars* (Ace), though sharp and darkly intelligent and cutting, shows all the signs of a Scientific Romance mind trapped in the wrong imperium. The result is a space opera whose excesses of intellect are a form of self-injury. Ian McDonald's *Desolation Road* (Bantam), though written with a striking presentness of style, makes too close an homage of Gabriel Garcia Marquez's *One Hundred Years of Solitude* (trans. 1970), and the fantasia he presumably intends does not quite reach take-off velocity, unlike Garcia Marquez's own soaring sacerdotal *Love in the Time of Cholera* (trans. 1988; Harpers). Rachel Pollack's *Unquenchable Fire* (Century/Legend), on the other hand, closely resembles nothing one might care to dream of. It is perhaps 1988's strangest novel, and one of its strongest. The premise is odd enough — in an alternate America whose physics may well be based on the Neoplatonic shamanism of the Crowley who read Frances Yates and wrote *Aegypt*, a redemptive Pregnancy has been imposed upon the unwilling woman at the heart of the tale — but the eerie hypnopompic tranced serenity of Pollack's telling of her story, and the medusoid cruelty of the exemplary fables she interweaves into the text, make reading *Unquenchable Fire* almost like having a nightmare.

It is like stepping into the full silliness of day to speak next of Paul Preus, soon to be sharecropping his *nous* with the rest of the staff; but *Starfire* (Tor), most unusually, is a hard-SF novel it is possible to read without gloves. Its proselytizing for the exploration of space is unstained by rant about commie liberals; its protagonists are larger than life but not more vicious; and its science, perhaps because the tale takes place in the near future, does not give off the stink of charlatanry that pinpoints the *real venue* of most hard-SF novels as being Orange County. We do not speak of the Orange County Kim Stanley Robinson would like to believe in, the Orange County soon to be revealed — it is hoped — in the utopian leg of his ongoing exploration of various futures we of the West may live to face; but *The Shining Sea* has not yet appeared. We must rest content with *The Wild Shore* (1984), which deconstructs the skim-milk pastoralism of the California Right in terms so humane some critics misread the book as invertebrate eulogy; and *The Gold Coast* (Tor), a dystopian version of Orange County fifty years hence. Distressingly, nothing much in the book is radically dissimilar to what we might expect to see next week, if the fog lifts. In this fine grave slightly obdurate book, what we see of the spoliation of Orange County is what we see in our daily papers, written in clear. In *Wetware* (Avon), zany brutalist Rudy Rucker continues the robot series begun in *Software* (1982) with hardware out of Barrington Bayley, headware out of John T. Sladek, and caviare out of I Click as I Move. And Hilbert Schenk continues to stick to his New England last in *Chronosequence* (Tor), most recent in a series of odes to the ocean, to oceanography, to ships and shipwrecks, to women of knowledge and independence, to the unguent of love. It is a grown person's guide; and *Steam Bird* (Tor) is a grown person's cap in the air. Highly silly — a steam-driven nuclear bomber takes off from Maine and circles the world for locomotive hobbyists and democracy — and remarkably affectionate, 'Steam Bird,' the novel-length tale which takes up most of the volume, glows with an innocence only available to real folk on holiday.

Lewis Shiner's *Deserted Cities of the Heart* (Doubleday Foundation), like so many novels and tales set in the guernica shambles of Central America, finds Conrad at the heart of the stew, and stirs elegantly; Mirrorshades and Mayans copulate in the foam. A cognate catholicity in the use of source materials also marks out Bruce Sterling's *Islands in the Net* (Arbor) as a novel of the Twilight Years of science fiction, as though Galveston a few years hence were a suburb of the Dying Earth. Nothing is new in Sterling but the most important thing of all: the new junctures he creates: the Medusa raft he hacks into shape to bear us on. In *Catspaw* (Warner), Joan D. Vinge puts on cyberpunk like a coat of many colours, but the lass inside is far more interested in unpacking a tiresome old space-opera tale than she is in miscegenating, bright of hue, like Bruce. The noise level of Jack Womack's *Terraplane* (Weidenfeld/USA), on the other hand, owes nothing to accidents of style, though is is a very noisy writer. At its electric heart — which is a dystopian alternate 1939 in Manhattan — *Terraplane* jumps with disquietude and anguish, judders through its capsizing plot-turns like a rhino in the funhouse. And finally David Zindell, springing full-grown from the brow of Gene Wolfe, gives us *Neverness* (Donald I. Fine), a galaxy-spanning space opera of cosmology of very considerable ambition. Its protagonist, a thin dark domineering memorious cruel prig, who has solved all the problems of the plot, almost against his will, and who has trouble relating to his parents, tells his story in the form of a written confession, composed years afterwards for the benefit of the people he now rules. It is a tribute to Zindell's strength of mind that despite the numbing Autarchy of its model *Neverness* does slowly manage to become itself.

And that was the colour of the flame in this year of the golem, year of the Twilight hotspurs, year of the small bright hopes. See if they thrive. See if they do. Look for hard rain.

[illegible] of the [illegible] for the benefit of the [illegible]

And that was the [illegible] of the theme in this year of the [illegible] of the Twilight [illegible] of the small [illegible]. See if they do. Look for [illegible].

THIS WAS THE FUTURE
by
DAVID S. GARNETT

'The straight science fiction books currently being published are mainly British reprints of American titles. This creates the unfortunate situation that excellent and readable books that are "British only" are rather scarce.'

An Unfortunate Situation

1988 was the year that Clifford Simak and Robert Heinlein died.

They were two of the first science fiction authors that I ever read, and the same must be true of countless other readers. In my case, those novels were both written in the early sixties — when the authors were in their late fifties. That was probably the best time to encounter Heinlein and Simak, because the material they wrote after that was never as good. The former went on to become a bestselling author, writing longer and more unreadable books; the latter kept on doing what he had always done, though not as well. With luck, both will be remembered for the fiction they created in the earlier parts of their careers, not their later ramblings.

Heinlein won four Hugo Awards for best novel: *Double Star*, *Starship Troopers*, *Stranger in a Strange Land* and *The Moon is a Harsh Mistress*. In 1975 he was given the first Grand Master Award of the Science Fiction Writers of America. Simak won the International Fantasy Award for his novel *City*, the Hugo for his novelette 'The Big Front Yard', his novel *Way Station*, and his short story 'Grotto of the Dancing Deer' — which also won him a Nebula. He collected the SFWA's second Grand Master Award in 1977.

Simak was born in 1904, Heinlein in 1907, and the world of science fiction was very different when they began their careers. Simak's first publication was in 1931, a short story entitled 'World of the Red Sun' in the magazine *Wonder Stories*; Heinlein's was in 1939, with a story called 'Lifeline' in *Astounding Stories.*

Way back then, this was the invariable route into print. Authors wrote for magazines, because there was no such thing as a science fiction book. If an author wrote a novel, his (because 99% of the authors were male) only hope of publication was as a serial in one of the magazines. Sometimes a serial might be reprinted in book form, but that was very rare.

Half a century later, the situation is almost the reverse. More sf novels are published each year than short stories. The route to book publication is no longer through the magazines. It is by no means uncommon for an author's first ever sale to be a novel, to have a book published before any short stories. (This happened in my case, back in 1968, with a novel sold to an American publisher. And I want to emphasise this, in case what I have to say later is interpreted as being less than enthusiastic about American sf publishing . . .)

To sell a short story, it first has to be written, sent up to a magazine or anthology, where it is in competition with hundreds of other manuscripts. But these days novels can be sold before they are even written. Editors have better things to do than read books, and it is much simpler to commission novels on the basis of a few sample chapters or even on an outline. The majority of science fiction novels now published have been sold before they were even written. Publishing is an industry, it turns out a 'product' — and the product is books. Not only is it easier for a new author to sell a first novel than a first short story, it is often easier to sell three — unwritten — novels than one!

This doesn't happen in short fiction. The majority of stories in the sf magazines and original anthologies have been written 'on spec'. Editors do occasionally commission short fiction, and sometimes they buy 'name' authors just so they can have that name on the cover. But on the whole, short stories and novelettes are published on merit — unlike novels, where a prime consideration is whether the author can deliver the correct number of words at the right time.

Unlike novels, short stories are far less of a commercial proposition. An author invests his or her time and effort in a story without any guarantee of publication. Short stories produce the best work from both the new and old names of science fiction, because they are written for love not money. Word for word, the financial rewards of short fiction are far less than for a novel; word for word, short fiction is also more difficult to write.

New names are the future of sf. In science fiction, authors often do their best work at the start of their careers — and many do still start their careers with short fiction, where the freshest of ideas and themes and treatments can be found. The 'big names' who continue to write short stories do so in the belief that short fiction is the heart of sf. They return to the form because they know the short story offers so much to both the writer and the reader: precision and immediacy — not the leaden effect of the multi-paged airport terminal (and terminal brain function) 'bestsellers' churned out by today's global media corporations.

Down in the corporate basements, where books are never mentioned but instead the talk is all of 'shifting units', the latest sf marketing notion — as John Clute has earlier discussed — is 'sharecropping'. At least the books which had the names of 'Heinlein' and 'Simak' on their covers were written by Heinlein and Simak, which is not necessarily the case with many other authors today.

To take an example: Piers Anthony's first sf novel was *Chthon*, perhaps his best book. As so often happens, he later wrote a sequel; as so often happens, this wasn't as good. Then Anthony started turning out his endless series of endless fantasy series, and so two sequels to the sequel to *Chthon* have been written by someone else, Charles Platt.

Similarly, there are 'Arthur C. Clarke' books which have not been written by Clarke. The same is true of 'Roger Zelazny' and 'Philip Jose Farmer' and 'Isaac Asimov'. Their bylines have become trade marks, brand-named books written by authors whose own names appear in much smaller letters on the covers — if at all. Instead of writing their own work, many writers are grinding out books set in universes 'created by' the big name authors of a previous generation.

What came first — a demand by readers for more of the same, more 'Isaac Asimov' books than even Asimov can write (although, considering his output, that seems impossible)? Or did the idea come from the publishers, knowing that it's simpler and safer to turn out more of the same old stuff than it is to find new work? Probably packagers must take the ultimate blame. A 'packager' isn't a publisher, isn't an agent, isn't a writer, but is a middleman who comes up with the 'concept' and arranges the whole deal. Instead of the publisher paying the author for the book he has written, it is the packager who is paid. After paying off the 'name' author, then taking a huge slice for himself, the packager pays whatever is left from the publisher to the guy who really wrote the book — who probably also has to pay a percentage to his agent.

The latest vogue in sf franchising — to give this wonderful idea the kind of derivative, mercenary name it deserves — is for sequels to famous stories to be written by different authors, so that the original and the sequel can be published together as a book. Thus Harry Turtledove writes a sequel to L. Sprague de Camp's 'The Wheels of If', while David Drake writes a sequel to Henry Kuttner's 'Clash by Night', and so on.

It used to be newer authors who did this kind of thing. They needed the money, and they worked cheaper. But now the sums of money involved can be much higher, and more famous authors are prepared to sell their names. Gregory Benford is writing a sequel to Arthur C. Clarke's novel *Against the Fall of Night.* Robert Silverberg and Isaac Asimov are turning three of Asimov's short stories into novels. One wonders what possible reason they can have for doing this — but apparently there are over a million of them . . .

Asimov's *Foundation* trilogy began as a series of stories published in *Astounding.* Recently, as part of linking all his material into a single 'future history', Asimov wrote a novel called *Prelude to Foundation.* Now *Prelude* will have its own sequel, to which the *Foundation* books will then be the sequels — unless, of course, there's another prelude/sequel which will fit somewhere in between. But at least Asimov has been writing these himself.

Possibly the most successful sf series ever has been Frank Herbert's *Dune, Dune Messiah, Children of Dune*, etc. Herbert died in 1986. How long until someone writes the seventh *Dune* novel?

Franchises and sharecropping, sequels and prequels, packaging and shared worlds — such generic outputs are increasing at an alarming rate. And novelisations of computer games and television shows must not be overlooked. There have been over 40 *Star Trek* novels published in America, and they outsell almost every other sf title. At one time, book covers were supposed to represent the contents of the novel within — although few authors would agree that they did — but there is now a series of books based on an illustration: 'Inspired by the legendary painting, *Death Dealer*.' (Fantasy, of course. What else?)

This is the way the world of science fiction publishing is going, at least in America — and what is published in the USA is almost certain to appear in Britain.

Whatever happened to originality? That's what the very word 'novel' means. Isn't that what sf is meant to be — unexpected, fresh, surprising? Do readers really want the same thing over again? Maybe they do, which is why there are so many identical fantasy series published.

But if you prefer the real thing, the newest and the best in sf, you'll find it in the short fiction published in the magazines and anthologies — and in collections such as this *Yearbook*.

Fairy Tales

Another author who died during 1988 was Lin Carter (born 1930). In view of what is being published these days, in many respects Carter is a more influential figure than either Simak or Heinlein. He is one of those responsible for spreading the plague of fantasy, which has infected so much of science fiction.

Two decades ago, it wasn't that easy to publish bad fantasy. But Carter was a pioneer. His 'Thongor of Lemuria' sword and sorcery books are amongst the worst ever published. Theodore

Sturgeon once said that 90% of sf was crap — but so was 90% of everything. This has become known as Sturgeon's Law. When it comes to fantasy, however, Sturgeon's Law seems a severe underestimate.

Even bad books serve a purpose, however. One of the contributors to this *Yearbook* owes his career to Lin Carter. Having attempted to read one of the Thongor books, and unable to believe how awful it was, he decided that he could write far better than that. He did — and he does.

Also twenty years ago, Lin Carter served as 'Editorial Consultant, Ballantine Adult Fantasy Series'. Ballantine was the American publisher of Tolkien. Having made so much money from that series, they started looking for similar books. At first the line consisted of reprints of obscure 'classics'; then, under the Del Rey imprint, they began to publish original (if 'original' is the correct word) books, trilogies, series.

(One theory for the ascendancy of fantasy is that the majority of editors at publishing houses are now women. They prefer fantasy to sf, and so they publish more fantasy at the expense of science fiction. Also, the proportion of fantasy writers who are female is higher than the proportion of sf authors, and viewing the theory from this perspective tends to give it some validity. But, if it's true, what is the explanation for the expansion in the number of horror novels being published?)

Science fiction itself is very different from what it was twenty years ago. It is forever changing. Despite the best efforts of packagers, the trend is still onwards and upwards. The opposite is true of fantasy, which only looks back. *Another* retelling of the Arthurian legends? You got it. Tolkien in *denim.* How many volumes? Beowulf as a *woman*? Brilliant!

Good science fiction makes the reader think. Fantasy rots the mind, or other parts of the body. As John Clute expressed it in the first *Yearbook*: 'Bad fantasy is junk-food, an addictive mockery of the true meal, which sticks to the stomach, and eats it.'

The best sf is that which stretches the limits of the genre. Much of today's science fiction borders on fantasy, sometimes even crossing the boundaries of 'realism'. My definition of sf is that whatever is included in the *Yearbook* is science fiction.

There are, I admit, some excellent fantasy novels and stories being published. But these are not the kind of fantasy which spew from the publishing empires and are thrown up onto the shelves of the bookshops — the type of books which *can* be judged by their covers: the interminable series with kings and beautiful princesses (all princesses are beautiful, it's one of the job specifications) and wise wizards and cute elves and talking animals and epic guests and eternal battles between good and evil and magic magic magic . . .

Sf authors used to complain that the genre was always judged by its worst examples, and this is what now happens with fantasy. But there are so many bad examples!

Within the world of science fiction, there is a lot of hostility to fantasy of all kinds. The reason for this is because of fantasy's close association with sf. If it were a completely separate genre, sold on different shelves, had nothing to do with sf, then no one would care. But fantasy is seen as polluting science fiction, contaminating the true source of speculative literature, and this view is not without justification.

Publication of a fantasy novel is accepted as qualification for membership of the Science Fiction Writers of America, and more and more fantasy stories are being nominated for the Nebula Award. The 1988 award for best novel went to a fantasy novel for the first time — although *The Falling Woman* is as far from the formula fantasy novel as can be.

Horror books have also traditionally been associated with sf, perhaps because they are viewed as a branch of fantasy. This is another can of worms — often literally. Horror novels provide even worse examples of the depths to which literature can descend than fantasy books do. The only claim to 'imagination' that most horror can make is in providing ever more detailed descriptions of death and mutilation — all coming under the justification of 'catharsis', of course. Horror is the fastest expanding section of American publishing — which probably says it all.

Although it might not seem like it, there are still more sf books published than fantasy novels, at least in America. *Locus*, the invaluable US news journal, counted 317 new science fiction novels published during 1988 — plus 264 new fantasy novels and 182 horror books, the latter an increase of almost 100% over the previous year.

In Britain, *Locus* counted 198 sf novels, 193 fantasy, and 44 horror. Quantitatively, fantasy has almost overtaken science fiction. But in quality . . ?

Fantasy does have its place, on the shelves with children's books. (This isn't meant to be derogatory to children's fiction.) The best sword and sorcery books, such as those by Michael Moorcock, are ideal for boys (and girls, although they form a minority readership) in their early teens. They read that kind of stuff when they are young, then move on to more subtle, mature novels. Either that, or they give up fiction and instead turn to balance sheets as their only reading. And although the idea of 'humorous' fantasy seems a paradox — because how can most 'fantasy' be considered seriously? — there are some very good comic novels being published. There are also some very bad ones, apparently written by and for people without a sense of humour.

As for the majority of the fantasy genre: are these really the kind of books that grown-ups should be reading? 'Adult fantasy' seems a contradiction in terms, although publishers are still trying to persuade us otherwise.

An American publisher, Tor, has just started a new line called Fairy Tales. The first book in the series is *Snow White*, and the publicity announces: 'Fairy tales were originally written for adult readers — the Fairy Tales series is the first attempt in centuries to reclaim these delightful and mythical stories for their rightful readers.'

Whether fairy stories were ever 'originally written' is questionable, but this series isn't 'the first attempt' to publish this material for alleged 'adults'. Ace Books had already started its own series called, as one might expect, Fairy Tales.

This is what generic fantasy is — kindergarten stuff. It's all about familiarity and reassurance, formula fiction which never upsets the reader or causes the slightest flicker of mental activity. If we aren't careful, this is the way that science fiction is going. There have always been sequels and series, but when these begin to exceed the number of original books, we're in trouble.

Horror authors were always on the fringes of sf, but in 1988 they formed their own gang, the Horror Writers of America. And with any luck, it won't be long before the fantasy authors go off to play in their own safe nursery. Perhaps they could call themselves the Fairy Ring of America.

Prizes . . .

Once upon a time there was the International Fantasy Award, which sounds very grand — until you realise that it was dreamed up by a few London fans who chose the original winners themselves. The 'international' probably meant that, as usual, the winners were almost all Americans; neither were the books 'fantasy' — or not until the very last award. But the International Fantasy Awards were the first established honours in the genre, and they are remembered because of the (mostly) excellent books which were chosen.

There weren't many — the Award only lasted from 1951 to 1955, although it was revived one last time in 1957 — so they can all be listed:

1951	Fiction:	*Earth Abides* by George R. Stewart.
	Non-Fiction:	*The Conquest of Space* by Willy Ley and Chesney Bonestell.
1952	Fiction:	*Fancies and Goodnights* by John Collier.
	Non-Fiction:	*The Exploration of Space* by Arthur C. Clarke.
1953	Fiction:	*City* by Clifford D. Simak.
	Non-fiction:	*Lands Beyond* by Willey Ley and L. Sprague de Camp.
1954	(Fiction)	*More Than Human* by Theodore Sturgeon.
1955	(Fiction)	*A Mirror for Observers* by Edgar Pangborn.
1957	(Fantasy!)	*Lord of the Rings* by J.R.R. Tolkien.

By the time the International Fantasy Award ceased, the Hugo Award had become established. These are given out at the World Science Fiction Convention each year, voted for by the members of that year's convention. The majority of World Cons have quite naturally been held in the USA, although more frequently the venue is 'overseas' — in Britain in 1987, for example. After only two years back in the USA, New Orleans in '88 and Boston in '89, the World Convention will return to Europe in 1990, when it will be held in Holland for the first time.

The correct title for the Hugo is the Science Fiction Achievement Award. Somehow, it became named after Hugo Gernsback. He was either the creator of the genre, through founding the first ever science fiction magazine *Amazing Stories* in 1926, or else he was responsible for creating the pulp fiction ghetto from which it is still struggling to emerge . . . depending on your point of view.

The 1988 Hugo Awards were as follows:

Best Novel:	*The Uplift War* by David Brin
Best Novella:	'Eye for Eye' by Orson Scott Card.
Best Novelette:	'Buffalo Gals, Won't You Come Out Tonight' by Ursula K. Le Guin.
Best Short Story:	'Why I Left Harry's All-Night Hamburgers' by Lawrence Watt-Evans.

There are a *lot* of Hugo Awards given out, and more each year. These were the rest of the 1988 winners:

Best Non-Fiction:	*Works of Wonder* by Michael Whelan.
Best Dramatic Presentation:	*The Princess Bride.*
Best Other Forms:	*Watchmen* by Alan Moore and Dave Gibbons.
Best Semi-Prozine:	*Locus*, edited by Charles N. Brown.
Best Professional Artist:	Michael Whelan.
Best Professional Editor:	Gardner Dozois.

Best Fan Writer:	Mike Glyer.
Best Fan Artist:	Brad Foster.
Best Fanzine:	*Text Sf Inquirer*, edited by Pat Mueller.
Special Award:	The Sf Oral History Association.

'Other Forms' is a new award, apparently designed to cover everything that doesn't fit into one of the existing categories. Also nominated, for example, were the *Wild Cards* series of shared world anthologies edited by George R.R. Martin (one story of which, Howard Waldrop's 'Thirty Minutes Over Broadway!' appeared in the first *Yearbook*) and Harlan Ellison's screenplay for *I, Robot* — an unfilmed film based on the Isaac Asimov novel. *Watchmen*, the winner, was what used to be called a 'comic book' — but now they are known as 'graphic novels'. Writer Alan Moore and artist Dave Gibbons were the only two British Hugo winners in 1988.

And there was also the 'Special Award' which is — well, a special award.

Also on the same ballot as the Hugos, and voted for by the membership of the World SF Convention, is the John W. Campbell Award for best new writer. The 1988 winner was Judith Moffett.

The other major sf awards are the Nebulas. These have been given annually by the Science Fiction Writers of America (SWFA) since 1966. Sometimes there is an overlap with the Hugo Awards, sometimes there isn't. Last year there wasn't. In 1988 the members of the SWFA voted the Nebula Awards to:

Best Novel:	*The Falling Woman* by Pat Murphy.
Best Novella:	'The Blind Geometer' by Kim Stanley Robinson.
Best Novelette:	'Rachel in Love' by Pat Murphy.
Best Short Story:	'Forever Yours, Anna,' by Kate Wilhelm.

'Rachel in Love' was without doubt *the* story of 1987. As well as the Nebula, Pat Murphy's story won the Theodore Sturgeon Award for best short fiction; it won the *Locus* poll as best novelette of the year; the readers of *Isaac Asimov's Science Fiction Magazine* voted the story as best novelette; and it was beaten into second place for the Hugo by the narrowest of margins. The story was one of only two to be reprinted in all three of last year's 'best sf' collections: those edited by Donald Wollheim, Gardner Dozois — and me. (The other story was Kate Wilhelm's 'Forever Yours, Anna'.)

But back to the Nebulas: the Grand Master Award for a lifetime's work went to Alfred Bester. Bester was the author of two of science fiction's genuine classics, *The Demolished Man* (which won the first ever Hugo Award as best novel) and *The Stars My Destination* (known as *Tiger! Tiger!* in Britain). He died in November 1987, six months before the presentation.

The Nebula Awards are given for first American publication, the Hugos for first world publication. In effect, this is the same thing: only two non-Americans have ever won a Nebula — Brian Aldiss in 1965 and Michael Moorcock in 1967, both for novellas. But unlike the Hugos, which are dated by the year they are given out (so that the 1988 Awards are for works published in 1987), the Nebulas are dated by the year for which they are given. (Got that?) In May 1988, therefore, it was the 1987 Nebula Awards which were presented — for best novel, novella, novelette and short story of 1987. Except that the winning novel had been published in 1986 . . .

Perhaps more than most, authors hope to win praise and prizes. (Because very few will ever make much money.) The highest form of recognition for the majority of writers is the approval of other authors. Only a writer knows how difficult it is to create fiction, is aware of what went into the construction of every paragraph, every page. Cynical criticism is easy, a few clever words are much simpler to produce than even the worse fiction factory fantasy novel. In the sf field, the most tangible form of professional approval is the awarding of the Nebulas.

Apart from the honour of being chosen the 'best' of the year, winning either a Nebula or Hugo can also be translated into financial reward. An award-winning author can expect a higher advance for his/her next book. Theoretically, the best way to win one of the two major prizes is to make sure that the majority of voters have had a chance to read the story/book (hereinafter referred to as 'the work'). The longer a work has been available, the greater the number of potential voters who will have read it. A work which has been published earlier in the year stands a higher chance of winning.

The Nebula rules allow an author to withdraw the hardback edition of a book from the ballot in favour of the later paperback edition. This is what Pat Murphy did with her novel *The Falling Woman.* The hardback came out in November 1986, only two months before the deadline for nominations for the 1986 Nebula. The paperback came out in September 1987, and in May 1988 the book won the 1987 Nebula.

To increase their Nebula chances, the authors of two 1987 novels have also withdrawn their books in favour of later paperback publication. The hardback editions came out that year, yet the paperbacks are not being published until 1989. Which means that it won't be until 1990 that they (possibly) appear on the final Nebula ballot — three years after publication. (It is their publishers' fault that the paperbacks were delayed. Whatever happens, it's *always* the fault of the publisher . . .)

Similarly, some writers are withdrawing the first publication of their short fiction, hoping that later reprintings stand a better chance of being nominated.

It seems clear that Something Must Be Done to sort this out, or it will end up that the winner of one of the 1998 Nebulas was originally published way back in 1991. The voting procedure involves nominations, a preliminary ballot and then the final ballot, a system which has been perfected to such a refined state of complexity over the past twenty-five years.

There also used to be a Nebula for 'best dramatic presentation'. This was a category on the ballot for three years, won by those immortal classics of cinematic art *Soylent Green* (1973), *Sleeper* (1974) and *Young Frankenstein* (1975). And in 1977 one of those 'special awards' was given to *Star Wars.* The award was wisely dropped, but — as happens every few years — there is again talk of it being reinstated.

Locus — 'The Newspaper of the Science Fiction Field' — runs its own annual poll, and claims 'more nominations than the Hugo, Nebula, and all the other awards combined.' Technically, this might be correct, because for *Locus* a 'nomination' is the same as a vote. But the Hugos draw more final votes than the *Locus* poll.

There are as many categories in the *Locus* poll as the Hugos, including such categories as Best First Novel and Best Fantasy Novel. So I'm not going to list all the winners here. Or any of them.

Science Fiction Chronicle, which is the same as *Locus* only different, quite naturally has its own annual poll — with different results.

. . . Prizes . . .

The 1988 John W. Campbell Memorial Award for best novel of the year was won by Connie Willis for *Lincoln's Dreams*. This prize has no connection with the John W. Campbell Award for the best new author. But it does have a connection with the Theodore Sturgeon Award (won, as mentioned above, by Pat Murphy for 'Rachel in Love'). Both awards originate from the Campbell Conference at the University of Kansas, where James Gunn is the Director for the Study of Science Fiction.

John W. Campbell, who began his career as an author, was the editor of *Astounding* from 1937 until his death in 1971, by which time the magazine had become *Analog*. The Theodore Sturgeon Award is given as a memorial to one of sf's greatest writers, who died in 1985.

Another of the late greats for whom an annual award is named is Philip K. Dick (1928-82). This is given for the best book to have originally appeared in paperback. In 1988 the winner was Patricia Geary, for her novel *Strange Toys*. As well as the award, Geary collected $1000. Runner-up was Mike McQuay, who won $500 for his novel *Memories*.

Philip K. Dick was the author of *Do Androids Dream of Electric Sheep?*, which was filmed as *Blade Runner*. (Such are the strange ways of the movie world that the title was from a book by someone else, Alan E. Nourse.) Dick won the Hugo in 1963 for his novel *The Man in the High Castle*. His reputation was always higher in Britain and Europe than in his native America, and since his death it has increased even more. Many of the non-sf books he was unable to sell when he was alive are now in print. In 1973 a *Locus* poll placed him 12th as 'best all-time author'; by 1988 he was ranked number 5. (Heinlein was at number 1 each time. Speaking of which, it can't be long until there is a Heinlein Memorial Award. Or a Simak. Or both.)

And — although this is jumping ahead of the year under consideration — in 1989, in another 'all-time best' poll, the readers of *Interzone* voted Philip K. Dick into top position. And while we're — still! — on the subject of awards, the *Interzone* readers' poll is worth a mention.

Analog and *Asimov's* both run their own polls, but *Interzone* is unique in that it subtracts votes for negative responses. It is therefore possible for a story to have a minus score, by more people voting against it than for it. Such a method deserves much more attention. If, for example, it were to be applied to the British electoral system, we would have a different government because in the last general election far more people voted against the Tory regime than for it . . .

When *Interzone* was published quarterly, its annual poll did not cover a calendar year but instead spanned the Autumn to Summer issues. The winner of the 1986/7 poll was Richard Kadrey's 'Goodbye Houston Street, Goodbye' (reprinted in the first *Yearbook*); the 1987/88 poll was won by David Brin's 'The Giving Plague'. (Both these authors, incidentally, are American.)

Because of the way the poll was arranged, this led to an anomaly whereby the story which polled most votes for the calendar year of 1987 didn't win either of the ballots. The author* of that story therefore suggested that the readers' poll should in future be run from January to December. *Interzone* editor David Pringle recognised a Good Idea when he heard one, and so a ballot for the whole of 1988 was held. This partly overlapped the previous poll, but this time David Brin was beaten by Eric Brown's story 'The Time-Lapsed Man.'

Brown wins a 'modest cash prize' from *Interzone*, and such financial awards are becoming more common in science fiction. Amongst the earliest of these was the Futura Award. This *Yearbook* is published by Futura Publications, of which Orbit is

*Me

the science fiction imprint. One of the previous grand potentates at Futura decided to give £500 for the best sf novel published in Britain each year. This was back in the days when £500 represented 2500 pints of beer or 1000 paperbacks; and being a prize, it was also tax free. In 1976 Ian Watson — whose story 'The Flies of Memory' is reprinted in this *Yearbook* — won the first Futura Science Fiction Award for his novel *The Jonah Kit*. He also won the only Futura Science Fiction Award. It was never given again because Futura's boss was less than happy that a book from a rival publisher had won, or so the legend goes . . .

Now there is another award for the best novel published in Britain. This is the Arthur C. Clarke Award, which consists of an inscribed plaque — and £1000. (There is also *another* Arthur C. Clarke Award, which is given by the Arthur C. Clarke Centre for Modern Technologies. This is an award, not surprisingly, given in recognition of outstanding contributions to modern technologies.)

1988 was the second year of the Clarke 'best novel' award, which the jury gave to the Australian author George Turner for his novel *The Sea and the Summer*. (And under its American title, *Drowning Towers*, the novel became a 1988 Nebula finalist.) This was Turner's fourth sf book, although in Britain it was not published as science fiction. Winning the Clarke Award probably came as a surprise to the book's publisher, who believed that they had cleared their list of sf. A decade ago, this publisher had almost the best hardcover science fiction list in Britain. Then they remaindered all their sf and stopped publishing such books — except by accident.

The Clarke Award was announced at the British Easter convention, which in 1988 was called Follycon (because it began on April 1) and held in Liverpool. The convention allegedly had an American guest of honour, but he was almost totally invisible.

The British Science Fiction Association (BSFA) Awards were also announced at Follycon. Best novel was *Grainne* by Keith Roberts; best short fiction was 'Love Sickness' by Geoff Ryman, which had been serialised in *Interzone*. Ryman beat Garry Kilworth by one point. Kilworth was on the ballot for his

'Triptych', one part of which — 'Murderers Walk' — was in the first *Yearbook.*

By the time this book has been published, the Easter 1989 convention will have been held — where, it seems, some more new British awards will be distributed. Watch this space in the third *Yearbook.*

'Keskiyon mato Ikaalisissa' by S. Albert Kivinen was the winner of the 1988 Atorox Award. That's the Finnish science fiction award, of course. And it was won by a 'Cthulu Mythos' story — which probably means that in Finland they haven't yet inaugurated a fantasy award.

. . . Prizes

The first World Fantasy Convention was held in Providence, Rhode Island, in 1975, and the 'Howard' Awards have been given out at this annual convention ever since. The name does not come from Robert E. Howard, creator of Conan — or else the first Fantasy Convention would probably have been held in Cross Plains, Texas — but from H.P. Lovecraft (1890-1937), who lived most of his life in Providence. (That's where Paul Di Filippo, who has appeared in both volumes of the *Yearbook,* now lives. But there's absolutely no connection . . .)

Lovecraft was the creator of the Cthulu Mythos, a kind of supernatural and malignant cosmology which intrudes into our world from an alien and adjectival dimension. Or something like that. As well as Lovecraft, many other authors wrote Cthulu stories. It could be argued that this was the first 'shared world' series.

In 1988, the World Fantasy Convention was in Britain for the first time, held in London over Halloween weekend. And it almost seemed as though it was a US convention. Although it was far smaller than the 1987 World Sf Convention, the proportion of American authors, agents and editors who made the trip to London was much higher than travelled to Brighton the year before. There were also few natives there — although none of them won any of the World Fantasy Awards.

These prizes cover the complete spectrum of 'imaginative

literature' except for science fiction, which means that anything from heroic fantasy to supernatural horror can be in contention. These unlikely encompassments have, however, produced many notable winners over the years. The awards are decided by a jury, and they have (mostly) been given to the type of material that gives a fantasy a good name.

For the Hugo and Nebula, a short story is anything up to 7,500 words (7,499 to be precise); a novelette is up to 17,500 words; and a novella up to 40,000 words; anything longer is regarded as a novel — although now that many novels seem to be sold by weight, most publishers would consider this length far too short for book publication. The World Fantasy Awards, however, count a short story as under 10,000 words; above that is a novella.

As might be expected, there are lots of World Fantasy Awards. In 1988 some of them were:

Best Novel:	*Replay* by Ken Grimwood.
Best Novella:	'Buffalo Gals, Won't You Come Out Tonight' by Ursula K. Le Guin.
Best Short Story:	'Friend's Best Man' by Jonathan Carroll.
Best Collection:	*The Jaguar Hunter* by Lucius Shepard.
Best Anthology:	*The Architecture of Fear* edited by Kathryn Cramer & Peter D. Pautz.
and:	*The Dark Descent* edited by David G. Hartwell.

Amongst the other prizes, the Special Award (Professional) went to David G. Hartwell, who was one of the inventors of the World Fantasy Convention. And the Life Achievement Award went to Everett F. Bleiler, who (with T.E. Dikty) edited the first ever 'best science fiction of the year' series forty years ago.

The story by Ursula K. Le Guin had already won the Hugo Award, which demonstrates how difficult it can be to draw a line between 'science fiction' and 'fantasy' — and how pointless such differentiation sometimes is.

The short story winner, Jonathan Carroll's 'Friend's Best Man', appeared in the first *Yearbook.*

The British Fantasy Awards were also given out at the same

time, and the fiction awards went to:

Best Novel: *The Hungry Moon* by Ramsey Campbell.
Best Short Story: 'Leaks' by Steve Rasnic Tem.

Ramsey Campbell is British, and the prize he won is the August Derleth Award. Derleth (1909-1971) was an American writer, editor and publisher. Meanwhile, in America, there's a new award named after a British writer: Bram Stoker (1847-1912). These are the honours of the Horror Writers of America, whose first awards ceremony was held in New York in June.

But there is a limit to how many awards can be listed here. And this is it.

Late News: The Arthur C. Clarke Award, for the best new sf novel published in Britain during 1988, went to *Unquenchable Fire* by Rachel Pollack. And the Philip K. Dick Memorial Award, for the best novel published in (American) paperback during 1988, was a tie between *400 Billion Stars* by Paul J. McAuley and *Wetware* by Rudy Rucker (co-author of 'Probability Pipeline' in this volume).

The New Encyberpedia

1979 saw publication of *The Encyclopedia of Science Fiction*, produced under the general editorship of Peter Nicholls, and for which John Clute — who contributes the survey of sf novels of 1988 to this *Yearbook* — was the associate editor. Authoritative and accurate, complete and comprehensive, this immediately became the standard sf reference work.

But in many respects as much has happened in the genre since publication of *The Encyclopedia* as happened before. There have been more science fiction books published in the decade since 1979, for example, than were published in all the years previously. Because of this, the book has needed updating.

In 1988 another sf encyclopedia appeared at last. 1272

pages long, and 2½ inches thick, this was entitled *Lexicon der Science Fiction Literatur.* Published in Germany, it was also, as one might suspect, published in German.

Then, later the same year, came *The New Encyclopedia of Science Fiction*, edited by James Gunn. But beware: this new book has no connection with the original volume (which will henceforth be referred to as the *Real* encyclopedia).

The first thing one notices is that, despite the growth of the genre, the New encyclopedia is much smaller than the Real one. 524 pages compared to 672, and each page contains only two columns of information, not three, and they are printed in larger type. The New book contains far less than half the information in the Real volume.

My own copy of the New book is missing page *xii* — part of the endless list of contributors — but page *xiii* is printed twice. This is symptomatic of what is to follow.

In the first hour or two of browsing through the New encyclopedia, I discovered about a dozen errors. Without having to check against other sources, I *knew* what was printed was wrong, and these inaccuracies made me immediately suspicious of everything else. It could be argued that what I found were all minor errors, but in such a reference work there is no such thing as a minor error. An encyclopedia is the sum total of thousands and thousands of details, and even one mistake is one too many.

In the foreword to the New book, it is argued that the choice of writers had to be limited 'to include only authors who had a body of work or who promised, at this early stage in their careers, to develop a body of work.' But the selection of entries is, to say the least, eccentric, and many more authors could have been included if the New book didn't waste so much space on its media coverage. There are entries on hundreds of obscure movies and television shows, and also biographies of many of the insignificant actors who appeared in them.

To take an example, almost at random: the 1953 Hammer film, *Four-Sided Triangle*, has nearly a quarter of a page devoted to it in the New encyclopedia. Page for page, this works out at four times as much coverage as it was given in the Real volume. But has anyone ever seen this film since 1953?

Does anyone want to? The final few words of its listing in the Real book say it all: 'This is a low-budget film.'

The only way in which the New book improves on the Real one is that it is more up to date — and even here it can't be trusted. In almost every respect the New volume is inferior to the Real encyclopedia. The exception is that some of its media coverage is more comprehensive. None of that is necessary, however, because by now there are plenty of other books devoted to science fiction films. And the audience for this kind of material doesn't need an encyclopedia. They don't want to be bothered with all those words. They want picture books with full page, full colour illustrations.

What is necessary, however, is an updated version of the Real encyclopedia.*

One of the entries in the New encyclopedia is on 'cyberpunk', and 1988 saw publication of a double issue of *Mississippi Review* devoted to that very topic: opinions and articles, reviews and interviews, criticism and fiction. When such a detailed analysis as this is published, on almost any subject, it is fair to say that it serves as an obituary. Cyberpunk is dead; long live cyberpunk.

It has been claimed that William Gibson's 'Johnny Mnemonic' (1981) was the first cyberpunk story, that his *Neuromancer* (1984) was the first such novel. The term 'cyberpunk' has been credited to Gardner Dozois, editor of *Asimov's*. There was, however, a story by Bruce Bethke in the November 1983 issue of *Amazing* which was titled 'Cyberpunk' . . .

Others maintain that its roots lie back in the seventies, naming James Tiptree Jr.'s Hugo-winning novella 'The Girl Who Was Plugged In' as the original cyberpunk story. An equally valid case can be made for Ken Bulmer's 1972 novel *On the Symb-Socket Circuit*, which pre-dates the Tiptree by a year.

The fact is that 'cyberpunk' was an evolutionary movement, a natural stage in the development of science fiction, growing

*Since writing this, John Clute has told me that negotiations are in progress for a new edition of *The Encyclopedia of Science Fiction*, to be co-edited by Peter Nicholls and him. Let's hope they prove successful.

out of what had gone before. The New Wave of twenty years earlier, however, was more of a revolution, a reaction against what had gone before. In retrospect, it is perhaps difficult to understand why the New Wave caused such controversy. It has since been absorbed into the mainstream of sf, and science fiction has never been the same since. The same is already true of cyberpunk, although the absorption has been swifter and the after-effects less obvious.

Looking back at Michael Swanwick's article 'A User's Guide to the Postmoderns', which was published relatively recently (*Asimov's*, August 1986), the whole cyberpunk/humanist schism seems so dated and irrelevant. (You haven't heard of the 'humanists'? Probably neither had most of the authors who discovered that was what they were. Anyhow, it's all over now.)

An interesting point in the Swanwick piece was where he stated: 'Samuel Delany, Thomas Disch, R. A. Lafferty, Norman Spinrad ushered in the New Wave.' Which seems strange, because at the time most people believed that it had something to do with J.G. Ballard, Michael Moorcock and *New Worlds*. What will they be saying about cyberpunk in twenty years' time..?

The two authors at the focus of cyberpunk were Gibson and Bruce Sterling, who have now collaborated on a novel called *The Difference Engine*. This sounds suspiciously like a 'steampunk' novel. There is no argument where this phrase originated: from a letter in *Locus* by K.W. Jeter. He probably suggested it less than seriously, but 'steampunk' is now the usual description for the Victorian fantasies of such authors as Tim Powers, James P. Blaylock, and Jeter himself.

This is a sub-genre usually set in an alternate Victorian London. All these books are written by American authors. But let any British sf author write a novel set in Britain, then try and sell it to an American publisher. What happens? It will be rejected as being 'too English'.*

The whole cyberpunk/neuromantic/Movement episode

*To be fair, British authors don't need to use British locales to provoke this response from American editors. Novels set in the far future, on other worlds, in different dimensions — they are all 'too English'.

caused a welcome burst of interest and argument, however, which had been sadly lacking in sf for some time. And at least what the cyberpunks were writing was the real thing, science fiction.

What the genre needs is more excitement, more experimentation, more dangerous visions. For his original anthologies, Harlan Ellison coined one of the best phrases for what good sf should be. He keeps promising that *The Last Dangerous Visions*, which was first announced in 1971, will be published real soon now. Meanwhile, 'noted futurist' Ellison appears in American television adverts. There's a free car given away with every copy of his new book. Or maybe it's the other way around. One hopes that the Ellison anthology will finally be published, although considering the majority of its stories were written 15-20 years ago they can't have much relevance to the next decade — and the next century.

Time is catching up with science fiction. The Kubrick/Clarke movie *2001* was released in 1968, set 33 years in the future. But as I write this, there are less than 12 years until 2001: the next century — the next millennium!

Can science fiction last that long?

Old Brits and New

The universe of science fiction is mainly an American universe. The quote at the beginning of this review of the year — about how 'excellent and readable books that are "British only" are rather scarce' — came from the September 1953 issue of *Astounding.* American domination of the genre is not new. Quite simply, there are more of them than us.

In Britain, there are far more books by American sf writers on sale that there are by British authors. But the same is true in other fields: thrillers, romances, family sagas, S&F (not to be confused with F&SF), even Westerns.

This cultural colonisation isn't confined to literature. People who work in television are concerned by the amount of American material shown on our screens. What we see at the moment is the *best* of American (and Australian!) television.

Tune into your not-so-local satellite tv station and see what else is on offer. (Arthur C. Clarke has got a lot to answer for!) Film makers are forever predicting the death of the British cinema industry, suffocated by the Hollywood 'product'. And what about sport? Have you noticed how much American football there is on television these days . . . ?

When it comes to sf, it's no good complaining that there isn't enough British science fiction, or debating why this should be so. The answer is simple:

Don't talk, write.

Fortunately, it seems that more and more British authors are doing exactly that.

This book has a British editor and is published in Britain, so this survey of the year has probably emphasised British sf more than would be appropriate on a statistical basis. But when it comes to the stories selected for inclusion, I have been strictly neutral. The fiction has been chosen on merit, not by nationality.

In the afterword to the first *Yearbook*, I referred to the fact that only one of the twelve stories in that book was by a British author — Garry Kilworth. Another story was by Lisa Tuttle, however, who has lived in Britain since 1980. Born in America, she now considers herself a British author. I said that possibly the second *Yearbook* would contain more stories by British writers than the first volume. And that is what has happened, with three stories by British authors being included — although two of these three were first published in America.

J.G. Ballard has written sf for over thirty years and, despite his recent success with *Empire of the Sun*, he has not disowned the genre and still considers himself a science fiction author. His story in this *Yearbook*, 'The Secret History of World War 3', is reprinted from the literary magazine *Ambit* and is a further reflection of the way Britain is influenced by the imagery and iconography of the USA.

Ian Watson is one of the few British authors whose stories are regularly published in the American magazines. Watson published his first novels during the seventies, and he is probably the most successful of the British authors who first came to prominence during that decade.

And it may well be that Ian McDonald will become the most successful from the eighties. The word 'young' is applied very flexibly when it comes to authors, but in McDonald's case it is not inappropriate: he is still under 30. So far, his name is probably better known in America than in Britain — as evidenced by his appearance on the 1988 Nebula ballot — although his first short story was published in *Extro* in 1982. This was a short-lived magazine based in Belfast, which also published new stories by Garry Kilworth, Ian Watson, John Sladek, James White, Richard Cowper and Bob Shaw — and which ceased publication as soon as it published a story by the editor of this *Yearbook.*

Both Watson and McDonald have revised their stories from the original published versions, making minor changes and also 'translating' the American spellings back into English.

No stories for this *Yearbook* have been selected from British sf publications, which in 1988 consisted only of *Other Edens 2* and *Interzone.* The former was the second volume of an original anthology series, edited by Christopher Evans and Robert Holdstock. I included two stories from Chris and Rob's first volume in my first volume, but this year the *Other Edens* material that I short-listed didn't make the final lineup.

There was, in fact, another original anthology published in Britain last year. *The Drabble Project*, edited by Rob Meades and David B. Wake, consisted of 100 stories each 100 words long. This started as a fan project, but ended up becoming a limited edition hardback volume. According to its introduction: 'Drabble is played sitting around a fire, while sipping brandy and partaking of pleasant conversation with friends. The first person to finish a novel wins. The first game of Drabble, a name coined in a Monty Python sketch, was played at the beginning of the last century. The winner was Mary Shelley with *Frankenstein*, and Polidori, who didn't actually finish during that stormy weekend, came second with *The Vampyre.*'

The idea of publishing 100 stories exactly 100 words long is of course a gimmick. The stories were written by fans as well as professional authors, and they vary greatly in quality — although it is by no means the former who produced the weakest results. There is some excellent material in the collection, but you'll have to buy the book to find out because none of it is reprinted in this *Yearbook. The Drabble Project* costs a fiver (100 shillings): £5.50 (including postage) from Beccon Publications, 75 Rosslyn Avenue, Harold Wood, Essex RM3 0RG. All the proceeds go to charity, to produce a 'talking book' for the blind. (Which will be a science fiction book.) A second volume, *Double Century*, is planned for 1990.

And another good cause well worth supporting is *Interzone*, the only British sf magazine, edited by David Pringle and published bi-monthly. *Interzone* publishes news and reviews, criticism and comment, interviews and profiles, opinion and articles, all of which make it the best sf *magazine* available anywhere. And some of the stories are also very good, although none of them made it to this volume of the *Yearbook*.

The main criticism that can be levelled at *Interzone* is that it publishes too much non-fiction. (Although it is all relevant to contemporary sf.) Only half the pages consist of fiction. The most recent issue, for example, includes book reviews by *ten* different people. The magazine is publishing more fiction than ever, but some of the extra pages devoted to articles should be assigned to adding another story per issue.*

Interzone is more than simply a British magazine. Much of its best material has come from American authors, the kind of fiction which is seldom published in the more conventional (or 'commercial') US magazines. *Interzone* is now distributed throughout Britain. A sample copy is £1.95 (£2.50 overseas/ $4 U.S.A.) from 124 Osborne Road, Brighton BN1 6LU.

Three new magazines, all bearing some connection to the genre, appeared in Britain during 1988, although 'new' is probably the wrong description for a magazine that has been published since 1977. *Fantasy Tales* was previously a small press magazine, but will in future appear in paperback every six months, sold in bookshops. This is probably what *Interzone* needs. It should be on sale where sf paperbacks are displayed — not hidden away among the caravan/computer/car magazines

*As I said last year: the articles in this *Yearbook* are extra — even without them, there would be no more stories . . .

on newsagents' shelves. But that's where the bi-monthly *Fear* can be found. This is a glossy magazine which, amongst various tasteful illustrations and restrained movie/video stills, published three stories in each of its three 1988 issues. *Fantasy Tales* is 'A Paperback Magazine of Fantasy and Terror', while *Fear* is 'The World of Fantasy and Horror'. *GM*, the new monthly gaming magazine, is also publishing one story each issue — a fantasy story.

Fantasy, fantasy, fantasy — but what about a new science fiction magazine?

Many new sf magazines have been announced over the years, in America as well as Britain. Some of them have even been published. But the mortality rate is very high. (*Twilight Zone* the media/fantasy magazine founded in the USA in 1981, has become the latest casualty.)

As I write, the first issue of *The Gate* is due to appear. It is already late. This will be the first new British science fiction magazine since *Interzone*, which made its debut in early 1982. At the same time, *Extro* published the first of its three 'professional' issues. *Extro* grew out of an amateur magazine — and, like so many others, failed. Let's hope *The Gate* does better. Assuming the first issue appears, it will be mentioned in this article in the next *Yearbook*. Maybe it will even have published a few issues by then, but I wouldn't bet on it.

Even so, 1989 promises to be an exceptional year for British science fiction. The third *Other Edens* will appear, as will *Arrows of Eros*, a new collection edited by Alex Stewart. And the first volume of my own *Zenith* will also be published, an anthology of twelve new stories by British authors. With *Interzone* now bi-monthly, there will be more sf stories published in Britain than there have been for twenty years.

Maybe science fiction does have a future.

This article began, long ago, with a quotation from *Astounding*, long ago. So let's conclude with a quote from its successor, *Analog*, taken from a story in the December 1988 issue:

'There was no question about it. The old Brit knew how to string words together.'

The old Brit? That was Tennyson (1809-1902), who is

probably no longer remembered for his scientifiction.

Perhaps it's about time an award was named after him.

LUCIUS SHEPARD has established his reputation with his short fiction. His first stories were published in 1983, and in 1985 he won the John W. Campbell Award as best new writer. He won the Nebula in 1987 for his novella 'R&R', and the World Fantasy Award in 1988 for his collection *The Jaguar Hunter.*

His novel *Life During Wartime,* based on several earlier stories, is currently in pre-production with Twentieth Century Fox; his story 'On the Border' is now being cast for a movie.

His most recent book is another collection, *The Ends of the Earth,* and 1989 will see completion of three new novels: *The End of Life as We Know It, True Hearts Like Yours and Mine,* and another book as yet untitled. And he is still writing short fiction — such as 'The Off-Season' . . .

BRIAN ALDISS has done everything in science fiction, everything and more: author and editor, historian and critic, thespian and winner of almost every award that sf has to offer. His most recent books are *Ruins,* a novella, and *Forgotten Life,* a novel — neither of which are sf — and *Science Fiction Blues,* the text of his stage show. Within the genre, his latest books are the collections *Best Science Fiction Stories of Brian Aldiss* and *Best Fantasy.* He is now working on a book of his writing life, *Bury my Heart at W.H. Smith's.*

JOHN CLUTE is the foremost critic of science fiction — anywhere. He writes about authors and their work, but this is what two of sf's finest authors have written about him and his work:

'Clute is *formidable*; an urban literary wit whose grasp of the genre, and of its place in the wider world of letters, are very likely unequalled in our time and language.' (William Gibson.)

'The most far-ranging, authoritative, and sheerly enjoyable body of critical writing in the field.' (Thomas M. Disch.)

DAVID GARNETT has written many novels, some of them even under his own name. His short fiction has been reprinted in three other 'best' anthologies and appeared on the final ballots for both the Hugo and the British Science Fiction Award. He is also the editor of *Zenith*, a series of new sf stories by British authors. And he wants to make it clear that the musical *Aspects of Love* has nothing to do with him.